Praise for *A Lasting Impression*

"Tamera Alexander has once again written a novel rich in storytelling and history, peopled with living, breathing characters who made me laugh, and cry. Better than sweet tea on a veranda, *A Lasting Impression* is a winner. I want to live at Belmont!"

—Francine Rivers, *New York Times* best-selling author of *Redeeming Love*

"Tamera Alexander paints vivid scenes, not with oils on canvas but with words on the page, as she sweeps us away to the cafés of New Orleans and the hills of Tennessee. In Claire Laurent we find a true artist, ever doubting her talents, ever questioning her calling. And in Sutton Monroe we meet a hero whose bright mind is eclipsed only by his tender heart. A lovely story, sure to please anyone who treasures a good romance."

—Liz Curtis Higgs, *New York Times* best-selling author of *Mine Is the Night*

Beautifully written and brimming with "real life" history, *A Lasting Impression* captures a slice of American history, and an era the South will not soon forget. Nor should we. As Director of the Belmont Mansion for the past twenty-five years, I highly endorse *A Lasting Impression* and invite you to visit the home of Mrs. Adelicia Acklen to see, in person, the beauty and elegance that defines both Adelicia's home, and this novel.

—Mark Brown, Executive Director,
Belmont Mansion, Nashville, Tennessee

"*A Lasting Impression* is a wonderful start to a new series. With writing that is rich and textured, Ms. Alexander paints a portrait of Belmont and Nashville after the Civil War that will pull you in and almost make you believe that you are living there yourself."

—Robin Lee Hatcher, bestselling author of *Belonging*

Praise for Tamera's TIMBER RIDGE REFLECTIONS

"Alexander exposes pain and loss, then paints a picture of true redemption and trust. In her iron-willed characters we find the rugged individualism and courage that the people of the American frontier are known for, and fans of inspirational historical fiction will be moved by how friendship turns into desire."

—*Booklist (Within My Heart)*

"Alexander crafts a pleasing and well-written romance that is filled with adventure and intrigue. Subtly weaving in the main character's steadfast faith in God, the book is full of faith and full of life. Readers who enjoy romantic novels but also want to feel inspired will definitely enjoy this satisfying read."

—*Publishers Weekly (Within My Heart)*

"Tamera Alexander paints scenery with the written word, and her characters, stories, and insights linger long after the book is read."

—Cindy Woodsmall, *New York Times* bestselling author of *When the Heart Cries*

A Lasting Impression

Books by Tamera Alexander

Belmont Mansion Novels

A Lasting Impression

A Beauty So Rare

A Note Yet Unsung

Fountain Creek Chronicles

Rekindled

Revealed

Remembered

Fountain Creek Chronicles (3 in 1)

Timber Ridge Reflections

From a Distance

Beyond This Moment

Within My Heart

Women of Faith Fiction

The Inheritance

Belle Meade Plantation Novels

To Whisper Her Name

To Win Her Favor

To Wager Her Heart

To Mend a Dream (novella)

A Belmont Mansion Novel

A Lasting Impression

Tamera Alexander

Bethany House Publishers
a division of Baker Publishing Group
Minneapolis, Minnesota

Published by Bethany House Publishers
11400 Hampshire Avenue South
Bloomington, Minnesota 55438
www.bethanyhouse.com

Bethany House Publishers is a division of
Baker Publishing Group, Grand Rapids, Michigan

Printed in the United States of America

Library of Congress Cataloging-in-Publication Data

Alexander, Tamera.
A lasting impression / Tamera Alexander.
p. cm.
"A Belmont Mansion novel."
ISBN 978-0-7642-0622-1 (pbk.)
1. Women artists—Fiction. 2. Upper class—Tennessee—Fiction. 3. Southern States—History—1865–1877—Fiction. I. Title.
PS3601.L3563L37 2011
813'.6—dc23 2011027176

Unless otherwise indicated, Scripture quotations are from the Holy Bible, King James Version.

Cover design by Jennifer Parker
Cover photography by Mike Habermann, Minneapolis
Cover background photograph by Photolibrary/Flirt Collection
Author represented by Natasha Kern Literary Agency

18 19 20 21 22 23 24 14 13 12 11 10 9 8

For Deborah Raney
In lieu of the world's best Peanut Butter Twist,
I offer this . . . and my gratitude, dear friend.

"For we are God's masterpiece. He
has created us anew in Christ Jesus,
so we can do the good things
he planned for us long ago."

Ephesians 2:10 NLT

Preface

Most of the novel you're about to read is purely fictional, though there are bits of real history and people woven throughout. For instance, there really is a Belmont Mansion in Nashville, built in 1853, that still stands today. And Mrs. Adelicia Acklen, a character in the novel, is the dynamic, born-before-her-time woman who lived there.

In addition to Adelicia Acklen, many of the other characters in the novel were inspired by real people who lived during that time—people who worked at Belmont and who visited there. But the characters' personalities and actions as depicted in this story are of my own imagination and should be construed as such.

The first time I stepped across the threshold of Belmont Mansion and learned about Adelicia and her extraordinary personality and life, I knew I wanted to write a story that included her, her magnificent home, and this crucial time in our nation's history. After over two years of research and writing, *A Lasting Impression* is the culmination of that dream, and I invite you to join me as we open the door to history once again and step into another time and place. Thank you for entrusting *your* time to me. It's a weighty investment, one I treasure, and that I never take for granted.

Thanks for joining me on yet another journey,
Tamera

1

French Quarter, New Orleans, Louisiana
September 7, 1866

Claire Laurent studied the finished canvas on the easel before her, and though *masterpiece* hardly described it, she knew the painting was her best yet. So why the disappointment inside her? The fiendish fraudulence trickling its way through her like tiny beads of sweat beneath layers of crinoline and lace. She ran a hand through her curls and dropped the soiled paintbrush into a cup of turpentine, full well knowing why. And knowing only deepened her guilt.

Her gaze fell to the lower right-hand corner of the canvas, the one reserved for the artist's signature. She hadn't yet been able to bring herself to sign this one. Not with *that* name. Because of all the landscapes and still lifes and portraits she'd painted, none had truly felt like hers . . .

Until this one.

A breeze, moist and swollen, heavy with the certainty of rain, wafted in through the open second-story window, and she peered from her bedroom over the town, breathing in the tang of salty air moving in from the gulf. She viewed the Vieux Carré below, the Old Square she'd painted so many times she could close her eyes and still see every detail—the rows of pastel-colored buildings clustered together and edging the narrow streets, their balconies of decorative black cast iron boasting hanging baskets that cascaded with late summer blooms. The combination lent a charm and beauty unique to this part of the city.

No wonder she'd fallen in love with New Orleans so quickly, despite the hardship of recent months.

The steady *tick-tick-tick* of the clock on the mantel marked the seconds, and she released her breath with practiced ease. She rose from her stool and stretched, paying the toll for retiring so late in recent evenings and for rising so early, but there was no avoiding it. This painting had taken longer to complete than she'd estimated.

Much longer, as her father kept reminding her.

Almost half past two, and she needed to "take leave of the gallery no later than three," as her father had insisted. She knew she shouldn't allow his request to bother her. It wasn't the first time he'd demanded she leave while he "conferred" with gallery patrons. And it wasn't as if she didn't know what he was doing during that time. What they did as a family business.

His increasing agitation in recent weeks wasn't helping her attitude toward him, however. Though not a gentle man, by any means, he wasn't customarily given to a sharp tongue. But in recent days a single look from him could have sliced bread hot from the oven.

"Claire Elise? *Où es-tu?*"

She stiffened at his voice. "*Oui,* Papa. I'm up here."

She glanced back at the canvas, fighting the ridiculous urge to hide it. Something within her didn't want him to see the painting. Not yet. And—if it had been within her control—not ever. Maybe she could tell him it wasn't finished yet. But one look at her, and Papa would know. Pretense was a skill she'd never mastered—not like he had.

Hurried steps coming up the stairwell told her there wasn't enough time to stash the painting in the empty space behind the wardrobe, and throwing a drape over it was out of the question with the final brushstrokes only moments old. Maybe if she told him how much this particular painting meant to her, he would let her keep it.

But she had a feeling that conversation would go much like the one six months ago, following her mother's passing—when she'd told him, as forcefully as she dared, that she didn't want to paint "like this" anymore. Her father had never struck her, but she'd sensed he'd wanted to in that moment, and she hadn't considered broaching the subject again.

Until now.

"Ah . . ." His footsteps halted in the doorway behind her. "Finally, you have finished, *non?*"

His tone, less strident than earlier that morning, tempted her to hope for an improvement in his mood. "Yes . . . I've finished." Readying herself for his reaction—and critical critique—she stepped to one side, a tangle of nerves tightening her insides.

He stared. Then blinked. Once, twice. "*Jardins de Versailles* . . . again." A muscle tightened in his jaw. "This is not the painting upon which we agreed." He looked at her, then back at the canvas. Keen appraisal sharpened his expression. "But . . . it does show *some* improvement."

Claire felt her nerves easing at the merest hint of praise. Until she saw it. . . .

That familiar flicker in his eyes. Her father appreciated art, in his own way, but he was a businessman at heart. His pride in her artistic talent ran a losing footrace with the profit he hoped to make through selling her paintings.

Her paintings . . .

The irony of that thought settled like a stone in her chest, which sent an unexpected—and dangerous—ripple of courage through her. "Papa, I . . ." The words fisted tight in her throat, and he wasn't even looking at her yet. "I need to speak with you about something. Something very important to me. I know you're not—"

His hand went up, and she flinched.

But he seemed not to notice. "This isn't the landscape we agreed for you to paint this time, nor is it what I described to the patron, but—" He studied her rendering of Louis the XIV's palace and the surrounding gardens, then gave an exaggerated sigh. "Given we are out of time, and that the patron very much desires to own a François-Narcisse Brissaud . . . it will have to do." He nodded succinctly, as though deciding within himself at that very moment.

"Yes. I'm certain I can convince him of its worth. After all"—he smiled to himself—"the larger galleries in Paris often ship the wrong painting. But next time, Claire . . ." He looked down at her, his gaze stern. "You must render, to the smallest detail, the painting upon which we have agreed."

Claire searched his face. His words stung, on so many levels. But the most disturbing . . . "You've secured a buyer for this painting? Before they've even *seen* it?"

A satisfied smile tipped his mouth as his focus moved back to her work. "I told you this would happen. Word is spreading. After two years of tireless effort, our humble little gallery is finally earning the recognition it deserves in this city. As well as our patrons' trust, as I knew it would, given time. And *my* negotiating skills." His head tilted to one side. "Though I must admit, your mixture of lighter and darker shades, the hues in the garden, the way you blended them this time . . . I see you took my advice to heart."

Claire said nothing, having learned that was best when it came to comments about taking his counsel.

His expression turned placating. "If I were to stand closer"—he did just that—"I am almost certain I could catch a whiff of lilac warmed by the noonday sun."

He stilled, and she followed his gaze to the lower left corner of the painting. The added detail was subtle, so subtle one might miss it if not looking. So she wasn't surprised it had taken him so long to notice.

"Abella . . ." His voice barely audible, her mother's name on his lips sounded more like a prayer than any Claire had ever heard. Not that she'd heard many, and never from him. "Y-you . . . painted her," he whispered.

Emotion stung Claire's eyes, prompted as much by the halting break in his voice as from missing the woman in the portrait. She'd painted her *maman* barefoot on the cobbled pathway, half hidden behind a lilac bush, a basket of flowers dangling from one arm. Her chin was raised ever so slightly as though she were looking for someone, waiting for them. And her cascade of auburn curls, mirrored in Claire's own, lifted in the imagined breeze.

Claire stared at the image of her mother until the delicate brushstrokes blurred into a pool of color. Ten years had passed since that afternoon at Versailles, their last visit to the palace before leaving Paris, and France, forever. She'd been nine at the time, but the memory of afternoons spent there with her parents—wandering the gardens, nurturing childish dreams of what it would be like to live in such a place—had nestled deep, and were still so vivid to her senses. The air fragrant with blossoms, nature's symphony in the rustle of the trees, the thriving sea of color—every detail locked away, secure.

Memories of those days were the happiest of her life. And those of the past six months . . . the loneliest.

She thought she'd been prepared for her mother's death. For over a year, she'd watched the sickness devour her from the inside out. And while she felt relief knowing her mother wasn't hurting anymore, there were days when a void, murky and dark, yawned so wide and fathomless inside her that she feared it would swallow her whole.

"She was so beautiful." Her father's voice was fragile, weary beyond his forty-two years. He reached out as if to touch the painting, then stopped. His hand trembled.

Claire looked at him more closely. The shadows beneath his eyes . . . How long had those been there? And the furrows in his brow. Etched by regret, perhaps? And worry, most certainly. But worry about what? Rent being late again? Selling the expensive pieces of art he'd purchased on credit, and against her better judgment?

She looked back at the painting. "I didn't plan on including her in the painting, Papa. She just . . . appeared . . . from the tip of my brush."

For the longest moment, he said nothing. Then his breath left him in a long, slow sigh. "The truth of a painting must first be birthed in the artist's heart before it can be given life on the canvas."

Claire felt a quickening inside her. Her mother's first lesson in painting . . . but from long ago. She couldn't believe he remembered. She, on the other hand, remembered everything her mother had taught her. If only she'd inherited Abella Laurent's giftedness. Her mother had insisted she had, and more so. But Papa had made it clear she hadn't.

He'd never said it outright, of course—that nothing she did was ever quite good enough. Yet she knew he thought it, just the same. She knew it by what he didn't say.

Her father's hand moved at his side, and in a briefly lived dream, Claire imagined he was going to cradle the side of her face, as she'd always wanted him to do, as her mother had told her he used to do, but Claire couldn't remember back that far. She waited, breath trapped in her throat, feeling less like a woman and more like a child.

He turned away. "I miss her too," he whispered. "Never think that I don't."

Feeling foolish, telling herself she should have known better, Claire bowed her head to hide the hurt. "I don't think that, Papa."

There had been times in earlier years when she'd questioned the love between her parents. But mainly her father's love for her mother. In the final days, especially. When it became apparent that the medicine wasn't working and the doctors had given up hope, and when

Claire had pleaded with him to send her mother to a sanitarium. "People like Maman go there and some of them get better," she'd told him. But his anger had erupted. "Those places cost money, Claire Elise! Money we don't have. Unless you can paint in her stead. Faster and better than you're doing now."

So she'd worked, night and day, for months on end. Caring for her mother as her mother continued to instruct her—just as she had since Claire was a little girl—sometimes from bed, when her mother was too tired to sit or stand. But in the end, no matter how much Claire pleaded or how much she painted, Papa had held his ground, and her mother had died in this very room.

Her father cleared his throat. "Fortunately for you, of the seventeen times Brissaud painted *Jardins de Versailles,* he included a different detail in each."

Claire nodded, aware of that fact, as he well knew. And also aware that every one of the seventeen original *Jardins de Versailles*—plus the four she'd painted before this one—were in circulation. If anyone ever devised a way for those four, soon to be five, proud owners of a François-Narcisse Brissaud "original" purchased from the European Masters Art Gallery in New Orleans to know details about the other seventeen . . .

Her father gestured to the clock on the mantel, then looked pointedly back at her before descending the staircase.

Claire retrieved her reticule and turned to follow him, then glanced back at the painting. Not giving herself time to think about the consequences, she grabbed a brush, dipped it in paint, and signed the portrait—with *her* name—hand shaking as she did. She'd have to change it later, she knew.

But for now, seeing her name on something she was so proud of—and knowing Papa wouldn't like it—felt good, if not a bit rebellious.

As she passed through the kitchen, she saw that the door leading into the art gallery had been left open—something Papa never permitted. Stepping through that door was like stepping into another world. Plush rugs and bronze chandeliers, oil paintings and sculptures, burgundy silk paper lining the gallery walls that matched the velvet cloths draping the tables. Every item purchased on credit when they moved into this building two years earlier, and purchased with the intent of creating an air of affluence and wealth, however flimsy and paper-thin that veneer.

Confronted again by the stark differences between the gallery and the living quarters, Claire paused at the back door. Hand on the latch, she summoned courage. "Papa . . . about the painting I finished today. I'd very much like to discuss with you about keep—"

"No. It's out of the question."

Unexpected heat shot up through her chest. "But this one is special. To *me,* at least. I'll paint another one, faster, exactly as you detail. Whatever you—"

"The answer is *no*!" Anger darkened his features. "The painting is already sold."

"But it has Maman—"

"We need the money, Claire Elise! Creditors are waiting to be paid, and your dawdling has cost me dearly. Yet again."

Knowing she was already treading dangerous ground, she pushed a little further. "I have another painting, Papa. One of my own, which I haven't shown you yet. Perhaps the patron might—"

"He wants a Brissaud! Have I not made that clear enough for you?" Fury mottled his throat a deep red. "Our patrons are not interested in the trite, inconsequential renderings of a—" As though hearing the harsh bite of his own voice, he exhaled and shook his head. "I'm sorry, Claire. But it's done. There's nothing left to discuss. In time, perhaps we can sell your own paintings. But for now, your talent simply lacks any . . . unique quality. Nurturing talent takes time. You're best served to stay with copying for now. You do that quite well."

Bitterness tinged her mouth, and Claire felt an unexplained severing deep inside her. She wanted to respond, but she wanted not to cry even more, and if she opened her mouth now—

"You must understand . . ." He squeezed his eyes tight. "This is what we've been working toward all these years. Having our own gallery, making a name for ourselves."

"Yes, Papa. A name. But *our* name. *Our* work. Not someone else's, where we—"

"Think of your mother and how hard she worked. For us as a family. For *you.*"

His expression took on a tenderness Claire barely recognized, and one she didn't fully trust.

"Your *maman* sacrificed so much to give you this gift, Claire. And a better life in America. Why do you think we came here? Why do you think we both worked so hard all those years? It was all for you. . . ."

She'd heard all of this before, and while she was grateful for everything her mother—and father—had given her, she also knew their efforts hadn't been *only* for her benefit. They were for his. Her mother had said as much. Her mother had said a great many things in those last days. Whether it was the laudanum speaking or the truth finally breaking free, Claire couldn't be sure.

But she wanted to believe that her father had her best interests at heart. After all, he was her *papa*.

Staring up at him, seeing the hard set of his shoulders, his iron resolve, she felt the fight within her drain away. She opened the door, then remembered and held out her hand, feeling like a beggar and resenting him all the more for it.

Her father pressed three coins into her palm. One more than usual. She turned without a thank-you or a good-bye.

"Enjoy your time at the café, but don't be gone overlong. We have work to do this evening." His tone had lightened, falsely so. It always did when she acquiesced. "And be sure to bring home a sweet for Uncle Antoine and me."

Claire halted midstride. "Uncle Antoine is back?"

He nodded as though the news were inconsequential, when he knew it was anything but. "He'll be here shortly to assist me. I'll ask him to stay so you can say hello, if he has time. Now hurry on." He gave a swift wave. "Leave the business details to us. That's where *our* talents lie."

Claire cut a path across the brick-paved street, pushing down the well of hurt inside her, like always. She dodged wagons and carriages as they rumbled past, hoping to reach her destination before the swollen skies delivered on their steely threat.

They'd lived in New Orleans for two years, the longest they'd lived anywhere since arriving in America, and the city had finally begun to feel like home. Which probably meant they would be moving soon. Just the thought of moving stirred a dread inside her.

Uncle Antoine had promised her he wouldn't let that happen again, that he would dissuade her father from making that choice. But she knew only too well how strongheaded Papa could be.

Uncle Antoine.

Feeling a portion of her angst drain away, she waited for a carriage to pass before crossing the street. Uncle Antoine had a way of easing the tension between her and Papa.

Close to her father in age, Antoine DePaul was no more related to her than she was to Louis XVI, but she adored him as though he were family. He traveled frequently, and business had called him back north for well over a month now. Too long. She could hardly wait to see what latest fashion boot he'd purchased. Alligator boots were his trademark, but upon a recent trip to New York, he'd purchased ostrich and anaconda. Only Uncle Antoine . . .

Turning the next corner, she purposefully inhaled, and wasn't disappointed. The comforting scent of yeasty beignets and chicory-laced coffee strummed the heartstrings of her childhood home and triggered such vivid memories. And that with Café du Monde still over a block away.

Her spirits began to lighten, as they always did when she ventured outside and took walks, when she was away from the gallery.

She recalled the first time she'd laid eyes on Antoine DePaul—in New York City, upon their arrival in America ten years ago. She'd thought him so tall and dashing. He could make her laugh without even trying. Such a lucky twist of fate, meeting him as quickly as they had after disembarking. And he having recently arrived from France as well. "A small world, even in this very large and new one," Papa had said. An experienced art broker himself, Uncle Antoine had a charm about him that seemed to draw patrons—and female admirers—by the dozens. He had soon become her father's business partner.

And, eventually, like a member of their family.

With a crack of thunder, the gray skies unleashed their weighty promise, and Claire made a mad dash for the café's striped awning. Feeling a little like a drowned rat and knowing she probably looked the part, she shook the moisture from her skirt and tucked her damp curls into place as best she could.

"*Bonjour, madame!*" She smiled at the woman behind the counter and placed her order, glad to see the café wasn't overcrowded.

Balancing two beignets on a plate along with two bagged for home, she grabbed her coffee and found an empty table. A previous patron had left behind the day's paper, so as she scanned the news, she relished the pastries between sips and licked the powdered sugar from her fingers, careful that no one was watching.

After a while, she folded the paper and laid it aside and enjoyed the last of her coffee. She brushed the powdered sugar from her lap, but the black fabric of her only mourning dress was reluctant to give up the dusty white. Had it really been six months since her mother had died? It seemed like much longer, and yet also like yesterday.

Seeing the rainfall had subsided, she started for home at a leisurely pace, surprised at how quickly dusk was approaching and at how warm and heavy the air still was. With purpose, she turned her thoughts toward which piece of art, if any, her father might have sold in her absence.

She thought of her *Jardins de Versailles* but knew it was safe for another day or two, at least. Because a painting from François-Narcisse Brissaud, a lauded "master artist of Paris" whose work was highly sought after, couldn't very well be sold in a New Orleans art gallery with the oils still tacky to the touch.

The majority of their patrons came into the gallery requesting copies of famous paintings. Once Papa received their deposit, she gladly filled their requests, signing her own initials—all that he would allow. Americans seemed to love anything and everything European, and owning a well-rendered copy of a renowned European artist's work was quite in vogue.

Doing that didn't bother her. In fact, she enjoyed it. Because those people *knew* they were buying a copy. A fake. A forgery.

But when someone came in and purchased the work of acclaimed artist François-Narcisse Brissaud—whose style her mother had studied relentlessly and learned to imitate, as had Claire—they believed they were getting something of real worth.

But in truth, the artist's name on the canvas was as counterfeit as the documents her father and Uncle Antoine forged attesting to the painting's authenticity. What they did was wrong, and she knew it. It was stealing.

She never understood *why* her mother had agreed to do it in the first place. Maman had never said, and Claire hadn't forced the issue, even at the end. It had seemed a trivial question as life painfully and surely ebbed away.

She still remembered, some years back, the first time she'd seen a landscape her mother had painted, but with someone else's name on it. At the age of eleven, she thought someone had made a mistake. Or that the man—whoever he was—had forged her mother's work.

Shortly thereafter came a series of boarding schools. But by the age of seventeen, she knew the truth. And when her *maman* had grown too ill to hold the paintbrush herself, Claire had forged her first painting—and the name François-Narcisse Brissaud at the bottom—with her father standing close behind her.

The weighty mantle her mother had worn for so many years had been bequeathed to her. And the *responsibility,* as her father called it, hung heavy and rough on her shoulders.

With every step closer to home, she felt herself tensing.

When she was away from the gallery, away from her father, she almost felt like a different person, living a different life. When, for the rest of the time, she only wished that were true. She had to find a way to make him listen, to make him understand.

Surprisingly, she didn't have to think long about what she wanted to say. *"Papa, I've decided I'm going to keep this painting of Versailles. I'll pay you for it, if you insist."* Though she didn't know how she would manage that. He handled the finances, and earnings from the gallery had been slow in past months, he'd told her repeatedly, even though paintings were selling. *"But I'm keeping it. And what's more, I won't be party to this any longer. I'll paint whatever you want me to paint, as long as it's* my *name I sign on the canvas."* There. She exhaled. The words flowed so easily when she wasn't standing in front of him, when he wasn't staring her down.

She entered through the kitchen. The building was quiet, and she felt a stab of disappointment. Had Uncle Antoine already left? Had she missed him entirely?

She plunked her reticule down on the kitchen table, along with the bag of beignets. Dinner needed to be started, but she wasn't hungry. Yet she knew Papa would be. She opened the door to the gallery and peered inside. A single candelabra flickered on a bureau against the wall, leaving the bulk of the room to shadows and dusk. "Papa?"

She noticed that *The Duchess of Orléans*—a reproduction of Alexandre-François Caminade's original that she'd painted two months ago, signed with *her* initials—was absent from its easel. The pedestal beside it displaying *Nydia, the Blind Flower Girl of Pompeii,* a small-scale original statue by Randolph Rogers, renowned sculptor and her personal favorite, was also empty.

Apparently, it had been a very profitable afternoon.

She'd scolded Papa when he'd bought the Rogers statuary. It was much too expensive a piece for them to purchase without a confirmed buyer, yet he'd done it anyway, saying that it was wise to have a true original on hand every now and then. And it would appear he'd made a sound decision for once, selling it in only a week's time.

She shook her head, turning to go find him. How smug he would be about it all too, reminding her how he'd—

Something crunched beneath her boot. She looked down. Shards of glass, everywhere.

Then she heard a low moan coming from somewhere behind the door.

Slowly, she gave the door a push, the creak of hinges sounding overloud in the silence. It took a moment for her eyes to adjust to the dim light. Then she spotted him across the room, lying facedown on the floor.

"Papa!" She ran to him, broken glass splintering beneath each step. "Papa, are you all right?" She bent close and gave his shoulder a shake. No response. "It's me, Papa. Claire . . . Can you hear me?"

His breathing was labored, as though he were in pain.

With effort, she turned him onto his back, as gently as she could. He groaned, and she flinched, afraid she was hurting him. She shoved her hair back to keep it out of her face, and felt a dampness on her hands, something sticky.

She looked down, and felt the room tilt.

A dark stain soaked the front of her father's shirt, the same stain slicking the palms of her hands. Her head swam. Dreading what she would find, she tugged the hem of his shirt from his trousers to reveal a gash in his abdomen. Judging from the loss of blood, the wound was deep. *Oh, Papa . . .*

"Open your eyes," she whispered, heart in her throat. "*Please,* open your eyes."

He didn't.

She raced to the bureau and grabbed a stack of fresh polishing cloths from a lower drawer, and then the candelabra. She needed to apply pressure to the wound—she knew that much. The arc of candlelight followed her movements, flickering and sweeping across the burgundy-papered walls. Wherever the light fell, the room took on a pinkish glow.

Something caught her eye, and Claire stilled.

She squinted and raised the candelabra higher, wanting to make sure that what she was seeing—or wasn't seeing—was real. But it was.

Every piece of art in the gallery was gone.

2

Claire shivered, feeling as though she and her father weren't alone. Yet clearly, no one else was in the room. She worked to stanch the blood flow, questions pressing. Who had robbed the gallery, assaulted her father? Who would chance such a bold undertaking on so busy a street? And where was Uncle Antoine?

But the most disturbing question, the one she couldn't silence—like the pounding at the back of her head—was what had her father done? What kind of *deal* had gone wrong that someone would do this to him?

Based on experience, she knew better than to think him innocent.

Wetness slicked her hands, and she knew she needed to get help. To get a doctor. But she couldn't leave her father alone.

"Claire . . ." Her father's eyelids fluttered open.

"Yes, Papa." She slipped her hand into his. "I'm here."

He blinked as though having trouble focusing.

"What happened, Papa? Who did this to you?"

His grip tightened with more strength than she would have thought possible. Uncertainty furrowed his brow. "You're not . . . hurt?"

She shook her head. "No, Papa. I'm not hurt."

The briefest trace of a smile . . . then he tried to sit up.

"No, you need to lie still," she urged. "Don't move. You're bleeding. You need a physician."

"What I need"—he winced, each breath hard-earned—"is for you to leave here. Now! It's not safe for—"

"I'm not going anywhere, Papa. Except to get you a doctor."

Despite her efforts otherwise, he pushed himself up to a sitting position. Sweat poured from his face. "Men . . . were here, Claire. Men"—he grimaced and huffed a humorless laugh—"who were *less* than satisfied with their purchase of one of the Brissaud paintings."

Claire tried to read the look in his eyes. "Do you mean . . . they *know*? About . . . the forgeries?" She could barely say it aloud.

"They suspect." He stared hard, his jaw rigid. "They asked who painted them."

The air left her lungs. "W-what did you tell them?"

"No one knows about you—yet." He exhaled. "Which is why you must leave. If they come back and find you here—"

A floorboard creaked above them, in her bedroom, and Claire went cold inside. "Papa, what should we—"

"*Shhhh!*" he whispered, his expression fierce. "I told you it's not—"

Footsteps pounded the staircase. Coming down. Fast. Fear widened her father's eyes. She'd never get him out by herself, and she couldn't leave him behind. She *wouldn't.* Not like this. No matter what he'd done. She stood and looked for something to brandish as a weapon and reached for the candelabra.

The door leading from the kitchen to the gallery flew open.

"Uncle Antoine!" Claire released her breath in a rush. "Where have you been? Papa's hurt. He's bleeding and needs—"

"I know. The physician's on his way." Three long strides brought Uncle Antoine beside them. His clothes, always pressed and stylish, were rumpled and stained. A gash marred his upper left cheek. The skin around the cut was swollen and purpling.

Claire rose, her legs none too steady beneath her. "What happened? Who did this?"

Uncle Antoine shot a look down at her father, who looked away.

Claire scoffed. "One of you needs to tell me. I deserve to know what—"

Uncle Antoine grabbed her wrist, hard enough to make her wince. "You must listen to me, *ma chère.* Very carefully. We have little time, and none for your foolish questions." An unfamiliar edge razored his voice. He let go of her and pulled a leather pouch from his coat pocket. "Everything you need is in here."

She stared at the pouch, then back at him, realizing what it contained. What it *meant.* Her mother always carried a similar pouch whenever the two of them left on "surprise adventures," as her mother had called them when Claire was younger.

"No," Claire heard herself whisper, the word out before she could think better of it.

Surprise sharpened Uncle Antoine's expression.

Claire hadn't moved an inch but she felt off balance, as if the rug had been ripped out from beneath her, yet again. Ironic . . . This life she would have traded away just an hour earlier suddenly held meaning and familiarity she wasn't eager to throw away, despite its many unhappy parts. "I'm tired of running, Uncle. Of moving from place to place." She included her father in her stare. "I know I can't stay here, but I don't want to do this anymore. I've told you that, Papa. And you said yourself that no one knows I'm the one who paints them. I could move somewhere else in town, and—"

"You're not listening, Claire." Uncle Antoine's voice lacked any trace of warmth. "We don't have time for this conversation. They could be back any moment." He glanced at the door. "It's not safe for *any* of us here. Not after today."

Claire squared her shoulders and willed her voice to be as strong and as certain as his. "And I don't think you're listening to *me,* Uncle. I know Papa never has." Her throat suddenly felt like sandpaper. "If you and Papa want to go and do this somewhere else, then go. But I'll no longer be a part of it." She swallowed, nearly choking on the words, and at the fury she saw in her uncle's face. "I'll make my own way. I'll—"

His hand came from nowhere, hot across her cheek. Claire would have fallen had he not grabbed her arm.

"Listen to me." Uncle Antoine pulled her close. "You're going, *ma chère.* It's for your own good. You must trust me in this. Your passage has been arranged. Now stop acting like a spoiled child and go pack your satchel."

Her face on fire, Claire felt as though she were looking at a stranger. Never had he spoken to her in such a manner, much less laid a hand on her. His gaze was flat and unyielding, and slowly, the pieces of an all-too-familiar puzzle jarred painfully into place. "You knew. . . ." Truth narrowed her eyes, and she saw it reflected in his. "That's why you were gone so long this time. Back north . . . You *knew* we were leaving again. And yet you—" He'd lied to her. Just like Papa. "You promised," she whispered, tears knotting her throat. "You promised we wouldn't—"

"Antoine's right, Claire. You're acting like a child."

Tears blurred her vision. She dragged her gaze back to her father.

His features were stony, without the least hint of remorse. "You've known this day would come again." He clutched the blood-soaked rag to his side. "I'm only grateful your *maman* isn't here to see this. Your selfishness would have pained her."

Claire blinked. *Her* selfishness? And this from her own father, who hadn't said a word when Uncle Antoine slapped her.

Uncle Antoine loosened his hold on her arm. "Family was most important to your mother, *ma chère.* She would want us to stay together. You know that."

Claire looked down to where he held her and, as she had earlier that day, felt something rend deep inside. Forcing a nod, she looked back, hearing again what her mother had whispered over and over in her fitful laudanum-induced sleep—"*Be careful who you love . . .*" Whether her mother had meant it as a warning for her, or perhaps as a reminder to herself, Claire didn't know. But for the first time in her life, she realized it was possible to love someone whom you *thought* loved you in return. Only to discover . . . that they didn't. And maybe never really had. "Where are we going . . . Uncle?"

Uncle Antoine relaxed, his expression conveying relief that she'd come to her senses. "Far from here, *ma chère.* Your father and I will follow shortly. We have . . . business to attend to first." He raised his hand, slowly this time, and touched her cheek. It was all Claire could do not to turn away. "*Je suis désolé,*" he whispered. "I lost my temper. But only because I'm so worried about you."

Claire said nothing.

Finally, he motioned. "Now go, pack a satchel. Only what you need. A carriage will be here anytime. And, Claire . . ." He gave her a quick downward glance.

Claire did likewise and cringed at what she saw.

". . . be sure to change your dress."

Upstairs in her room, Claire lit an oil lamp, her hands shaking. She fumbled with the buttons on her bodice, mindful of the clock on the mantel.

She caught sight of herself in the mirror, and the reflection was one she wouldn't soon forget. Betrayal, anger, and hurt darkened her eyes. And a weariness that went bone deep.

She stripped down to her chemise and underskirts, then scrubbed her hands and face in the basin on the wash table. The water was tepid, the air warm, but still she felt a chill. Wishing she owned another mourning dress, she searched the wardrobe for the darkest dress she could find. A deep russet would have to do. She made a mental list of items to pack in her satchel.

How could she have been so foolish? So gullible. So . . . taken in. She should have seen this coming. She expected such behavior from Papa. But from Uncle Antoine? His actions resulted in a whole different kind of hurt.

And what of the men who had attacked her father and stolen the art? What if they came back? Or discovered she was the forger? What would they do to *her*?

Hurrying faster, she wrestled with the tiny pearl buttons on the front closure of her dress, finally choosing to leave the ones at her collar unfastened. She pulled another dress from the wardrobe, rolled it up and shoved it in the satchel, then pushed down the swell of emotion rising again inside her.

Hands shaking, she hurriedly tucked the remaining items from the bureau drawer into her satchel, along with her mother's locket watch. Then she turned to get the painting.

But her *Jardins de Versailles* was gone.

An hour later, standing on the deck of the *Natchez,* Claire watched the lights of shore grow dimmer, swallowed up by dark of night. The boat shuddered, its enormous paddlewheel churning the murky waters of the delta, its steam engines roaring, sending vibrations through the wooden deck beneath her as it forged a steady path northward up the Mississippi.

She gripped the boat's side rail, numb with exhaustion and fear. Hot, silent tears slipped down her cheeks. She sneaked furtive glances at the passengers around her, her mind still on the men who had pillaged the gallery earlier.

But no one even looked her way.

All the art—gone. No telling how much money it represented. How would her father and Uncle Antoine recover from such a loss?

Maman had tried to persuade her father to take out insurance on the more expensive pieces, but Papa had said that would only encourage inquiries, which could lead to suspicion, which could lead to their ruin.

But it seemed ruin had found them anyway.

The moon hung full and bright, its light stretching out across the water, rippling and breathing in the wake. The air was so redolent with brine she could taste it in the back of her throat.

A part of her had wanted to stay and take care of her father. Though, as she'd waited at the gangplank with Uncle Antoine standing beside her—she lifted a hand to her cheek, the sting long gone but not the hurt—she'd realized that the desire sprang more from a sense of obligation than from tenderness. The stark truth of that distinction had been sobering. Still, she prayed he would be all right.

The physician had arrived only moments before the carriage. "Your father's lost a great deal of blood, Miss Laurent. But he'll be fine, I assure you."

"You're certain?" she'd asked.

The physician nodded. He wasn't the same doctor she'd seen in town before. He was younger, more succinct in manner. "I've no doubt. So journey without concern, ma'am."

Claire frowned, listening to the waves lap the hull. How had the physician known she was readying to travel? Then again, she guessed he'd overheard her conversation with Uncle Antoine. Their exchange had been revealing.

Tennessee.

That was where he'd said they would find their new start. And in Nashville, of all places. She'd glimpsed parts of that city two years earlier, when they'd passed through Nashville on their way to New Orleans, and it had hardly seemed like the Athens of the South, as Uncle Antoine called it. Her clearest memory of Nashville was of how despondent the people appeared. Discouraged and beaten. Even the land itself had seemed in mourning, if that were possible.

The rain from earlier in the day returned, and she found refuge inside the steerage cabin. The cabin was long and dimly lit. Rows of benches bracketed narrow aisles, making the space feel smaller than it was. There were few passengers, and most of them male.

Claire sought a bench on the far end of the room and claimed a spot near the only family—a father and mother with four small children. She folded the coat she'd brought along and used it as a makeshift pillow, then closed her eyes, feeling the sway of the boat and imagining she was in a hammock, the kind her father had promised for years that he would buy for them.

But never had.

A day and half later, the *Natchez* steamed its way into port in Mobile, Alabama. Parched and famished, her food supply depleted, Claire disembarked and located the train station. After taking care of personal needs, she hurried across the street to the general store.

The first train whistle hadn't sounded yet. She still had time.

She chose a sleeve of crackers wrapped in brown paper and a drink, and a wedge of cheese from a case on the counter. Thinking better of it, she turned and discreetly counted the money in her change purse, then started to put the cheese back—and paused.

She was so hungry. . . .

Almost two days remained before she would reach Nashville. She'd *told* Papa and Uncle Antoine she needed more money, but they'd insisted they'd given her enough.

She glanced around but saw no one. She looked at her open reticule, then back at the cheese. Then at the store's fully stocked shelves. Surely the proprietor did well enough that he wouldn't miss—

With swift decisiveness, Claire returned the cheese and withdrew her hand as though it might be burned. *I will not do this anymore.* No more deceit. No more stealing. Or lying.

"Will there be anything else, ma'am?"

Startled, Claire turned. The apron-clad proprietor wore a smile, but something in his features told her he'd seen what she'd been about to do. She lowered her head. "No, thank you. This will be plenty." Face heating, she counted out the coins, with a penny left over.

The train whistle blew. Twice.

Twice? Looking out the window, she saw the porter hoisting the step stool onto the passenger car. She turned to grab her purchases and her reticule slipped from the counter. Its contents scattered across the floor.

Gritting her teeth, she knelt and snatched up the items, then grabbed the cloth bag the gentleman held out. "Thank you, sir!"

His kindness never dimmed. "God be with you, ma'am."

Claire ran for the train, calling out to the porter. He gave her a low-browed warning, and by the time she found an empty bench in the last car, the train had long pulled away from the station.

Shaky with hunger, she reached into the cloth bag for the package of crackers and—

Her hand closed around something.

Slowly, not trusting her sense of touch, she withdrew a wedge of cheese wrapped in wax paper, along with the crackers and her drink. Still feeling a slight weight at the bottom of the sack, she peered inside and saw the coins she'd paid.

Tears threatening, she recalled the proprietor's parting words. *"God be with you, ma'am."* She ate the crackers and every morsel of cheese, vowing to repay his kindness. She didn't know how or when, but someday, she would do something kind for someone else, the way he'd done for her.

She leaned her head against the window, the rhythm of steel wheels against iron rails lulling her to rest. She wondered how her father was, all while wishing her ticket could take her far, far away from both him and *Uncle* Antoine, though it was difficult to even think of him as such anymore. She touched her cheek, a spike of anger returning. With each passing minute, as the distance separating her from them mounted, so did her resolve to stand up to them both, and to make a fresh start for herself.

She withdrew her mother's locket watch and checked the time, then touched the miniature likeness of her mother's face. So pretty . . . She'd always liked it when people had said how much they favored each other.

The rocking of the train gradually conspired with her full belly until her eyes slipped closed. *"God be with you, ma'am . . ."* She hoped what the proprietor had said was true. That God was with her. But even more, that He knew where she was headed.

She wished she'd thought to pack the Bible she'd read from to her mother during those last days, the one she'd been issued at boarding school. But she hadn't even thought about it. Until now. Although she couldn't remember the Scriptures themselves, she remembered how the words, the promises, had comforted her mother. And her too.

Sleep swam toward her, and as the waves of drifting consciousness carried her farther out, she found herself wanting to trust that remembered peace, wanting to believe that the Author of Life had a plan for hers.

And the following afternoon, when she stepped onto the station platform in Nashville, she wanted to believe it more than anything else in the world.

3

Claire followed the flow of passengers outside onto the train platform, pausing only after she'd picked her way through the crowded station. A late-day September sun hung hazy in the west, and a breeze wonderfully absent of smoke and soot brushed warm against her neck. Without a doubt, every speck of sand and dirt between Louisiana and Tennessee was now embedded into the pores of her skin. Either that, or layering her bedraggled curls.

Every inch of her itched, and ached, and felt utterly and completely spent. She was relieved to have finally arrived, and yet—staring out across the city of Nashville—she wasn't.

Surely this must have been a beautiful city, even charming, before the war. Yet she couldn't escape the sense of loss and defeat. Rows of buildings, constructed mostly of brick but with a few clapboard thrown in, huddled the narrow streets. The majority of structures were vacant, windows boarded up. Those not were cracked and broken, long since abandoned, by the looks of them. Some blocks away, a church steeple, barren of decorative touch and lonely on the horizon, rose like a bewildered beacon.

Street signs, what few there were, leaned to one side, bent and stooped beneath an invisible weight. And where trees had once flourished—she could imagine stately poplar and sycamore dotting the nondescript streets even now—the dirt sprouted burned-out stumps and piles of rubble and debris. And the people . . .

Their expressions mirrored their surroundings.

Soldiers still clad in the uniform of a once-proud army stood in clusters of two or three, the gray woolen fabric now tattered and threadbare, coats hanging limp on their too-thin shoulders. Negroes populated the streets—far more than in New Orleans—yet not one of them wore the exuberant smiles of recently freed men and women. On the contrary, their countenances mirrored the same despondency as those of the broken men who had fought—at least in part—to keep them enslaved.

Only a month ago, she'd read in the *New Orleans Picayune* that the state of Tennessee had finally been readmitted into the Union, over a year after the war had ended. But looking out over the city, seeing the lingering aftermath of war, Claire couldn't escape the feeling that the battle was still being waged.

And *this* was where Papa and Uncle Antoine had chosen to come?

She reached into her reticule for her mother's locket watch to check the time, and her fingers brushed against a piece of paper. She pulled it out. The address Uncle Antoine had written down on a torn piece of stationery. From one of his many trips, she knew. This one to New York, to the Perrault Gallery. New York was a place she never wished to visit again either. However, in comparison to Nashville . . .

Uncle Antoine had instructed her to report to the residence as soon as she arrived, and assured that she would be well taken care of until they joined her. Papa had said the same just before she'd boarded the carriage. But with nearly five hundred miles separating her from them now, she didn't feel the same pressure to comply as she had the night she'd left.

And yet . . .

She had no arrangements other than the ones already made, whatever those were. And no money left either, having spent the few coins she'd had on meager rations of food along the way. Standing there, satchel in hand, her brief dream of independence and adventure puddled pathetically at her feet, and her choices narrowed to one.

"Sir?" She flagged down a porter. "Would you be so kind as to give me directions to this address?"

"Surely, ma'am." He glanced at the paper. A brow rose. "That's a ways from here, but not a bad walk on such a pretty afternoon. And a nice part of the city too. Lots of shops and galleries."

Encouraged by his comments, Claire focused as he told her the way, drawing a map with her mind's eye. She thanked him and set out but had barely reached the end of the station platform when an oversized wooden crate being unloaded from one of the freight cars drew her attention.

As did one of the men beside it.

The man definitely wasn't an employee of the railroad, Claire surmised—not with the expensive cut of suit he wore. And not with the way the other men looked to him for instruction.

"Careful, gentlemen. Please!" Shedding his suit coat, he came alongside the dockworkers and lent his strength as they eased the crate down the ramp. Judging by the strain on the men's faces, the crate's contents were considerable.

"Care to inspect it, Mr. Monroe?" a dockworker asked, wiping his forehead. A trace of Ireland lilted his voice. "Before we load it on the wagon, sir?"

"No, that's all right, Jacobs. We'll do that out at the house. If there's a problem, I'll contact the gallery."

The gallery? Claire took a step closer, grateful for the signage partially concealing her curiosity.

"This one came all the way from Rome, sir?" a worker asked Mr. Monroe. "Rome, Italy?"

"It did." Monroe smiled. It was an easy gesture, one that seemed to come as natural to him as breathing. "But the sculptor is an American."

An American . . . Claire strained to see writing on the side of the crate, anything that might yield more information, but she saw nothing.

"I ain't hardly believin' that, sir," another worker chimed in, his drawl rich with the South, his skin dark as burnished coffee and glistening in the sun. "That fine lady, she crosses that big ocean only to go and buy somethin' one of our fellas made. . . ."

"*One of our fellas* . . ." Claire grinned, pleased to see Mr. Monroe doing the same.

Monroe tipped each of the workers and shook hands with Jacobs, gripping his forearm like older men sometimes did, even though he was younger than Jacobs by half. It was a friendly gesture, sincere, intimate. Which was surprising given Monroe's obviously high social rank. What wasn't surprising was to learn he was married.

"*That fine lady* . . ." Mr. Monroe's wife, Claire guessed. Still, she found it far more appealing to imagine that the *fine lady* was his mother, or older sister, or perhaps a rich elderly aunt. It made the world a much more interesting place.

Emboldened by her invisibility, she studied him more closely.

Handsome could've been used to describe him, but that would have been like calling Michelangelo's *David* "adequate." The fact that watching this man summoned the naked statue of *David* to mind made her blush. But not enough to look away, or to keep her from smiling.

Taller than average and of strong build, Mr. Monroe had an ease about him, a sincerity. And he moved with an unassuming confidence that drew a person's attention, not unlike his smile.

Monroe picked up a leather satchel, much like the one Uncle Antoine carried for business. "I'll look for the wagon later tonight, and will help you unload it." He strode to a waiting carriage. And quite a conveyance it was, for quite a man. . . .

He climbed inside the carriage, and with two raps of his hand on the door, the driver slapped the reins.

Not sure why, Claire waited until the carriage was a good distance down the street before she moved from behind the sign and continued on her way. How she wished she could see the contents of that crate! A statuary of some sort, because Mr. Monroe had mentioned an American sculptor. Carved from marble, most likely. But perhaps molded of brass.

Her imagination sparked, she combed through the American sculptors she was familiar with and quickly settled on one. She giggled aloud.

What if the crate contained a statue by Randolph Rogers! The very possibility quickened her step. How exciting that would be. And how expensive the statue must have been. Rogers's fees were handsome enough, she knew, but to ship something of that weight all the way from—

Hearing the thread of her own thoughts, Claire resisted the urge to roll her eyes. She was getting far too carried away. Oh, but it was good to feel this way. To feel so *light* inside. Almost . . . carefree.

Half an hour later, she located Elm Avenue, a quaint street lined with shops, tucked off a busier thoroughfare. But when she reached her destination, she paused to check the address in the written instructions, wondering if she'd misread it.

She looked down, then up again.

The address number matched the number on the brass plate over the threshold. While Uncle Antoine hadn't said what they would be doing in Nashville, she'd assumed his and Papa's *business* would be the same. Maybe, *hopefully,* she'd been wrong. Not that it mattered for her in the long run. She was more determined than ever to break free of their plans for her. Though she had no idea how to go about that yet.

Taking a deep breath and hoping—*trusting*—God had a plan, she opened the door.

4

Good evening, dear. How may I help you?"

Closing the door behind her, Claire smiled at the elderly woman seated behind the desk. "Good evening, ma'am." She set her satchel down, glad to be free of the weight. "I'm here to see a Mr. Samuel Broderick, if he's available. My name is Claire Laurent. I believe Mr. Broderick is expecting me."

The woman frowned, looking a bit lost. "That name doesn't sound familiar to me, dear. I'm sorry."

Claire's hope plummeted. She glanced back at the stenciling on the store's front window. "This *is* Broderick Shipping and Freight Company, is it not?"

"Yes, it is!" A bright smile replaced the woman's vagueness. "And *I'm* Mrs. Broderick!" She reached over and patted Claire's hand with exuberance. "It's so nice of you to drop in and say hello, dear. My husband's not here right now, but I'll be sure and tell him you stopped by to visit. Saturday afternoons are so *very* busy for us, you know." The woman's smile never dimmed, but clearly, she expected Claire to leave.

Knowing she shouldn't stare, Claire was unable not to. She got the distinct impression that sweet Mrs. Broderick wasn't quite "all in the moment." And it wasn't only because this happened to be a *Monday.* She hated to press the woman for more information, but under the circumstances, she had no other choice. "Do you happen to know when your husband will be back? It's urgent that I speak with him."

"When my husband will be back . . ." Mrs. Broderick whispered, blinking. She looked down at the desk, and began straightening the already tidy stacks of paper. The vague look crept back into her features. "I . . . I don't think he's coming back. My Samuel . . . he's . . ." She pressed a hand to her chest and let out a cry. "Oh dear . . ."

Claire raced to the other side of the desk, afraid the woman was about to faint. "Mrs. Broderick, are you all—"

"Mama!" A man appeared through a side door, moving with a swiftness that belied his tall stature. "What are you doing down here?" His tone firm, he slipped an arm around his mother and patted her shoulder. He glanced at Claire, then looked back a second time, his gaze more encompassing this time, and not altogether gentlemanly as it inched downward.

Claire knew the buttons on her bodice were fastened but couldn't resist checking, just to be sure. When she looked up again, he looked away.

"It's all right, Mama," he whispered. "I'm here. Take some deep breaths. . . ."

Mrs. Broderick did as she was told, leaning against her son, appearing calm again.

Claire took a step back, feeling awkward and yet responsible, and more than a little tired. The days of travel were catching up to her. "Please, let me offer my apologies. I didn't mean to upset her."

"It's not your fault. Don't blame yourself." He shifted his considerable weight and pointed in Claire's direction, as though having just figured something out. "If I'm right, and I'm guessing I am . . . you're Miss Laurent."

For reasons Claire couldn't explain, she wished she could say no. "Yes, I am." She knew she should probably be relieved that this man knew her name, because that meant he'd been expecting her, which meant she was where she was supposed to be, according to Uncle Antoine's plan. But she couldn't shake the overwhelming feeling that she was *not* where she belonged. Already guessing his name, she asked anyway. "And you are?"

"Samuel Broderick. The *second,*" he added in a way that made her think he was attempting to impress her. Unsuccessfully so. "I inherited this business from my father . . . who passed away a few years ago."

Claire gave a little nod. "I'm sorry about your father, sir. And about your husband, Mrs. Broderick." She included the matron in her nod.

Mrs. Broderick straightened, her attention fixing on Claire. "Do I know you, honey?"

Claire smiled. "My name is Claire, Mrs. Broderick. We met just a moment ago."

It looked as though a light came on behind the woman's eyes. "Ah . . . You're the woman that nice man told us about. I overheard him and my son talking about you." She took hold of Claire's hand, looking as though she might cry again. "I'm so *sorry* to hear about your fa—"

"Time to get you back upstairs, Mama!" Mr. Broderick stepped between them and took hold of his mother's arm. "You know how you love dinner!" He guided her toward the door, talking over his shoulder. "I'll be back down in a few minutes, Miss Laurent. Then you and I can get better acquainted."

Claire waited, moments passing, and she fought the urge to leave. Getting better acquainted with Samuel Broderick wasn't at the top of her list, much less even on it. She got a prickly feeling being around the man, and Maman had counseled her often enough to listen to that inner voice. If she'd had anywhere else to go—or means to pay for a hotel—she would have left without a backward glance.

Surmising from the quality of furniture in the office and the general surroundings, she guessed that Mr. Broderick ran a profitable business. Her question was: How did operating an art gallery in Nashville figure into a partnership with a freight company?

Broderick returned moments later and bolted the front door. Claire got a shiver as the lock thudded into place but told herself it was for naught. After all, she saw through the window that other shopkeepers were closing as well.

"Mama's a real sweet woman, Miss Laurent. But you'll have to forgive her. Sometimes she doesn't think too clearly."

Claire nodded, not really knowing what to say.

"May I offer you something to drink? I've got tea and coffee or"—he smiled a tight smile—"something a little stronger that'll help cure the ails of travel. . . . Along with a warm bath, perhaps. I can draw one for you upstairs."

Claire blushed even as she cringed. "What I'd really appreciate, Mr. Broderick, is to know which boardinghouse Mr. DePaul arranged for me to stay in. I'm exhausted from traveling and would like to get settled."

"Oh . . ." He laughed as though he were embarrassed, though she doubted he was capable of being such. "There's no need for a boardinghouse, Miss Laurent. Mr. DePaul and I agreed that you'd stay here with me until they arrived. And"—he glanced toward the stairs—"with my mother, of course. Here . . . let me show you to your room."

Not at all eager to go anywhere with the man, Claire weighed her options and reluctantly followed him upstairs. The residence portion of the building was more spacious than she would've thought, and just as nice, if not nicer, than the business downstairs. Broderick Shipping and Freight did indeed fare very well.

She followed Samuel Broderick, *the second,* down the hallway to a room at the far end. He pushed the door open and entered ahead of her.

She fingered the lock on the door and found it to be broken.

"Oh yes." He moved closer. "I've been meaning to fix that. I'll get right to that tomorrow."

Nodding, Claire put some distance between them and ran her hand over a sturdy rail-back chair just begging to be wedged beneath the doorknob. But the bed . . . Already, she could feel herself curled up between the sheets. The bed looked heavenly.

"Mr. DePaul told me you're a gifted artist. And that *your work*"—his tone held a hint of amusement—"is very much in demand. DePaul seemed eager for you to resume your painting. He said several requests are waiting to be filled. And when you're done"—his expression turned conspiratorial—"your paintings will be shipped all the way from Europe, arriving with certificates of authenticity, of course."

Claire eyed him, hearing her earlier suspicions about Papa's and Uncle Antoine's intentions confirmed. She guessed—at least in part—what Broderick's role would be in the scheme. Forging the shipping documents. An integral part of what they did, she knew.

But—she promised herself yet again—they would be doing it without her.

"I hope you'll be comfortable here, Miss Laurent." Mr. Broderick's gaze moved over her, warming in a way that made her skin crawl.

Not wanting to encourage further conversation, or anything else, Claire stood straighter, trying to appear more confident than she felt. "I'm very tired, Mr. Broderick. I believe I'll just turn in for the night."

He glanced toward a footed tub situated in the corner. "I'll be happy to draw you a bath, if—"

"No—thank you. I'm fine."

"Perhaps in the morning, then." His smile came slowly. "If there's anything you need, anything at all, all you need do is let me know. My bedroom is right across the hall." He pointed. "And I'm a light sleeper."

Wishing she had somewhere else to go, Claire decided to seek other lodgings first thing in the morning. "Thank you, Mr. Broderick. I've got everything I need."

Claire closed the door and laid her reticule on the dresser. She looked around for her satchel, then exhaled, gritting her teeth. She'd left it downstairs by the desk.

After waiting for several heartbeats, she opened the bedroom door a fraction of an inch, then another, and peered down the hallway. She did *not* want to risk further interaction with her host.

The hallway was empty, and she was halfway to the stairs when voices drifted toward her. She hesitated, then made a mad dash by an open doorway, praying she wouldn't be seen.

Feeling a little foolish that she was tiptoeing down the stairs, as though she were doing something wrong, she crossed the room and retrieved her satchel. A burnished glow from outside caught her eye, and she paused for a moment to peer out the window.

Gas lamps lining either side of the street burned brightly, the flames flickering orange-gold within the smoky glass. So pretty against the purple dusk. It made her homesick for—

Her hand tightened on the leather handle. Homesick for *what*? A place to call home? For Maman? Always . . . For Papa, and the relationship she'd always wanted with him but had never had? Perhaps . . .

Unwilling to give those thoughts further rein, she tiptoed back upstairs. She paused at the top of the second-floor landing, listening for any sign of her overly friendly host.

"It just seems right to me, Samuel, that she be told about such a thing."

Claire grew very still.

"She *will* be told, Mama. When that nice man comes back. You remember Mr. DePaul. He brought you flowers and candy. He said in his telegram that *he* wants to be the one to tell her. That we're not to say anything about it. He knows best, and we need to respect his wishes."

Claire didn't move for fear the creak of a floorboard would give her away. Uncle Antoine wanted to tell her something himself. But what? From inside the room, came the clink of dishes and shuffled steps. At any moment, she expected Mr. Broderick to walk into the hallway and discover her standing there. And then what would she—

"And be nice to her, Mama. We're supposed to keep an eye on her until he comes again. He made that clear. She'll be helping to take care of you now. Won't that be nice? No more of my cooking. And you'll have another woman to talk to."

Claire frowned. Helping to take care of Mrs. Broderick? And cooking?

A light sigh, then the creak of a rocker. "All right, Samuel. But I still think a daughter deserves to know her father has died."

Claire blinked, her world grinding to a halt. She heard the words all too clearly but had trouble making them make sense. An instinctive step backward—

And nothing but air met the heel of her boot. She dropped the satchel and grabbed for the handrail. And missed. She slipped a step, then another, before gaining hold. The satchel slid down the stairs and landed at the bottom with a thud. Heavy footsteps sounded, and Broderick appeared at the top of the stairs.

"Miss Laurent! Are you all right?" He reached her and practically lifted her up the stairs.

"My father," Claire whispered. *"A daughter deserves to know her father has died."* The words kept replaying in her mind, and what little air there was seemed to evaporate.

"Here—" His arm came tight about her waist. "Let me help you to your room."

Claire tried to push him away, but he was strong, and insistent.

"I'm sorry you heard that. But . . ." He led her into the bedroom and over to the bed, where he sat beside her. "I received the telegram this morning. I'm so sorry you had to find out this way." He stroked her back, his hand caressing, moving downward.

Claire scooted away. "Don't!" She put up a hand. "Please, just leave me—"

"You're upset, as well you should be." He moved and slid an arm around her shoulders again. "I know what it's like to lose a parent."

Claire tried to stand, but his arm tightened around her. Only then did she realize he'd closed the door to the bedroom.

"I want to help you, Miss Laurent." He reached for her hand. "I believe that we'll—"

"Let go of me!"

But he didn't. And the previous warmth she'd seen in his eyes graduated to a heat. Even inexperienced as she was, Claire knew that wasn't good. Feeling sick, she purposefully went limp for a second, felt him relax beside her, then jumped up and ran.

She flung open the door and was to the stairs before she heard his footsteps behind her. Fighting the instinct to look back, she gripped the handrail and took the stairs in twos. At the bottom of the staircase, she grabbed her satchel. But she'd forgotten about the bolt on the door!

Bracing for the pain, she slammed at it with her fist. The lock slid open.

"Miss Laurent, come back! I think you misunderstood my inten—"

Claire ran out the door and down the street, hearing him behind her. The memory of his hands on her pushed her forward, down the next street and the next, and the next, until she lost count and lost her way. Until her lungs burned and her side ached. Her satchel felt as if it held the weight of the world, the straps digging deep into her shoulder.

She ducked into an alley, dropped the satchel, and doubled over, hands on her knees. She leaned against the side of a building for support, holding her head, listening, but unable to hear anything but the rush of her own breathing. Her stomach spasmed, but the involuntary action proved futile. She hadn't eaten in hours. Yet she wasn't hungry. Not anymore.

Papa was gone . . . *dead.* She choked down a sob. It didn't seem real. The doctor had told her he would be fine. The fire in her lungs lessened by a degree, but the throb in her chest didn't. A noise at the far end of the alley drew her head up.

A man rounded the corner, his gait swaying and irregular, a bottle of some sort in his hand. She didn't think he'd seen her, and she wasn't about to give him the chance. She picked up the satchel and looked both ways down the street, not knowing where she was going.

She only knew she couldn't stay here.

5

Claire reached the next intersection and took in her surroundings, trying to gain her bearings in the unfamiliar town. It didn't feel that late, but the streets were empty. The streetlamps illuminating the darkness no longer held the charm they had earlier, and her feet ached from running so far in heeled boots.

Her gaze snagged on the rise of a steeple a couple of blocks over, and she headed toward it, remembering another night much like this one, when she and her mother had gone on ahead on one of their "surprise adventures." *Oh Maman, I wish you were still here.*

After trying the front doors, Claire made her way around to the back of the church. The first door was locked, as was a window. But the second door . . .

The latch lifted.

She ducked inside and closed the door noiselessly behind her, eyes wide in the darkness. Barely breathing, she stood statue-still, listening for the slightest indication that she might not be alone.

All she heard was the thunder of her own heartbeat.

Pale moonlight framed a curtained window on the opposite wall, and gradually her eyes adjusted. She was in a storage room of some sort. She felt her way across the cramped space to a closed door. The knob turned easily in her hand, and she peered through the slight opening, a draft of air hitting her face. She caught a faint whiff of something and sniffed again, thinking her mind was playing a trick on her. But there was no mistaking the lingering smell of antiseptic, however slight, veiling the sanctuary.

She stepped inside and found her gaze drawn upward.

High-reaching windows, naked of covering, dominated the two-story room, sending variegated shadows across the rows of wooden pews. Intending to walk to the back, where it was darker, she came to a bench in the middle and stopped.

This pew was cushioned. The others weren't.

Her decision made, she unlaced her boots and slipped them off, and sighed as she rubbed her aching feet. She withdrew her coat from the satchel to use as a blanket and lay down and curled up on her side, then bunched the satchel beneath her head.

Exhaustion washed over her, and her eyes slipped closed. She could see Papa's face so clearly, but it was her mother's she sought to remember. She hugged the satchel tighter against her cheek.

Tired beyond anything she could remember, she wasn't certain whether God was listening at the moment or not. She believed Him capable of hearing every thought. And though, sometimes, that belief was more irritating than comforting, right now she clung to it. And she prayed He would hear her heart.

Because she needed His help now, more than ever before.

Claire awakened, blinking, sunlight bright on her face. Shielding her eyes, she rose up slightly. A sharp gnawing clawed at her belly as the knowledge of where she was and how she'd gotten here returned in splintered pieces.

Papa . . .

She lay back down and stared at the carved beams far above, mourning him and the decisions he'd made, and the relationship they should have had. Yet she couldn't ignore two undeniable truths. As much as losing him hurt, the loss didn't begin to compare with the emptiness she'd felt at her mother's passing. Which, for some reason, only added to her present grief.

And the second truth—even *thinking* it felt wrong—was that his passing, however much she wished he were still alive, confirmed within her that her decision to make a new life for herself was the right one. The opportunity hadn't come in the guise she'd expected, but she was taking it.

Uncle Antoine had told Samuel Broderick—*repulsive man*—not to tell her about Papa's passing. No doubt he wanted to tell her himself after he arrived so he could coerce her, try to convince her to stay and continue the "family business." How could she have ever thought Antoine DePaul genuinely cared about her? And how could she have thought so fondly of him? She'd been so naive, so gullible.

"*Be careful who you love . . .*"

With her mother's words replaying in her mind, she turned on the narrow bench, her back aching from having slept too long in the same position. She moved to stretch—and whacked her elbow on the back of the pew. Pain exploded up and down her arm, white hot and prickling, and she groaned—

Until the overloud creak of a door silenced her.

"Are you *sure* we're supposed to be in here?" a female voice whispered. "It's awfully early."

"It's fine!" a second woman answered. "The doors open at seven o'clock for prayer, but no one else is here, so come on!"

Judging by the swift tread of footsteps, Claire guessed the women were in a hurry. And they were coming straight down the aisle, right toward her.

Hoping their footsteps would mask any noise she made, she grabbed her satchel and coat, rolled off the pew, and scooted back beneath it. She yanked her skirt and belongings close, praying she wouldn't be seen. Seconds later, two young women swept past her toward the front.

"I didn't know you went to church here."

"I don't." Impatience abbreviated the second woman's tone. "But this is where *she* goes. And I want that position! That should count for something. Besides, everybody knows it's better if you pray in a church."

"Why is it better?"

Interested in hearing the answer to that question, Claire rose up on one elbow, careful not to hit her head on the bottom of the pew.

"Because, *silly*"—a bothered huff—"it shows God that you care enough to actually get up and do something, which puts you ahead of the other people who don't. It also increases your chances of Him giving you what you're asking for."

Claire found the woman's explanation lacking. There'd been plenty of times in her own life when she'd done everything she could to please God, when she'd acted on what she thought *He* wanted her to do, instead of what she *knew* she wanted to do.

Yet, in the end, He'd still said no.

From her vantage point, Claire could see one of the women kneeling. Only then, be it right or wrong, did she start to feel self-conscious about overhearing their conversation.

"What makes you think you're going to get the position anyway? Half of the girls we know have interviewed for it and were turned away."

"Because I'm the most qualified, Susanna. *I* know what it's like to move in her circle. Father says Mrs. Acklen thanked him *by name* the last time she was in the bank."

"Yes . . . but the advertisement calls for applicants skilled in filing and able to manage details. You have trouble keeping the perfume bottles on your bureau straight. And you don't speak French either."

Claire bumped her head on the bottom of the pew—then froze.

"What was *that*?" came a harsh whisper. The skirt of the woman standing swished as she turned this way and that.

Claire held her breath.

"It was just a wagon or something else outside. And *excusez-moi*! I do *so* speak French. *À quelle heure arrive le train?*"

Claire let out her breath and then inhaled again. The woman interviewing for the position did have a passable French accent. But *passable* didn't mean she truly knew the language.

"Susanna, are you going to pray with me or not? The interviews end today, so this is my only chance!"

Claire watched Susanna go to her knees beside her bossy friend and wondered how long they were going to be. She hoped not too long because she would hate to be caught hiding beneath—

Only seconds had passed before the overly forward woman stood. Claire smiled to herself. Apparently, when attempting to sway the Almighty's opinion, the length of the prayer was of little importance.

"I need to go get ready for my interview."

Susanna rose. "I thought you said it wasn't until noon."

"It isn't! But I need for everything to be perfect. You've seen her in town. You know what she dresses like, how she always looks so perfect. I have to look that way too. And I need for you to help me. *Please . . .*"

A tired sigh. "All right, I will. But you have to promise you'll put in a good word for my younger brother, if you get the job."

The woman gave a tiny squeal. "I will. I promise. But I can't guarantee anything."

Hasty steps portended their approach, and Claire lay perfectly still.

"Your brother is going to have to work very hard in order to get that job, and then to keep it. I won't put my reputation on the line for just anyone. . . ."

The front doors to the church creaked open and closed again, and Claire breathed a sigh of relief.

She waited a moment longer to make certain she was alone, then scooted out from beneath the pew, dragging her belongings with her. When she reached down to retrieve her boots, she noticed her dress. She was covered in dust! Every inch of her, from bodice to hem, including her stocking feet.

Huffing, she brushed herself off as best she could, her plans for the day entirely altered by what she'd just learned. She hadn't the slightest idea how she would accomplish it, but she needed to obtain an interview with . . . *Mrs. Acklen,* whoever that was—today! Because she needed a job, and money to pay for food and a place to live. After all, she could file and manage details and she spoke *fluent* French!

She frowned. Her underskirts were so twisted, and no wonder.

She reached beneath her dress and gave them a good rustle, then—alternately balancing each foot on the edge of the pew—she took the opportunity to straighten and secure her stockings. Feeling her corset and chemise off kilter too, she remedied that with some quick tugs and coercive boosts, then tried to make some sense of her hair. Grit and dust layered her scalp, so she knew excessive efforts there would be wasted.

What she needed was a long hot bath, a change of clothes, and an interview with Mrs. Acklen—all before this afternoon. Which meant, she needed a miracle. Or several.

Her gaze traveled toward the front of the sanctuary, where the two women had knelt just moments earlier. She stared, contemplating going up there and *formally* asking God for His help. But a niggling discomfort rose to the surface. It felt awkward, and unfair to think of asking Him for so large a favor when she hadn't done anything even remotely worthy of such generosity.

Feeling daunted and ill-equipped, yet already framing the petition in her mind, she turned to retrieve her boots from the floor, when she saw a man—and not just any man—leaning on the pillar at the end of the pew. Watching her!

And judging by the wry smile tipping one side of his mouth, he'd been doing just that for quite some time.

6

In the space of a blink, Claire silently recounted every womanly alteration she'd just made—and her face went hot. Wishing she could turn and run, she saw the amusement in Mr. Monroe's expression and grew warmer still. Why, of all men, did *this* one have to walk in on her just now? Michelangelo's *David,* in the flesh, albeit fully clothed. He was taller than he'd seemed at the train station yesterday, and far more observant.

He advanced a step. "My apologies, ma'am, if I startled you." In the custom of Southern gentlemen, he bowed at the waist, his gaze never leaving hers. "Typically the sanctuary is unoccupied at this early hour." The same heritage that instructed his gentility also velveted the deep timbre of his voice.

Humor shadowed his expression, which only deepened Claire's discomfort. Yet it wasn't the same discomfort she'd experienced under Samuel Broderick's leer. She wouldn't mind this man's attention in the least, just not when she was . . . arranging herself.

Needing to say something—*anything,* in her defense—she grasped what shreds of decorum remained. "A proper gentleman would have made his presence known, sir. At the very outset." The reprimand didn't come out nearly as convincingly as she would have liked.

"Indeed, he would have." His smile remained undeterred. "As I did. *Twice.*"

She narrowed her eyes.

He held up a hand as though requesting her patience, then proceeded to clear his throat. Loudly—not once, but twice. Until he choked in the process. Or at least pretended he did. Rather convincingly too, going so far as to clutch his chest and reach for the back of the pew for support.

Despite her embarrassment, Claire fought back a giggle—the response he'd hoped to elicit, she felt sure, considering the watchful glint in his eyes. He'd caught her in a most embarrassing moment, but just *how* embarrassing, she wasn't sure. Had he actually seen her crawl out from beneath the pew where she'd hidden? Certainly she would have noticed him standing there, if so.

Regardless, she recognized what he was offering her now—the opportunity to make light of the situation and save face. And she grabbed it with both hands, hoping she would be halfway convincing, and that he wouldn't notice her stocking feet.

"While that was a fairly convincing demonstration, sir"—her unease lessening, she still held her smile in check—"I fail to see how I could have possibly turned a deaf ear to so flagrant a display."

His dark brows inched higher. And the swift manner in which he masked his reaction told her he knew how to play this game, probably better than she. "Which accounts for my surprise, dear lady. And frankly, my keen disappointment when you failed to come to my aid. I could have choked to death. Right here, on this very floor."

"And what a loss that would have been for us all."

He frowned, feigning hurt and disbelief. Feigned, she knew, by the barely perceptible upturn of his mouth.

Under normal circumstances, she would never have entered into such casual repartee with a stranger, but this man didn't feel like a stranger to her. At least not completely. Having observed him with the workers at the train station, she'd glimpsed his lack of pretense, his sincerity of character, and she found herself wanting to trust that first impression.

Very much.

To her surprise, he walked toward her, the entire length of the pew, and stopped a respectable distance away. At least two feet separated them, but the distance felt much closer. *He* felt much closer.

He offered another bow. "I've been remiss in my manners. Mr. Sutton Monroe at your service, ma'am."

She offered her hand, and he took it in his. His breath was warm against her skin, his lips soft, and his release all too swift. Claire had a difficult time not staring. *Sutton* Monroe. The name suited him.

Acting on a whim, she gave a sweeping curtsy worthy of Emperor Napoleon's court, careful to keep her stocking feet covered. "Miss Claire Elise Laurent . . ." She lifted her head as she rose. "Pleased to make your acquaintance, Mr. Monroe. And my deepest apologies for endangering your life as I so obviously did with my earlier negligence."

His smile turned dangerously disarming.

It occurred to her that perhaps her casual banter was giving him the wrong impression about what sort of woman she was. She looked into his sea-blue eyes and detected an inviting sparkle—and knew without a doubt that she was in trouble. Not because of any flaw in his moral fiber, but because she couldn't stop looking at him. . . . At the quiet confidence residing in his features, the resilient strength in his manner. The smooth-shaven jawline and the fullness of his mouth. The way his dark hair fell in carefree fashion across one side of his forehead and curled at his temple.

Her gaze lifted. And there again were those eyes. . . .

Warmth spread through her, similar to moments before, only . . . *different* this time. But a good different. A *very* good different.

His playful behavior fully convinced her that the *fine lady* mentioned in conversation yesterday by one of the workers must have referred to either his mother or a rich elderly aunt. And not a wife. Because she couldn't imagine that this man—once having made a vow of faithfulness and oneness of heart—would ever do anything to tarnish it. Even a little.

"Permit me an inquiry, Miss Laurent?"

She lifted a brow. "*One,* Mr. Monroe."

"Do I detect a trace of France in your voice?"

"*Oui, monsieur.* I was born in Paris." She tilted her chin. "*Parlez-vous français,* Monsieur Monroe?"

He gave a hesitant shrug. "*Un peu.* And not very well. But—" Pleasure crept into his expression. "I very much enjoyed your country."

All playfulness fell away. "You've been to France?"

"*Oui,* Mademoiselle Laurent." His graveled tone and French accent touched places inside her that Claire hadn't known words could reach. "I was in Paris this past March, in fact."

She mentally counted back. *Only six months ago.* "What was it like? What did you visit while there?"

His look turned puzzled.

She rushed to explain. "My family left Paris when I was but nine years old. I haven't had occasion to return." Vivid scenes rose in her mind, accompanied as always by the familiar scents. "What I remember best are the smells. The gardens of *Les Tuileries,* passing the open doors of *pâtisseries* on nearly every corner."

"*Mmmm* . . ." He briefly closed his as eyes as though he too were remembering. "Fresh *croissants,* steaming *café au lait* . . ."

"*Pain au chocolat,*" she whispered, her mouth watering.

"And another pastry"—he squinted—"made in layers with vanilla cream and—"

"*Napoléons,*" Claire supplied, feeling a pang of hunger. She pressed a hand against her stomach to quell the gurgle. "And did you happen to visit the Palace of Versailles?"

The delight in his eyes answered before he did. "*Oui, mademoiselle.* We enjoyed the privilege of breaking our journey there for a night."

"You *stayed* at Versailles? In the palace itself?" Who *was* this man . . . "Your family must be most influential, Mr. Monroe." The thought—intended to be kept to herself—slipped past unrestrained.

Staring at her, he blinked, and an abrupt awareness moved over him. He looked away, and an almost boylike shyness—or was it sadness—overtook his expression.

"I beg your pardon, Mr. Monroe. I didn't mean to speak out of turn or—"

"No." He shook his head, his smile slowly returning, still genuine, though more guarded than before. "It's all right, Miss Laurent. No offense taken. I assure you." His posture, already arrow straight, became more so. "Would you permit me one more question, Miss Laurent?" His gaze grew contemplative. "One . . . far more to the point."

The moment between them had passed, and the change in the tone of their conversation was not one Claire welcomed. Yet she had no choice but to nod. "Of course, Mr. Monroe."

"Do you make it a habit, ma'am, of . . . hiding beneath church pews?"

So he *had* seen her crawl out.

She looked away, then quickly realized that was what Papa had always done when he lied to her. Thinking of her father brought the threat of tears, but she restrained them—more easily than she would have thought—by remembering how his lying had made her feel.

She looked back and met Mr. Monroe's discerning gaze. She didn't want to lie. But how much of the truth to tell this man was another matter entirely.

"No, Mr. Monroe, I don't. As it happened, I saw this church and decided to come inside." She tried to add a smile, thinking it would help lessen the tension of the moment, but she found herself unable to sustain it. "Two women came into the church sometime after me." She motioned to the front doors, but his focus remained steady on her. Very steady. "They didn't see me when they first walked in, and I hated to interrupt their conversation, which quickly took a more private turn, so I . . ."

She licked her lips, realizing she was rambling, and that she was absolutely no good at this. At telling a more condensed version of the truth while still not telling a lie. But one thing she did know. . . .

Saying the least she could would serve her best.

"So I hid beneath the pew. Not with the intention of eavesdropping, I give you my solemn oath. But only to prevent them from—" Hearing, inside her head, what she was about to say, she winced, realizing there was no excuse for her actions, however innocent they'd been. She'd known it then, and she knew it now. "I did it to prevent them from seeing me, and from feeling uncomfortable . . . once they discovered that I was privy to their conversation."

The blue of his eyes took on a steely cast. He looked around the sanctuary. Searching for what, she didn't know. Then his gaze snagged on her unlaced boots lying on the floor.

Telling doubt registered in his face, followed by swift question, and Claire raced to think of something to say that would explain it away. Then he looked at her again, more thoroughly, as though seeing her for the first time, and every possible explanation that flew to her tongue suddenly fell flat.

His gaze, patient in its perusal, traveled the length of her body. Not in a lewd manner, but in one more akin to a detective working to solve a mystery. Or worse, a crime. Comprehension replaced the question in his eyes. And Claire's embarrassment returned in a flood.

Seeing herself through his eyes, she became painfully aware of her rumpled dress, and her sagging, matted-down curls. What hurt the most was the realization that, of all the men she'd met since coming of age, this man was one she would have liked to have known better.

Even more, she would have liked him to think well of her, maybe even desire to know her better too.

She lowered her eyes. "I can explain, Mr. Monroe. I arrived in Nashville yesterday, and the place where I had been instructed to stay last night was . . . regrettably unsuitable."

He looked down at the pew, then back at her. "So you slept *here*? All night?" He asked the question as though such a thing was unbelievable. But of course, to a man of his wealth and position, his social rank and connections, it would seem impossible to believe.

"I give you my word, sir, I didn't disturb anything in the church. I simply came in"—she nodded past him—"through that door there. The outside door had been left unlocked. And I went to sleep. I was readying to take my leave when I looked up and saw you standing there. *Watching* me."

She'd almost held back the last two words. But she'd detected a slight culpability in his expression as she spoke, and was glad now that she'd said it. Perhaps prodding his guilt would help her case.

For a long moment, he didn't answer. And she imagined he was trying to decide what to do with her. Whether to report her to the authorities for trespassing perhaps, or take her before the bishop or minister or whoever was in charge of this church. Either way, it didn't bode well for her, or for the fresh start she wanted to make.

She thought about leaving, just grabbing her belongings and striking out the front door, but she'd never outrun him. Even if she had her boots on.

But she would never attain an interview this afternoon with Mrs. Acklen by standing here, explaining herself to him.

He finally shook his head, more to himself, she thought, than to her. "Do you have a safe place to stay tonight, Miss Laurent?"

Claire eyed him, relaxing a little. So he wasn't going to put her through an interrogation. Her first impression of this man's kindness had been accurate after all. "Thank you for your concern, Mr. Monroe. And yes, I have plans to find such a place."

He opened his mouth as though to say something else, then closed it, sighing. "I hope you can understand my position, ma'am. I don't wish to overstep my boundaries. That's not my intention, I assure you. But . . ."

In his brief hesitation, Claire got the niggling feeling that the interrogation she thought she'd escaped might still be forthcoming.

"Neither can I in good conscience simply let you—"

The front door to the sanctuary opened, drawing their attention.

A man entered, carrying a box. He turned to his left, then stopped and pivoted back in their direction, peering over the load in his arms. "Monroe? You're still here?"

Looking between the two men, Claire prayed this was the opportunity she'd been waiting for, and she wondered how quickly she could run in stocking feet.

Beyond the walls of the church, the distant clang of a bell began to sound. Mr. Monroe withdrew his pocket watch from his vest and flipped open the gold lid.

Just as quickly, he closed it again. "Good morning, Father Bunting. You're just in time. This young woman would like to meet with you."

Claire didn't miss the knowing look—deftly given, she'd grant him that much—that Mr. Monroe sent Father Bunting.

Bunting set the box down on a pew. "Is that so . . . *Mr.* Monroe?"

Monroe indicated for Claire to precede him down the aisle, which she did, begrudgingly, satchel, coat, and boots in hand. She wished the floor would open up and swallow her whole. And take Sutton Monroe right along with her.

"*Father,* may I present Miss Claire Elise Laurent of . . ." Monroe turned to her. "I apologize, Miss Laurent. I fail to remember from where you said you hailed."

Because she hadn't mentioned it, which he knew full well. She could tell by the way he was watching her. "From Louisiana, Mr. Monroe. I arrived in Nashville yesterday, as I *do* recall telling you earlier." Two could play at this game.

"Louisiana . . ." He repeated, as though this new piece of information held special interest to him. "Father Bunting, may I present Miss Claire Elise Laurent of Louisiana. She has a matter of . . . personal importance that I believe she'd appreciate discussing with you. *If* you have a moment available, sir?"

It was Bunting's turn to look between them. "Yes, of course I do. Miss Laurent . . ." The priest gestured for her to sit on a nearby pew, and Claire did as he indicated, setting aside her belongings.

She stared up at Sutton Monroe, who wasn't the least shy in meeting her gaze. On the contrary, he seemed bent on capturing it. If he only knew how much she really needed to confess, he wouldn't have let her off so easily. She wished now that she'd confided in him more fully about the events of recent days. Perhaps then he would have been more understanding.

But that opportunity was past.

"Miss Laurent . . ." A crooked smile tipped one side of his mouth. "It was a pleasure to meet you, ma'am. And also . . . insightful. Now, if you'll both excuse me, I have obligations across town. Should you require my assistance"—his attention settled on the priest—"you know where to reach me." He strode from the church, never once looking back.

Claire watched the door close behind him.

As enjoyable as meeting Sutton Monroe had been, a part of her wished she'd never laid eyes on the man. As she relived their conversation, she wondered whether the tiniest seed of something that might have been special—in another time, another place—had just walked out of her life.

And in a strange way, she mourned the loss.

7

"You're in need of confession, my dear?"

Claire finished lacing her boots and turned her attention back to the priest. How did he know she needed to—

Wait. He was a priest. Of course he knew. She felt herself shaking on the inside.

"Yes, sir. Yes, *Father,* sir . . ." Though her parents had practiced Catholicism—at least back in France, they'd told her—they'd never taken her to church. So she'd never made confession to a priest before.

She took a deep breath and attempted to make the sign of the cross, but was fairly certain it came out looking more like a star. "Be with me, Father, for I . . ." She squeezed her eyes tight. *What are the words?* "I have committed a grievous wrong."

She waited, then peered up.

The priest was smiling. "If I'm not mistaken, Miss Laurent, I believe it's 'Bless me, Father, for I have sinned.'"

She let out a held breath. "Of course." She gave a tiny laugh. "That makes more sense."

"And it's shorter," he added, his eyes gracious, without a trace of condemnation.

Claire nodded, grateful she'd gotten a patient priest. Tempted to glare again in the direction of the door, she resisted. "You'll have to forgive me, Father. I'm a little nervous."

"That's understandable, Miss Laurent. Take your time."

The man before her, absent his white collar, looked remarkably less like a priest and more like a normal man, which helped to set her at ease. She leaned forward. "I have a confession to make. Before the main one," she added, to clarify. And then whispered, "I'm not usually Catholic."

At that, he laughed, then leaned forward just as she had done. "I figured as much. And I'll let you in on a little secret." He glanced around as though making certain they were alone. "I'm not usually Catholic either."

She stared, uncertain, as a trace of mischief colored his expression. "I don't understand. I thought that you—"

"I'm not a priest, Miss Laurent. I'm a reverend." He waved his hand in indication of their surroundings. "I'm the minister of this church. First *Presbyterian* of Nashville." He eyed her. "I went along with Mr. Monroe just now because, without saying it outright, he made it quite clear that you have something you wish to tell me. Or, more likely, that you *need* to tell me." He paused. "Mr. Monroe is a trusted member of this church and of this community. I count him as a personal friend, and am grateful that he considers me as such. So . . ." Relaxing, he rested an arm along the back of the pew. "If you'd like to tell me whatever it is that's troubling you"—he shrugged in a noncommittal way—"or whatever might be on your mind, I'd like to hear it. While I cannot accept your confession as would a priest, I'm ready to listen to you as a man who tries his best to follow Christ, and who will help in whatever way I can. If you're inclined to share."

Claire took all this in, imagining what mirth Sutton Monroe must have felt when he'd exited the church minutes earlier. Leaving her there to confess what she'd done to a "priest." If not for wanting to wring his muscular neck, she might have seen some humor in it. "So, if I understand what you're saying, *Reverend* Bunting . . ."

He waited, ever patient.

"If I were to decide that I didn't want to . . . *confess* anything, I don't have to."

He nodded.

"And if I wanted to get up from here right now and leave, you wouldn't try to stop me."

"That is exactly right."

An enormous weight lifted from her shoulders. She could breathe again. Tempted to go ahead and tell the reverend what she'd done, she decided that really—when taken as a whole—her actions hadn't been horrendous. She hadn't broken anything or taken something that wasn't hers. And the door *had* been unlocked, after all.

"Well . . ." She rose. "That's wonderful to know because . . . I really don't have anything to confess. Not a horribly grievous sin, anyway."

The table at the front of the sanctuary, where the women had bowed earlier, caught her eye, and silently, she thanked God for answering her prayer of deliverance. She was now free to go and pursue that interview—she glanced down at her dress—looking like a travel-worn vagabond. And with not a single coin left in her—

My reticule!

She glanced about but saw only her satchel.

She raced down the aisle to check the pew where she'd slept. Nothing. Then a picture formed in her mind, and knowledge hardened like a pit in the bottom of her stomach. She'd left her reticule at the shipping office, on the dresser in the bedroom. Oh, how could she have been so—

Feeling sick, she frantically searched the pockets of her skirt, reaching deep inside, praying she'd feel the familiar touch of metal. But her pockets were empty. She closed her eyes as regret knifed deeper. She'd left her mother's locket watch in her reticule.

Tears rose, and she could do nothing to stop them.

"Is there a problem, Miss Laurent?"

Hearing Reverend Bunting behind her, Claire kept her face turned away, unable to speak. Assuming that Samuel Broderick *the second* was the kind of man she thought him to be, he would already have plans for what to do with the contents of her reticule. And surely he'd have found it by now. And he could have it all. She didn't care—except for that locket watch. She wanted her mother's most treasured possession back.

She sniffed, and a handkerchief appeared over her shoulder.

"Miss Laurent, I'd be most honored to offer assistance, ma'am, if you'll only tell me how I might do that."

Gingerly, she took the handkerchief, wiped her tears, and dabbed her nose. Finally, her voice returned. "I have nothing. No money. No family. No place to stay. No place to go." She turned back to him. "And . . ." Oh, she hated to admit it. "I slept in your church last night. Right there." She pointed to the only cushioned pew, tears renewing. "And when two women came in this morning for prayer, I hid beneath the pew so they wouldn't see me. So I wouldn't get in trouble. And then I overheard their conversation, which was wrong, I know." She hiccupped a sob. "And then I got up and"—she made motions with her hands—"I was . . . *fixing* myself, only to look up and find Mr. Monroe watching me. He saw me crawl out from beneath the pew, and . . ."

Expression attentive, Reverend Bunting nodded.

"Mr. Monroe, he was kind, and then . . . he left me with you. And"—she took a breath, the weight of recent days bearing down hard—"I learned last night that my father died."

Reverend Bunting patted her arm, and she cried, telling him everything. She left out the details about the robbery in the art gallery—and about what she and her parents used to do. Sharing that bit of information would surely hinder her fresh start.

Besides, all that was behind her now. Or soon would be.

"I'm sorry," she finally whispered after a long moment. "I've gone on too long and have taken up too much of your time."

"*Shhhhh* . . . Don't you worry about a thing. You're exactly where you need to be, Miss Laurent. Of that, I'm certain."

She sniffed, reminded of something she'd noticed last night. "Your church smells like a hospital."

He took a breath, his brow wrinkling. "I don't smell it anymore myself. I guess I've grown used to it. The church was used as a hospital during the war. All the pews were moved out and over a thousand cots were crammed in from corner to corner." He scuffed the floor with the tip of his boot. "The wooden planks seem reluctant to give up the stains. And the smell too, I guess."

Claire dried her eyes, hearing the somber note in his voice. She looked around, viewing the sanctuary in an even more reverent light, and slowly, oddly, began to calm.

"Better?" he said softly.

She shrugged, then nodded. She did feel surprisingly better having confessed everything. Well, almost everything. "There is one thing I can think of that I need help with, Reverend Bunting. But it's a lot to ask."

"It may not be as much as you think, my dear."

She briefly looked away. "The women I told you about . . . the ones I overheard . . . ?"

He nodded.

"One of them spoke about interviewing for a position with a lady in town. A lady who attends this church."

Comprehension moved across his face. "I believe Mrs. Adelicia Acklen would be that lady's name." He studied Claire for a moment. "Do you have any idea who Mrs. Acklen is?"

Feeling as though she should, Claire shook her head.

Reverend Bunting glanced back at the door. "And do you know anyone in her employ? Say, someone who could give you a personal recommendation, by chance?"

Again, Claire shook her head, feeling her chances lessening by the second. "But I think I might be qualified for the position." She lifted one shoulder and let it fall. "From what I overheard," she added more softly.

"And you'd like to interview for it."

She nodded. "But the interviews end today. And I need a fresh dress and a place to clean up, and—"

"Say no more, Miss Laurent. I can tell you right now that this task is far beyond my skills and abilities."

Claire's heart fell. "I underst—"

"But! I know of a saint whose guidance we can seek. Saint Chrissinda is her name."

Claire looked up. "But I'm not Catholic." She arched a brow. "And neither are you, Reverend Bunting."

Grinning, he picked up her satchel and motioned her toward the door that led to the storeroom. "Let's head out the back way. Chrissinda is my wife, Miss Laurent. But she's a saint if I've ever known one."

Claire gathered her things and preceded him into the storeroom, noticing how much smaller the space appeared in the daylight. "Will she object to your bringing a stranger home unannounced?"

"If my wife knew the situation and that I failed to bring you home, Saint Chrissinda would tan my backside, as we say here in Tennessee."

Claire laughed, imagining the scene and tickled that he'd said such a thing. She paused at the back door through which she'd entered last night, feeling the need to complete her confession. "This is how I got in, Reverend. I guess someone forgot to lock it."

Reverend Bunting touched the latch. "I didn't forget, Miss Laurent," he said softly. "I left it open last night—just as God urged me to."

"Be careful how you proceed, Monroe. If you push these men too far, they may push back—like they did with your father."

Sutton Monroe studied the blackened soil in his palm and would've sworn he could still smell the smoke. Charred remains of his family home—blackened chimneys and a wood-burning stove leaning crippled to one side—emerged from the rubble as though begging not to be forgotten. As if he could ever forget. He fisted the dirt tight, then let it sift through his fingers. "You're saying I shouldn't pursue this, sir?"

"I'm saying to be careful as you *do.*"

Hearing both warning and cautious consent in the older man's tone, Sutton glanced back.

Sitting astride his mare, wearing his trademark tall black hat, Bartholomew Holbrook eyed him, much as his own father might have, if he were still alive. "I know better than to try to dissuade you once you've set your mind to something, son." Holbrook's sigh held reservation. "Justice may be on your side, but justice always comes with a price. And you're all your mother has now. Remember that. Whatever price you pay, she'll be forced to pay as well. And mark my words—it will hurt her more." He leveled his stare. "As it will a certain young woman who shall remain unnamed."

Sutton let his mentor's counsel settle inside him, aware of what the venerable attorney was asking—in that indirect manner of his. Bartholomew Holbrook was renowned not only for four decades of practicing law in Nashville but also for his ability to ferret out information.

Yet Sutton had learned a thing or two from the older gentleman in their years together—like how to evade such an attempt. He wasn't ready to discuss this particular topic with anyone. Because he hadn't fully decided the issue within himself.

He'd hoped the few days spent with Cara Netta LeVert and her family in New York last month would have helped make his decision clearer. Easier. But it hadn't.

Cara Netta was a fine young woman. Intelligent, thoughtful, pretty. They'd known each other for years and got along well. She possessed a dowry that had every unmarried Southern male vying for her hand.

Everyone said he and Cara Netta would make a perfect pair. Frankly, he had a hard time seeing how anyone could say he would make a good match with any woman these days. He had precious little to offer a wife in terms of financial security. The war had seen to that.

And he'd be hanged before he allowed a woman to provide for him.

Cara Netta knew about his circumstances—as though it were a secret—which spoke even more highly of her character. Over recent months, they'd developed an understanding between them, one of a more romantic nature, and she'd told him, more than once, that his financial standing didn't matter to her. But it did to him. Though he had yet to formally propose, he knew she was waiting, expecting it, as were her mother and sister.

Yet the timing hadn't been right. And still wasn't. Not until he knew for certain that this new government wasn't going to take his land and rob him of his birthright. Once that was all set to rights, he would be ready to move forward with the marriage. At least that's what he told himself.

And for the most part, he believed it.

He stared at the land that had been in his family for three generations. Laurel Bend, as his grandparents had named it. Land that would be stripped of his family name if the Federal Army had their way. In his mind's eye, he saw where the barn and stables had once stood, and the smokehouse behind which his grandfather had taught him how to shoot.

His gaze traveled purposefully back toward the charred remains of his childhood home, and another image returned—of his father lying facedown in the dirt only yards away from where he stood now. His blood ran hot. Resolve hardened within him like steel. "Have you learned the name of the man chairing the Federal Army's review board, sir?"

"Not yet. But he's a high-ranking Federal officer. All the evidence has been turned over to him." A moment passed before Holbrook continued. "One of the men on the board informed me privately—which is, of course, how I'm informing you right now. . . ."

Seeing the question in the older man's eyes, Sutton nodded his agreement.

"He told me they were most impressed with the written defense you made on your father's behalf. He said it was the most thorough and well-authored account they'd received to date. Which is saying a great deal."

"I still wish they would allow me to testify in person."

Holbrook sat straighter in the saddle, the leather creaking as he moved. "There are too many of these cases, and that would take far more time than they're willing to allow. Besides, testifying personally makes far too much sense, which means the government would naturally oppose the idea."

Sutton responded with a semblance of a smile, but inside his gut churned. His father had been a peaceable man. The most gentle, loving man he'd ever known. His life shouldn't have ended the way it had. And while Sutton knew, on one level, that it wasn't his own fault, on another, he was certain it was.

It was *his* fault his father hadn't signed the Oath of Allegiance to the Union that day. Remembering his last conversation with his father in that regard, Sutton felt something inside him give way. He would have given anything to go back and have that conversation again.

"One last thing, son. Decisions by the review board are final. No appeals will be heard. No matter who brings it. No matter how well written."

Sutton gripped the reins to his stallion and swung up into the saddle. Truxton snorted and pranced beneath him, eager to outrun the wind and be free. Desires Sutton understood. Only . . . what *he* yearned to be freed from was something he feared he might never be able to outrun.

Bitterness curdled inside him. The injustice of it all. The North stood determined to rob him of everything. They'd already killed his father and burned the family home. Now they wanted to take his land, his heritage, and his future. He thought of his mother. In a way, they'd taken her from him too. She would never be the same. Not after what she'd witnessed.

If only he'd been there the afternoon it happened . . .

He briefly closed his eyes. His mother had recounted every excruciating detail. The Federal officer riding up to the house, escorted by full military detail. His father meeting the officer at the top of the porch steps, hand outstretched in greeting. His mother said accusations ensued, followed by threats—and a final ultimatum. Then the captain drew his gun and fired point-blank.

Almost two years had passed, yet still it seemed surreal.

And now the government was alleging that his father had been the first to draw a firearm. His father—a pacifist, a physician committed to saving lives. His father who had never owned a gun in his life, at least that Sutton could remember. As a boy, he'd learned to shoot from his grandfather because his father refused to teach him, something Sutton had never understood, and guessed he never would.

If only he could speak with one of those board members. Make a personal appeal. Closing arguments were his greatest strength as an attorney, or so Mr. Holbrook had told him, time and time again.

Forcing the last lingering image of his father from his thoughts, Sutton urged the stallion forward and fell into step beside Holbrook's mare. Side by side, he and Holbrook rode in silence down the cedar-canopied drive to the main road, then on toward town.

Church bells tolled some distance away, traveling over the rooftops and drawing Sutton's attention to a much closer steeple, two streets over. *Mademoiselle Claire Elise Laurent.* A name, and woman, not easily forgotten. He welcomed the pleasant intrusion in his thoughts, especially one so captivating, but knew he probably shouldn't in light of his relationship with Cara Netta.

Still, he wished he'd had the time to spare earlier that morning. He'd wanted to help Miss Laurent more than he had. Then again, Reverend Bunting was the person the young woman had truly needed to see. For many reasons.

He felt the tug of a smile. The look on her face as he'd turned to leave . . .

Like she'd wanted to skin him alive.

She was feisty, for sure. But he'd detected a shyness about her too. An almost frightened quality. Which was understandable if she'd arrived in town only to find herself with nowhere to go. No place to stay. But what lady traveled unescorted and with no confirmed destination?

"Mildred received a letter from your mother yesterday."

Pulled from his reverie, Sutton glanced beside him, and tried to read Mr. Holbrook's expression. His mother had written him too, three months earlier. He'd answered her letter promptly but hadn't received a response. A wider gap than usual in their correspondence, but no cause for worry. At least he hadn't thought so.

His mother had always had spells, when she found it difficult to be at rest within herself and when she wrestled to get her thoughts onto the page, but those spells had worsened after his father's death.

"Mildred permitted me to read the letter, feeling certain it wouldn't break a confidence. And it didn't." Holbrook seemed to choose his next words more carefully. "Your mother sounds . . . some better."

Sutton returned his attention to the road. "Which, when interpreted, means she still doesn't appear to be well. At least not well enough to return."

Holbrook's silence was answer enough. "She mentioned returning, someday, perhaps. But coming back to Nashville is going to be difficult for her, no matter how much time passes. I believe—and Mildred agrees—that encouraging a few more months of rest would be prudent. Judging from what your mother wrote, staying with your aunt is pleasant and like a good tonic."

Sutton started to comment, then nodded instead. If his mother wanted to present her relationship with Aunt Lorena as pleasant and like a good tonic—he could hear her using those exact words—so be it. But he knew better. Still, he missed her.

But her return to Nashville would be far more difficult now. For them both.

When he and Holbrook reached the crossroad where they were to part ways, Sutton started on ahead, then reined in when Holbrook spoke his name.

The elder attorney fingered the rim of his black hat, his expression growing sober. "Don't attempt to contact the review board directly, Sutton. You'll not only be going up against some very powerful men, you'll be challenging an edict from the United States government."

Sutton nudged his thoroughbred closer. "A government that murdered my father, robbed him of his honor, and burned his home to the ground. And that now aims to destroy his name and everything he spent his life working for. That's not the government of a more perfect union, sir."

"No," Holbrook said. "But it is *de lege lata*."

Sutton sighed, familiar with the Latin phrase. *What the law is.* "And what about *de lege ferenda*." *What the law ought to be.*

Holbrook's gaze was unyielding. "It takes time to heal a nation. Especially when the hearts of its people are still wounded and bleeding.

On both sides." He leaned forward. "As I remind myself every morning . . . 'Vengeance is mine, sayeth the Lord.' That same Lord ordains that we obey the laws of the land and submit to our rulers. And the—"

"But when our rulers are bent on—"

Holbrook held up a hand. "May I please finish, Mr. Monroe?"

Stung by the gentle rebuke and mindful of what Bartholomew Holbrook meant to him, Sutton nodded. "Yes, sir. My apologies."

A telling gleam lit Holbrook's eyes. The old man enjoyed arguing a case as much as he did.

"As I was saying, the Lord calls His people to be just, flawed beings though we are." A bushy eyebrow rose. "But government, in and of itself, can no more be fair and just than any one of these businesses here." He indicated the storefronts lining the street. "Justice does not reside in institutions, Mr. Monroe. But in the hearts of men. *If* those men seek Him with all their hearts." His eyes narrowed. "And that, my promising young friend, is what I am petitioning the Lord for on your behalf. That the review board will seek God's face, and that they'll rule on this issue justly. But I'm also praying that *you* would seek justice within your own heart as well, and make peace with the past, whether justice comes in the guise you expect, or not."

As always, Bartholomew Holbrook spoke eloquently, but Sutton still found himself wanting to argue. Yet from years of experience—and having heard the church bell toll three times, meaning he was going to be late for his next appointment if he didn't hurry—he knew it would be pointless.

Today, anyway.

He dipped his head forward. "I'll take your counsel under strictest consideration, sir."

A sad smile crept over Holbrook's face. "You're like a son to me, Sutton. You're bright and talented, more capable than I ever dreamed of being at twenty-seven. And no matter what it feels like now, you *will* recover from this loss. Don't allow yourself to be consumed with the same hatred that prompted those men to kill your father. If that happens, they will have won for a second time."

Hearing the faint and cherished voice of his father in the man's counsel, Sutton had to look away. He tugged at the edge of his collar.

Holbrook reached over and gripped Sutton's forearm. "I know your legal plate is rather full right now with work for your esteemed employer, but I have a proposition for you. One I believe you'll find most intriguing. And likewise, at least I hope, most difficult to turn down."

Sutton waited, his interest mildly piqued.

"It's a case that, if I were younger, I wouldn't dare share. Not even with you, dear boy."

Sutton smiled, his interest holding steady. He was familiar with Holbrook's persuasive powers.

"It will involve a great deal of work and long hours. That's why I'm offering to bring you in. I need your youth and stamina, your tenacity."

"What's the case about, sir?"

Holbrook held up a hand. "If we were to win this case, Mr. Monroe, your name would be on the front page of every newspaper in the country and at the top of every law firm's hire list. Your financial future would be set."

"What is the case about . . . counselor?" Sutton repeated again, his interest having edged up several notches due to that last comment alone.

Holbrook chuckled. "The usual—theft, greed, and deceit. Qualities that make humanity such a fascinating—and tragic—study." Holbrook leaned closer. "A long-standing client of the firm purchased an original Raphael from a gallery in New York, only to discover upon having the painting insured . . . that while it was indeed an original, the painting's certificate of authenticity had been forged, for some reason. Which then led our client to question the validity of another *original* he'd purchased from the same gallery two years earlier. That painting, as it turns out, was a forgery. The gallery denies having known that, though evidence indicates otherwise. But in preparing to go to trial, we've uncovered yet another layer to this sordid affair."

"And what layer would that be, sir?"

Zeal punctuated Holbrook's expression. "Our client has what you might call a rather sizeable investment in art, as do his peers. He's hired investigators, and their reports indicate that these dealings could be more widespread than originally thought. Our client wants to sue this gallery for financial damages, of course. But he also wants whoever is at the top to answer for this as well. And he's willing to pay us, quite handsomely, to work with the investigators to ensure that happens."

Sutton nodded, his appetite more than a little whetted.

When first considering studying the law, the choice to become an attorney had been the means to an end for him—to what he really wanted to do with his life. But over time, and influenced by Bartholomew Holbrook's mentoring, the law had come alive and instilled within him a passion for its truth. But as much as he loved the law, he loved something else equally well, if not more.

He fingered Truxton's reins, remembering how many years he'd saved to buy this thoroughbred, as well as the others the North had confiscated during the war. His childhood dream had about as much chance of coming to fruition now as he did of receiving a fair rendering from the review board.

Mr. Holbrook knew about his other aspiration, and Sutton wondered if offering a part in this case was the old man's way of helping him pick up the pieces of that dream the war had shattered.

"Consider my offer, Sutton, and when you've made your decision, let me know. One stipulation . . . Under no circumstances—whether you accept my proposal or not—can you inform anyone that the firm is working on this case. If news of our client's investigation were to get out, I fear the evidence we're seeking, and that we need, would be buried before it sees the light of day."

"I understand, sir. And I appreciate your trust." Sutton reached for Holbrook's hand and appreciated the man's still-firm grip. "I'll have an answer for you within the week."

"And when I get word of the board's decision," Holbrook continued, "I'll inform you straight away."

Sutton nodded. "Thank you, sir. For . . . everything."

Holbrook made to go, then paused. A memory-laden smile eased the tracks of time and loss etched in his face. "Sometimes, Sutton . . . when I look at you, I can still see him. He loved you, you know. Like a brother."

Sutton felt a wash of yesteryear move through him. "I loved him too, sir, and carry him with me every day."

Seconds passed unhindered, and finally, Holbrook adjusted the brim of his hat. "Well—" He inhaled sharply. "Wish me luck. I'm off to meet with an investigator. I haven't done this in years. Makes me feel like a first-year attorney again. Never mind that I'll be reaching for my rheumatism medicine by noon."

They parted ways, and Sutton rode on through town. When he reached his turnoff, he headed south, urging Truxton to a canter. He knew Holbrook didn't agree with his petitioning the military board to review the case surrounding his father's death. The man didn't consider it wrong—just pointless, under the circumstances.

Yet he also knew that Bartholomew Holbrook understood.

Because Mr. Holbrook had lost his only son on a battlefield not fifteen miles south of town, just a handful of days after Dr. Stephen Monroe had been shot point-blank on his porch in front of his wife. Sutton had been the one to tell Holbrook about his son, because he'd cradled Mark Holbrook—his best friend since the age of six—as death snatched Mark's life away mere seconds after the minié ball had blasted a hole in his chest.

Sutton urged the stallion to a canter, then a gallop, then gave the thoroughbred his head. Vengeance belonged to the Lord—he knew that. But sometimes the Lord seemed slow in meting out justice.

Too slow for the thirst that ached inside him.

8

"How much farther to Mrs. Acklen's estate, Reverend?" Nerves edging out her eagerness, Claire leaned forward on the buggy seat and peered past *Saint* Chrissinda to Reverend Bunting, who gripped the reins.

"The turnoff's just ahead." He tossed her a reticent smile. "I told you it was on the outskirts of town."

Two miles from Nashville proper, the Reverend had said, just before insisting that he and Mrs. Bunting accompany her. Claire was grateful for the companionship, and the ride.

The farther they got from town, the more beautiful the views. Stalwart pines stood shoulder to shoulder with lush-leafed oaks and maples to flank the sunbaked dirt road. Every so often, the timber soldiers would break rank and part to reveal sweeping views of the rolling countryside. Even with the numerous stumps of mighty felled trees—a result of the war, no doubt—she would never have guessed the area surrounding Nashville to be so lovely. Especially after what she'd seen in town.

She could have traveled the distance on foot—she was accustomed to walking much farther—but the afternoon heat and humidity were enough to bear, even riding in the buggy. And the dusty roads would have ruined the elegant emerald dress and matching jacket Mrs. Bunting had loaned her.

She'd glimpsed the contents of Mrs. Bunting's wardrobe, and while the rest of the woman's dresses were certainly nice, this ensemble was without question her best. Claire hadn't had the heart to remind Mrs. Bunting that she was still in mourning for her mother. And her father too.

She silently recounted the couple's kindness and the small miracles Mrs. Bunting had performed in so short a time. Who would have imagined a reverend's wife could arrange hair so elaborately? She fingered a curl dangling at the nape of her neck.

"I'm guessing that thick hair of yours isn't completely dry just yet, dear." Mrs. Bunting patted her arm. "But no one will notice—take my word. You look lovely." She pursed her lips and eyed Claire's hair. "What I wouldn't do for those curls. Not to mention that color."

Recognizing the attempt to lessen her nerves, Claire smiled her appreciation. Her hair *did* feel wonderfully clean, like the rest of her, thanks to the luxurious lavender-scented bath Mrs. Bunting had poured. She could have soaked in that warm, sudsy water for days.

Afterward, she'd told Mrs. Bunting everything she'd told the reverend, and she quickly discovered that Chrissinda Bunting was every bit the saint her husband claimed her to be.

Reverend Bunting peered over at her. "When we arrive, Miss Laurent, I'll accompany you inside and make the introductions. Then I'll wait outside with Mrs. Bunting until you're done."

"I'm going inside too!" Mrs. Bunting nudged him. "Don't think for one minute, Robert Franklin Bunting, that I've come all this way only to sit and wait in this buggy." She winked at Claire. "I never miss an opportunity to see Belmont."

Certain the estate and home were lovely, Claire also felt sure they would fall short of others she'd seen in Louisiana. Not that she would ever voice such an impertinent opinion.

Remembering *another* rather blunt opinion she had given voice to—just that morning, in fact—she felt a sense of misgiving. *Sutton Monroe.* Little had the man known that his attempt to coerce a confession would result in such a boon to her! But despite his intentions, whatever they'd been, she wished he did know. She wished she could tell him. And thank him.

She'd been tempted to ask the reverend about him, knowing they were acquaintances. But that might be construed as forward on her part, and she hated to add *improper* to her already somewhat tarnished first impression. It wouldn't speak highly of her character, and she wanted the Buntings to think well of her. They'd been so generous. . . .

Which only increased her guilt at not having been totally truthful with them about her circumstances. But how could she just come right out and tell them and still expect their help? She couldn't. And she needed this opportunity. She needed this job! A way to provide for herself.

She wondered whether her father's death had changed Antoine DePaul's decision about coming to Nashville. She could only hope that it had, and that she wouldn't have to face him again.

The buggy dipped, and Claire gripped the edge of her seat. "Thank you again, Reverend and Mrs. Bunting. I appreciate everything you've done for me."

"It's our pleasure, dear." Mrs. Bunting squeezed her hand.

"My wife's right. We're happy to do it, Miss Laurent. But we're only giving you the proverbial foot in the door. The rest is up to you. In the note I sent to Mrs. Acklen earlier, I relayed no specifics about you or your experience. I only gave your name and requested that, upon my recommendation, she grant you an interview this afternoon."

Which Mrs. Acklen had done without delay, Claire noticed. Which spoke most highly of the woman's regard for the reverend. Mrs. Acklen had also responded with extreme brevity. The missive, written on fine linen stationery and in flawless handwriting, simply stated, *"Dear Reverend Bunting, Request granted. I'll expect you at half past four. Warmest regards, Mrs. Adelicia Franklin Acklen."*

Adelicia Franklin Acklen. A very distinguished-sounding name.

Mrs. Acklen was a widow—a very wealthy widow, the Buntings had told her—and had four children ranging in age from six to sixteen. After breakfast, Mrs. Bunting had shown her the previous day's newspaper that contained the advertisement for the position.

Claire pulled the clipping from her skirt pocket and perused the qualifications again, speculating on what questions might be asked during the interview and rehearsing what she would say.

The advertisement hadn't been listed with the other requests for assistants, clerks, and secretaries, but occupied a section all its own. Neither was its description abbreviated, as were the others. Apparently, Mrs. Adelicia Franklin Acklen wasn't concerned with paying by the word.

The title of the position made Claire smile. The list of qualifications did not.

LIAISON TO MRS. ADELICIA FRANKLIN ACKLEN

Desired: Young woman of impeccable character and pleasant disposition who possesses exemplary skills in letter writing, bookkeeping, and coordinating social events. Must be meticulous and thorough in nature, possessing initiative and maturity. Fluency in both English and French required. Résumé and recommendations to be reviewed prior to interview being extended at Belmont.

"I know what you must be thinking," Mrs. Bunting whispered, eyeing the newspaper clipping. "Does such a woman exist who can meet such expectations?"

Claire folded the paper and slipped it back into her pocket, her confidence waning. "Yes, ma'am. That's precisely what I was thinking." What on earth was she doing trying to interview for such a position? She was detail-oriented and fluent in French, of course. That wasn't the problem. It was the *exacting* tone of the advertisement that worried her. Such high expectations written between each line.

She fingered the lace-bordered sleeve of her borrowed jacket, wishing she knew more about this Mrs. Acklen before the interview. But before she could articulate the thought into a question, Reverend Bunting slowed the horses and turned onto a side road, guiding the buggy through massive columns of chiseled limestone.

Claire leaned forward, her focus inexplicably drawn, lured by the wealth of land and richness of beauty sprawling before them.

Immersed in every imaginable shade of earthy green and sun-drenched yellow, the vista looked like something that belonged more on a canvas than it did in reality. Yet it was the mansion in the distance, rising in a flourish of mauve splendor atop the hill, that captivated her most.

Reverend Bunting chuckled softly beside her, as did his wife. "Welcome to Belmont, Miss Laurent. The home of Mrs. Adelicia Acklen."

9

Lovely didn't begin to describe the resplendence of the Belmont estate. *Breathtaking* came closer but still fell short. The buggy wound its way along the tree-studded path, past a carriage house and stables, and again Claire noted the remnants of years-old felled oak and pine, their burned-out stumps testimony to battles fought.

Claire spotted a deer—or more rightly, a stag—lurking in the shadow of a pine. Only, this was no ordinary stag.

Made of cast iron and capturing the true animal's regal stance, the statue stood alert, its antlered head lifted heavenward, eternally seeking a scent on the wind. Delighted, Claire grinned as other animals appeared—dogs, lions, and several deer—all cast from iron like their dauntless leader, either nestled among the shady trees or standing watch beneath flowering shrubbery.

The road gradually widened and turned, and the estate extended its second formal welcome in the presentation of lavish gardens containing every imaginable color. The mansion sat atop the hill, in full view, though still some distance away, and Claire drank it all in. Belmont—or *Belle Monte* in French, meaning "beautiful mountain"—was an artist's paradise. And she marveled at the lengths Mrs. Acklen had gone to create such a lavish impression on her visitors.

Three circles comprised the formal gardens, the largest circle located nearest the mansion, while its smaller counterparts descended downhill, diminishing in size. The buggy rumbled past intersecting walkways that connected the circles, and bubbling fountains overflowed amidst a sea of roses, star jasmine, and boxwood. Gardeners dotted the expansive grounds, clipping and planting, pruning and sheering.

A tower stood a short distance away, and Claire imagined how far a person might be able to see from that vantage point. Something ahead glinted in the sunlight, and she shielded her eyes to get a better look.

Marble statuary—too many to count at a glance—dotted the expansive gardens. Reflecting the afternoon sun, the sculptures shimmered dazzling white against the grassy carpet of green. And gazebos, standing a softer white against the late summer blooms, extended an invitation to come and rest.

She laughed to herself. It was all so—

"Beautiful, isn't it?" the reverend said.

She exhaled. "*Overwhelming* was the word I was thinking of."

"You haven't seen the half of it yet." A smile lit his voice. "Right over there"—he pointed to an octagonal-shaped building—"is the bear house."

Claire frowned. "I beg your pardon?"

Mrs. Bunting nodded. "The bear house, dear. Mrs. Acklen keeps wild animals on her property. Her late husband"—her voice lowered a notch—"God rest his soul, often kept a lion or tiger for the delectation of his guests and himself, or so we've been told. Mr. Acklen passed away before we moved to Nashville, so we never had the honor of meeting him. But—if what I'm told is correct—in recent years, Mrs. Acklen has limited her interest in larger animals to bears."

"And alligators, let's not forget," Mr. Bunting supplied.

Claire looked to see if he was jesting. But his expression said he most certainly was not.

The reverend gestured. "In that direction is a lake where Mrs. Acklen keeps the alligators. She had them shipped from Louisiana."

Claire instinctively recoiled. What type of person brought alligators all that way? And kept them at their home?

The clomp of horses' hooves drowned out the fountains they passed, and she spotted a marble statue, one of a young woman trimming vines about an arbor. The woman, forever fixed in stone, was missing her left hand, and all the fingers from her right, save one.

"It was damaged in the war."

Claire turned to find the reverend looking at the same statue.

"When the Federal Army took control of the grounds. Soldiers were encamped everywhere. Their generals took command of the house." Traces of bitterness crisped the edges of his voice. "One of the last battles was fought here, around the house, then on up toward town. Most of Mrs. Acklen's neighbors lost everything, including their homes. But Belmont came through relatively unscathed."

Looking out across the estate, Claire tried to imagine the scene. Soldiers everywhere, campfires burning, the chaos of battle, the smoke and echo of gunfire. Such a stark contrast to the present bliss.

The mansion loomed ahead, and a tangle of nerves twisted inside her. She wished now that she hadn't eaten those extra biscuits and ham at lunch.

Reverend Bunting guided the mares around the wide arc of the circular drive and brought the buggy to a stop before a limestone walkway. An elderly Negro man—dressed in a dark suit with shoes shined to a high polish, his shaved head bearing a similar sheen—stood waiting.

He bowed at the waist. "Welcome, Reverend Bunting, sir. Mrs. Bunting . . . an honor to see you again, ma'am." He spoke with distinction, every syllable perfect.

"Good afternoon, Eli." The reverend set the brake, then helped his wife down from the other side of the buggy. "We have an appointment with Mrs. Acklen at half past four."

"Yes, sir, Reverend. Lady Acklen's waiting for you all inside." He assisted Claire as she stepped down.

His hand dwarfed hers, and she noticed his fingers—thick, work worn, as ancient as his voice. Yet his grip remained oak tree strong.

"Afternoon, ma'am." He gave Claire a smile that demanded one in return. "I'm Mr. Eli." He dipped his head. "Welcome to Belmont."

"Thank you, Mr. Eli." Claire offered a brief curtsy, pleased when his smile edged wider. "I'm Miss Claire Elise Laurent."

"Yes, ma'am." A twinkle crept into his dark eyes. "I believe you are."

A breath of wind stirred. And as if the mansion had whispered her name, Claire lifted her gaze in answer.

The first things she noticed—besides the enormity of the residence—were the Corinthian columns that framed the entrance to the home. Next was the mansion's color. Distance lent it a pinkish hue, but closer inspection revealed the stucco's true color. A warm reddish-brown, set off perfectly by white trim. Cast-iron balconies dotted the front of the mansion, their black lacelike railing reminiscent of New Orleans and the Old Square she'd so dearly loved.

Standing at the foot of the stairs, Claire let her focus trail from the base of one of the columns all the way up to the octagonal cupola crowning the mansion. Head tipped back, a tremor skittered through her. Both of anxiety and of possibility. So much rested on the next few moments.

"Shall we?" the reverend asked.

Claire turned to find him and Mrs. Bunting waiting.

She followed them up the stairs to the ornate front entrance, mindful of the full hoop skirt and concentrating to keep from tripping on the decorative hem. Though she tried to buoy her hopes, she knew chances were good she wouldn't be invited back, so she attempted to memorize every detail about the mansion that she could.

Panels of etched, rose-colored Venetian glass accented the front door as well as the transoms above. Even the side panel doors framing the main entry boasted colored-glass panes of green, red, and purple. On either side of the walkway, stone lions guarded enormous cast-iron urns overflowing with blooms of purple and yellow and white, their sweet scent heady.

Claire drank in every detail. *Exquisite.* Every place the eye lit, beauty dwelled.

She glanced behind her at the opulence of the gardens—the statues, the fountains—and though she knew it was foolish, she couldn't shake the niggling feeling she'd been there before. Then she realized what it was she was feeling. This sense of *déjà vu* . . .

In many ways, the Belmont estate was a miniature American Versailles.

The front door opened, and an older woman greeted them and bid them entrance. Her wardrobe resembled that of a well-dressed housekeeper, and though she was handsome and might even have been considered beautiful in younger years, Claire knew instantly—as one knows better than to grasp a rose stem too tightly—that this woman was not to be trifled with.

"Good afternoon, Reverend. Mrs. Bunting." The woman closed the door behind them and peered at Claire over dark spectacles resting midway down an elegantly slender nose. "Miss Laurent." It wasn't a question. "I'm Mrs. Routh, the head housekeeper at Belmont."

Claire curtsied, afraid for a moment she'd forgotten how. "A pleasure to make your acquaintance, Mrs. Routh."

The head housekeeper's stoic expression said she doubted that was true.

Reverend Bunting stepped forward. "Mrs. Routh, I would consider it an honor to introduce Miss Laurent to Mrs. Acklen, if it would—"

"None of the other applicants has required a personal introduction, Reverend." Mrs. Routh's tone teetered between pleasant and patronizing. "I'm certain Miss Laurent is capable of presenting herself in this situation. If not," —she gave Claire an appraising look—"then perhaps we should reconsider the judiciousness of her appointment altogether."

Claire stared between them, waiting. Mrs. Bunting did the same.

Finally the reverend laughed softly, seeming unbothered. "Of course, Mrs. Routh. You're right. Miss Laurent is most capable of conducting herself with every manner of grace and decorum."

"Very well, then." Mrs. Routh gestured to her right. "Would you and your wife care to reside in the *tête-à-tête* room until Miss Laurent completes her interview? We'd be pleased to serve you *croissants* and *café au lait* while you wait. Mrs. Acklen brought the recipes back with her from the family's recent grand tour of Europe. The refreshments have swiftly become favorites of the Acklens, as I'm sure they will the city of Nashville once Mrs. Acklen introduces them at her next ball."

"How generous of you, Mrs. Routh." Reverend Bunting's patient expression never wavered. "Yes, we'd be pleased to accept your invitation. And the refreshments sound delightful." Thanking Mrs. Routh again, he indicated for his wife to precede him into the *tête-à-tête* room, which Mrs. Bunting did, after smuggling Claire a last fleeting glance that said "good luck."

And that's when Claire saw the statue on a pedestal before the fireplace. She hadn't noticed it before because the Buntings had been blocking her view. Her eyes watered with emotion as all else around her faded.

She was in the same room with a Randolph Rogers masterpiece. And not only a masterpiece, but his *tour de force.*

She had seen this sculpture in print form before but never dreamed she would ever see it in person. She stepped closer. The smooth lines of the woman's perfectly sculpted marble face, her expression poignant, so full of adoration and love. And the way Rogers had carved the woman kneeling, looking upward, her gaze beseeching, oblivious to her robe having slipped from her slender shoulder to reveal a rather shapely right breast.

Which—enamored though Claire was with the statue and its sculptor—made her question the statue's placement in the middle of the front entrance hall. Quite bold a choice of venue. But question of placement aside, *Ruth Gleaning* was Randolph Rogers's first work and, in a widely held view, his greatest. She instinctively reached out to touch *Ruth*'s delicately extended right hand.

"Miss Laurent!"

Flinching, Claire jerked her hand back, feeling oddly off balance. And completely out of line.

Judging by the level-eyed stare Mrs. Routh aimed in her direction, Claire guessed the head housekeeper agreed. She also had a feeling the woman had asked her a question. One she hadn't heard. "Yes, ma'am?" She curtsied again, in apology, then read further disapproval in Mrs. Routh's eyes and wished she could take the curtsy back. "I'm sorry, ma'am, but I—"

"My name is Mrs. Routh, in the event you've already forgotten, Miss Laurent."

"No, ma'am, I . . ." Claire shook her head. "No, Mrs. Routh, I haven't forgotten. I was simply taken aback by this sculpture. It's so beautiful, and I've long admired—"

"Belmont is an exquisite estate, Miss Laurent." The woman's left eyebrow arched in a way that looked painful. "And Mrs. Adelicia Acklen is a highly cultured woman of great wealth who possesses an unsurpassed eye for only the finest of art. You will do well to remember that."

Claire opened her mouth to respond.

"*And* to appreciate the art in this home for whatever length of time you are privileged to be in it." Mrs. Routh's gaze swept her up and down. "Which, if my guess proves correct, will likely be most brief."

Claire wanted so badly to say something in her own defense but knew it would only drive the wedge further between her and this woman. So she kept her mouth shut and her features schooled as best she could. Yet she couldn't help envying the woman's ability to speak her mind so thoroughly, without a hint of hesitation.

How many times had she wanted to do that with her father? But never had . . .

Mrs. Routh took a step closer. "Have I made myself perfectly clear, Miss Laurent?"

Resisting the urge to blink, Claire met her gaze straight on. "Quite, Mrs. Routh. You express yourself with great clarity and directness."

"Acquired traits that would serve *you* well, Miss Laurent."

Claire might have taken offense at the counsel—had it not been true.

"You will wait here, please." Mrs. Routh turned. "I'll let Mrs. Acklen know you've arrived."

Mrs. Routh strode through the doorway to the left of the marble fireplace, the rich red-and-gold floral carpet muting her already quiet steps. Even on the black-and-white-tile-painted floor beyond, Mrs. Routh's boots barely made a sound. And Claire imagined many an under housekeeper at Belmont experiencing moments of utter terror when sensing a presence behind them only to turn and find Mrs. Routh peering down, her dark spectacles resting at half-mast.

Alone in the entrance hall, Claire took sum of her surroundings and her feelings of inadequacy multiplied a hundredfold. To her right a portrait hung on the wall of a strikingly handsome man dressed in a dark suit and trousers and with what was, she guessed, the Acklen tartan. The late Mr. Acklen, she assumed, had apparently been of Scottish descent. She wondered how long ago he had passed away. The Buntings hadn't said.

On her left hung another portrait, larger, almost life-size. A woman holding hands with a little girl. Mrs. Adelicia Franklin Acklen, mistress of Belmont, she felt certain. The woman was elegant, beautiful with her delicate cheekbones, the wide-set eyes and porcelain skin.

But there was something about her air, in the slight tilt of her chin and the focused intensity of her gaze, qualities the artist had captured with masterful skill, that seemed to deepen her physical beauty. Almost mystified it. Making a person wonder what—or *whom*—had occupied Mrs. Acklen's thoughts while the artist's brush captured her likeness.

Claire looked more closely at the woman in the portrait and searched her eyes. Something lingered within them, a knowledge, perhaps. Or a question. She couldn't be sure. Artists were often much *kinder* to their painted subjects than nature and time had been, and she wondered . . . Was Mrs. Acklen as fair of face, and as striking and confident as the artist had portrayed her?

Exhaling the air kept too long in her lungs, Claire looked about the entrance hall, knowing she would soon find out.

Every inch of her view, from floor to ceiling, seeped wealth and privilege. From lavish draperies and richly patterned wallpaper, to the flowered English Wilton wall-to-wall carpet, to the marble fireplace, to the carved moldings framing a magnificent bronze chandelier, illuminated by gas, from the looks of it.

And the plethora of oil paintings . . .

Claire peered down the hallway where Mrs. Routh had disappeared, found it empty, and took two cautious steps toward a side room containing well-appointed bookcases. The library . . . She peeked inside, and felt her pulse edge up a notch.

Two landscapes adorned the wall above the desk, painted with such realism she felt she could almost step right into them. Breathtaking in color, the paintings depicted lush Italian countrysides with vineyards ready for harvest. She chanced another step closer to gain a better look and spotted a statue in the corner.

She couldn't contain her smile.

Though not as large as *Ruth,* the piece also was one she recognized. *Rebecca at the Well.* It was a C.B. Ives, she was almost certain. A shudder of excitement whisked through her. Belmont Mansion wasn't merely a home. It was an art gallery.

Giddy with excitement, she wondered what other treasures were tucked away in this—

Footsteps sounded in the hall.

Heart in her throat, Claire bolted back to the spot where she'd been standing, slightly out of breath and certain whoever was coming would hear the thud of her pulse.

A young girl entered through the opposite doorway through which Mrs. Routh had exited. Her skin was the loveliest tawny brown and her lithe shape dallied on the cusp of womanhood. Spotting Claire, she stilled. "Good afternoon, ma'am." Her voice was feather soft, her drawl its only weight. "May I be of assistance?"

Claire smiled at the girl's question. She was well spoken for one so young. "I have an interview with Mrs. Acklen. Mrs. Routh requested that I wait here until she returns. My name is Claire Laurent."

The girl ducked her head. "Mine's Eva. Eva Snowden." Eva's gaze lifted decidedly from Claire's, a measure of formality having left her voice. "You got mighty pretty hair, ma'am," she whispered, glancing behind her before continuing. "How do you get it to do that?"

Claire touched her hair, wondering what it was doing and whether she had time to fix it before Mrs. Routh returned. She glanced at herself in the gilded mirror above the fireplace, and frowned. "I'm not sure what you mean." Her hair looked like it usually did. Except maybe nicer, with Mrs. Bunting's touches.

Eva peered to one side. "How you get it to curl that way? And stay?"

"Oh . . . *that.*" Claire smiled. "It curls naturally. But it isn't nearly as pretty when it rains."

Eva nodded, as though imagining the results in her mind. "Goes all wild? Like a soured mop?"

Claire blinked, unsure how to respond . . . and having no time to.

Mrs. Routh strode through the doorway. She stopped abruptly by the statue of *Ruth,* and peered down. "Eva?"

"Yes, Mrs. Routh?" The young girl's voice heightened with respect.

"What is this?"

Claire looked at the carpet where Mrs. Routh pointed, then back to Eva, who was already closing the distance.

Eva knelt and picked up a single piece of straw. "I'm sorry, Mrs. Routh. I guess we missed that one, ma'am."

"Yes, that would seem to be the case." Mrs. Routh's mouth thinned, her patience apparently having done the same. "One would think you would have had ample time to have cleaned up the mess by now. After all, the statue was delivered last night."

Claire saw the hurt on Eva's face and felt for the girl—until Mrs. Routh's comment registered. *"Delivered last night . . ."*

Claire looked from Mrs. Routh to the statue again, her thoughts spinning as memory pulled her back to the train station yesterday. And to the crate. And to the man helping unload it. Her eyes narrowed. What were the chances that *Ruth Gleaning* was the—

No . . . It couldn't be. And yet . . .

Monroe had said something to the workers about helping them unload the crate later that evening. And about the statue within being carved by an American sculptor. And Randolph Rogers was an American sculptor.

The scale of possibility tipped with a jarring clang—and not in Claire's favor.

Sutton Monroe knew she was guilty of unlawfully entering a church building and then spending the night curled up on one of its pews like some common vagrant. Earlier that day, she'd wanted to thank him. Now all she could do was pray he had no connection whatsoever with Belmont, or Mrs. Adelicia Acklen.

Because if he did, she had the feeling he wouldn't be nearly as trusting as Reverend and Mrs. Bunting, who were helping her largely—she knew—because of that silent nudge the reverend had felt to leave the door to the storeroom open.

A door that had also opened this one, and which Sutton Monroe could slam shut with a single word. Which would mean that her interview for the position of liaison was over before it had even begun.

10

"Come with me, please, Miss Laurent. Mrs. Acklen is waiting."

Claire blinked, heart in her throat. "Y-yes, Mrs. Routh. Of course." Managing a halfhearted smile in Eva's direction, she followed, stealing a last look at the statue and hoping her suspicions about Sutton Monroe were unfounded.

"*Today* would be preferable, Miss Laurent."

Turning back, Claire discovered Mrs. Routh already a good six strides in front of her. She hastened her step, her heels clicking on the black-and-white-tile-painted wooden floor.

They passed a cantilevered staircase that rose from the grand salon opening before them. The spacious room's vaulted barrel ceiling and double colonnade of Corinthian columns were a work of art in themselves. A mural painted in pastel tones covered the expanse of the ceiling, giving the room a larger, more open feel. Mrs. Routh turned to the left and Claire did likewise, but not before chancing a quick look behind her.

Plush red carpeting—that *her* boots would likely never touch—accented the mahogany stairs. Halfway up, the staircase divided and spiraled to the left and right before continuing to the second floor. *So elegant . . .*

Working to keep pace with Mrs. Routh, Claire imagined what it would be like to attend a party at Belmont. To descend those stairs to the swell of stringed music and the lilting conversation of guests, bronze chandeliers flickering with gas flames, china and crystal—

Mrs. Routh stopped abruptly by a set of glass-paneled double doors, and Claire nearly ran into her backside. She took a quick backward step to compensate, but Mrs. Routh's heavily lidded gaze communicated plenty.

Mrs. Routh rapped softly on the glass pane, then turned the knob and indicated for Claire to precede her.

The instant Claire saw Mrs. Adelicia Acklen—seated on a curved settee in the center of the room—she knew that the artist who had painted the portrait of Belmont's mistress in the entrance hall had not exaggerated his subject in the least. Mrs. Acklen was stunning.

Though some years older than the woman depicted in the portrait in the entrance hall, she still embraced the qualities of a rare dark-haired beauty. Her complexion was flawless with a hint of summer rose in her cheeks, and she possessed an old soul's gaze that an artist's brush begged to immortalize.

Even seated, Adelicia Acklen had a commanding presence. Unmistakably feminine yet undeniably formidable. And every one of Claire's doubts dug in their talons and drew fresh blood.

With a sweeping wave of her arm, Mrs. Routh inclined her head. "May I present Mrs. Adelicia Acklen. Mrs. Acklen, this is Miss Claire Laurent, here for her interview."

Claire curtsied, feeling like a pauper in the presence of royalty. "It's an honor to meet you, Mrs. Acklen." She lifted her gaze. "*And* to be in your home."

Mrs. Acklen gave a measured nod worthy of a queen. "My appreciation, Miss Laurent." Her gaze shifted. "Mrs. Routh, would you see that dinner is served promptly at six o'clock, please? And that the children are present. It seems I'll be venturing out later this evening, after all."

"Yes, ma'am. Dinner at six. I'll tell the children."

"And ask Eva to ready my ivory lace dress, Mrs. Routh. The one with beaded pearls. I desire to dress before dinner."

"As you wish, ma'am."

Ask Eva to ready her dress . . . Was the young girl Mrs. Acklen's personal maid, perhaps? Claire heard the latch of the door click into place behind her and noticed a second door, also closed, off to her left. She looked back at Mrs. Acklen, wishing she knew more about proper etiquette in such situations. Especially with someone of such vast wealth.

But common sense alone told her to wait for Mrs. Acklen's invitation before drawing closer.

With the slightest movement of her hand, Mrs. Acklen gestured her forward, then glanced at the companion settee directly opposite her own. Claire swiftly took a seat where indicated and smoothed her skirt—or Mrs. Bunting's skirt—all while attempting to emulate Mrs. Acklen's impossibly perfect posture.

A whiff of cinnamon and cloves wafted toward her, so homey and comforting a scent for such grandiose surroundings. Claire was tempted to take inventory of the room—the furnishings, the statue she could see from the corner of her eye even now, as well as the paintings adorning every wall—but she didn't dare. Not with Mrs. Acklen staring so intently.

Mrs. Acklen gestured toward a silver service on a side table. "Would you care for a cup of tea? It's a special blend that Cordina, Belmont's head cook, makes for us every fall." A knowing smile hinted at indulgence. "I requested it early this year. I don't know what she puts in it, but it's delicious."

Claire opened her mouth to accept when three jarring images flashed through her mind—of breaking the delicate china of her possible future employer, of spilling spiced tea all over Mrs. Bunting's best ensemble, and of not getting the job. Her mouth went dry at the thought of declining, but she shook her head. "No thank you, ma'am. But thank you for your generosity."

Inclining her head, Mrs. Acklen sipped from her china cup. "Reverend Bunting obviously thinks most highly of you, Miss Laurent. And since *I* think most highly of Reverend Bunting . . ." She smiled, her gaze observant. "That is why you now find yourself seated in my sitting room this late-afternoon hour on the final day of interviewing for the position of my personal *liaison*."

Appreciating Mrs. Acklen's French pronunciation of the word, Claire quickly gathered from whom Mrs. Routh had honed her penchant for being so direct. She also wondered whether the mistress of Belmont might not have an affection for all things French.

If so, that could work to her advantage.

Already, her back was beginning to hurt from sitting so erect, so she squared her shoulders and tried to appear at ease, and as if the future direction of her life didn't hinge on the outcome of these next few moments. "I'm grateful for the opportunity to interview with you, Mrs. Acklen. Reverend Bunting and his wife have been most kind to me. I think the world of them both."

She dearly hoped Mrs. Acklen wouldn't inquire about how long she'd known the Buntings. For the Buntings' sake, as well as her own.

With a queenly nod, Mrs. Acklen returned her cup to its saucer with a soft *tink* and set it aside. She arranged her hands demurely in her lap, as though preparing to sit for a portrait, then reached up and touched the pendant on the front of her dress.

Only then did Claire realize she was staring at it. "I'm sorry, Mrs. Acklen." She gave a nervous smile. "It's just so beautiful. And distinctive."

"It's a hunting horn and a hound's head." She fingered it delicately. "A gift from Emperor Napoleon and Empress Eugenie at *Les Tuileries*, following our fox hunt."

Claire blinked. France was *her* birthplace, and yet this woman went fox hunting with the emperor and empress? She felt more insignificant by the second. "It's lovely."

"*Merci beaucoup, mademoiselle.*" Mrs. Acklen smiled, eyeing her with deeper interest. "Perchance, have you been to that lovely country?"

"*Oui, madame,*" Claire said softly, not nearly so eager to reveal her heritage now that she knew the extent of Mrs. Acklen's social connections. "I am originally from Paris. But I grew up here in America."

Mrs. Acklen nodded. "You're not the first French girl to interview for this position." She smoothed the sides of her upswept hair. "There have been several, as you might imagine."

"Oh yes. I'm sure." Claire felt a sinking inside as a much-needed advantage slipped away.

Mrs. Acklen resumed her poised position. "Now, let us turn to the business at hand, shall we? May I see your résumé, Miss Laurent?"

Claire summoned her readied response. "Actually, I didn't bring a résumé, ma'am. I learned about the position only this morning, so I didn't have time to prepare one. However, with your permission, I'm prepared to tell you about myself and why I believe I would perform quite well in this very important position."

Claire smiled, hoping it would bridge the gap between expectation and reality. But her smile went unreciprocated.

Mrs. Acklen raised a forefinger, not even a whole hand. But that tiniest of gestures carried a weight of displeasure. "Allow me to clarify my understanding of your situation, Miss Laurent."

Claire waited, finding the stiff cordiality of the woman's tone less than reassuring.

"Between the moment you learned of the position this morning and"—Mrs. Acklen briefly looked past her—"a quarter before five o'clock in the evening, you could neither find the time, nor pen and paper, I presume, to list your experiences and talents. To briefly define your individual, God-given characteristics that would aid in convincing me that you are indeed the right young woman to serve in this *very important position.* Is that the understanding I am to form from what you have relayed to me thus far?"

Claire's cheeks burned as though she'd been slapped. Every intelligible thought vanished.

She broke out in a cold sweat, which only deepened her concern about the borrowed ensemble. She *had* to focus. She had to think of something to say. "I could have listed all of that on a piece of paper, yes, ma'am. But it wouldn't have been a *formal* résumé, which I knew someone in your position would expect."

"So instead of bringing less than what was expected, Miss Laurent"—Mrs. Acklen's old-soul eyes held hers without mercy—"you brought nothing?"

Wordless with embarrassment, Claire felt a coolness on her tongue and realized her mouth was hanging open. She promptly closed it. She tried to take a deep breath, but her rigid posture—and the corset she'd tied extra snug in the hope of appearing more fashionable—prevented it. The image of seeing herself fainted dead away on Mrs. Acklen's pristine floral carpet spurred her on. "If you will allow me to give account of my knowledge and skills, I believe they will prove to be more than adequate." *More than adequate!* She barely masked her grimace. That's not what she'd planned to say! "What I meant was . . . if you will allow me to expound on my strengths, I'm—"

Irritation clouded Mrs. Acklen's features, and Claire hastened to regain lost ground.

"I'm thoroughly experienced in bookkeeping and am very detail-oriented by nature. I've organized a library." She forced a smile, which died a quick, pathetic little death. And with good reason. She *had,* in fact, organized a library. Her family's, which had consisted of thirty-eight sad little volumes and a ponderously large dictionary.

She'd been only five at the time, so the feat—completed on her own initiative—had seemed quite an accomplishment.

Before viewing it through Adelicia Acklen's eyes.

Claire licked her dry lips, then wondered if that was poor etiquette. "I'm fluent in French, and have been told that I'm quite gifted in communicating. Although . . ." Her self-deprecating laugh came out more like a high-pitched squeak. "I'm certain it doesn't appear that way at the moment. Lastly, I also possess excellent handwriting. I'd be happy to demonstrate, if you'd like."

Interpreting Mrs. Acklen's lack of response as a clear *no*, Claire waited, wondering if she should continue or simply excuse herself and flee the mansion without a backward glance.

Silence thundered in her ears, and it was all she could do not to give in to the stranglehold of emotion tightening her chest.

Following an excruciating pause, Mrs. Acklen reached for her teacup. She took a sip and set the cup down again, then drew an unhurried breath and exhaled. "Miss Laurent . . . am I to understand by your lack of provision up to this point that you also came to this interview without the requested recommendations?"

Through sheer willpower alone, Claire maintained the woman's gaze. What had she been thinking, coming here? But that was just it. She hadn't known where *here* was. Nor had she known how demanding a woman Adelicia Acklen would be. "No, Mrs. Acklen. I'm sorry. I did not bring recommendations with me. I've only recently arrived to Nashville, so I haven't had the opportunity to—"

To what? Everything she thought of to say felt like a flimsy excuse. Either that, or a partial lie. And worse, she sensed Mrs. Acklen knew it too.

The silence grew thicker, and Claire felt the hot prick of tears as her hopes for this interview, and what it could have meant for her, came to a crashing halt. But she would not cry—she bit the inside of her cheek—not in front of this woman who had probably never shed a tear in her privileged, wealthy life.

Staring at her hands twisted tight in her lap, Claire thought of the man's portrait in the entrance hall, and knew she wasn't being fair. Yet, look at all this woman had. How could someone like her understand what Claire was feeling?

The hollow *ticktock* of a clock somewhere in the room marked off the seconds.

This wasn't the way she'd thought her life would turn out. She couldn't exactly pinpoint, in that moment, what she'd dreamed it would be. She only knew this wasn't it. Three months into her nineteenth year, and she had no family, no home, no means of provision. Everything she owned was in her satchel at the Buntings' home. She didn't even have a place to sleep tonight. And she could encroach upon the Buntings' kindness for only so long.

Feeling Mrs. Acklen's intense stare, she sensed the woman was waiting for an explanation as to why her valuable time had been wasted. And rightly so. No matter how curt Mrs. Acklen had been with her, Claire knew she'd wasted *both* of their time.

Apology was on the tip of her tongue when she spotted a magazine peeking from beneath a cushion on the settee where Mrs. Acklen sat. Recognizing the cover, she felt a twinge of tenderness.

Godey's Lady's Book.

The monthly publication had been a favorite of Maman's and hers for years. They'd read it together and had traveled the globe through the magazine's collections of stories and poems. They'd delighted in learning about fashion and culture from around the world. Seeing the magazine—and learning that a woman like Adelicia Acklen read it too—brought both a warmth, and a renewed yearning for her mother.

Despite the shambles of her interview, Claire knew she was qualified to be Mrs. Acklen's liaison. And something inside her whispered that this wasn't an accident, her being here, her having overheard those women in church earlier that morning. If only Mrs. Acklen knew what she'd been through to get to this moment, and how much the opportunity meant to her. How much she needed the job, the opportunity to start over again.

And what better place to pursue her own art than Belmont? She would be surrounded by timeless works of beauty that could—and *would,* she felt it in her bones—inspire her to create something truly worthy. Another painting like her rendition of *Jardins de Versailles,* perhaps. Or better.

And being at Belmont held another advantage. . . .

If the right people saw her work, people who moved in Mrs. Acklen's social circle, perhaps they would recognize her talent, and—Claire felt her desperation narrow to a single point of focus—that would enable her to gain the recognition she sought, that she could almost taste. Then like Randolph Rogers and his *Ruth Gleaning,* she would create something that would inspire. That would affirm her talent. Something with *her* name on it that would earn her the respect and attention of critics.

She took a breath and released it with practiced ease. But how to get Mrs. Acklen to change her mind? And then it occurred to her. It was almost too simple and had been right in front of her the entire time.

She lifted her gaze. Only seconds had passed, but it felt like much longer. "Mrs. Acklen, you're right. I apologize for coming here today so ill-prepared for our interview. I need to confess something to you, but before I do, I ask that whatever opinion you form of me, you will not hold Reverend or Mrs. Bunting responsible for my failure to make a favorable impression."

Mrs. Acklen studied her with a glimmer of renewed interest. "Very well, Miss Laurent. You have my assurance. After all, it's only proper that one take responsibility for her own shortcomings."

The razor-edged comment cut, but sensing the sand pouring through the hourglass, Claire plunged ahead. "I arrived to Nashville only yesterday. And through a series of unfortunate events, late last night I found myself at a chur—"

She jumped at the sharp knock on the door behind her.

Looking equally surprised, and bothered, Mrs. Acklen glanced in that direction. "Yes, come in."

The smooth glide of recently oiled hinges announced someone's entry.

"Mrs. Acklen," a man said, "I need to speak with you about—oh, my apologies for interrupting, ma'am. I didn't realize you were entertaining a guest."

Recognizing his voice, Claire didn't move—except to turn her head slightly away so that Sutton Monroe wouldn't see her face.

11

Claire sat absolutely still, feeling as though she'd been caught with her hand in the cookie jar. Any second now, Sutton Monroe would recognize her, and her chance to win Mrs. Acklen's trust would be lost. If that chance had ever been hers to begin with.

Mrs. Acklen looked past her and smiled with a sweetness heretofore unseen. "That's quite all right, Mr. Monroe. You're never an interruption. I'll be finished here shortly. Can you wait?"

"Certainly, ma'am. I'll be in the study."

"Very well." Mrs. Acklen nodded. "Thank you."

Hearing Monroe's retreating steps, Claire took a much needed breath. How had he not recognized her? Yet considering she'd been sitting with her back to him, and remembering how she'd looked that morning at the church building, no wonder he hadn't—

"Oh! And Mr. Monroe?"

Claire tensed again.

Mrs. Acklen gestured to the side table directly to Claire's left. "While you're waiting, would you mind reviewing a document for me? Mr. Olensby had the file delivered today while you were away. He's requesting an answer no later than tomorrow morning, and I assured him we'd have one for him by then."

Hearing Mr. Monroe draw closer, Claire bowed her head and pretended to be distracted by a thread at the edge of her sleeve. She could see his hand as he reached for the folder.

"I'll review it immediately, Mrs. Acklen," he said. "And again, please accept my regrets for interrupting your visit."

Mrs. Acklen waved as though dismissing his apology. "It's an interview, Mr. Monroe. Not a personal visit. And we're nearly finished. I'll join you in a moment."

Claire silently counted Monroe's steps to the door as the niggling thread magically fixed itself.

Mrs. Acklen's attention returned to her. "Now, Miss Laurent . . . you were saying?"

Monroe's footsteps halted. And Claire cringed, feeling the lid to the cookie jar clamp viselike on her hand. And on her future.

Mrs. Acklen glanced past her again. "Is something wrong, Mr. Monroe?"

Claire heard him approach a second time and knew there was no use trying to hide her face as she'd done before.

"Miss *Laurent*?" Disbelief weighed his tone.

Her heart pounding so hard she felt breathless, Claire attempted a pleasant countenance as she lifted her gaze. "Mr. Monroe . . ."

Mrs. Acklen leaned forward. "You two *know* one another?"

Calculation and suspicion darkened Monroe's features, and Claire quickly realized he was leaving Mrs. Acklen's question for her to answer. "N-no, ma'am. We don't know one another. Not formally, anyway. But our paths *did* cross briefly this morning at the . . . First Presbyterian Church."

Claire waited for him to say more. But he didn't. He only stared.

"I see . . ." Mrs. Acklen looked between them, curiosity evident in her gaze. "Then allow me to make the proper introductions." She rose and Claire did likewise. "Mr. Monroe, may I present Miss Claire Laurent, who is interviewing for the position of my liaison. Miss Laurent, this fine gentleman is Mr. Willister Sutton Monroe, the most promising young attorney in the state of Tennessee. Mr. Monroe is responsible for managing interests pertaining to Belmont, as well as my other business holdings. I could not do without him."

Claire curtsied, encouraged by Mrs. Acklen's use of the present tense "*is interviewing.*" Meaning, perhaps there was still hope. But as she lifted her gaze and met that of *Willister* Sutton Monroe, she read the very opposite in his eyes. "It's my pleasure to make your *formal* acquaintance, Mr. Monroe."

He offered a stiff bow. "On the contrary, Miss Laurent. The pleasure is all mine."

The way he said it, his voice velvet smooth, made Claire tremble.

But not in a good way. Reluctantly adhering to custom, she offered her hand and he kissed it briefly, just as he'd done that morning. But this time, as he drew back, he squeezed her fingers the slightest bit and gave her a smile heavy with meaning. Without knowing exactly how she knew, Claire understood that he intended to have words with her. Words she would not welcome.

"I'll leave you two ladies to finish your interview." Folder in hand, he turned. But he paused at the door. "It's slightly stuffy in here, Mrs. Acklen. Would you prefer that I left this open?"

Mrs. Acklen nodded. "Yes, please do, Mr. Monroe. Thank you for your attentiveness."

Claire didn't miss the look Mr. Monroe threw in her direction as he left. Which confirmed what she already knew. *Attentiveness* was the last thing on the man's mind. He wanted to hear their conversation. Not that she could blame him.

Mrs. Acklen reclaimed her seat on the settee and indicated that Claire do the same. "Miss Laurent, in the interest of time, I must be frank with you."

"Please, Mrs. Acklen, if you'll only allow me to—"

That same silencing forefinger rose. "I'm an excellent judge of character, Miss Laurent. And while I appreciate your interest in the position and the courage you've shown in coming here today"—a sly little smile tipped her mouth—"as well as the manner in which you conducted yourself in the face of grave embarrassment, *and* accepted responsibility for your lack of readiness . . . I fear the nature of this position and its strenuous demands—especially when considering upcoming events—would stretch you beyond your current abilities. You're a young woman yet, Miss Laurent. You have much to experience and to learn. However, I *do* see promise in you."

Claire didn't know whether the gripping ache in her chest was due to Mrs. Acklen's rejection of her for the position, or to the unexpected compliment the woman had just paid her. Or the unnerving prospect that *Willister* was listening to it all outside the door.

Whichever it was, she felt unusually emboldened. And coupled with the memory of Reverend Bunting intentionally leaving the storeroom door open, she knew that if she left without saying what she'd planned to say, she would regret it forever.

She took a fortifying breath. "Up until this morning, Mrs. Acklen,

I had never heard of Belmont." She spoke softly, above a whisper so as not to appear like the beggar she felt, and yet hushed in the hope that her voice might not carry to the next room. Sutton Monroe obviously thought poorly of her already. No reason to give him further evidence to support that opinion. And though she cared—far more than she should have—about his estimation of her, saying what she needed to say to Mrs. Acklen mattered more. "And please know that what I say next, ma'am, I say with the utmost respect. . . . I had never heard of you either. But despite that, I find myself sitting here, in this room, speaking to you now. And I'm beginning to believe that some of the events that led me here—or perhaps all of them, I don't know—happened on purpose."

Mrs. Acklen listened wordlessly. And somewhere in between the faint glimmer in the woman's eyes and the downward tilt of her delicate chin, Claire sensed a spark of renewed interest. And she grabbed it, determined to make the most of the opportunity.

However fleeting or ill-fated it might prove to be.

Sutton stood on the other side of the open doorway, in the central parlor, intent on protecting his employer's interests.

Though hidden from the ladies' view, he was certain Miss Laurent knew he was there. He'd given her a look that said he would be listening.

He didn't trust her.

And though he found what she was saying now—about arriving in Nashville yesterday—credible enough, he didn't believe her statement about never having heard of Belmont or Mrs. Acklen. He fingered the folder in his hand. He'd been told that particular story before.

How many fortune seekers had he chased off in the past? And how many times had complete strangers shown up on the front porch claiming to be related to Adelicia? Or what of the parade of ne'er-do-well Northerners who came armed, portfolios at the ready, with their "no-lose" investment opportunities. Even far-reaching family members occasionally came calling under the guise of wanting to reconnect with a "loved one." Adelicia Acklen being that loved one. And yet each time they all wanted the same thing.

Money. And one of his responsibilities was to make sure they didn't get it. Or that they got only what Mrs. Acklen desired that they have.

Granted, on the surface, Miss Laurent didn't seem like one of those charlatans. Still, something about her felt . . . not quite right. That could be due to his knowledge that she'd spent the previous night in the First Presbyterian Church—and on Adelicia's personal cushioned pew, no less.

Something Miss Laurent had failed to mention thus far.

"After I left the train station, Mrs. Acklen, I discovered that the lodgings where I had planned to stay were . . . regrettably unsuitable. So . . ."

Regrettably unsuitable. The exact description she'd used with him that morning. Not that this meant she was lying. . . . It simply seemed like too much of a coincidence to him. Her showing up in town when she did, and then at the mansion, on the last day of interviews. Not to mention she was French. Hardly a coincidence, given that Adelicia, as most everyone knew, loved anything French.

The woman had adored Paris. That's where she'd gotten the idea to hire a personal liaison in the first place—after his none-too-gentle suggestion that she do so. She needed the talent of a female counterpart who shared her interest in planning parties, creating guest lists and menus, selecting flower arrangements for tables, and creating the artistic aura that Adelicia demanded for her evenings of elaborate entertaining.

Hence, the liaison.

"So when I saw the church building, I decided to check the doors to see if it was open. And . . ."

Sutton's train of thought stopped cold. So Miss Laurent *was* telling Adelicia about the church. Then again, of course she would. Because she would know that if she didn't tell her, he would. He listened, finding her next statement hard to believe.

She'd entered through a storeroom door that had been left unlocked? That seemed unlikely. Reverend Bunting was a thorough man. Bunting wouldn't have mistakenly left a door open.

Sutton smiled as Adelicia questioned the validity of that statement too.

"Yes, ma'am, I give you my word. I found the door unlocked. And as it turns out, that doesn't seem to have been an accident. Reverend Bunting told me that . . ."

Unexpected laughter coming from the *tête-à-tête* room drowned out Miss Laurent's words, and Sutton frowned at the interruption.

Who else was Adelicia entertaining this afternoon? The woman was becoming a veritable socialite. And he knew who to blame for that—

Cara Netta's mother, Madame Octavia Walton LeVert. She and Adelicia had fast become intimate friends.

"So I am to understand, Miss Laurent, that you *slept* in the church last night?" Incredulity edged Adelicia's tone. She wasn't a woman easily won over.

"Y-yes, Mrs. Acklen. That's what I'm saying. But you must understand, I had nowhere else to go. I know no one in this town, and . . . my funds are rather limited at present."

Sutton studied the carpet beneath his boots, Miss Laurent's last statement reverberating inside him like a warning bell.

"Very well, Miss Laurent. And is the church where you met Mr. Monroe?"

"Yes, ma'am. I was readying to leave—after not having disturbed anything in the sanctuary—when I turned around and . . . saw him standing there."

As Miss Laurent told of their encounter—her reflections on the moment similar to his—Sutton smiled as he relived it again in his mind. He'd opened the side door to find this young woman—a very beautiful young woman—*arranging* herself and her undergarments. Not something he typically saw in a sanctuary. Or anywhere else, for that matter.

The sanctuary being a place of worship wasn't what had drawn him there that morning, and other mornings. Rather, it was revisiting the place where so many of the men—and boys—he'd known, his friends, had died following battle. And the place where he'd lain, staring up at the rafters, wondering if he would die too.

"You stated earlier that you came from New Orleans, Miss Laurent. Why exactly did you leave?"

A long pause followed Adelicia's question.

"I would have stayed in New Orleans, ma'am . . ." Her voice was hushed, sad sounding. "But staying wasn't an option any longer. Maman—my mother—passed away six months ago. And my father . . . he—" Miss Laurent's voice caught.

Sutton found himself leaning forward. Listening. Waiting.

"He died most unexpectedly. I received word of his passing only after I arrived in Nashville."

Sutton bowed his head, feeling like an intruder now—especially knowing she knew he was there.

"Please accept my sincerest condolences, Miss Laurent." Adelicia's voice held uncustomary softness. "Both on your most recent loss, and the loss of your *maman*."

Recalling how quickly his own life had changed with the news of his father's death, Sutton felt for Miss Laurent and what she was going through. A familiar sense of loss resurfaced—for his father, for Mark Holbrook, and so many others. At least now he knew why she'd worn such a frightened, lost look earlier that morning. *If* she was telling Adelicia the truth, he quickly reminded himself.

Which, for the most part, he thought she was. But as an employee of Mrs. Adelicia Acklen, he was paid to not trust easily. Because if Miss Laurent really was in mourning, why wasn't she wearing mourning garb?

"I hope you will understand my need to ask this, Miss Laurent. But if what you're saying is true, why are you not dressed for mourning?"

Sometimes it frightened him how much he and Adelicia thought alike.

"My only mourning dress was soiled just before I left New Orleans. And as I said earlier, ma'am, I arrived in Nashville yesterday. My trunks were shipped separately, so I temporarily find myself without my wardrobe. In fact, this dress I'm wearing belongs to Mrs. Bunting."

"Yes . . . I recognized the ensemble when you entered the room."

Sutton shook his head. *Adelicia*. Always frank.

The silence lengthened.

"Miss Laurent . . ." Adelicia sighed. "I appreciate you telling me all of this. You've been very forthcoming, and your honesty is to be commended. However, again, in light of the specific duties this position requires and of your lack of experience in—"

"Mr. Monroe? You doin' all right, sir?"

Sutton turned to see Cordina eyeing him from across the room.

He'd forgotten he'd left the door to the entrance hall ajar, and seeing her wary expression, he felt even more uncomfortable. Because he knew Cordina. And that dubious look of hers told him she knew he was eavesdropping.

And furthermore, the hand perched on her ample hip said she did not approve.

12

Sutton crossed the central parlor to where Cordina stood, not wishing for Adelicia or Miss Laurent to hear him. "Yes, Cordina. I'm fine, thank you. Mrs. Acklen is interviewing someone, and I was . . . waiting to see if she needed my assistance." Belmont's head cook didn't need to know his real reason for standing there. Though she knew just about everything else that went on at Belmont.

Cordina nodded toward the sitting room. "You ain't trustin' whoever it is with Mrs. Acklen, are you, sir?"

He curbed a smile, accustomed to her blunt—and discerning—nature. "I never said that."

"No, sir, you didn't." She gave him the up-and-down look she'd been giving him since he was thirteen. "But I heard it, just the same." She leaned closer. "You think the Lady done made up her mind on which one she gonna hire?"

The Lady. A title some of the older Negroes had bestowed upon Mrs. Acklen years earlier. He shook his head, glancing back toward the sitting room. "Not yet. Mrs. Acklen and I will discuss it later, though, I'm sure." Adelicia had agreed to let him offer his input before she made her final decision, since he would also be working closely with the young woman.

"You think the Lady might pick that highfalutin' little thing that sashayed her fancy little bottom through here a while earlier?" Cordina made a sashay movement herself, and Sutton smiled.

"Heaven help us all if Mrs. Acklen hires her." Which she would do over his dead body.

Cordina let out a deep chuckle. "I done saw the way that sweet gal been eyein' you when she was here, sir. *Mmm-hmm* . . ." She firmed her lips while laughter danced in her eyes. "You best watch yourself, Mr. Monroe. That little snippet of a woman got somethin' more than helpin' the Lady on her mind."

"Thank you for the warning, Cordina. It's duly noted."

She smiled and patted his hand, her palm rough from kitchen work. He didn't know how old Cordina was, and knew better than to ask. He marveled at how one woman could manage what Cordina did, while also keeping up with every morsel of gossip pertaining to both the house and grounds staff.

If she was ever in a mood and unwilling to talk—which happened on occasion—he went to Eli, her husband, who knew how to sweet-talk the woman into just about anything. Cordina and Eli were as much a part of Belmont as anyone. And despite the war that had been fought and lost, the Negro couple had stayed on with Adelicia. And he admired their loyalty.

Some of Belmont's slaves—*servants,* he silently amended—had disappeared immediately following the end of the war. Which they were free to do, in this new order. His own family's slaves, all seven of them, ran off shortly after his father was killed and his family home was razed. Not that there was much to stay around for after that.

Still, they could have at least stayed to help his mother in the days following. Shown some measure of gratitude for how his parents had always treated them—with fairness and honesty. More like hired hands than slaves, and a lot better than other owners he'd known. But now all of that had changed, yet not all of the changes were sitting well with him.

"I best get myself back down to the kitchen, sir. Make sure dinner's cookin' right." Cordina glanced at the clock on the mantel, and Sutton did likewise.

It was later than he'd thought. "I sure smelled something good when I walked by the stairs earlier."

She raised a brow. "Roasted chicken with white beans, and fresh corn with cream sauce. And blackberry cobbler for dessert. But not if I don't get back to it. Mrs. Routh told me six o'clock sharp, and I ain't been late with dinner yet. Ain't startin' tonight either. No, sir . . ."

She bustled off, and Sutton headed for the study, then decided to wait in the entrance hall instead, hoping to conduct his own brief *interview* with Miss Laurent. Though not for the same reason he'd interviewed the previous ladies.

He sat down and attempted to review the file in his hand, but his mind drifted back to Mr. Holbrook's earlier proposition. Though he had yet to weigh all the variables, he already knew he would say yes to working on the case. How could he refuse? It sounded like a lawyer's dream, and he needed the money.

The door to the *tête-à-tête* room opened, and he looked up to see Reverend and Mrs. Bunting.

"Monroe!" The reverend extended his hand. "I was hoping to see you while we were here today." Bunting motioned to his wife. "Mrs. Bunting and I were headed out to the gardens for a brief jaunt. Would you care to join us?"

Sutton shook the reverend's hand, not having to wonder long about what—or whom—had brought them all the way out here. He glanced toward the sitting room and spotted Adelicia and Miss Laurent conversing by the door. Miss Laurent's head was bowed, and Sutton couldn't hear what they were saying. "I appreciate the offer, Reverend. But I'll have to decline. I'm waiting to see Mrs. Acklen."

"So are we, in fact." Mrs. Bunting's tone held a trace of anticipation. "At least, we're hoping to be able to say hello to her. *If* she's not too busy, that is."

Sutton smiled. "I'm certain Mrs. Acklen will welcome the opportunity to see you again, Mrs. Bunting. She appreciated you sharing your cherry cobbler recipe with her. Cordina made a pan of it last week." He leaned closer, lowering his voice. "Don't tell Mrs. Acklen, but her William and Claude both licked their plates clean when she wasn't looking."

Chrissinda Bunting beamed. "Boys will be boys, Mr. Monroe."

"Yes, ma'am, they will be." And at age eleven and nine respectively, William and Claude were definitely putting that commonly used phrase to the test. Eager to cast off the things of childhood, William seemed bent on mischief and drafted his little brother into the fray at every turn. Their younger sister, Pauline, was often the brunt of their antics. But Pauline was proving to be her mother's daughter and could hold her own quite well.

"Reverend and Mrs. Bunting!" Adelicia entered the front hall, hands extended in a gracious welcome. "What a pleasure to see you again. And how kind of you to accompany Miss Laurent to Belmont."

With Adelicia engaging the Buntings in conversation, Sutton seized the opportunity to do the same with Miss Laurent. Despite her not getting the job, he still had a few questions he wanted to ask, mainly to satisfy his own curiosity.

She stood off to the side, quiet and tentative-looking, which was understandable. Questions at the ready, he approached. She seemed hesitant to look at him, and he wondered if she was intentionally avoiding his gaze. He opened his mouth to say something just as she looked up. Her red-rimmed eyes were wary and watchful—like those of a doe caught in a rifle's sights.

Keeping his reaction in check, Sutton quickly gathered that Adelicia had been none too gentle in refusing Miss Laurent the position. *Adelicia Acklen* . . . He was grateful for the opportunities the woman had given him, but sometimes her straightforward manner came across harsher than he thought she was aware.

All the questions he'd planned to ask Claire Laurent evaporated. Save one. "Pardon my candor, Miss Laurent, but . . . I hope you're not feeling unwell?" He kept his voice low, not wishing to draw the others' attention and embarrass her further.

Her smile was unconvincing. "No, Mr. Monroe. I'm fine. Thank you." She glanced in Adelicia's direction, and her hand went to her midsection.

An unconscious gesture, Sutton felt sure. But telling, all the same. He tried to think of something to say that would be an encouragement to her but that wouldn't come across as condescending.

"May I pose a question to you, Mr. Monroe?"

Caught off guard by her request, he nodded. "Of course, Miss Laurent."

"What is *your* opinion of my interview with Mrs. Acklen?"

Her question, innocent enough on the surface, was actually anything but. She was telling him that she knew—or strongly suspected—he'd eavesdropped on their conversation. As a lawyer, he appreciated her sly tactic. Likewise, he hoped she would appreciate his equally direct rejoinder. "The answer to your *insinuated* question, Miss Laurent . . . is yes. I happened to overhear—"

"*Happened* to overhear?"

Despite her pallor and the evidence of tears, Sutton sensed a steely determination in the young woman. Either that or desperation. But for the moment—if he was correctly interpreting the stubborn tilt of her chin—her frustrations were aimed at him. "As you are now aware, Miss Laurent, I am an employee of Mrs. Acklen. In light of that, and considering the circumstances under which you and I met, I'm certain you can appreciate why I deemed it imperative to *intentionally* listen to your exchange."

She opened her delicate little mouth to respond.

"And"—he inclined his head to mimic hers—"in answer to your stated question . . ."

She frowned, and looked so much like a little girl that if not for the intensity of her expression and the outcome of her interview, he might have been tempted to smile.

"I thought you presented yourself to Mrs. Acklen with great decorum. Especially under the circumstances." Although, he still doubted whether she would have told Adelicia the truth about where she'd stayed last night had she not suspected he was listening.

"And may I assume you heard me explain about how we met?"

"Yes, ma'am, you may." He debated whether to be forthcoming about his doubts regarding the motivation behind her honesty. Force of habit told him yes, but considering their paths would likely not cross again—a thought that disappointed him more than he would have imagined—he decided to keep that observation to himself. "And let me assure you that despite a little good-natured fun on my part, I actually happened into the sanctuary toward the latter stages of your . . . public ablutions."

He watched her, hoping the words would coax a blush. He wasn't disappointed.

"Public ablutions?" A hint of pink crept into her cheeks. "That makes it sound even worse than it was."

"You're right." He eyed her. "Would *female capers* be more appropriate, Miss Laurent?"

"Not mentioning it again would be more so, Mr. Monroe." Her eyes brightened the littlest bit, like someone had struck a match deep inside her.

And in a way Sutton couldn't have explained if he'd tried, he felt honored to be on the receiving end of that light.

Adelicia had made the right decision in saying no to her. Claire Laurent was not the best candidate for the position. He knew that, and his instincts rarely failed him in that regard. Yet, he would have liked the chance to get to know her better. Which, when considering his understanding with Cara Netta LeVert and the uncertainty of his own financial position, made that desire both untoward and unwise. And best dismissed.

But he'd say one thing for Miss Laurent, for having appeared to want the position so badly, she was taking the rejection well. And he sought to encourage her in that regard. "As I'm sure you're aware, Miss Laurent, there were many applicants for this position, so please don't let it—"

"Miss Laurent?"

He turned. Miss Laurent did the same.

Adelicia stood by the open front door, alone. She gestured. "As you can see, the Buntings are waiting for you."

Sutton looked outside, and sure enough, the reverend and his wife were already seated in their buggy. He hadn't even heard them leave.

Miss Laurent hurried to the door. "Mrs. Acklen, I . . ." Lips pressed together, she bowed her head. "I-I want you to know that . . ." She slowly looked up, as though meeting Adelicia's gaze would be painful.

Which, for her, Sutton guessed it would be.

"Miss Laurent, I believe that you have already said everything to me that is required." Adelicia glanced outside and returned Mrs. Bunting's wave with a gracious smile. When she looked back, her smile had cooled. "And I'm quite certain I have made myself abundantly clear to you. Have I not?"

Miss Laurent's lower lip trembled. "Yes, ma'am," she whispered, not looking up again. She curtsied and left without a backward glance.

Adelicia closed the door before Miss Laurent even reached the bottom step, but Sutton could still make out the young woman's form through the rose-colored glass of the side window. Eli assisted her into the buggy, and Reverend Bunting guided the horses down the lane.

Adelicia turned in the direction of the study. "If you'll join me, Mr. Monroe, I'm interested in hearing your thoughts."

Sutton didn't move. He only stared at his employer, knowing he needed to take care with what he said next. He'd witnessed Adelicia's occasional callousness before. Wealthy beyond what most people realized, much less could fathom, she was a woman accustomed to having her way. Willing to fight to get it, and to keep it.

He recalled the journey they'd made to Louisiana during the latter part of the war, and a cool wind of realization blew through him. What that decision had almost cost her . . . cost them all.

But in the end, it had paid off, as they said at the horse track. And paid off royally.

He'd worked for her, or her late husband, in different capacities over the past eight years, and he'd known her and her family on a personal basis even longer. She had moments of generosity that left him speechless, but she could be critical of others when they didn't meet her high standards. Even then he'd never seen her treat someone of lesser rank with such lack of feeling and in so offhanded a manner.

She paused and looked back. "Is there a problem?"

"Yes, ma'am. There is."

She took a step back in his direction. "You're upset with my decision."

"No, ma'am. Not with your decision, but in the way you summarily dismissed her."

Adelicia held his gaze. Then slowly, a spark lit her eyes. "Dismissed her?"

He nodded, not wishing to be manipulated the way he'd seen her manipulate others. She could be most persuasive when she put her mind to it, and so kind in the process that, often, the person being swayed didn't realize that what they had agreed to wasn't of their own choosing.

She pursed her lips. "Am I to understand that you believe I acted rudely just now when saying good-bye to her?"

"That's just it, ma'am. You didn't say good-bye. You simply . . . showed her the door. It's not like you to treat someone like Miss Laurent with so little graciousness."

"Someone like Miss Laurent?" she repeated. "Meaning?"

"Meaning someone of far lesser rank than yourself, Mrs. Acklen. And someone who, only moments earlier, shared some very personal—and painful—insights with you, ma'am."

"Ah . . ." The word came out slowly. "Thank you for clarifying that. Perhaps I should clarify something for you, Mr. Monroe."

Sutton caught the subtle steel in her voice and knew he'd touched a nerve. Something he didn't do often with her, and with good reason. He waited.

"I didn't *summarily dismiss* Miss Laurent just now. I prevented her from thanking me again."

He gave a sharp laugh. "Thanking you? For what? Not hiring her? Demeaning her?" He sighed, wishing now that he'd never broached the subject. "I agree with your decision not to hire her, Mrs. Acklen. What I'm saying is that I would have appreciated—"

"But I *did* hire her, Mr. Monroe." Her eyes narrowed. "Miss Laurent didn't inform you of that fact?"

For a moment, none of what she'd said made sense. Then a sudden heat rose inside him. "You *hired* her? Without discussing it with me first?" As soon as he said it, Sutton realized he'd overstepped his bounds. "I'm sorry, Mrs. Acklen. What I should have said was—"

"What you *should* say is never of interest to me, Mr. Monroe. I have enough people in my life who say what they think I want said. The reason I hired you, and one of the reasons you're still here—after countless others have attempted to take your place—is because you say exactly what you believe. What you think is right. You always have."

Something akin to admiration softened her expression. "That's something Colonel Acklen admired in you, God rest him . . . And I prize that quality too. The courage to speak aloud what resides in your heart." She glanced past him toward the front door. "Miss Laurent possesses that quality as well, when coaxed. Though I dare say"—her focus centered back on him—"she lacks the skill for it that you have so masterfully acquired."

Hearing a trace of humor in her tone, Sutton let out the breath he'd been holding. "I'm guessing that's because I've had considerable more practice at it, ma'am."

She laughed. "*Touché,* Mr. Monroe. *Touché . . .*"

Tired and confused, he ran a hand along the back of his neck. Though he resisted admitting it, part of him felt almost hopeful at the prospect of seeing Miss Laurent again. But the greater part of him, the part responsible for protecting Mrs. Acklen's personal welfare and financial empire, did not. "Would you help me understand why you hired her, ma'am? We both know she's not the most qualified. And"—he felt a pounding begin at the back of his head—"what I find especially frustrating is that we had an agreement—at *your* suggestion—that we would discuss the candidates before you made your decision."

"I'm fully aware of that, Mr. Monroe. But . . ." She shrugged. "She's a most persuasive young woman. And I'm not a woman easily persuaded, as well you know."

He stared, knowing he didn't need to respond.

She moved to the window where the late-afternoon sun shone through the Venetian glass, casting a warm glow on the entrance hall. "The main reason I hired her is because she doesn't know who I am." She pressed her palm flat against the window and spread her fingers wide. "She's the only applicant who didn't look at me in judgment, and with veiled disdain. Because she's not from here. . . . She doesn't know what everyone else in town does."

The ache in Sutton's head intensified. *This again?* He thought she'd moved beyond it. "The other candidates didn't look at you in judgment, Mrs. Acklen. Granted, some were overeager to impress you and had their priorities misplaced, but I didn't sense any disdain toward you."

"Nor would I expect you to." She glanced back. "You're a man, after all." She returned her gaze to the gardens in bloom. "But it was there. I felt it. With everyone . . . except her."

Sutton rubbed the back of his neck again, wishing he were astride Truxton right now, flying across the open fields. He would never understand women. Especially this one.

Adelicia faced him. "Anyone else in my position would have done what I did. You said the same yourself."

"And I still hold to that, ma'am. You made the right choice in going to Louisiana. It was a difficult decision and one that's had its consequences. But—"

"Consequences I underestimated."

"But they're temporary, ma'am. Give it time. You've only recently returned from your trip abroad. This prevailing attitude will pass. You'll see."

He could tell she was tired by the slight droop of her shoulders.

At her core, Adelicia was a very private person, and the interviews had taxed her. As had the past two years. The clink and rattle of dishes from the family dining room announced the dinner hour, and his thoughts returned to the reason for their conversation.

"One last question, ma'am. . . . Why, if Miss Laurent knew she had the job, did she look so ill at ease when she left?"

Adelicia pursed her lips and looked off to one side, and he recognized the reaction. Something was afoot.

She absently touched the pin on the bodice of her dress. "She was thrilled when I told her she would be my personal liaison. But our interview ended on somewhat of a . . . more somber note."

"Somber, ma'am?"

"My agreement with Miss Laurent is on a trial basis." Her chin took a slightly upward tilt. "I told her that if she fails at the task I give her, I will terminate her employment immediately and see to it that she's never hired in Nashville or Tennessee again."

Sutton exhaled in disbelief. "You should try being more direct next time, ma'am. Put the fear of God into her."

Adelicia waved his comment away. "She already has a healthy respect for the Almighty, Mr. Monroe. It's belief in herself that she lacks. She needs someone to nurture that quality. To push her, if necessary."

"And how do you know that?"

"Because when I look at her"—she hesitated, a fleeting glimpse of vulnerability shadowing her ever-present confidence—"I see myself . . . another lifetime ago."

Sutton was so taken aback by her honesty, he could say nothing.

She averted her gaze, and her attention moved to the statue delivered the previous evening. She stared at it, her expression growing reflective. After a moment, she cleared her throat. "Have you any idea when the next statue will arrive?"

Hearing a definitive end to their discussion, Sutton knew better than to push. And frankly, he was ready to take his leave. He'd already excused himself from dinner with the family, eager for time away from everything and everyone. But the statue she inquired about—the last she'd purchased in Rome—held special meaning to her.

"No, ma'am, I don't. But it should be arriving soon. I'll check again with the shipping company."

"Very good, Mr. Monroe. Thank you."

He sensed a truce in her smile, and returned it.

She started toward the grand salon, then paused. "One last thing, Mr. Monroe. Watch Miss Laurent closely. I don't know what it is, but she's hiding something. Or from something. . . . I can feel it."

He nodded, neither surprised at her observation or her request. He sensed the same thing. "Yes, ma'am, I'll do that. I'll conduct the usual formalities that we do with everyone who's hired here."

"Very good. But I'd like to go one step further with Miss Laurent. She said she's from New Orleans. I want you to contact a colleague in that area to verify that what she told me in her interview is true. You *were* standing outside the door listening . . . were you not?"

He gave a not-so-sheepish smile. "Yes, ma'am, I was. I'll mail the query this week."

As Sutton made his way across the estate grounds to the stables, and as he saddled Truxton and urged the stallion into a canter toward the lower fields, he thought again of Mrs. Acklen's request. She wanted him to observe Miss Laurent, who he wholeheartedly agreed was hiding something.

He only hoped the young woman's motivation for being at Belmont wouldn't prove damaging to the estate, or to Adelicia. Because if it did, he would personally see to it that she paid the price in full. Not that Claire Laurent would have much of a reputation left once Adelicia Acklen was through with her.

13

Best watch them boots, Miss Laurent. With it rainin' buckets like it is, you might wanna give them another good brushin' 'fore you step inside here, ma'am. The Lady's got some mighty nice carpet and rugs layin' around."

Claire looked down and saw traces of mud still clinging to her heels, and quickly did as the Negro woman bade, her insides knotted tight. Just as they'd been since she left Belmont yesterday.

She'd awakened in the Buntings' guest room during the night and had broken out in a cold sweat, the realization of what she'd done hitting her full force. She heard again what Mrs. Acklen had said. *"If you fail to meet my expectations, you'll be terminated immediately."* But it was what Mrs. Acklen had said next—about seeing to it she would never work in Nashville or Tennessee again—that sent a shiver up Claire's spine.

Perhaps working for the richest woman in Nashville—or maybe Tennessee, for all she knew—wasn't going to be the key to achieving her dreams after all. Yes, Mrs. Acklen prized art and had connections in that realm. But *original* pieces were what she, and everyone else, truly valued. What would Adelicia Acklen do to her if the woman ever discovered that her personal liaison was a forger? Or had been . . .

Claire ran the soles of her boots across the boot brushes again, feeling her palms go sweaty. The woman who had answered the door—a cook, Claire guessed from the freshly starched apron she wore—had introduced herself just seconds earlier, and Claire knew she should remember her name. But with the tussle of nerves inside her, she'd already forgotten.

She was just thankful it wasn't Mrs. Routh. The head housekeeper scared her almost as much as Mrs. Acklen did.

"You got yourself some tiny little feet there, Miss Laurent."

Claire managed a smile, liking the way the woman pronounced her last name—*Lowrent*—with a rich drawl that somehow drew the name into three syllables. Papa would have corrected the woman's enunciation immediately. Which, oddly, made Claire determine never to do so.

Certain that the bristles from the boot brushes were about to poke through to the bottoms of her feet, Claire checked the soles of her shoes again.

"Looks like you done got it all this time, Miss Laurent." The woman grinned. "We could just 'bout eat offa' them now, I reckon. Now get your bag there, missy, and come on in outta the wet."

Claire retrieved her satchel, catching a last glimpse of Reverend Bunting's buggy as he guided the team up the lane. She appreciated his and Mrs. Bunting's kind offer of lodgings last night. Though she'd scarcely slept a wink.

Stepping across the threshold of the mansion, she couldn't shake the feeling that she was stepping into an animal's lair—of her own disastrous making. The opulent beauty of the mansion hadn't changed overnight, but her realization of the seriousness of her predicament had. And she only had herself to blame.

Despite her fears and the endless possibilities of what could go wrong whirling in her head, she was determined to make the most of her opportunity. But her first assigned duty—to plan a birthday celebration for Mrs. Acklen's recently turned eleven-year-old son, William—was already challenging that intent.

Not having met William, she'd tried to imagine what a boy of his age and upbringing would enjoy. She believed the ideas she'd prepared to present were rather creative, things she would have adored when she was his age. And she knew Mrs. Acklen could well afford the expenditures.

Claire followed the woman through the entrance hall, taking in the ever lovely and stone-silent *Ruth*. The door to the library was closed, and she wondered if Mrs. Acklen was inside working. She hoped Mrs. Acklen wasn't waiting on her.

She was arriving much later than planned. The inclement weather and muddy roads hadn't helped any, but it was a stop at the train station to check on the arrival of her trunks that had caused the delay.

After a quick perusal of the ledger, the porter had said they had no record of her trunks arriving. But if they had, by chance, arrived, Claire knew they would have been delivered to Broderick Shipping and Freight, according to Antoine's instructions. When the porter asked where to send her trunks, she'd nearly answered Belmont, then caught herself, not wanting to risk that Antoine would try to visit her there. She assured the porter she would stop back in a few days.

Claire followed the apron-clad woman into the grand salon. A savory whiff of herbs layered the air, and Claire inhaled. "Something smells delicious."

"That'd be my pork roast, Miss Laurent. I baked it with rosemary and thyme picked fresh from the garden this mornin'. 'Bout melts in your mouth. But you'll find that out soon enough." She paused and gestured to an out-of-the-way corner. "Just stow your bag right over there for the time bein'. They's all waitin' on you."

Claire stilled. "Waiting on me? *Who's* waiting on me?"

"Mrs. Acklen and her children, and Mr. Monroe. They's all in the family dinin' room down the hallway here. Ain't been there long, though. They's still workin' on their soup."

"Working on their soup? But I didn't realize . . ." Panicking, she shoved her satchel into the corner and started hand-pressing the wrinkles from her dress. She glimpsed the splotches of mud staining her hem and grimaced, trying to remember . . .

She was certain Mrs. Acklen hadn't mentioned anything about dinner. She'd simply said to arrive sometime during the afternoon. *Oh* . . . Claire cringed. Late on her first day! The look Mrs. Acklen was going to give her . . .

"Calm yourself down there, missy." The woman gently touched her arm. "Ain't nothin' to get worked up over. It's only dinner, child. And they's eatin' a mite early on account of the Lady goin' out this evenin'." Smiling, she puffed out her generous bosom as though making airs. "She be goin' to a fancy opera in town."

Claire shook her head. "But I'm not properly dressed for dinner, and I—" Seeing a mirror, she chanced a quick look, and sucked in a breath. The curls she'd worked so hard to tame were a mass of frizzy ringlets. What had the young girl asked her yesterday, about what her hair did when it got wet? *"Goes all wild? Like a soured mop?"* Claire tried to tuck the curls back into place, but with little success.

The sharp tinkle of a bell sounded.

"That's the Lady," the woman whispered. "That means they done with their soup and they ready for the main course." She winked and took hold of Claire's hand, her grip firm, like a man's. "We'll just serve you up right alongside the pork roast. Come on now."

Claire had no choice but to follow.

Feeling smaller with each step, she found herself clinging to the woman's hand. Just before they entered the dining room, the woman loosened her grip, and Claire let go. All eyes turned, and conversation around the table fell silent.

"Miss Laurent is here, Mrs. Acklen. You asked me to bring her on in, ma'am."

The woman's introduction urged Claire forward.

Claire curtsied and lifted her head. Her gaze brushed that of Mr. Monroe's, then quickly found its way back there again, and lingered. Wearing a black coat with freshly starched white shirt and cravat, he looked nothing less than dashing. Claire gathered he would be attending the opera too.

Mr. Monroe stood, as did the two boys seated beside him, one of whom looked considerably older than the other and who bore a striking resemblance to the man in the portrait in the entrance hall. Claire's gaze swept the table.

Mrs. Acklen, donned in a stunning blue dress, was seated at the head, her attention unyielding, her expression inscrutable, and her brief up-and-down gaze . . . telling. To her left sat a young girl whose silky dark hair was caught back in a decorative-beaded band. Her eyes were dark and inquisitive. Beside the girl perched the youngest boy seated forward in his chair as if ready to spring at any moment. His eyes were the identical shape and striking brown of his siblings'.

"Welcome, Miss Laurent." Mrs. Acklen, her smile gracious, motioned Claire toward the empty chair directly across the table from Mr. Monroe. "How lovely that your schedule has finally allowed you to join us."

Hearing the subtle reprimand, Claire halfway wished she could announce that on the way the Buntings' buggy had overturned in a horrific accident, and that only after clawing her way through the carnage had she barely managed to escape with her life, and that was why she was late. But of course she couldn't say that, and the real excuse felt flimsy by comparison.

Standing beside the empty chair, Claire dipped her head, grateful the table hid her muddy hem. "My sincere apologies for being late, Mrs. Acklen." The silence in the room lay heavy without an accompanying excuse, and Claire bit her tongue to keep one from slipping out, knowing it wouldn't help her cause.

"Allow me, Miss Laurent." Mr. Monroe appeared behind her and held her chair as she took her seat.

She glanced up at him, catching a hint of bayberry and spice. "Thank you, Mr. Monroe."

"My pleasure," he whispered, his eyes not meeting hers. He returned to his place.

The same woman who had answered the door returned with three other women, all carrying platters and dishes laden with food. Within seconds, the table was transformed into a mouthwatering buffet. Creamed sweet potatoes, whipped light and fluffy, mounded the scalloped edges of an ivory compote, and thick slices of herb-encrusted roasted pork loin adorned a silver platter. Lima beans in a white cream sauce and a bowl of buttery corn followed, but it was the baked apples still bubbling in their sugary cinnamon bed that drew an "Ah . . ." from Mrs. Acklen's daughter.

Claire had never seen the likes of such luscious offerings. Did the Acklen family eat in such a fashion every night? She couldn't begin to imagine. . . .

But it was what filled her glass, and everyone else's, all the way to the brim, that truly amazed her. *Ice.* Which cracked and popped as the servants poured what looked to be lemonade.

"Would you care for a roll, miss?"

"Yes, please." Claire looked up to see Eva, and almost felt as if she was seeing a friend. "Thank you, Eva."

Eva gave a delicate, proper nod older than her years. "You're welcome, ma'am."

Only then did Claire notice her dinner plate. Fine scalloped china with the name *Acklen* painted in gold lettering in the center. She touched the gold-rimmed edging, not having to wonder whether or not the gold was real.

After everyone was served, the servants left the room. All except the woman who had escorted Claire in. "Is there anything else you be needin', Mrs. Acklen?"

Mrs. Acklen gave a sigh heavy with approval. "I can't think of a thing, Cordina. You've outdone yourself yet again."

Cordina . . . Claire made mental note of the woman's name.

"I 'preciate that, Mrs. Acklen. But it wasn't just me, ma'am. I have lotsa good help in my kitchen." She dipped her head. "Hope you all enjoy your dinner."

As Cordina exited the room, Mrs. Acklen bowed her head, as did the rest. Claire followed suit.

"For what we are about to receive, dear Lord, and for what we have already received in such great bounty . . ." Mrs. Acklen's voice held a humility and quiet reverence that drew Claire's gaze.

Barely lifting her head, Claire peeked from the corner of her eye, just in case any of the children were looking. They weren't. Their heads were all dutifully bowed and their eyes closed, as hers should have been.

She chanced a look across the table and felt her breath catch. Mr. Monroe's head was bowed, but only slightly. And he was watching her. She offered a meager smile, which he barely returned before looking down again.

"Grant us wisdom and discernment to be good stewards of all you have bestowed . . ."

Claire felt a slight frown. Based on her exchange with Mr. Monroe yesterday, she'd thought the two of them had reached a friendly truce. But what she'd seen in his eyes just now hardly resembled a warm welcome.

A thought occurred. One that didn't bring comfort.

He'd started to say something to her yesterday, just as she was leaving, but they were interrupted. She'd been so preoccupied at the time, she hadn't thought anything about it, until now. He'd said something about there being a lot of applicants, so she shouldn't let it—

Bother her . . . Claire blinked. Was that what he had been about to say? That she shouldn't let it bother her . . . that she hadn't gotten the job. He'd assumed Mrs. Acklen had said no to hiring her.

". . . and may we always be mindful of those less fortunate. . . ."

Claire stared through the steam rising from the food. She

surmised that Mrs. Acklen relied heavily on Mr. Monroe for legal counsel. But she sensed a more personal bond there too. So securing his good opinion was paramount to making this a more permanent arrangement.

"In the name of Jesus, we pray . . ."

Claire quickly bowed her head again and closed her eyes.

"Amen."

"Amen," Claire echoed softly with everyone else, careful not to look in Mr. Monroe's direction.

Fork raised, Mrs. Acklen gave a queenly nod, and dinner ensued. "Children, I'd like to introduce Miss Claire Laurent. I've already told you a bit about her. She'll be working with me over the next few days to plan William's birthday celebration."

Claire smiled at the boy sitting beside Mr. Monroe, fairly certain that he was William.

"You may remember that Miss Laurent was born in Paris," Mrs. Acklen continued.

Her daughter leaned forward and peered down the table. "We just got back from there." Her lower lip pudged. "It's so pretty!"

Claire smiled. "Yes, it is. But it's also very lovely here."

The little boy next to her leaned closer. "Mama knows the emperor of France. Do you know him?"

"I'm afraid I haven't had the pleasure of meeting him." Claire sipped her lemonade, relishing the cold against her throat, as well as the boy's short attention span and apparent affinity for sweet potatoes.

"Miss Laurent, allow me to introduce my children." Mrs. Acklen looked at the older boy seated to her right. "This is my eldest son, Joseph. He's sixteen and will be returning to school. So he'll only be with us through the weekend."

Joseph was a handsome boy with a head of thick, dark brown hair, and was undoubtedly the son of the man in the portrait.

"William is our birthday boy. He turned eleven while in New York, on our way back from Europe, and I assured him that we'd celebrate in style upon our return." Mrs. Acklen beamed. "Sitting next to you, Miss Laurent, is Claude, who is nine. He's as sharp-witted as he is precious, so be on your guard. And this"—she patted her daughter's arm—"is Pauline, who is six . . . going on twelve." She smiled. "My children are my greatest treasures."

Claire looked around the table. "And I can see why. It's very nice to meet all of you."

Joseph nodded, again in a manner much like his mother, while William eyed her with meager interest. Only Claude and Pauline offered welcoming smiles.

Claire returned them, directing her next comment to the youngest Acklens. "Do you both enjoy attending school? Seeing all of your friends?"

Silence rewarded the questions, and Claude and Pauline looked to their mother.

"Actually, Miss Laurent, the childrens' *private* tutor returns to Belmont in two weeks." Mrs. Acklen's tone, though genteel, held a touch of correction, and Claire nodded as Claude and Pauline let out yips of excitement. Mrs. Acklen quieted them with a hushing hand. "Miss Heloise Cenas has been with us for many years now. She oversees the children's studies in remarkable fashion. I don't know what we would do without her."

Claire started to say "How very nice" but decided that simply nodding again and concentrating on her meal was the safer choice.

A moment passed, the only sound the tinkling of silver cutlery on delicate china.

"I'm certain, Miss Laurent," Mrs. Acklen continued, "that you're dreaming up some wonderful plans for William's birthday celebration."

Hearing a request in the woman's tone, Claire hurriedly swallowed the bite of lima beans and washed it down with a gulp of icy lemonade, which rushed a chill to her head. "Yes, ma'am." She smiled at William for good measure, though he still didn't return the gesture, and she wondered whether the details were meant to be a surprise for him. "I had intended to discuss them with you first . . . privately."

Mrs. Acklen shook her head. "I think William would be interested in knowing what you have planned." She glanced at her son, whose expression conveyed considerably more interest than moments earlier. "So . . . do tell us all, Miss Laurent. What are your thoughts at the moment?"

Claire rested her fork beside her plate, eyeing her remaining sweet potatoes. She dabbed her mouth with her napkin. "Well . . ." Excitement rose inside her as she imagined the scene in her mind. "Turning eleven is a special time in a child's life, and . . ."

She glanced at William, whose features instantly dulled.

"And . . ." Scrambling to regain her thoughts, she wondered what she'd said to provoke such a response. "I was thinking that we could invite his friends, of which I'm sure there are many."

The boy's air of disinterest plummeted to full-fledged boredom.

Claire decided to skip her rehearsed introduction and jump ahead to the best part. "This morning, I browsed in town and found the most wonderful puppet shop. I thought we could—"

"Not puppets *again*!" Claude sighed. "We saw those in Europe. Over and over . . ."

Pauline sat straighter. "I like puppets! Especially when they *hit* each other!" She smacked her fork against her spoon. But only once. A cowing look from her mother saw to that.

William exhaled. "Puppets are for children." He rolled his eyes. "And I'm not a child anymore."

"Now, now . . ." Mrs. Acklen lifted her chin. "You will keep your comments to yourself and allow Miss Laurent to finish her thoughts. I'm certain she has other ideas."

She told herself not to, but Claire glanced across the table only to discover Mr. Monroe's gaze now confined to his plate, which somehow only deepened her embarrassment.

"Yes, ma'am . . . I have other ideas." She took a breath, willing her forced enthusiasm to sound authentic, and hoping Mrs. Acklen wouldn't consider this next idea too indulgent. "I'll need to explore the logistics, of course, but imagine how exciting it would be to ride in a hot air balloon!" She paused to let the idea take flight, as it were. "We could hire a balloonist to take the chil—" She caught herself. "To take William and his friends for a ride. We would have the balloon tethered, of course, so that it would be secure. Less risk for injury or mishap."

Claire had trouble gauging their reactions to the idea, so she pressed on. "I've actually seen these balloons before. Once," she admitted. "They're *quite* beautiful, and the experience looks like it would be a memorable one."

The expressions of Mrs. Acklen and her sons could best be described as complacent. Little Pauline, her eyes wide, seemed close to bursting with excitement yet remained compliantly silent. It was

Sutton Monroe's expression—the flicker of compassion, however fleeting—that explained everything.

Claire's throat tightened. Her face burned with embarrassment. "You've already done that too, I suppose."

"In Paris," William said, his tone gloating. "We flew the balloon over the city. Without a tether."

"However"—Mrs. Acklen cast a sharp glance at her middle son before looking back at Claire—"your description of the experience is most accurate, Miss Laurent. It was a memorable part of our journey."

It was all Claire could do to nod.

"Well . . ." Mrs. Acklen rang the silver bell beside her place setting. "I think that's enough conversation about the party for now."

Claire bowed her head as familial conversation resumed. She sensed Mr. Monroe's attention but didn't dare look across the table. The last thing she wanted to see was his pity.

Hearing footsteps in the hallway, she glanced at the others' plates. All empty. Hers was still half full. Despite having failed miserably to impress them, she was still hungry, but she wasn't about to ask to be given more time.

A dessert plate was placed where her dinner plate had been, and the serving of *petits fours glacés* blurred in Claire's vision. Her mother had always loved these tiny little iced cakes. Claire gritted her teeth until her jaw ached, refusing to give in to the slow-burning truth flickering inside her. She knew she didn't belong. In this house, in this position, in this make-believe kind of world.

And what was worse—she slid a look across the table—Sutton Monroe knew it too.

14

May I have a word with you, Miss Laurent?" Sutton could tell by the way she'd avoided his gaze during dessert, and how she'd bolted from the family dining room, that a word with him was the last thing she wanted. And he couldn't say he blamed her. Not after what she'd just been through.

He understood her desire for a hasty retreat and empathized with her embarrassment, but he needed to properly congratulate her on getting the job, regardless of how he felt about it. And equally as important, he wanted to lay the groundwork for their working together. However brief a time that might prove to be.

She paused by the staircase and turned back, wearing a pasted-on smile and tugging nervously at her dress. "Yes, Mr. Monroe, you may. But please don't allow your conversation with me to make you late for your opera."

Telling by the faint flicker in her expression, Sutton gathered she'd tried to keep the hurt from her voice, but a thread of it had needled its way through, and he felt its prick. "There's time yet before we need to leave, ma'am. And, I promise, I'll be brief." He smiled in the hope of setting her more at ease, but the tiny lines at the corners of her eyes only knit tighter. "Allow me to extend my formal welcome to Belmont, Miss Laurent, as well as my congratulations to you on being chosen for the position. If I can be of assistance to you, I hope you'll consider me at your service."

"That's very kind of you, Mr. Monroe. And your offer is most generous."

Sutton studied her, wondering if she was aware of how truly poor a liar she was. Not that she was lying, *per se*, but she definitely wasn't speaking her mind. Adelicia was right. That apparently took some coaxing.

With silent deliberation, he checked his pocket watch. If the two of them were going to work together—which Adelicia had made clear they were, at least for the time being—they needed to get some things straight. But the grand salon wasn't an appropriate setting.

He glanced to where Mrs. Acklen was bidding her children goodnight, then back to Miss Laurent. "The gardens are especially lovely this time of evening, Miss Laurent. Would you care to view them with me?"

"That's most kind of you, Mr. Monroe. But I have no intention of making you late for your plans. And I still need to be shown to my—"

"Miss Laurent . . ." Apparently, he needed to take the more direct approach. "I'm requesting an opportunity to speak with you privately. I'd prefer to do that now, if you are agreeable. Or we can meet following breakfast in the morning."

Emotions flitted across her pretty face—fear, dread, and finally, begrudging acceptance. With a frown, she nodded, her auburn curls bouncing. He gestured for her to precede him, smiling at her back.

Adelicia caught his attention and gave the faintest nod. He returned it. She hadn't specifically requested that he have a conversation with Miss Laurent. It was simply understood that he would. Adelicia would view it as his responsibility to keep an eye on the young woman.

The air outside was cooler, and he welcomed the breeze. The rainfall had ceased, leaving behind a world of deeper green and a veil of moisture that clung to every surface. He breathed in and caught the scent of Adelicia's innumerable roses and was grateful the heavy days of summer were behind them.

He offered Miss Laurent his arm as they descended the steps. She slipped her hand through, then promptly removed it the second her little boot touched level ground, which only renewed his smile. The poor liar, who had trouble speaking her mind, possessed an independent streak. Interesting combination.

They strolled toward the main fountain and as far as the first tiered garden before he broke the silence. "I appreciate your taking the time to speak with me, Miss Laurent. And I'm wondering . . ." He peered over at her. "Would you like to go first, or shall I?"

Her steps slowed. "What do you mean?"

"I mean that we both have things we want to say to each other. I'll go first, if you'd like. Or you may."

She came to a stop. "I'm afraid you've misread me, Mr. Monroe. I . . . don't have anything *pressing* that I want to say to you."

"Are you certain?"

She blinked as though checking her own thoughts. "Quite."

"Very well, then." He motioned toward a gazebo, thinking she might like to sit, but she shook her head. So they continued their stroll. "First, may I say, ma'am, that I believe you handled the situation in the dining room with grace and decorum."

She peered up at him. "Yes, you may, Mr. Monroe. And I thank you. But . . . I doubt that's what you brought me out here to tell me."

He let his smile show, appreciating her candor. It was a step. "You're right. It's not. The main thing I want to say to you, Miss Laurent"—he prayed he would speak with a fraction of the genteel honesty he'd always admired in his father—"is that, while I was not in favor of Mrs. Acklen hiring you for this position, I do respect her choice. And I was most sincere earlier when I offered to assist you in whatever way I can."

As they rounded a curve in the path, he glanced back toward the house to make sure the carriage wasn't waiting, dreading the evening before him. He'd gotten his fill of opera for a lifetime in Europe, as well as the social politics that accompanied the event locally.

They walked in silence until Miss Laurent paused by one of the many statues Adelicia had collected through the years. "Why did you not want me to get the position?" Her voice was quiet, her attention fixed on the polished marble of a young woman trimming vines next to an arbor.

Studying her profile, Sutton debated how to phrase his answer, not wanting to intentionally hurt her. But not wanting to mislead either. And certainly not wanting to reveal a confidence between him and Mrs. Acklen. "Because I didn't feel as though you were among the most qualified applicants, Miss Laurent. I'm sorry. . . ."

She stared at him, then nodded, slowly, as though having to accept his response in increments. They continued down the walkway, and when they came to a fork in the path, Sutton chose the direction leading back toward the mansion.

"What position do you hold here at Belmont?" she asked after a moment.

"I'm Mrs. Acklen's personal attorney. I also help manage the financial holdings of her estates, which—among other things—means protecting her, and her wealth, from people who would seek to take advantage of either, or both." He gauged her expression, watching for a reaction—a trace of guilt, perhaps, a sign of discomfort.

And saw traces of both—just before she looked away.

As they neared the main fountain, he spotted the carriage in the distance, coming up the lane. "Shall we?" He offered his arm as they ascended the steps to the front portico. Once inside the entrance hall, he heard Adelicia's voice, and Mrs. Routh's, coming from a nearby room. "Has Mrs. Routh shown you your quarters yet?"

"Not yet."

"Then allow me. It's through here." He led the way across the grand salon to the northeast wing. "Others might disagree, since your room doesn't overlook the gardens, but I think you have one of the most beautiful views Belmont offers." He opened the door to the bedroom, working to sort the culpability he'd seen in her features a moment earlier with her seeming innocence. "I know because I stayed in this room when I first came here."

"You don't live at Belmont anymore?"

"I do. But in another building. The art gallery has guest quarters. I live in one of those."

Her eyes lit. "Belmont has an art gallery?"

He nodded, feeling a little as if he were seeing the estate for the first time again, through her eyes. "Come and see your view." He pulled the curtains back to reveal the lush rolling meadows that encompassed the majority of the one hundred eighty acres surrounding the manor. Acreage he and Truxton knew by heart.

She stepped close to the window. "It's like a painting," she whispered. "All the colors . . ."

"And it's not even at its best yet." He pointed to the tree line in the distance. "Those are all maples. Give it a few weeks and that entire hillside will be on fire with autumn."

She sighed, and her breath fogged the glass pane. "Autumn was my mother's favorite time of year. It's mine too."

Sutton studied her profile, remembering her recent losses. "I'm sorry about your father's passing, Miss Laurent. And that of your mother."

"Thank you, Mr. Monroe." A moment passed before she looked back at him. Silent tears marked her cheeks.

Knowing he needed to go, Sutton found he didn't want to. He hated to leave her melancholy. "Is there anything I can do for you, Miss Laurent? Believe I leave . . ."

She dabbed her cheek. "Actually, there is. You can stop calling me Miss Laurent. That's getting rather bothersome, don't you think?"

He smiled. "With your permission, then, may I address you as Claire, in less formal settings?"

"You may." She looked up at him. "But only if I can call you Willister."

Sutton realized he'd walked directly into her trap. "You may. But only if you don't want me to respond." He crossed to the door. "I'm certain Mrs. Routh will be by soon enough to answer any questions you may have." He gave a brief bow. "Good evening, Claire."

She curtsied. "Good evening . . . Willister."

It wasn't until the curtain fell after the third act that Sutton realized his misstep earlier that evening. He tugged at his collar, the lead soprano's excessive vibrato gnawing at his patience. In his effort to be upfront with Claire Laurent, he had in all likelihood driven a wedge between them, and he'd undermined his pledge to Mrs. Acklen to keep an eye on her.

He'd admitted to Claire that he didn't believe she was qualified for the position, which meant she wouldn't dare seek his advice on anything, because that would only prove his point. So instead of nurturing their working relationship, which would further his employer's goal, he'd actually given Claire a bona fide reason not to confide in him. Or trust him.

Seated in the row behind Mrs. Acklen in her box seats, he stared out over the crowd of Nashville's elite. As much as he despised the name Willister, he'd certainly earned it this time.

15

While these are not wholly unappealing possibilities for a party, Miss Laurent, I was certainly hoping for something with a little more . . . creativity from you." Mrs. Acklen eyed her across the library desk. "This needs to be an event that William and his friends will remember, that their parents will talk about, instead of a celebration centered around . . ."

Claire cringed in her chair as Mrs. Acklen reached over the desk for the list of ideas she'd stayed up past midnight last night compiling. Around the same time Mrs. Acklen and Sutton returned from the opera.

". . . clowns, sack races, croquet, rolling hoops, hopscotch, and . . ." Mrs. Acklen peered over her reading glasses to look at her. "*Donkeys?*"

Disapproval and fatigue lined Mrs. Acklen's features, and Claire lowered her gaze.

With a sigh, Mrs. Acklen pushed the piece of paper back toward her. "I assume, Miss Laurent, that you're aware of the zoo on this estate. So correct me if I'm wrong, but I fail to see how a game with donkeys—ones fashioned from paper, no less—is going to enthrall forty-seven children."

In a brief moment of lunacy, Claire considered correcting her employer's use of the word *children*—knowing William would have had he been present—but she quickly regained her senses. "Yes, ma'am, I'm aware of the zoo. But the donkeys I referred to are actually *piñatas.* A *piñata* is an object made of *papier mâché* that is filled with—"

"I know what a *piñata* is, Miss Laurent! What I'm telling you is that none of these ideas appeal to me. And I'm certain they won't appeal to William." Mrs. Acklen removed her glasses and massaged the bridge of her nose. "Nine days, Miss Laurent. Nine days . . . That's all that remains before the party." She gave a tired laugh. "And we don't even have the menu selected. But of course we can't do that until we have an idea for the theme."

Part of Claire wanted to gently remind the woman they were only planning a child's birthday party, not Nashville's social event of the year. Then again, this "child's birthday party" *was* the deciding factor in whether or not she got this job. And she needed to succeed.

"I'm sorry, Mrs. Acklen." Claire rose, eager to return to her task. "If you'll excuse me, I'll go and prepare some new ideas."

"*Creative* ones this time, please, Miss Laurent. And what of the party favors? Have you ideas for those?"

"Party favors?"

Mrs. Acklen's eyes fluttered closed, then opened. "Yes, party favors, Miss Laurent. A small token of appreciation given to a guest to convey the host's gratitude for their attendance."

Claire felt her face heat. "Yes, of course, ma'am. I'm going into town this morning. Right this minute, actually, and will return with possibilities for those as well."

"Have you arranged for a carriage yet?"

Hand on the doorknob, Claire shook her head. "No, ma'am. I thought I would walk. It's so nice outside, and I enjoy—"

"Take one of the carriages." Mrs. Acklen peered over the desk. "Your hem is already caked in dust. I'd hate to imagine what it would be like after tromping the streets of Nashville after yesterday's rain."

Claire looked down. She'd spent half an hour brushing the skirt of this dress, since her only other dress was still splattered with mud. "Yes, ma'am."

"And am I to assume, Miss Laurent"—Mrs. Acklen's tone softened by a degree—"by your lack of mourning garb that your trunks have not arrived as of yet?"

Claire fingered her skirt. "No, ma'am, they haven't. But I'll be sure to stop by the train station when I'm in town and check again."

"Yes, please do that. And tell the steward to have them sent here. No need to continue making needless trips into town when there's so much to be done. In fact, I have several contacts in New Orleans. We could wire them and ask them to check on your belongings and—"

"No, ma'am," Claire said quickly, panic clawing its way up inside her. The last thing she needed was for an acquaintance of Mrs. Acklen's to visit the gallery where they had lived. "What I mean is . . . that won't be necessary. I'm sure the trunks will arrive soon enough."

Mrs. Acklen looked pointedly at her. "If your trunks don't arrive today . . . then other arrangements will need to be made."

"Other arrangements, ma'am?"

"Yes, Miss Laurent." Mrs. Acklen smoothed the front of her own immaculately pressed pastel dress. "We're having dinner guests tomorrow night, and you need a suitable *ensemble* for that occasion. As well as an appropriate mourning dress."

Claire tightened her grip on the doorknob, summoning her nerve. "I understand what you're saying, but I'm rather short of funds right now, and buying even one dress—"

"Oh yes, I remember you saying as much. Not to worry, I'll deduct the dresses from your wages." With a fountain pen, Mrs. Acklen wrote something on a piece of stationery and held it out. "Visit this shop and ask for Mrs. Perry. She'll assist you."

Claire took the fine linen paper and stared at the name of the shop, then the address, wondering why the street sounded so familiar. Her grip tightened on the page as realization dawned.

"Do you have a question about what I've written, Miss Laurent?"

Claire looked up. "No, ma'am. There's no question. Thank you." She opened the door to leave, existing solely for the moment she could close it behind her.

"Miss Laurent?"

Masking her dread, Claire looked back. "Yes, ma'am?"

"One does not say they're sorry when they have committed no wrong. While you were mistaken in thinking that your ideas for the party were worthy of serious consideration, you committed no *wrong*. Offering an apology for an offense and admitting you were mistaken on a subject are two quite different responses to two quite different circumstances."

Claire stared, waiting, wondering if Mrs. Acklen was finished. "Yes, ma'am. I understand. I'm sor—" She caught herself. "I'm *so* very grateful that you pointed that out to me. Thank you." Sweat beading beneath her chemise, Claire thought she caught the flicker of a smile in Mrs. Acklen's eyes. As she pulled the door closed, she looked again to be sure, and knew she must have imagined it.

The latch clicked into place behind her, and Claire leaned against the doorjamb in the entrance hall and sighed.

"That bad, was it?"

She quickly straightened. Mr. Monroe—*Sutton*—was standing in the hallway leading to the grand salon.

Gathering her wits, she shook her head. "No, everything's fine." She recalled his admission last night, and while having suspected his opinion of her, hearing him say he didn't consider her qualified for the position stung.

Determined to appear more confident, she pasted on a smile. "I'm simply weary from a late night. And I have a busy day ahead. So if you'll excuse me . . ." She headed toward her room, not really knowing why. Only that she wanted to appear confident and as if she knew what she were doing.

He fell into step beside her. "And what does that busy day entail . . . Claire?"

"It entails going into town . . . Sutton."

"Have you requested a carriage?"

She stopped midstride. "I was going to do that right now."

"Well done, then."

Aware of his deepening amusement, she took a step and glanced about, wondering where to go and whom to ask about a conveyance. Mrs. Routh had given her a brief tour of the main floor of the mansion last evening, but the head housekeeper had left the rest of the mansion to her imagination, stating rather coolly that "the family's *private* quarters are upstairs." Which Claire had taken to mean she wasn't supposed to go up there.

Sutton cleared his throat. "Eli would be happy to send for a carriage." He motioned. "He's out front."

Claire nodded. "Of course." She should have known that. She headed toward the entrance hall.

Sutton followed. "Ask for Armstead, Mrs. Acklen's coachman. I'd be happy to accompany you too, if you desire."

"No," Claire said quickly, a little too quickly, she realized after the fact. "Thank you, Sutton, but . . . I imagine your day is rather full, and I have several errands." One of which she was still debating the wisdom of making, but she certainly couldn't see to if he were along.

"I understand." He motioned for her to precede him into the entrance hall. "Have you decided on a theme for the party yet?"

She gave him a look, and he held up his hands as if declaring a truce. "It was merely a question."

"I'm still working on it. But I'm getting closer." It wasn't exactly a lie. Even though she still had no clue what she was going to do, she *was* getting closer simply by the process of elimination. The cumulative number of ideas inhabiting the universe pertaining to children's birthday parties was shrinking rapidly due to their lack of appeal to Adelicia Acklen. Which therefore meant she was getting closer.

The door to the library opened, and Mrs. Acklen stepped out. Claire sucked in a breath.

"Oh, Mr. Monroe, I'm glad you're here. I just opened a telegram. . . ." Mrs. Acklen held up a piece of paper. "It's one I believe you'll find most encouraging." With a nod, she included Claire in the conversation, and Claire saw a definite glimmer in her eyes this time. "The LeVerts will be departing New York soon and have requested to break their journey at Belmont. They'll be here the first week of October."

"October . . . That's barely three weeks away." Sutton's voice had changed somehow. "That *is* wonderful news."

Claire looked beside her. She didn't know Sutton well, by any means. But she knew him well enough to know he didn't truly consider that *wonderful* news.

Mrs. Acklen folded the telegram. "Miss Laurent, the LeVerts are a fine family with whom we traveled while in Europe. Madame LeVert is a dear friend, and she tells me that her daughters will be in her company as well." She gave Sutton's arm a quick pat. "I should ask Cordina to prepare onion soup like you and Cara Netta shared that one evening. Remember? At the café near the Louvre. It will be like Paris all over again."

Sutton agreed, returning her smile, but his exuberance seemed forced. In fact, it appeared he was rather uncomfortable about the LeVerts' visit.

The only question Claire had, much to her surprise, was who was Cara Netta?

Claire hated to admit it, but Mrs. Acklen had been right. If she had tried to walk into town, it would have been a disaster. The roads were a mucky mess of mud and dung. Simply walking across the street without slipping or stepping in something vile was an accomplishment. And the smell . . .

She grimaced, dodging a pile of something she didn't care to dwell on. The afternoon's warming temperatures were only making conditions worse.

"Here, ma'am—" The carriage driver jumped down from his perch. "Let me take that for you."

Claire handed him the package. "Thank you, Armstead." She accepted his outstretched hand and did her best to knock the mud from her boots before climbing into the carriage. The same carriage she'd seen Sutton get into at the train station. She'd known from the carriage's exterior that it was nice. But inside . . . Supple leather and thick crushed velvet. The definition of elegance.

"You ready to head back now, Miss Laurent?"

Claire peered out the window and down Elm Street, still debating. She breathed out, barely able to read the name *Broderick Shipping and Freight* on the sign above the door at the far end of the avenue. Something inside told her to go back to Belmont, as Armstead suggested.

But she wanted her mother's locket, and it grated on her to think of a man like Samuel Broderick having it. If he still did.

She'd already done her shopping and had stopped by the train station. According to their records, no trunks had arrived in her name, which led her to think that Antoine DePaul hadn't arrived either.

Looking down the avenue, she weighed her options, and finally decided. "I have one more stop to make, if you don't mind, Armstead. It's down this street a short way."

"Wherever you wanna go, ma'am. Just say the word."

When the carriage reached the corner, Claire rapped on the side of the door as Armstead had told her to do. He stopped the carriage and offered his assistance, glancing at the cigar shop behind them. "This where you wanted to go, Miss Laurent?"

"No." Claire smiled, surveying the street, hoping not to see any familiar faces. "But I'd rather walk from here. I won't be long."

"All right, ma'am." He tugged on his hat. "I'll be waitin' right here for you, ma'am."

She thanked him and made her way toward the Brodericks' storefront, slowing her pace the closer she got. Taking a deep breath, she peered around the corner and inside the shop. Mrs. Broderick sat at the front desk just as she had at their first meeting.

Feeling more than a little conspicuous, Claire waited. Heart pounding, and seeing no sign of Samuel Broderick *the second*, she opened the door and stepped inside. It felt as if weeks had passed since she'd been here, instead of days.

Mrs. Broderick looked up. "Good afternoon, dear. How may I help you?"

Claire watched for a spark of recognition in the woman's eyes. "How are you today, ma'am?"

Mrs. Broderick's expression turned bothered. "I'd be much better if we weren't so busy."

"Yes." Claire glanced around the empty shop. "I can see that. By chance . . . is there anyone else here?"

"No, dear, there's not. I'm afraid I'm the only one . . ." A stricken look came over her. "Oh dear . . . I'm not supposed to tell anyone that. Oh, gracious me . . ."

"It's all right." Claire reached over and patted her hand. "I won't tell anyone. I promise." She glanced at the staircase that led to the second floor. Mrs. Broderick clearly didn't remember her and wouldn't after this visit either, she felt certain. "I'm wondering, ma'am, if anyone has turned in a reticule in the last few days. Or . . . perhaps a locket of some kind?"

"A locket . . ." Mrs. Broderick started searching the top of the desk. "I used to have a locket. But someone took it." Tears welled in her eyes.

Claire glanced out the front window again before moving around the desk, feeling only a touch of guilt over what she was about to do. After all, it *was* her reticule. "Mrs. Broderick, would you like to go upstairs for a while? You might feel more comfortable there."

The older woman nodded. "I do like it better up there. It's not so busy. And people don't take things."

Mrs. Broderick teetered as she stood, and Claire slipped an arm about the woman's frail shoulders to steady her. They navigated the stairs with little issue, and once the matron was settled in her rocker,

Claire got her a glass of water and the woman sipped, then leaned back and closed her eyes.

Claire discreetly searched Mrs. Broderick's room, then left the door ajar and tiptoed down the hallway, listening for the slightest sound. She searched the bedroom where she'd left her reticule, then what appeared to be Samuel Broderick's quarters, eager to be out the second she stepped inside. She searched the other bedrooms last, but her search proved fruitless.

She turned to leave when a door at the end of the hallway caught her eye. A linen closet, maybe—just where a man might stash a woman's reticule. She covered the distance on tiptoe and winced as the door creaked open. It was not a linen closet. It was another bedroom, and men's toiletries littered the top of the bureau.

But it was the familiar leather satchel on the chair—with the initials A.D.—that raised the hair on the back of her neck. *He's already here. In Nashville.*

Suddenly feeling as though she were being watched, Claire turned to look behind her. But no one was there. She started to close the bedroom door, eager to leave, when she hesitated. She wouldn't get another chance to search his room again. Because once she left she was never coming back. Trembling and with perspiration trickling beneath her chemise, she searched every drawer, every cubby, even his leather satchel, careful to put every item back in the same place.

It wasn't the thought of facing Antoine DePaul again that frightened her so much. He was a swindler and a liar, and expert at both. And despite how he'd slapped her that one time, she was confident he wasn't a violent man. But with a word he could ruin her, and her opportunity at Belmont. And something told her that once he knew she wasn't going to paint for his benefit anymore, he would do just that.

And he would revel in it.

No reticule. No locket watch. Nothing of her father's or mother's either. And no trunks, that she could see. Forced to accept that the locket watch was gone, she closed the door and hurried down the hallway, hearing Mrs. Broderick's soft snoring as she passed the woman's bedroom.

Claire paused at the top of the stairs, listening to make sure no one had come in, then started down. But the squeak of a door opening in the shop below stopped her cold.

16

Frozen on the third stair from the top, Claire heard the door close in the shop below, then the hollow thud of footsteps. She skirted back upstairs and pressed her back against the wall. She hadn't noticed a second-floor exit in her search, so the only way out of the building was down the stairs.

The footfalls grew closer, and she held still, unwilling to take another step for fear a squeaky plank would give her away. *So foolish . . . coming back here.* Was it Samuel Broderick? Or Antoine? She wasn't sure which one she dreaded most.

"Broderick, are you here?" a man called out.

Claire took a much-needed breath. The voice wasn't Antoine DePaul's. Still, how was it going to look if she came waltzing down the stairs? For what felt like forever but was, she was certain, only a moment or two, she waited to hear the door to the shop open and close again. But it didn't. Was the man waiting for Broderick to return?

Claire chanced two steps and peered downstairs. She didn't see anyone. *They* might want to wait for him, but she certainly didn't. Piecing together a plausible excuse for her presence, she headed down.

A distinguished older gentleman seated in a chair by the desk looked up as she descended. He stood and removed his tall black hat. "Good day, ma'am."

Claire did her best to appear at ease. "Good day, sir."

He glanced beyond her. "Broderick's not hiding somewhere up there, is he?"

The twinkle in his eyes told her he was jesting. "No, sir. He's not.

Per his mother, he'll be back in a little while." She gestured toward the stairs. "I was helping Mrs. Broderick back up to her bedroom. She didn't seem too steady on her feet."

"Ah . . ." He nodded. "That was most kind of you, young lady. We infirm, older folks need some help every now and again."

Claire smiled, but *infirm* was not a word she would have used to describe the gentleman. He was getting on in years, true, but his gaze was keen, and she guessed his mind to be equally so.

Eager to leave, she curtsied. "I hope you have a good afternoon, sir."

"I plan on making it one, ma'am."

He met her at the door, apparently having decided to leave as well. Claire opened the door and, out of deference for his age, gestured for him to go on through.

He shook his head. "No, ma'am. It's always ladies first."

"Thank you, sir." She smiled and walked on down the street, mindful of passersby and praying none of them would have a familiar face. When she reached the carriage, Armstead was waiting.

"Get what you need, Miss Laurent?"

"No," she said after a brief pause. "I didn't. But . . . it's all right." She accepted his help into the carriage and leaned back into the cushioned seat. Of all the gifts her mother had given her, the locket watch had been her most prized.

As soon as the thought came, Claire knew she was mistaken. She still had her mother's *two* most precious gifts. One was tucked deep inside, as deep as a mother's love could reach. And the second—she bent her fingers as though they held a paintbrush—was also nestled safely where no one could ever take it away.

The carriage started forward with a jolt, and she gripped the side of the door. She assumed that her trunks had already been delivered—and were wherever Antoine was storing them. But the forfeiture of items in those trunks—much like the loss of her mother's locket—was nothing compared to the chance to start over again, fresh and clean.

Nor were they worth all she stood to lose if Antoine ever found out where she was or if Mrs. Acklen or Sutton ever learned about her past.

She could never have imagined ending up at a place like Belmont, and she hoped Belmont was the very last place Antoine DePaul would ever look for her. Sooner or later, he would move on—like she was determined to do.

As the carriage rounded the corner, Claire glimpsed the elderly gentleman she'd seen in the shop, his black hat making it easy to spot him in a crowd. He was climbing the stairs to a tall redbrick building. She read the name of the business on the brass placard hanging to the right of the double cherrywood doors.

Holbrook and Wickliffe Law Offices.

She looked back to the man and, to her surprise, found him looking in the direction of the carriage as it passed. He raised a hand as though waving to her. Uncertain whether he was looking at her or not, she raised her hand in return, and he smiled.

The next morning, Claire awakened before sunrise, still tired but unable to sleep. She'd awakened several times during the night, worrying about Antoine and that he might somehow find her. And each time, she'd consoled herself with the sheer size of Nashville. Surely she could hide among twenty-five thousand people. Still, she would take extra care when venturing into town from now on, and would do everything she could to minimize those excursions.

She yawned and stretched, dreading having to leave the warmth of her bed. She'd promised Mrs. Acklen after dinner last night that, in addition to answering a stack of correspondence, she would present the entire plan for the party to her this afternoon. The sack containing the sample party favors sat in a corner across the room and she thought Mrs. Acklen would approve, especially with the extra touches she planned to add.

But as of yet—Claire exhaled in the dark—she still hadn't thought of an idea for an activity that the Acklen family hadn't already experienced while visiting some foreign country halfway around the world. "*We flew the balloon over the city. Without a tether.*"

She rolled her eyes, recalling William's comment and also her brief conversation with him yesterday afternoon—that yielded no help whatsoever.

All the boy had said was that he wanted a grown-up party, where they really did something. And he'd said it with such sincerity that she almost forgave him for his previously high-and-mighty attitude. Almost.

What must it be like to be raised in the midst of all this? To never know anything but elegance and plenty? She feared that with young William's present outlook, life after Belmont might prove to be somewhat of a disappointment for him. As it would for her too, all too soon, if she didn't get up and start accomplishing something.

She pushed back the covers and lit the lamp on the bedside table, wondering if there wasn't one special idea Mrs. Acklen was waiting for her to discover. Planning this party was a test. Mrs. Acklen had made that clear. But a test of what?

At first, Claire would have said it was of her own ability to coordinate details, as the advertisement had listed. But now she wasn't so sure. Was it a test of her patience? Her creativity? Her fortitude? Her dedication and desire to work for Mrs. Acklen? Perhaps all of those. Whatever it was, she asked God to show her what to do, because she was all too swiftly coming to the end of her own abilities.

After using the chamber pot, she lathered a cloth with soap in the tepid water in the basin on the washstand and ran it over her skin. She rinsed the cloth in fresh water and repeated the process, then dried off with a fresh towel. By the time she finished, the skin on her arms and legs resembled gooseflesh.

Dressing hurriedly, she chose one of the two dresses she'd brought with her to Belmont, grateful to whomever had washed the mud-splattered dress and returned it to the wardrobe freshly pressed.

Contrary to Mrs. Acklen's instructions, she'd purchased only one dress in town yesterday, and even that had seemed exorbitant considering her meager finances. She hoped Mrs. Acklen would be pleased with her choice, but that remained to be seen.

She brushed her teeth and pinned up her curls, appreciating her accommodations. The bedroom, with its modest pine furniture, cotton draperies, and unadorned fireplace, lacked the opulence of the rest of the home, but it was nicer than any bedroom she'd ever had. And its simplicity suited her.

She especially liked it because this had been Sutton's room at one time. Somehow that made it feel more familiar. And appealing.

The clock on the mantel above the fireplace read half past five when she grabbed her shawl and slipped noiselessly from her bedroom and down the darkened corridor toward the grand salon. Mrs. Routh's bedroom, she'd learned, was off this hallway too, but farther down in the opposite direction. Thank goodness. Her limited interaction with the head housekeeper had been civil thus far, though she could tell Mrs. Routh still wasn't overjoyed about her being hired.

Claire paused just inside the doorway leading to the grand salon, still not believing she was actually living in such a place—for the time being.

Pale moonlight bathed the salon in silver shadows, and not a sound stirred the silence. Something about standing in the middle of this grand mansion filled with people sleeping all around was comforting. She'd always wished she'd come from a larger family, and she envied the Acklen children's sibling relationships far more than their privileged upbringing.

Her hunger dictating her first destination, she crossed the salon, the moonlight allowing her to pick her way around the tables and chairs arranged in groupings about the room. Not for the first time, she admired the nearly life-sized painting of Queen Victoria hanging at the head of the staircase landing leading to the second story. The royal red of Queen Victoria's robe appeared gray in the dim light. She'd been surprised at the enormous size of the portrait but not at its presence in this home. Especially not with the royal connections Mrs. Acklen seemed to enjoy.

She continued down the hallway toward the family dining room, stopping when she reached the stairs leading down to the kitchen in the basement. Mrs. Routh hadn't included the basement on her abridged tour, and Claire felt a little daring at the thought of venturing down there on her own.

She peered down the dark stairwell, thinking she heard the rattle of a pan. Mrs. Acklen had invited her to join the family for breakfast whenever she desired, but Claire had a sunrise walk in mind and needed a day-old biscuit or corn muffin—and a cup of coffee, if possible—before she set out.

She held the rail as she descended to the first landing, then peered down and around the corner to see a faint glow from beneath the kitchen door. The hope of sustenance urged her on. She felt for the doorknob in the dark, couldn't find one, so finally gave the door a little push. It swung right open.

The comforting aroma of eggs and bacon greeted her, as well as the promise of coffee, but she wasn't prepared for who was standing at the stove. "Sutton!"

He turned, wearing a somewhat guilty look. "Shhhh . . ." Smiling, he held a finger to his lips. "If Cordina catches me in here again, I'm a goner."

Claire giggled and let the door swing shut behind her, surprised at how delighted she was to find him down there. "What are you doing up so early?"

"Couldn't sleep. And you?"

She shook her head. "Me either."

"You hungry?" He pointed to a bowl of fresh eggs on the counter.

"Starving."

"Here—" He gestured her closer. "Keep stirring this, and I'll crack a couple more."

Claire did as he asked, feeling as though they were getting away with something. And it felt rather good. The kitchen was surprisingly well lit, with oil lanterns affixed to the walls. Only three flickered with a flame, but the white plastered walls seemed to multiply their efforts. "I meant to ask you yesterday . . ." She assumed a more formal tone. "How was the opera Wednesday evening?"

He sighed. "Long, and wasted on me."

She laughed again, stirring as he added the two eggs he'd whipped in a separate bowl. He lifted the lid on a second pan set off to the side, revealing eight slices of bacon fried up brown and crisp.

She peered up at him. "You're a tad hungry."

"Always. But I'm willing to share." He transferred the slices of bacon to a plate. "What about you? Do you enjoy the opera?"

Claire kept her gaze on the scrambled eggs, reliving a tinge of the "out of place" feeling she'd experienced at dinner her first night at Belmont, yet she was determined not to show it. "Actually . . . I've never attended an opera." She made a face. "But I'm guessing it would probably be wasted on me as well."

He flashed a smile, and she knew she'd said it convincingly enough. She was getting better at masking what she didn't want others to see. She scooted the pan off the burner. "The eggs are ready."

"And so are"—Sutton grabbed a towel—"these." He opened the oven door and withdrew a pan of golden brown biscuits.

Claire looked from him to the pan, then back again. "Where did you learn how to cook? Most of the men I've known"—not that she'd known that many, she realized, thinking mainly of her father and Antoine DePaul—"didn't know the first thing about anything culinary. Except the eating part." She took the plates he handed her.

"You don't get to be my age without learning your way around a kitchen. Not if you want to eat."

She held the plates as he dished up the food. "Come, come, Mr. Monroe. You're not that old." She smiled sweetly, guessing him to be only a handful of years older than she. "You're at least a good decade away from needing a cane."

He feigned a frown. "Such impudence after I made you breakfast."

She inhaled. "Which smells wonderful!" She carried the plates to a small side table and claimed one of the two chairs. He followed with coffee, steam rising from the cups.

As she picked up her fork to start eating, she noticed Sutton's outstretched hand and read the soft intention in his eyes. Uncomfortable at having revealed she didn't follow the same routine, she returned her fork to the table and wordlessly slipped her hand into his.

He bowed his head. "Father God, we thank you for this food and for the gift of friendship—" He spoke as if the One he addressed was seated right next to him instead of in another realm. "And for grace that is wholly undeserved, Lord. But upon which our souls depend. In Jesus' name . . ."

"Amen," she whispered in unison with him, aware of how he gently squeezed her hand before letting go.

"So . . ." He forked a bite of eggs. "What's on your itinerary for the day?"

Claire heard the question but was still thinking about his prayer . . . So simple, so honest. And he'd called her a friend. She was more touched by that than she should have been. But it had been a long time since she'd had a *friend*. Since boarding school. And even then, she'd never truly been close to any of the girls. She'd always felt on the outside. Different. Never quite able to bridge the gap.

Aware of Sutton watching her, she directed her attention back to his question. "I have a meeting with Mrs. Acklen this afternoon about—"

"The party." He gave her a playfully ominous look.

She nodded. "I'm afraid I'm still not quite ready for the meeting yet. But I will be! I thought an early-morning walk might help stir the imagination."

He raised his coffee cup in a mock toast. "That always works for me. Has anyone given you a tour of the estate?"

She finished a piece of bacon and wanted to lick her fingers, but refrained. "Mrs. Routh gave me a tour of the main floor of the mansion. But no, I haven't seen the grounds or any of the other buildings yet. This morning though, I'd planned on walking the fields you can see from my room. And may I add . . ." Fork in hand, she pointed to her plate. "This is delicious, *kind sir,* thank you."

"You're most welcome, m'lady." He winked, those bluish-gray eyes intent on hers, and something inside her went soft and warm. She felt a tightness begin to unfurl, like a wood shaving being devoured by the flame. Whatever the feeling was, it felt *good.* And inviting. So inviting, it almost scared her. What was it about Sutton Monroe that did that to her? That made her want to open up to him? To be closer, somehow.

It would have been different if he were *trying* to gain her attention, as other men sometimes did. But Sutton didn't seem to be the least aware of the effect he had on her.

"The fields are a good choice for your walk." He sipped his coffee. "It's beautiful back in there. There's an old Indian trail you can follow that leads down to a creek." He drained his cup, eyed the coffeepot, and started to rise.

Claire held up a hand. "Please, allow me." She retrieved the coffeepot from the stove and refilled his cup, then hers, enjoying the chance to look at him without him looking at her.

"So tell me, Claire . . ." He leaned back in his chair. "How long did you live in New Orleans?"

Her guard heightened at the unexpected question. Not that it was overly personal. But it had to do with her past. "We lived there for about two years."

"Did you enjoy the city?"

She returned the coffeepot to the stove. "Yes, for the most part."

"Where did you live? Chances are good I'll know where it is. I've been to New Orleans many times for Mrs. Acklen on business."

Claire reclaimed her seat and took a sip of coffee, buying herself a little time. From her experience, most people enjoyed talking about themselves. She didn't. And she wasn't about to give him the name of the street where they had lived. Not when that could lead him straight to the gallery. "We lived not far from the Old Square, in the French Quarter."

His eyes widened. "So I'm sure you know Café du Monde."

She smiled, but only to cover her unease. Her two worlds were becoming far too close, far too fast. "Yes. I've been there before, but"—she waved a hand, eager to turn the subject away from her—"you asked me about my day. . . . Now what about yours? I'm guessing it's busy, and that you have lawsuits to be fought and won, closing arguments to be delivered . . ."

He stared at her, and for a second, she got the feeling he knew she was intentionally changing the subject. Then he smiled that easy smile.

"No lawsuits, and no closing arguments either. But yes, it's on the busy side. But first, another question."

He leaned forward, forearms on the table, and Claire tensed. *I will not lie. I will* not *lie.*

"Would you allow me to give you a tour of the estate this evening? I'd enjoy showing it to you."

A weight lifted from her shoulders. "I'd love that, Sutton. . . . But didn't Mrs. Acklen say something about having dinner guests tonight?"

He winced, nodding. "The Worthingtons. I'd almost forgotten."

Claire reached for another biscuit. "Judging from your reaction, I'm guessing that whoever the Worthingtons are . . . they're not listed among your favorite dinner guests."

"No, no. The Worthingtons are a very nice couple. And I'm certain dinner conversation will be quite lively."

Claire took a bite of biscuit and waited, eyebrows raised.

"The Worthingtons appreciate fine art. Mrs. Worthington, especially. She and Adelicia—Mrs. Acklen—attended an art auction in town last year, one to benefit an orphanage, and they ended up bidding against each other for a painting. It was all quite civil, but Mrs. Worthington's interest in the painting greatly increased once she realized Mrs. Acklen was also interested. There was a small scene. It made the papers the next day."

Claire took his words in, acting as though the mention of art auctions and paintings and biddings gone wild were of only passing interest to her. "I would imagine that type of situation happens frequently with Mrs. Acklen. And that her opinion of art, and everything else, is highly esteemed by the rest of the community."

Sutton took his time in answering. "Mrs. Acklen's opinions and actions never go unnoticed. You can say that with full certainty."

Claire sipped her coffee as the reality of her situation once again stared her boldly in the face. Belmont was both the best—and absolute worst—place she could be. Mrs. Acklen's sphere of influence with art in Nashville was far-reaching and highly esteemed. If Adelicia Acklen were to bestow her approval on a painting, or—Claire could hardly imagine such a thing happening—if by chance, she could paint something worthy of Mrs. Acklen's bidding on that painting, others would certainly take notice. Mrs. Worthington along with everyone else.

As sweet as that imagining was, an equally bitter thought overlaid it. If Mrs. Acklen were to uncover the truth about her family's business and what she had done, Mrs. Acklen would see to it that she never worked in the state of Tennessee again. Much less, painted.

And that was one promise Claire had no difficulty believing.

Sutton stood and stacked their plates. "I have meetings in town this morning and afternoon, but I should be back in time for dinner. Which leads me back to *my* original question. If we have time after the meal, I'd be honored to show you the estate. Otherwise, sometime this weekend. Mrs. Acklen wants you to know what and where everything is for the day of the party."

Claire's heart sank a little. So Mrs. Acklen had asked him to show her around. Not that that made any difference. She and Sutton were colleagues, after all. And, not to forget, he'd told her point-blank that he didn't consider her qualified for the job. Sobered by the collection of thoughts, she reached for a smile. "I would appreciate your showing me the estate, Sutton. Thank you."

She gathered their cups, still grateful she'd ventured down to the kitchen, and remembering the look on his face when she'd opened the door. Which reminded her . . . "You said you'd be a goner if Cordina found you down here again. Why is that?"

"I be tellin' you why's that, Miss Laurent."

Claire nearly dropped the cups. She spun around to see Cordina standing behind her in a doorway she hadn't even noticed was there. Hands on hips, Cordina wore a look that said somebody had better do some explaining. And fast!

17

Cordina huffed, eyeing the kitchen stove. "Here you go again, Mr. Monroe. Just helpin' yourself to my kitchen. Like I ain't even here."

Claire stared, wide-eyed, not knowing what to say. Or if she should say anything at all. She couldn't believe Cordina was speaking this way to a man! Much less to Sutton Monroe. She didn't even seem like the same woman who had welcomed her to the mansion. Claire started to volunteer to clean up their mess but hated to make things worse. She looked to Sutton for direction.

His expression was surprisingly calm. "Now see here, Cordina. We've talked about this before. I'm quite—"

"Comin' in here, usin' my stove this way. Fixin' them plain ol' eggs like you do." Cordina picked up the egg pan and sniffed. "Not a shred of cheese in them things. *Mmmph . . .*" She shook her head and glowered at the remaining biscuits. "I'm bettin' you didn't even give this poor girl any butter for them ol' hard things either. Or any of my jelly." She tossed up her hands. "Lawd, help me! This man's stealin' my joy."

Slowly, it dawned on Claire what Cordina was frustrated about. It wasn't that Sutton had used *her kitchen*, but that he'd cooked his own breakfast. Feeling a tickle of humor, she tried to get Sutton to meet her gaze. But he wouldn't. As humorous as the situation seemed to her, she also sensed a thread of genuine irritation from Cordina.

Almost without thinking, she feigned a cough, and Sutton's and Cordina's attention angled to her.

She took a little gasp. "I nearly choked on those dry old biscuits," she whispered, holding her throat. "If only I'd"—she coughed again—"had some jelly." Uncertain whether she could hold back a grin, she found the determination to when seeing the start of their smiles.

Sutton eyed her, shaking his head. "Are you serious?"

Cordina let out a laugh. "Good for you, Miss Laurent! Us womenfolk, we got to stick together."

Claire finally allowed the hint of a smile, pleased with herself for her small performance—but even more, with the glint of humor in Sutton's eyes.

"Women," he said beneath his breath, then looked at Claire, his gaze appraising. "I wouldn't have thought you capable of such duplicity, Miss Laurent. Seems I underestimated you." A wry smile tipped one side of his mouth. "I won't make that mistake again."

Cordina laughed, and so did Claire, outwardly. But not so much on the inside. Perhaps it was her imagination, but she'd heard a touch of seriousness in Sutton's tone, and once again she was reminded of how important it was to keep him on her side.

Both as a colleague, and a friend.

By the time she left on her walk, the sun had risen, though a hush still lay over the house. True to Sutton's word, a well-worn path wound its way through the grass-covered meadows and across the maple-dotted ridge to a creek bed below.

She spent the next hour searching and exploring, enjoying the discovery of wildflowers and foliage in the area and spying glimpses of approaching fall, little clues of color nature had hidden. Having missed taking walks in recent days, she reveled in the canted sunlight through the trees, the blue of sky, and longed for a fresh canvas, paintbrush, and palette with which to capture it all.

As she walked, she thought about the events that had led her to Belmont, and try as she might, she couldn't see them as anything less than orchestrated. *"Things happen for a reason, Claire."* She could hear her mother's voice clearly in her mind. No telling how often her mother had said that to her. Looking back, she wondered if her mother had said it to encourage her, or to convince herself.

The soft, drawn-out coo of a mourning dove drifted toward her from over the hill, and Claire stared up into the cloudless sky. Until leaving New Orleans and arriving in Nashville, she hadn't realized how heavy she'd felt inside. Not just lonely and alone but weighted down. Which didn't make sense. How could she feel so empty and yet so weighted down with guilt?

She told herself it wasn't her fault. She hadn't wanted to forge those paintings. But she'd done it. And, God forgive her, she would do it again if it meant providing money for her mother's medicine. If it meant buying a chance that her *maman* might still be alive.

But to think that her mother had lived with that same anvil of shame for so long . . . The guilt her mother had carried became undeniably clear the day before she'd passed.

Claire sank down onto a flat lichen-covered rock and drew her legs up against her chest, still able to see her mother lying in the bed so clearly.

"*Water,*" her mother had whispered, and Claire felt a flush of emotion as the folds of memory loosened and smoothed, offering up recollections of those final hours like jewels on a blanket. Claire had filled the cup and held it to her lips. But her mother shook her head. So Claire dipped a fresh cloth in the cool liquid and sponged her fevered forehead and face. But again, her mother objected, tears coming. It broke Claire's heart to see her cry. Her mother never cried. And when Claire held the water to her mouth again, her mother had whispered something she hadn't understood. . . .

"*Pour it over me,*" she'd begged, and Claire had stared down, not understanding, believing the laudanum had addled her mother's reasoning. But her mother had known what she was asking, even if Claire hadn't, at the time. So Claire had done exactly as her mother asked. Cupful by cupful, she'd poured the water over her mother's frail body until the mattress was soaked and her mother was weeping. But tears of contentment this time, not of frustration. "*Merci beaucoup, l'amour de moi,*" Maman had whispered, a peace easing the traces of pain and illness from her face.

A peace that still eluded Claire, but that she craved with everything in her.

Claire wiped her cheeks and looked around. The meadow was empty, and from where she sat, she could barely see the top of the mansion. She was alone. She recalled how straightforward and honest Sutton's prayer had been, and wanted to word her request to God just like that, as if He were right beside her. But the words that came to mind seemed forced.

No, more than that. They seemed *coercive*. Like she was trying to bargain with God, convince Him that she was worth His time and attention, when really, deep down, she knew the opposite was true. Because she knew what she was. A fake. A forgery. Not good enough. And it wasn't the paintings she was thinking of any longer. It was *her*.

She sat for a while, wishing away the fear inside, wishing she could feel the sun's warmth on her heart as she felt it on her face.

By the time she started back, she guessed it had to be approaching nine o'clock. She'd thought of other ideas for William's party on her walk, but none seemed worthy of presenting to Adelicia Acklen. But the idea would come. It had to.

As she neared the mansion, she was tempted to take a brief detour to explore the building Sutton lived in, the one housing the art gallery. But work came first.

A carriage pulled up to the front of the mansion, and she slowed her steps. She didn't think the carriage belonged to Mrs. Acklen but couldn't be sure. The woman had several. When two gentlemen climbed out and young Pauline and Claude ran down the steps to greet them, Claire decided to find a door leading in through the back. She didn't want to chance interrupting a meeting between Mrs. Acklen and her guests.

Behind the mansion, rolling hills and meadows extended as far as she could see. Off to the side, between the manor and the stable and carriage house sat five brick cottages, identical to one another, all lined up in a neat row, clustered alongside a bank of unwieldy pines. She assumed the servants lived in them and couldn't help noting the contrast between those structures and others she'd seen made of rotting plank wood and timber. It made her feel better about Mrs. Acklen, in a way. And still . . .

Brick or timber, it didn't change what the people who lived inside those structures were. Or had been. From what she'd seen since coming to Nashville, the war might have abolished slavery, but it hadn't eliminated the scar. Or even started to close the wound.

Continuing on around, she spotted a Negro boy crouched beneath a tree some distance away, nine or ten years old, judging from his size. He dug in the dirt with something. A broken stick, perhaps.

Suddenly he stilled, bent low, and reached into the hole he'd made. He felt around and pulled something out.

He held the object up close, blew against it, eyed it again, then grinned and stuffed it in his pants pocket, and started digging all over again. Claire watched, amused. Whatever he'd found and whatever he continued to search for, it had him spellbound, the little scavenger.

She saw a door on the back of the mansion and tried it. Locked. She knocked. No answer. She tried a second door. Locked as well. She knocked on it too, but again, nobody answered.

She turned back to the boy, certain he would know how to get inside. He didn't hear her approach.

"Excuse me, but—"

The boy jumped up to his full height, his eyes wide as saucers. "Lawdy, ma'am, you done scare't me good."

Claire tried not to laugh. "I'm sorry. I didn't mean to."

He started giggling, which tickled her even more, because when he laughed, his ears wiggled. Actually *wiggled.* She couldn't keep from laughing now.

"You the Lady's new helper, ma'am?"

"I am. At least for now." Claire extended her hand. "My name is Claire Laurent."

He looked at her hand good and long before giving it a quick shake. "I'm Ezekiel. But I go by Zeke." His attention drifted upward. "That's some right pretty hair you got, ma'am. My aunt done told me about it."

"Thank you, *Zeke.*" She gave a little curtsy. "And who is your aunt?"

"Aunt Cordina. She runs the kitchen for the Lady." He gestured toward the mansion. "She and Uncle Eli been with the Lady long 'fore I was born."

Cordina? And Eli? "Your Aunt Cordina and Uncle Eli are married?"

He grinned again. "Yes'um. They ain't never had no kids, though." He shrugged his shoulders. "So they do their dotin' on me and my brothers and sisters."

"May I ask you something, Zeke?"

"Yes'um."

"What were you digging for when I walked up?"

He smiled and reached into his pocket. "I's lookin' for bullet shells this mornin'. But I found me a nickel too." He held up the coin, proud as could be. "I dig around some." He scuffed the toe of his shoe in the dirt. "I just like findin' things, I guess."

"Well, how would you like to find something for me?"

"What you lookin' for, ma'am?"

"A way back into this house without having to go all the way around front."

Those ears of his wriggled, and just as she'd thought, he knew precisely which door was unlocked.

Zeke led her through the maze of rooms comprising the basement of the home. She'd had no idea how massive the space was from her brief visit to the kitchen, and how much storage it boasted. Shelves of food and supplies lined the plaster walls. Yet she hadn't seen crops or fields anywhere on her walk. She asked Zeke about it.

"Yes, ma'am. We got us a farm. Over back behind the fancy flower house."

Behind the conservatory, Claire thought, nodding.

"We grow us all sort of things over there. Watch your head, Miss Laurent. It's kinda low through here."

Claire ducked through a doorway.

"The Lady, she gots her own plantations too. In Louisiana. They grow cotton, mostly. But I ain't never seen those places."

Mrs. Acklen had cotton plantations in Louisiana? In addition to all of this? The sources of Mrs. Acklen's wealth were becoming clearer by the minute. She wished she could ask Zeke a few more questions, but he'd led her into the kitchen, where she and Sutton had eaten that morning. The space was bustling with activity, and the aroma of baking bread made her mouth water.

Women cooking at the stoves and stirring bowls at counters turned and looked. Claire smiled, noting that Cordina wasn't among them.

Zeke sidled up to one of the smaller women. "This here's my mama, Maria. She cooks for the Lady and her family." He said it proudly, hugging his mother's waist.

Claire curtsied, remembering having seen the woman serving dinner. "Maria, it's nice to meet you. You have a delightful son."

"Thank you, Miss Laurent," Maria said in a soft voice, cradling her son's head.

Claire didn't wonder how Maria already knew her name. News traveled fast at Belmont.

"And this here"—Zeke pointed, continuing on down the line—"is Rena and Harriet and Ive and MaryAnn. They work down here in the kitchen too, but sometimes upstairs with Mrs. Routh."

Claire nodded a greeting.

"This here's Amanda. She's a cook too. And Miss Betsy, over there"—Zeke motioned to an older woman seated at a table, a set of silver service and oilcloths spread out before her—"she's Amanda's and Ive's and Harriet's mama. She's been with the Lady longest of anybody, exceptin' Eli."

"It's nice to meet all of you," Claire said, noting the familial relationships and wondering how many servants worked at Belmont. She asked Zeke that as they started up the stairs leading to the mansion.

"There be eleven of us, I think. Not countin' the gardeners and workers the Lady hires."

The soft pitter-pat of footsteps sounded from above, and Eva met them on the stairs, a bundle of clothing in her arms. She dipped her head politely in Claire's direction, then turned a glare on Zeke. "Eli's been askin' for you, boy! The Lady's got guests, and their horses need waterin'. You best get yourself upstairs right now, or you're gonna get what for from Eli—*and* your mama once I tell her!"

Zeke bolted, throwing a hasty "Good-bye" over his shoulder as he raced up the stairs.

"That boy . . ." Eva shook her head, but Claire detected a smile in her voice, as though she enjoyed bossing him around. At least a little.

Claire eyed the laundry. "Are you the one responsible for cleaning my dress, Eva? The one that was splattered with mud?"

Question lit the girl's expression. "Yes, ma'am. Was everything all right?"

"Oh yes! More than all right. I just wondered who to thank, that's all."

Eva smiled. "I help with the laundry, mostly. But my mama's Mrs. Acklen's personal maid. I'm trainin' to take her place."

"Well, you do a very fine job, Eva. Thank you."

Eva continued down the stairs, a spring in her step, and Claire continued up, hoping Mrs. Acklen hadn't been looking for her. She'd been gone longer than she'd planned. Almost to her room, she thought of Zeke again and the way his ears wiggled when he smiled. And something he'd said returned to her.

"I just like findin' things, I guess."

She paused in the hallway leading to her bedroom. That was it! The idea she'd been searching for! She raced to her room, eager to capture on paper the perfect theme for William's party, all while beginning to think that maybe, just maybe, God was listening to her after all.

18

Knowing dinner with the Worthingtons was long over, Sutton reined Truxton in by the stables as the sun made its final descent in a haze of dusky orange. He dismounted, frustrated at being so late but even more so by the summons from the St. Francisville, Louisiana, attorney that had been delivered to the law offices that afternoon.

For over two years the lawsuit had been dragging on, and he was beginning to wonder whether the whole cotton debacle would ever be resolved. He rued the day they'd ever involved Mr. Alexander Walker. But one thing he knew for certain—Adelicia was not going to be pleased.

He led Truxton into the stable, welcoming the brief walk to the house in order to gather his thoughts.

"Evenin', Mr. Monroe."

Sutton looked up. "Good evening, Zeke. How are you tonight?"

"I'm good, sir. You comin' in awful late."

Sutton sighed. "Later than I'd planned."

"Here, let me see to him for ya, sir." The boy grasped Truxton's reins in one hand while making a show of holding something out in his other.

Amused, Sutton squinted in the dim lantern light as if not already knowing what was in the boy's palm. "You find something in your digging today?"

"Yes, sir, I did. Somethin' special." When Zeke grinned, his whole face took part. "I told you there's treasure buried round here."

Sutton peered closer at the coin he held. "You're kiddin' me. You found that out there?"

"Yes, sir. Sure did. Found these too." Zeke dug into his pocket again and held out a collection of spent shotgun shells. "I reckon these are from the battle that happened right here."

Sutton nodded. "I'm sure they are." He knew how much the boy enjoyed hearing stories about the war, especially the battles that took place nearby. But talking about those experiences was never easy for him, and he just couldn't right now. Not tonight.

"I need to get on up to the house. Mrs. Acklen's expecting me." At Zeke's nod, he gave the boy's head a playful rub. "Congratulations on finding that coin. And thank you for seeing to Truxton. You always do a good job. And Truxton likes you."

The boy grinned. "Thank you, sir."

Sutton took long strides, the muscles in his legs tightened up from the ride from town. He loosened his tie and angled his neck from side to side. The mansion loomed ahead, the open windows in the front study aglow with lamplight. The curtains billowed in the breeze. As he grew closer, he thought he caught the murmur of feminine voices.

He pictured Claire again from that morning, when he'd asked her about whether or not she liked the opera. Recalling her response, he again felt properly chastised. She'd tried to mask her true feelings, but pretense wasn't her forte. She said she didn't have any interest in attending the opera, but that wasn't true. And it made him feel smaller inside somehow, for not appreciating something that she longed to experience.

Another image of her arose, and he grinned, remembering her pretending to choke. Adorable. She'd been so proud of herself, which made it even more comical. He'd tried his best not to stare at her over breakfast, but it hadn't been easy. He'd thought she was pretty the first time he'd seen her in the church, all mussed up and with her dress wrinkled.

But this morning in the kitchen . . .

She'd been downright intoxicating. That fresh look of sleep about her, the dimples when she laughed, the way she'd hopped right in beside him to cook the eggs. She hadn't even seemed to notice when their bodies brushed against each other in the process—he exhaled—but he sure had. He noticed details about her that a man who had an understanding with another woman shouldn't.

It wasn't that he never thought about Cara Netta. It was just that he never thought about her the way he thought about Claire Laurent. The realization wasn't reassuring.

Bits of conversation drifted toward him through the open window as he climbed the front steps.

"Yes, ma'am. That's exactly how I'm picturing it. I'm also imagining . . ."

"That idea actually appeals to me, Miss Laurent. The boys competing against the girls . . ."

Sutton shook his head. Adelicia *would* find that appealing. The woman had a competitive streak a mile wide. He had an inkling Claire did too. Heaven help these two women if they ever got into a competition with each other. Claire would probably allow her employer to win, as well she should, though he couldn't be certain. Mrs. Acklen would simply go for broke and never give up.

What a combination . . .

If only Adelicia had hired someone a little more homely. Someone who didn't have "that way" of looking at him that made him feel more like a schoolboy than a grown man. But it wasn't only Claire's loveliness that attracted him. He was often in the company of beautiful women, yet they didn't linger in his thoughts the way Claire Laurent did. They didn't make him want to invent excuses to see them again.

It wasn't prudent, he knew, his being so attracted to her. First, she was an employee of Mrs. Acklen's. Second, he was supposed to be watching her—which he was certainly doing, but at least in part for his own personal reasons.

The entrance hall was dark, save for the lamps in the small study. Their flickering glow cast a sliver of light onto the statue before the fireplace, giving *Ruth Gleaning* an almost ghostlike quality. He understood why Adelicia had purchased the statue. It was exquisite. But it still surprised him that she'd placed it in such a prominent place, where everyone entering the home would see it. A rather bold choice.

Looking more closely at the sculptor's lifelike detailing, he remembered the Biblical account and imagined what Boaz's reaction would have been to such a display, however unintended by dear, innocent Ruth. The poor man wouldn't have stood a chance against *Ruth's* doleful gaze and her lovely physical *attributes,* for lack of a better—

"Good evening, Mr. Monroe."

Startled at the voice behind him, Sutton turned. "Mrs. Routh . . ."

He smiled to mask his jumpiness. Somehow the woman always managed to sneak up on him. "I didn't realize you were here, ma'am. How are you this evening?"

"I'm well, sir. Thank you." She dipped her head in a subservient manner. "I heard you arrive and wanted to make sure you weren't in need of anything before I retire for the evening."

"That's very kind of you, Mrs. Routh. But no, I don't need anything. I'm simply here to meet with Mrs. Acklen. Then I'll be retiring myself."

"Very well, sir. Good evening, then." She took two steps and paused, then turned back. "I'm wondering, sir, if . . . I might pose a question." She lowered her voice. "One I prefer be held in strictest confidence."

"Of course, Mrs. Routh."

She gestured for him to follow her into the grand salon. Sutton was accustomed to Mrs. Routh's careful nature. A widow, the woman had been Adelicia's friend—and social equal—before the untimely death of Mrs. Routh's husband, Francis, several years ago. Since then she had been a faithful employee to Mrs. Acklen.

He'd questioned the arrangement at first. Having a good friend as an employee often spelled disaster. But the woman performed her head-housekeeper duties with excellence and kept the mansion in tip-top condition. She held a loyalty for Adelicia as well—and with good reason. But sometimes that loyalty led her to suspect trouble where there was none. Like now, he guessed.

Mrs. Routh stopped by the staircase, looked around, and leaned close. "It's about—" she glanced back toward the entrance hall—"the new hire."

His interest piqued. "Miss Laurent?"

She nodded, reluctance etching the lines of her face. "I don't wish to overstep my bounds, sir, but . . . I'm simply wondering what we know about her."

Had he not known better, Sutton would have thought she was fishing for gossip. But not Mrs. Routh. Honest and upright, she expected everyone else to toe the same line. "Has Miss Laurent acted in such a way that causes you to question her intentions?"

A stricken look crossed her face. "No, sir. And please don't hear me insinuating that the young woman has done anything improper. It's just that, well . . . Take this morning, for instance. I found her in the central parlor looking at one of Mrs. Acklen's statues. Just standing there, *staring* at it." She raised an eyebrow.

"You found her staring at a statue?" Sutton curbed a grin.

"The one of the little girl."

Sans Souci. Adelicia had purchased it in Rome on their trip. "Perhaps she was simply admiring it."

"That's what I thought too. At first. Then she crouched low and started searching around the base." She leaned closer. "When I questioned her, she said she was looking to see who had sculpted it."

Sutton smiled, able to imagine the scene between the two women quite well. "Maybe that's what she was doing."

Mrs. Routh eyed him as though he were naive, and then it occurred to him what she might be insinuating.

"Are you suggesting, Mrs. Routh, that you believe Miss Laurent has . . . less than honorable motives in being here at Belmont?" He couldn't begin to estimate the worth of Adelicia's art collection. Not only the statues and paintings, but the jewelry, the century-old books, and family heirlooms, the gifts from foreign dignitaries. He'd been after her for years to catalog everything, which would take weeks to do properly.

But Claire Laurent, an art thief? The thought was laughable.

Mrs. Routh suddenly looked away, guilt shading her expression. "I'm sorry, sir, for even broaching the subject. It was wrong of me to do so without a firm—"

Sutton touched her arm. "Mrs. Routh . . . it's never wrong of you to bring a concern to me when it involves Mrs. Acklen's welfare. I appreciate your care and concern, as does Mrs. Acklen. And rest assured, we closely evaluate every person who's hired to work at Belmont."

With an acquiescent nod, Mrs. Routh bid him good night, yet Sutton felt a twinge of unease walking back to the entrance hall, knowing he hadn't "closely evaluated" their most recent hire as thoroughly as he usually would have. At least not before she'd begun working there. Mrs. Acklen's hasty decision had seen to that.

He'd mailed the letter to his colleague in New Orleans, as requested, but it would be at least a couple of weeks before he could expect to hear anything. He'd considered sending a telegram. But the last time they'd done that with potentially delicate news, the findings had ended up as fodder for gossip. So until he received his colleague's reply, he would simply watch Claire more closely. And if he discovered her hauling statues out the front door in the middle of the night, he would confront her about it straightaway.

The thought made him grin.

Muffled voices came from within the study, and he drew closer.

"So tell me in greater detail about the pastries, please. Do you know how to make the *Napoléons*?"

Recognizing the subdued enthusiasm in Adelicia's voice, Sutton stepped closer to the study and found the door partially open. Whatever ideas Claire had finally come up with, Adelicia liked them. Liked them a great deal. Though he doubted she would openly convey that at this point. Generous at heart, Adelicia wasn't quick to trust. And he couldn't blame her after what she'd been through.

Which reminded him of the letter in his pocket.

He stepped around the corner and knocked on the door. It inched open. "Good evening, ladies."

Claire knelt by Adelicia's chair. Their heads lifted in unison.

"Good evening, Mr. Monroe." Adelicia waved him into the room. "You must have had a very busy day."

"Yes, ma'am. You could say that."

Adelicia locked eyes with him, and held. And without saying a word, he knew she was aware that he had bad news. But he also knew it would wait until Claire had taken her leave.

Adelicia's smile never faltered. "You missed a lovely dinner with the Worthingtons. Cordina outdid herself yet again, and Mrs. Worthington was especially fond of the new statue in the foyer."

Sutton eased down into one of the diminutive parlor chairs, finding it a little confining, as usual. "Did she offer to purchase it from you?"

"Actually, she did. In her own subtle way." Adelicia's eyes narrowed. "I graciously refused, of course."

Sutton shook his head, then turned his full attention to Claire, as he'd wanted to do ever since walking into the room. "What's this I hear about *Napoléons*?"

Claire's eyes lit. She put a finger to her lips. "It's one of the desserts we're having at William's party." She whispered as though someone might be eavesdropping around the corner. "I've written the recipe for Cordina"—she looked back at Adelicia—"and I'll arrange a time to help her make them early this week, along with everything else. A sort of . . . trial run for the desserts, so to speak."

Sutton caught the secretive look Claire gave him, and smiled. Adelicia did too, he knew, but she wanted to know what news he had as badly as he didn't want to tell her.

As if sensing the silent exchange between them, Claire rose. Sutton did likewise. Only then did he notice her dress. Or, more rightly, the way the dress looked on *her.* The rich charcoal gray set off her blue eyes, and the rest of the dress set off everything else. Realizing he was staring, he redirected his focus, only to meet Adelicia's all too observant gaze.

He cleared his throat and had to remind himself to swallow. "You look lovely this evening, Miss Laurent. Is that a new dress?"

She smoothed a self-conscious hand over the front, giving him a smile that made him wish he'd gotten there hours earlier. "Yes, it is." She glanced at Adelicia. "Seeing as my trunks haven't arrived yet, Mrs. Acklen encouraged me to purchase something a little more suitable to wear for dinner tonight, and . . . for still being in mourning."

Subtle meaning softened her voice, and Sutton nodded, remembering she *had* just lost her parents.

"Well . . ." Claire turned. "If you'll both excuse me . . ." She started gathering items from a side table. All things pertaining to William's birthday party, from the looks of them. "I'm going to say good night."

Adelicia stood. "Of course, Miss Laurent. It *is* getting late. Thank you again for your contributions at dinner this evening. I had no idea you were so well-informed about the world of art."

Sutton looked up, the comment standing out to him and gently prodding his doubt.

"Oh . . ." Claire looked away. "I'm not that well-informed, ma'am. But I do have an appreciation for art. For painting, in particular."

"So I can see." Adelicia picked up something from the table. "Mr. Monroe, have you seen what Miss Laurent has planned for one of the party favors? They're quite nice."

"Quite nice." That was high praise from Adelicia. She placed a toy in his palm. He'd seen children playing with the thick wooden discs when they were in Europe. A string was wrapped around the middle and the goal had seemed simple—to allow the disc to drop, then with a flick of the wrist, recoil again. A burgundy *A* had been painted in an elegant script on the side. Personalized, as it were.

Feeling both women watching him, waiting for his reaction, he nodded. "It's nice. Very nice."

"It's a *joujou,*" Claire said, stepping closer. "At least that's what we called them in France. It means little toy. With Eli's help, I contacted a woodworker in town this afternoon. He was kind enough to carve a sample for me."

"Turn it over, Mr. Monroe," Adelicia instructed, a smile in her voice. "See what Miss Laurent painted on the other side."

He did as she asked. And though he couldn't explain why, he felt a stir of caution mingle with his surprise.

19

Sutton moved into the lamplight and held the *joujou* closer, astonished at the detail with which Claire had captured a miniature rendition of the Belmont mansion. The tiny replica of the manor, painted on the *joujou* in a ruddy hue identical to the original, included the white columns, the balconies with black cast-iron trim, the cupola and parapets, even the statues adorning the roofline.

He studied it more closely, then realized . . . while she had depicted the major architectural details of the mansion, she'd somehow also captured that swept-away feeling one experienced when first glimpsing the magnificent estate. And on the side of a child's toy, no less. No wonder Adelicia was pleased.

He would have been pleased too, if not for a lingering sense of doubt about Claire. Mrs. Routh's comments from moments earlier only fed that concern.

"You painted this, Miss Laurent?" Hearing the disbelief in his own voice, he rushed to clarify. "I mean no disrespect, I assure you. I'm simply . . . surprised. And impressed."

"No offense taken, Mr. Monroe." Appreciation lit Claire's features. "I'm glad you're pleased. That you're *both* pleased. As Mrs. Acklen and I were just discussing, the theme of the party will be Hidden Treasures. All of the games and party favors will center around that theme. We'll put each *joujou* in the bottom of a drawstring bag, and then fill each bag with candy."

"And . . ." Adelicia reached for something on the table behind her. "We'll also be giving these away. It's called a *bombonnière,* which is French for *sweet box*. It was Miss Laurent's idea to paint them with a picture of the mansion as well, as you can see." She indicated the scene Claire had painted on the lid, similar to the one on the toy, only larger. "We'll give them to parents as a token of our thanks, and inside—hidden away like a treasure—will be a mixture of sugared almonds and roasted cashews."

"Well done, ladies." Sutton had to admit, the theme was brilliant. "It appears as though you have everything planned, and all in typical Belmont fashion."

"We do indeed." Claire's exuberance hinted at anticipation that Sutton wished he could share at the moment. As he helped her gather her items into a box, he considered that she probably had no idea how important this children's party was to Adelicia. It wasn't simply a birthday party for William. It was the first small step in Adelicia's reintroduction to society since the family had returned from Europe.

The grand tour had been the talk of Nashville while they'd been gone, or so he'd been told. And the lavish redecoration of the mansion and refurbishing of the gardens that Adelicia set into motion before leaving had only fueled the gossip. For months. So he especially appreciated Claire's attention to the details.

With a gracious curtsy, Claire bid them good night. And the fleeting backward glance she gave him at the door did his heart more good than it should have.

Adelicia immediately turned to him, but Sutton waited for a moment. He crossed the study, peered outside into the quiet hallway, and closed the door. He knew better than to sugarcoat the news. Adelicia always preferred the straightforward approach.

He pulled the envelope from his pocket and held it out. "It's from the attorney in St. Francisville, Louisiana. The district court has ruled that you must pay Mr. Alexander Walker twenty-five thousand dollars for his assistance in the sale of the cotton."

Stone-faced, Adelicia took the envelope, seated herself in her chair, and read the letter. Then she promptly refolded it, saying nothing. But Sutton could almost hear her thoughts from across the room.

He claimed the chair beside her. "We knew there was a chance of this happening."

Her lips firmed. "Mr. Walker's wife met us in New Orleans that morning over two years ago. She accepted the payment of five hundred dollars on behalf of her husband's involvement. Does that count for nothing?" She turned to him. "You were there. Their own attorney was present too. Their acceptance of the payment that day indicates willful compliance in the eyes of the law. Does it not, Mr. Monroe?"

Sutton knew he didn't need to lecture her on the finer points of the law. Adelicia had grown up reading the law books in her father's library and—according to her late husband, who had been one of the finest attorneys Sutton had known—she began arguing cases with her father at the age of eight. It was a frivolous thought, he knew, but she would have made a formidable lawyer herself.

"Mrs. Acklen, I wish the law were that clear-cut, but we both know it's not. In a perfect world—"

"Please spare me the perfect-world lecture, Mr. Monroe. In a perfect world justice would always be blind and all verdicts would be just." She stated it as though she were speaking to a first-year law apprentice.

Sutton bit his tongue, knowing she was upset, and disappointed. Just as he had been when he'd first read the letter. He'd had the luxury of the past three hours to digest the frustration. She'd had the past three minutes. And it was her money they were talking about. Not his. "My apologies, ma'am, if my words seemed trite. That wasn't my intention. But the fact remains . . ." With deep respect and concern for her, he leveled a stare. "You are an extremely wealthy and well-known widow who played a *very* deep game during a turbulent time in this country."

"I was attending to my own affairs, Mr. Monroe. In the manner *I* thought best."

"I'm well aware of that. But people haven't forgotten that you were accused by the Federals of being 'in complicity with the rebels.' And the Confederates labeled you a Union woman."

She scoffed. "You know my goal was to save that cotton. And I went to great lengths—and peril—to do so. Don't forget my imprisonment! For three days they kept me under house arrest!" She gave an exasperated sigh. "I couldn't simply stand by and allow three years' worth of labor and potential revenue to be burned to naught all because of one general's insatiable thirst for destruction."

Sutton leaned forward. "Of course, I understand. I was there," he gently reminded. "Please understand, Mrs. Acklen, I'm not questioning your motives or your actions. I'm only trying to illustrate how I believe the district court viewed this case."

"I see the argument you're making, Mr. Monroe. But I fail to see the connection between that and a man who agrees to accept one sum of money for his services, only to later change his mind and sue for a greater sum once he discovers how much money his employer received." Taking a deep breath, she stood and strode to the window. "The behavior is deceitful and wrong and ought not to be rewarded. Not by a court of law and *certainly* not by me!"

Weary in body, and of fighting this particular legal battle, Sutton rested his head in his hands, wrestling with how to phrase his next thoughts, but knowing they needed to be said.

Finally, he straightened. "I've encouraged you to put this whole situation behind you, and my counsel in that regard still stands. What's done is done. And as you stated, you wouldn't do anything differently. But . . . that said, though the war is over, tensions are still running high, and certain people's loyalties continue to be held in question."

"As in mine." It wasn't a question.

"Yes, ma'am. As in yours." Remembering what she'd said about how she appreciated his speaking the truth to her, he forged on, hoping she would still feel that way when he was done. "As you know . . . a court of law is only as fair and just as is the judge seated on the bench, or the people seated in the jury. People are responsible for interpreting the law, and yet we each come with our own individual backgrounds and experiences and, therefore, biases."

He looked back at her but she still faced the window. "At the end of the war, ma'am . . . when most people were struggling to find food and shelter for their families—many of whom still are—you managed to outmaneuver two armies and transport twenty-eight hundred bales of cotton through enemy lines. And you sold it . . . for one million dollars, and then set out on a grand tour of Europe. While others, say a judge or a jury of your peers"—he watched her closely, trying to read her posture—"returned to homes that had been burned to the ground and to lives that had been torn asunder."

He clenched his eyes tight. "*Please* hear me in this, Mrs. Acklen. I do not judge you. That's not what this is about. But I firmly believe that the district court's decision in favor of Mr. Walker *is* an indictment of your choices and of the fortune you amassed during that time."

Adelicia continued to stare out the open window, her shoulders rigid. And Sutton waited, the clock ticking, slicing off the seconds.

She turned back to him. "Mr. Walker will never get one penny more than the five hundred dollars he's already received, and that he first agreed to."

Sutton offered a conceding look. "That's precisely what I thought you would say. So I've already begun drafting an appeal to the Supreme Court of Louisiana. It could take months for their review and a final verdict, but I trust that if personal biases influenced the decision at the district level, those biases will be corrected in the Supreme Court's final ruling."

She nodded. "Very good, Mr. Monroe. *Very* good. I appreciate your due diligence, as always."

"You're most welcome, ma'am." He sighed. "Now, if there's nothing further, I believe I'll call it a day. Good night, Mrs. Acklen." He bowed briefly, then turned to leave.

"One more thing, Mr. Monroe."

Accustomed to her "one more things," Sutton turned back.

"Have you received word from the review board yet? As to whether they've rendered their verdict?"

The very mention of the review board dredged up a pile of emotions and regrets he was loath to deal with at the moment. "No, ma'am. Nothing yet. I'll be sure and let you know." He turned to go.

"Praying your forbearance, Mr. Monroe, but . . . I have one more question."

Swallowing a sigh, Sutton turned back again, and could tell by her expression that she knew he was finished with their conversation. But she wasn't.

Yet she seemed unable to sustain his gaze. "In order that sleep may eventually find me when I rest my head on my pillow tonight . . ." Her tone took on a fragile quality, and her manner grew tentative. "When thinking of your father, God rest his soul, and of what the government is seeking to do now—trying to take your family's land, your inheritance—has there ever been a moment, even in the briefest sense, when you've contrasted your circumstance to my own, and . . ." She briefly looked away. "Have you ever thought less of me for the choices I made, and for how those choices unfolded?"

The question caught him off guard. That she cared what he thought and feared he might be holding something against her personally brought a burning to his eyes.

He confined his gaze to the carpet. "As I understand it, you're asking me whether, when I ride up the road to Belmont and see this magnificent estate, I experience a sense of begrudging toward you because *you* didn't lose your home in the war . . . and if—when faced with the loss of my own wealth—I feel a sense of jealousy that your fortune, already immense at the time, was made even more so as a result of your choice to fight to protect your own interests during the war."

He finally looked up. "Have I correctly interpreted your question, ma'am?"

He could hear her breathing from across the room.

"Yes, Mr. Monroe. You have indeed. And with your usual thoroughness."

He took a step toward her, seeing sincerity glistening in her eyes. "I would be lying to you if I said those questions have never assailed me. They have," he whispered, "and still do, on occasion."

He swallowed, feeling the solid thud of his heart in his throat. "However, I don't judge you for your choices, or their outcome. You believed God was directing you to go to Louisiana. I watched you maneuver that cotton past the Confederate Army using Union wagons and mules." He felt the faintest hint of a smile, and saw the same in her. "But you weren't just saving your cotton that night, ma'am. You were protecting your late husbands' legacies, as well as the financial futures of your children.

"As for me . . ." He sighed. "I also live with the outcome of my choices, however less favorable. I refused to sign the Oath of Allegiance and took up arms against the Union. My father . . ." The burning in his eyes intensified. "My father was willing to sign the oath to keep the peace, to sow the seeds of a new nation, but I . . ." He took a steadying breath, remembering that last conversation with his father. "I convinced him otherwise, telling him that to sign would be a betrayal to his family and friends. But most of all . . . to me. And in the end, he paid the price that I alone should have paid."

"Mr. Monroe, you are not responsi—"

He held up a hand. "Don't," he whispered. "If you were in my place, you would feel the very same way."

Her expression sobered. She bowed her head.

"And for what it's worth, ma'am, in my eyes, God could have still burned that cotton even as you were fighting to save it, if that had been His desire. But He *allowed* you to salvage it, and to sell it. All for a divine purpose, I believe."

"And what purpose would that be, Mr. Monroe?"

He shook his head, reaching for the door handle. "*That,* Mrs. Acklen, is between you and your Maker."

He closed the door behind him. And as he lay in bed a while later, alone in the guest quarters of the art gallery with nothing but priceless paintings and statues for companions in the opposite wing, he pushed every bruising thought from his mind, and grasped at the first pleasant one within his reach.

Claire.

It was natural for him to think about her, he told himself. They were colleagues, after all. And friends. He let the word *friend* settle inside him. It didn't adequately describe his feelings for her, and he knew it. But picking at the thread of that thought would only lead to frayed ends.

Cara Netta's most recent letter lay on the bureau and he knew he needed to answer it. She would arrive soon, and he wasn't nearly as enthusiastic over the prospect of seeing her again as he should have been. Not with where they supposedly were in their relationship. In fact, part of him was dreading her arrival, which prodded his guilt.

He raised up, punched his pillow a couple of times, and tried to get more comfortable.

"I had no idea you were so well-informed about the world of art." Adelicia's comment to Claire replayed in his mind. As did what Mrs. Routh had said to him.

It wasn't that Claire knew how to paint so well that bothered him, it was that she'd not mentioned anything about it. Not a word, that he could recall. And it seemed far too much of a stretch that someone so gifted at painting—and apparently *"well-informed about the world of art"*—would just so happen to end up working for the richest and, arguably, most influential person within the art community in Nashville, Tennessee.

And possibly, the whole of Dixie.

20

Paintbrush in hand, Claire turned in her chair to check the clock on the mantel. If only she could make time stand still. The week had flown by far too quickly, and so much remained to be done. It was Friday evening. The party was tomorrow at one o'clock, precisely eighteen hours away, and she still had three *joujou* and four *bombonnière* left to paint, plus all the clues for the scavenger hunt to write and hide.

Still, she was enjoying every minute of the preparation. Especially the painting. *And* Mrs. Acklen's affirmation, which she prayed boded well for her retaining the liaison position. Mrs. Acklen had approved the theme, the party favors, the invitations, the menu—every last detail. Even William seemed excited about the plans for the day.

Claire arched her back and blew a curl from her eye. The muscles in her right hand started to cramp, so she paused to flex her fingers, then painted an *A* on the next *joujou,* adding some elegant swirls for richer depth.

Holding the toy by the edges, she carefully turned the *joujou* over and began painting the other side. Her eyes watered and she blinked to clear them, knowing the image of this mansion would be forever emblazoned on her memory now that she'd painted it dozens of times.

Minutes later, a knock sounded on her bedroom door.

"Captain Laurent?"

She smiled. "Come in, Willister."

No response.

Tempted to try and outwait him, she decided they didn't have the time. "Come in, please, Sutton."

The door opened without delay. "Reporting for duty, Captain Laurent." He came alongside her and offered a mock salute.

She grinned. He'd bestowed the silly nickname after he'd heard her enlisting the help of numerous servants during the course of the week. "At ease, Corporal."

"Corporal? Yesterday I was a lieutenant."

"Yes, but yesterday you brought me a piece of pumpkin bread." She peered up at him, waiting.

Gleam in his eye, he gave her shoulder a friendly nudge. "You're a spoiled officer."

Laughing, she turned back to her work. "A couple more minutes, and I'll be ready."

He knelt beside her. "How long does it take you to paint one of those?"

"Only about thirty minutes of actual painting time . . ." She completed the last tiny brushstrokes on the miniature mansion and set the *joujou* on its edge for the paint to set, careful to place it where it wouldn't roll off the desk. "But I have to wait for it to dry before I can add the detail to the mansion."

"*Hmmm* . . . Time-consuming."

"Yes." She placed her paintbrush in a cup of turpentine. "But worth it, I hope."

He straightened. "I have no doubt your party favors will be a huge success. As will everything else." He glanced toward the window. "We'd better get started, though. From what you said last night, it sounds like we have a lot to do, and it's getting dark earlier these days."

"Have they left yet?"

He nodded. "The carriage just pulled away. Mrs. Acklen said she and the children will be gone until well after dark."

"Perfect! That should give us enough time, if we hurry. If you'll get that basket there on the dresser, please." She gestured. "And I'll get these"—she grabbed the squares of oilcloth she'd cut earlier, along with blue and pink ribbons—"and then we'll be ready."

He was more casually dressed than she'd ever seen him, *sans* coat and tie, and she liked the change. Very much. His white shirt fit snugly across his shoulders and chest, and rolled-up sleeves revealed muscular tanned forearms. Tailored gray trousers complemented his physique just as nicely—from the ever-so-brief glance she allowed herself. Twice.

They'd seen each other throughout the week, but it was mainly at dinner and always with others around. He'd seemed somewhat preoccupied, and she'd wanted to ask him about it, wondering if it was due to something she'd said or done. Or whether it had more to do with the numerous closed-door meetings he'd had with Mrs. Acklen in the library throughout the week.

Whatever it was, the appropriate opportunity to ask him had never presented itself. Until now . . .

"I thought we'd start over there." She pointed to the vine-laced gazebo closest to the house. "I really appreciate your help with this, Sutton. I know you've been busy this week. Lots of meetings, it seems." She glanced over at him. "I hope everything's all right. That . . . nothing bad has happened?"

"Everything's fine. And it's my pleasure to help." He gestured for her to enter the gazebo, then followed. "For not knowing what you were going to do for William's party at the outset, you've certainly accomplished a great deal in a very short time, Claire."

Though his behavior seemed normal enough, she sensed he'd evaded her question, which made her even more curious about the purpose behind his meetings with Mrs. Acklen. As she set the pieces of oilcloth on the bench inside the gazebo, her curiosity made a random leap—and a sinking feeling set in.

What if they'd been meeting about *her*? About whether or not she was going to get the job? Or worse, what if they'd learned something about her? Or about the gallery in New Orleans? The very thought sent a shudder of dread through her. Aware of Sutton watching her, she cordoned off her fears as best she could. "Thank you, Sutton. I've had a lot of excellent help."

"You've had a lot of excellent ideas too. Mrs. Acklen is certainly impressed." He looked over at her. "As am I."

She stilled. "Thank you. . . . That means a great deal coming from you."

His expression turned sheepish. "Why? Because I told you I didn't think you were the most qualified for the job?"

"No." She reached for the basket of note cards he held. "Because I value your good opinion. And not to correct you, but"—she made herself look into his eyes, reliving the sting of his original comment—"what you said was that you didn't think I was even *among* the most qualified."

A stricken look came over him, and he clutched his chest as though she'd plunged a dagger into his heart. He staggered back, agony replacing the shock on his face. Then he fell backward out of the gazebo and landed in the grass on his *derrière.*

Eyes wide, she watched in disbelief, a hiccup of laughter bubbling up her throat. Shocked he'd done such a thing, she was also delighted. What he'd said to her that day had hurt her, and she'd wanted him to know it. And, oh . . . how *good* it felt to be able to say what she'd wanted to say, in the moment she'd wanted to say it. And to have it elicit such a reaction! It more than bolstered her courage.

She peered down at him and lifted a haughty brow. "If you're just going to sit and stare like that, this is going to take all night."

Grinning, he jumped up, dusted himself off, and bowed low. "Consider me at your service, *mademoiselle.* But first . . ." He joined her in the gazebo again. All traces of humor faded. "Please accept my apology. It was never my intention to hurt you, Claire. Honesty is something I value most highly. But . . . I realize that sometimes I can be *too* straightforward."

Claire studied him. And it was all she could do not to open up to him. To tell him about the forgeries and the gallery and her family's business. Contrary to the morning when they'd first met in church, she wanted to confess everything. And part of her believed that if she did tell him the truth right now, he would understand and forgive her.

But another part of her . . .

Told her how foolish that notion was. Sutton Monroe was an attorney-at-law. Laws she had broken. If she told him anything, that would mean the end of everything. And she couldn't risk that. Because she had nowhere else to go. And no one to go to.

"Apology accepted," she finally said, knowing she didn't deserve it. Or his kindness. On a whim, she extended her hand. "Friends?"

He stared for a moment, then slipped his hand—warm and strong—around hers, looking as if he wanted to say something else. And then came that smile. "Friends," he repeatedly softly, and gave her hand a firm shake.

Over the next two hours, they toured the estate and hid clues for each of the two teams for tomorrow's activity, writing them as they went. Twenty-four clues in all. And Claire was certain that if the partygoers had half as much fun as she was having, the party would be a huge success.

They wrapped each clue in oilcloth, then tied them with a pink or blue ribbon. Then they stuffed them into crevices of statuary, slid them into chinks of loose mortar at the top of the water tower, and sneaked them into the bear house, where the black bear slumbering behind bars never even stirred. They stuck clues in the ironwork of gazebos, in the craggy arms of ancient magnolias, and placed one in the mouth of a stone cobra coiled atop a fountain in the conservatory.

In the chill of the icehouse, Sutton climbed up a rock wall and left the boys' clue protruding from a crevice where they would easily see it. Claire first hid the girls' behind a large block of ice in the corner, but then thinking better of it, she stood, with Sutton's assistance, on a block of ice and shoved the clue into a crack between two rocks where it, too, would be seen.

Sucking on slivers of ice he broke off with a pick, they left the icehouse with only two clues remaining to be hidden. Claire fell into step beside him as they headed back across the estate to their last destination.

Almost giddy from the magnificence of the estate and the variety of buildings and architecture, she sighed. "How did Mrs. Acklen ever dream up all of this?" She looked back downhill toward the conservatory. "She has flowers and trees in there I've never even heard of before, much less seen. It feels like you're in a foreign land."

Sutton gave a nod. "She likes rare things. Beautiful things too."

"Did you already know Mrs. Acklen when she built the estate?"

"When she *and* her late husband built it," he gently corrected. "And yes, I knew her. Though not as well, of course, as I do now. That was about . . . thirteen years ago. My father was the Acklen family's physician for many years. Adelicia's late husband, Joseph, and my father were close friends. Mr. Acklen was also my mentor when I began studying law."

They walked in silence together, Claire letting that information sink in. She'd suspected a closer relationship between them, and this explained it. It also explained Sutton's devotion to Mrs. Acklen. Adelicia, as he'd called her before, wasn't simply his employer. She was a longtime family friend.

"Here we are!" Sutton climbed the stairs to the building that would house their last two clues. A building that, Claire felt sure, would be popular with the boys and girls tomorrow.

When first exploring the grounds, she had wondered what this long, narrow building was, and now she grinned to herself, thinking of the clue she and Sutton had just written and hidden in the icehouse. A clue that would—hopefully—lead the children here. Sutton had insisted that some of the clues rhyme, saying it would make them more interesting. She'd argued it just made them harder to write. But they were memorable.

"Approach with care," she recited the first line of the clue in the icehouse, "your eye down the lane. . . ." She stepped through the open door as he held it for her.

"Keep your aim steady," he continued, following behind her, "your mark good and plain."

"Ten little pins"—she stood for a moment and let her eyes adjust to the dimmer light—"all set and ready . . ."

"Awaiting the onslaught"—he came alongside her—"of a sphere *strong and steady*!" He finished on a deeper, more masculine note, like an actor in a play.

Claire laughed at his antics. "A bowling alley." Looking around, she shook her head. "Who would have guessed?"

"If you have a bear house, you have to have a bowling alley."

"Oh, indeed. No question about it. Because we both know how much bears like to bowl." Enjoying the sound of his laughter, she hid her clue in a finger hole of one of the smaller bowling balls, eager to get to the last stop on their tour—the building she'd been waiting to see since she'd first heard about it. The building she'd tried to slip into during the week but had found locked. She hoped Sutton hadn't forgotten.

He hid his clue, and once back outside, they found the sun dipping low in the west, swathed in a haze of pink. Ever the gentleman, Sutton offered his arm before they descended the steps, and Claire briefly slipped her hand through, half wishing she could leave it there when they reached the walkway. But she didn't.

Her thoughts returned to something he'd said before. "Your father . . . He's a physician?"

"*Was* a physician." His voice mirrored the hush of approaching night. "He died during the war."

"Oh, Sutton . . . I'm so sorry." She slowed her steps. But when his gait didn't follow suit, she hurriedly matched his pace again. "Was he killed in battle?" she asked after a moment.

He didn't answer immediately. "No," he whispered. "He was not."

She kept her focus ahead, waiting to see if he might say something more. "And . . . may I ask about your mother? Is she still living?"

His sigh held the semblance of a smile. "Yes, my mother's still living. But not here in Nashville. She lives with my aunt Lorena, her older sister, in North Carolina. She moved there after my father's death. Remaining in Nashville was too difficult for her. My mother has always had more of a . . . delicate emotional nature. Which only became more so after my father's passing."

Claire nodded, wondering about the "delicate emotional nature" comment, but believing she understood, at least to some extent, the part about his mother finding it difficult to remain after his father died. She couldn't imagine still being in New Orleans right now, living above the art gallery, with both her father and Maman gone.

Spotting the art gallery ahead, she smiled. He hadn't forgotten.

The two-story brick building loomed dark and stately, large enough to be a hotel, and certainly grand enough in appearance. At least on the outside. Darkness hid the precise definitions of the structure, but she already knew them by heart, having seen the building often enough since arriving at Belmont.

Airy, elegant balconies reminiscent of European architecture accented the front of the building, and white columns framed the main entrance, drawing the eye upward to an observatory that crowned the splendid edifice. Sutton withdrew a key and slid it into the lock.

"Your humble home," she said quietly.

"Hardly. Half of the building houses the art gallery. The rest comprises five guest suites for Belmont's visitors, along with quarters for their servants."

"All of whom like to bowl, of course."

"But only with bears," he countered, not missing a beat. He swung open the door. "After you, Captain."

Claire stepped inside, then paused, unable to see anything in the darkness. Windows lined the front of the building, but thick draperies—all drawn shut, she'd discovered earlier that week—blocked out the natural light. For the protection of the paintings, she knew.

But the curtains also served double duty in stifling the curiosity of nosy onlookers. Like her.

"Wait here." He touched her arm. "I'll get a lamp."

Sutton stepped beyond her line of sight, the echo of his footsteps lending the room a vast feel. "It's late, so I'll just give you a brief tour tonight, but you're welcome to come back some other time. I think you'll enjoy looking around. Especially since you're so . . . *well-informed* about the world of art."

His comment hung in the silence, and though she recognized it as something Mrs. Acklen had said, she sensed meaning in Sutton's tone she couldn't interpret, not without seeing his face. "Mrs. Acklen was being overly generous when she said that, Sutton. I'm not that knowledgeable, I assure you."

"And I can assure you, Claire . . ." He struck a match and fed the flame to the oil lamp. The halo of light arced back and forth on the walls as he retraced his steps. "Mrs. Acklen is *never* overly generous."

Something was on his mind. She could tell by his earnest expression. And whatever it was, she sensed he'd been waiting for the right time to broach the subject. Her first inclination was to feel baited—until she recalled having used the same ploy on him earlier that evening. However unsuccessfully.

"Mrs. Acklen was completely enamored with your contributions at dinner that night with the Worthingtons. I understand you made quite an impression."

Something in his voice seemed slightly *off,* but she couldn't place what it was. "I'd scarcely say that. I merely attempted to join the conversation when appropriate. Which was no small feat. In fact"—she tried for a conspiratorial tone, hoping to nudge the conversation back toward lighter banter—"Mrs. Worthington is *quite* the conversationalist, especially following a third glass of wine."

Giving her a less-than-convinced look, he indicated a hallway, and she fell into step beside him. The lamplight formed a golden glow between them as they walked.

"You're underestimating the weight of your comments that evening, Claire. Mrs. Acklen praised your knowledge of paintings. And she's not a woman whose praise is easily earned, as we both know. So I'm curious . . . What exactly did you say?"

Claire glanced over at him, wondering why he was so interested.

"During the course of dinner, Mrs. Worthington was discussing a number of paintings, and she attributed two of them to a certain artist. I happened to be familiar with that artist's work and knew he hadn't painted them, so—" she lifted a shoulder and let it fall—"I gently corrected the error and gave credit where it was due."

"I see . . ."

The *clickity-clack* of their footsteps echoed off the walls.

He paused by a doorway and gently took hold of her arm. "May I? It's rather dark inside, and I don't want you tripping over a Michelangelo."

Claire felt her mouth slip open. "Are you saying—"

"No." He smiled. "I'm playing with you. Mrs. Acklen hasn't purchased one of his pieces. Not yet, anyway."

They paused by a painting, and he raised the lamp. "*Marriage of Jacob and Rachel.* It's seventeenth century, by an Italian artist. I'm afraid I don't remember the name."

Still smiling over his Michelangelo comment, Claire didn't recognize the painting, and the scrawled signature didn't help to reveal the artist's identity. But the oil on canvas was stunning. "The colors are so rich, even in this light."

"This one here"—they moved a few steps—"is *Venus at the Forge of Vulcan* by . . ." Sutton hesitated, as though trying to remember.

Jan Brueghel, the younger. Claire recognized the artist's work, but she wasn't about to say anything, not in light of his earlier mention of her *knowledge of art.* "It's lovely." But *lovely* didn't begin to describe it. The detail in the brushstrokes, the movement. Flawless. She could have sat and studied it for hours.

Sutton looked over at her then, and for reasons she couldn't define, she got the feeling that his hesitation seconds earlier had been intentional, to see if she would fill in the blank. She quickly looked away, the loathsome weight inside her growing denser, heavier.

He led her into the next room. "Careful, there are some crates along through here."

Claire maneuvered around them.

He raised the lamp again. "And these four paintings . . ."

Claire saw the first painting and went weak in the knees. *Antonio Canaletto.*

". . . are some of Adelicia's favorites. The artist is Canaletto. This is the *Great Canal,* the next is the *Church of the Salute*, and then the

Rialto Bridge, and then finally"—he extended the lamp out to one side—"the *Church of the Friar.* I tend to remember the artists and titles of the most expensive ones."

Claire could hardly breathe. The actual title of the first oil was the *Grand Canal,* but again, she wasn't about to correct him. Grateful for the dim lighting, she did her best to mask her emotions, almost wanting to cry she was so moved at being in the presence of such masterpieces. "They're all . . . very nice."

She'd copied the first painting twice and had sold it as such with her initials. At the time, she thought she'd captured the colors of the original quite well. She'd been wrong. The cloud-feathered sky was more cerulean than azure, and the Venetian buildings along the canal more misty taupe than tawny brown. She looked around the room and saw more canvases, hanging one after the other, though she couldn't see the paintings themselves. "Are *all* of these originals?"

"Yes . . . though Mrs. Acklen *does* own a few select copies. But only those painted by an accomplished apprentice serving under the strict tutelage of the original painting's artist." He laughed softly. "Would you expect the Adelicia Acklen you know to own anything less?"

Claire felt a stab of reality. No, she wouldn't. Why would someone like Mrs. Acklen ever desire a cheap imitation of the real thing? Much less a forgery? The painting would be worthless. Not good enough. *Never* good enough . . .

Sutton held the lamp closer, and Claire resisted the urge to turn away.

"Why is it, Claire, that you never mentioned anything about your knowledge of art before? Or of how *very* accomplished you are at painting? It seems like that would have come up before now. Especially with an employer like Mrs. Acklen, and at an estate like Belmont."

Claire sensed a definite difference in his tone this time, and she read in his eyes what his voice had only hinted at before—suspicion and distrust. And she panicked, certain he knew the truth.

21

Claire looked down and squeezed her eyes tight, unable to think with him watching her so closely. How had he found out? She'd been so careful not to say anything, not to let anything slip. She needed to look up, but she couldn't. If she looked at him, he would see the truth in her face. But she had to look up. Because if she didn't, he would know she was hiding something.

She forced her gaze upward and saw a shred of question lingering in his eyes. Maybe he *didn't* know. . . .

Maybe he was just being an attorney and . . . doing whatever it was attorneys did. He'd told her himself that he was paid to be suspicious, and she'd been plenty evasive with him. Which, looking back, had not been a wise choice on her part.

"Sutton, I . . ." She half expected him to say something. Interrupt her, maybe. But he didn't. She'd never been on a witness stand before, but she felt as if she were on one now. She couldn't tell him the truth, and yet she also would not lie. "I never mentioned it before because . . . compared to all of this"—she gestured around them, hearing the next words in her mind just before they burned with shame on her tongue—"my knowledge, like my talent . . . is nothing unique."

If only he knew how honest she was being with him at that moment. More so than she'd been with anyone else in her life. Even Maman. "But I'm committed to learning, to improving. Over time, and with practice. And I give you my word, it won't interfere with my position as Mrs. Acklen's liaison. *If* I get the position, of course."

For the longest moment, he said nothing, and Claire bowed her head, waiting for him to tell her that he knew about the gallery in New Orleans, and about what her family used to do, and about what she was.

Then he reached up and brushed a curl from her temple. "Look at me, Claire."

Dreading what she would see, what he was going to say, she couldn't.

"Captain Laurent . . ." He laughed softly. "Look at me. That's an order."

Slowly, she lifted her gaze, and her heart responded to him in a way it had no business doing.

"I'll be the first to admit," he said. "I'm not an expert in the world of art. But take my word for it, Claire . . . your talent is anything but ordinary."

She let out her breath as a trickle of relief wound its way through her. And she suddenly grew very aware of the darkness around them, of how alone they were, and of just how attracted she was to this man. To his humor, his integrity, his warmth, his . . . *David*-like qualities.

"I'm going to ask you a question, Claire, and I want an honest answer."

Realizing he was waiting on her to respond, she nodded, feeling the other shoe about to fall after all.

"Did you, or did you not, seek the position with Mrs. Acklen with the purpose of using her social connections and reputation to further your own chances in the art world?"

"I did not," she answered with full honesty. "I didn't know who Mrs. Acklen was before I arrived at Belmont. I told her that in the interview. I'd never even heard of her before I"—she hated to remind him—"eavesdropped on those women in church. I give you my word, Sutton. And furthermore, I would never do anything that would bring reproach on her good name. Or yours."

His focus unrelenting, he studied her, and for once, she didn't flinch beneath his close attention.

Finally, a ghost of a smile appeared. "I appreciate that, Claire. Thank you. Now I'd better get you back. You have a big day tomorrow."

He took hold of her arm again as they maneuvered their way back to the lobby. Claire felt a closeness to him she hadn't before, and she sensed he felt it too, but couldn't be sure. She'd won his trust, though, and was determined to keep it.

He reached to open the door for her and paused. "I'm going to take a wild stab here, but I'm guessing that since you didn't know who Mrs. Acklen was before you came here, you also aren't aware of the art auction she helps sponsor every spring. Part of which features new artists and their work."

"New artists?" Claire asked, doing her best to sound casual, and knowing by his devilish smile that she'd failed.

"Well . . ." He opened the door for her. "I guess that answers that."

"Let's review the rules to make sure everyone understands the goal of the game. . . ."

Pistol in hand, Sutton listened to Claire address the crowd. Lovely in her gray dress, she stood on the top step in front of the mansion, her honey-autumn curls swept up and shining in the sun. An almost palpable excitement infused the warm September afternoon and a perfect breeze accompanied a cloudless blue.

Boys and girls pressed close on the lower stairs, already grouped in their opposing teams. They whispered to each other, smiles wide. Parents gathered in a group behind them wearing looks of youthful anticipation. Even Adelicia, dressed in a deep plum dress Sutton couldn't remember seeing before, appeared as though she wished she, too, could take part in the hunt.

"Remember, you must stay on course and go only where clues tell you to go." Claire seemed as excited as the children. "Just because the girls' team finds a clue in one spot doesn't mean the boys will also find one there. And some of the clues may be more difficult to decipher than others. That's especially true"—she glanced in Sutton's direction, tilting her head knowingly—"of the clues that rhyme."

He smiled, enjoying the private joke, and the opportunity just to look at her. He'd considered her pretty the first time they'd met, even with her hair mussed and her dress wrinkled. And her beauty had only deepened the more he'd gotten to know her. He'd enjoyed writing and hiding the clues with her last night. How long had it been since he'd laughed like that? He couldn't remember.

Then there'd been those moments in the art gallery. . . .

That fraction of a heartbeat when he'd partially lost his mind and had actually contemplated taking the woman in his arms and *kissing her*! He'd imagined cradling her cheek and tasting the wine from those full pink lips. He'd quickly come to his senses, of course, and knew he needed to get a rein on himself. And still did, apparently.

He took a deep breath and exhaled.

He and Claire were colleagues. *Friendly* colleagues who shared a good working relationship. And playful banter. And who could talk at length about many different subjects. But that was all. Claire had never given him any indication that she felt anything more than friendship for him. So he'd figured—up until last night—that the spirited back-and-forth between them was safe enough. But his surprising inclination toward her in the gallery was making him think otherwise.

He needed to tell her about Cara Netta. That would help things. Yet he hadn't been able to broach the subject. It was wrong for a man to foster daydreams about a woman when he was in a relationship—whatever that may be—with another.

Cara Netta was kind and good and gracious and sweet, and was from a well-established family whose name opened doors at the merest mention. She was everything a man could want in a wife, and she would arrive at Belmont in a matter of days and would be expecting a proposal. One he still wasn't prepared to extend.

But he could be, perhaps, if the review board rendered a fair verdict. Or if the case he had formally agreed to work on with Mr. Holbrook proved to be as promising as Holbrook thought.

The alleged incidents of art fraud were more numerous than first estimated, but gathering the necessary evidence would take the investigators time. It seemed like an almost impossible feat right now. Meanwhile, he and Holbrook were deposing clients and slowly building their case, piece by piece. And if they were to take this case to trial and win . . .

It would change everything for him. The financial reward for the firm—and his portion of that—would go a long way to starting a thoroughbred farm.

Pulling his thoughts back, Sutton refocused on Claire, and on the children's faces as she described the rest of the afternoon's activities. She'd worked so hard to make this party a success. And the fruits of her labors would go far, he knew, in rebuilding Adelicia's relationships with begrudging peers. If Adelicia didn't give Claire the job after all this . . .

He thought of the letter he'd sent to his colleague in New Orleans and felt a twinge of guilt. He quickly reminded himself that Adelicia had requested the query be sent. Still, having sent that query and now growing closer to Claire as he was made him feel like he was being dishonest with her somehow. Even though he knew he was only doing his job.

He was convinced she hadn't known about the art auction. A person couldn't feign that kind of surprise. Not Claire anyway. She could no more tell a lie than a bird could swim. And even though he believed everything she'd said, he also still believed she was hiding something. But he'd finally come to the conclusion it couldn't be of huge consequence.

Because he'd seen her sincerity. He'd *felt* it.

"All right, everyone! I've already given each team a hint as to where your first clues are hidden, so—"

Excited chatter rose from the youth, and Claire raised her hands to regain their attention. The chatter lowered to a simmering thrum.

"So when the signal sounds"—she looked back at Sutton—"that will be your cue to start. The first team to gather *all* their clues and meet back here at the stairs is the winner, and each member of the winning team will receive a prize. Now, do you have any questions?"

"Yes, ma'am," William called out, standing at the head of his team. "What are the girls gonna do when the boys get all of their clues first?" His team members snickered and thumped him on the back.

"We'll be waitin' right here on these stairs for you, William Acklen. That's what we'll be doin'!" a spunky little blonde retorted, her smile as competitive as it was pretty. Sutton had seen William talking to the girl earlier, and though they were a little young for thoughts about sparkin', as his grandfather had called it, he'd sensed an interest on the boy's part.

And the grin William sneaked her way now left no doubt.

Amidst the laughter, Claire glanced at Sutton and nodded. He raised the pistol high.

"On your mark . . ." she shouted.

Sutton cocked the gun. The boys leaned forward, eyes fierce with competition. The girls gripped their skirts, readying to bolt.

"Get set . . ."

Children and parents held a collective breath.

"Go!"

Sutton fired, and off the teams went. Girls in one direction, boys in the other, laughter coming from both.

"And to our remaining guests," Claire addressed, "we appreciate your attendance today. While our little scavengers are out hunting for their hidden treasures, Mrs. Acklen invites you to enjoy a variety of French pastries she recently discovered on her family's grand tour of Europe. On the tables to your left"—she gestured—"you'll find pastries with the name and description of each, as well as the history behind them. *Café au lait* is available at the table by the main fountain. And on behalf of Mrs. Acklen and everyone at Belmont, thank you again for joining us for William's eleventh birthday celebration. *Bon appétit!*"

Applause rose from the parents, and Sutton smiled. Nervous as she'd been before she'd gotten up there, Claire Laurent looked as if she'd been directing troops all her life. He sidled up beside her. "Well done, Captain."

She grinned up at him, then turned and made a face that only he could see. "I hope the teams can figure out all the clues. If they can't, I'm blaming you."

He laughed. "That's fine, but I'm pretty sure I can't go much lower than a corporal."

"Well, we'll just see about—"

"Well done, Miss Laurent."

They both turned to see Adelicia ascending the stairs, young Pauline and Claude racing up beside her. And—much to Sutton's delight—Adelicia's mother followed them.

"Mrs. Hayes," he said, bowing at the waist. "How wonderful to see you again, ma'am." Little Pauline reached up to him, and he scooped her up in his arms, relishing her little-girl hug.

Mrs. Hayes extended a lace-gloved hand, which Sutton kissed. "The pleasure is all mine, Mr. Monroe. I wasn't about to miss my grandson's eleventh birthday celebration. Especially not after Adelicia's lengthy description of the pastries, party favors, and games earlier this week. Although, I don't quite see the purpose behind intentionally setting the girls' team against the boys'. We all know that a *properly* bred young lady will always allow a boy to win. Any lesser behavior would be considered lacking in etiquette."

Sutton caught Adelicia's fleeting frown, and Claire's less than subtle look of confusion.

"It's simply a game, Mother dear," Adelicia said, her smile back in place. "And I dare say, Miss Laurent, that this is a party William and his friends, *and* their parents, will remember for years to come. As will I."

Her tone was exceptionally gracious, Sutton noted, and the affirmation lighting Claire's eyes lit something inside him too.

"Thank you, Mrs. Acklen." Claire curtsied. "I'm happy that you're pleased."

"Shall we treat ourselves to refreshments, children?" Adelicia asked.

"I want a *Napoléon*!" Pauline chimed in.

With a quick peck to Pauline's cheek, Sutton set her down, and off she went. Claude followed, racing her down the steps. Arm in arm, Adelicia and Mrs. Hayes descended in more graceful fashion. Sutton was glad to see his employer in the company of Nashville society again, although he noticed that the guests didn't exactly flock to her as they once had.

He offered his arm to Claire. "Are *you* ready for a *Napoléon*?"

With waning enthusiasm, she accepted. "Mrs. Hayes doesn't like the party."

"That's not true. She's simply more . . . old-fashioned in some of her opinions. But I can tell you from having known the woman for years that she was impressed with what you've done today. And with her daughter . . . for hiring you."

"At least temporarily." Claire gave him a deflated smile.

When they reached the bottom of the stairs, he covered her hand on his arm. "Don't let that one comment ruin the day. All right?" He playfully tweaked her chin, glad when her smile blossomed again.

"Thank you, Sutton."

"Oh, Miss Laurent! May we speak with you?"

"Do you hire out for parties?"

Seeing a hoard of purposeful mothers heading their way, Sutton made his exit, knowing Claire could manage them without his assistance. Visiting with guests, he feasted on pastries that took him back to the streets and the delectable bakeries of Paris.

Claire joined him about an hour later and they sat inside a gazebo, grinning along with the parents as they watched the boys and girls dart from statue to building, then building to statue, then back to the low-hanging magnolia branches.

For most of the hunt it seemed the teams were neck and neck—until he spotted the girls heading for the icehouse.

"Uh-oh," he whispered beneath his breath, then looked over to see Claire beaming. "Claire Laurent, how can you be responsible for William's party and yet want his team to lose? It's his birthday!" He checked to make sure Mrs. Hayes wasn't nearby. "Besides, it's completely lacking in etiquette."

She gave him a look. "I never said I wanted the girls to win. Out loud, anyway."

He shook his head. She and Adelicia were cut from the same cloth. A breeze stirred a curl at her temple, and he smiled to himself, thinking of what she'd arranged for the members of the winning team. Even the weather was cooperating according to the woman's plan. "I meant to ask you. How did you come up with this game?"

She lifted her chin. "I thought of it. All by myself." She looked down her pert little nose at him. "With no thanks to you, kind sir."

Sutton eyed her. The snippy little—

"I got the idea from Zeke."

He frowned, not following. "Zeke gave you the idea?"

She nodded, sipping her coffee. "I saw him one morning digging in the dirt. He was so intent on his task and having such fun. He'd found a nickel and some spent shells. Then later, I thought of Zeke again and began thinking of how much fun it might be for William and his friends to . . . What?" Her eyes narrowed. "Why are you smiling?"

Sutton looked at her, finding a satisfaction in her answer that he wasn't about to explain. "No reason, I just—"

She reached over and grabbed his arm. "The girls are leaving the icehouse," she whispered. "But here come the boys!"

Sure enough, Sutton looked up to see William leading the pack, running full out. The boys crowded into the icehouse and couldn't have been inside more than thirty seconds before they barreled back out, headed straight for the bowling alley. "So much for the clues that rhyme being harder to decipher."

The boys made a dash for their last destination, covering ground much faster than the girls, who were just reaching the steps of the bowling alley.

Sutton stood. "It's going to be close."

"Very close." Claire rose too and started toward the mansion. Sutton followed.

Several of the parents began moving back in that direction as well.

Not three minutes later, the girls' team burst through the doors of the bowling alley, decorum and propriety tossed to the wind, skirts hitched knee-high and hair ribbons flying. They raced back across the lawn, glancing over their shoulders and squealing the second they spotted the boys fast on their trail.

Sutton had never seen anything like it, and was certain Belmont hadn't either. He looked around to make certain Mrs. Hayes wasn't having the vapors. But the woman was cheering along with everyone else. For the boys, of course.

And more than that, the look on Claire's face was pure delight. As was Adelicia's, as she stood behind them on the stairs.

"Come on," he heard Adelicia whisper, and knew instinctively whose team she was rooting for. Apparently gender outweighed blood relations, at least in competitions. The parents rooted for the teams too, yelling encouragements as they raced toward the goal.

But the winner was clear.

22

The girls' team, led by the spunky little blonde who had spoken up earlier, stampeded up the stairs. With cheeks flushed and spirits high, the girls crowded together as though intent on guarding their territory as the leader pressed a neat pile of clues into Claire's hand.

"Here you are, Miss Laurent." The little blonde took a breath, her eyes bright. "All the clues, in order." She smiled. "Oh! That was fun!" Her friends nodded, giddy with triumph.

Sharing their moment of glory, Claire counted the girls' clues to make certain they'd found them all, and by the time William and his friends climbed the stairs, she knew the winner. Judging by William's poorly masked disappointment, so did he.

Claire stepped forward. "Congratulations to both teams for finishing so quickly. And now, the declared winner of the Hunt for Hidden Treasure is—the girls' team!"

Cheers went up from everyone, though the boys' applause seemed halfhearted at best. Even Mrs. Hayes was wearing a smile.

Waiting for the cheers and congratulations to die down, Claire turned to see Sutton retrieving the two large boxes stashed inside the entrance hall, right on cue. "Thank you," she mouthed, appreciating the man more each day. "And now it's time to award the winners their prizes." She reached into the first box and carefully removed a resplendent red-and-yellow kite, the one Sutton had helped her assemble that morning.

She held it high as the girls clapped in excitement, and as the boys lowered their heads. Then she had an idea. . . .

"As I give the girls their prizes," she continued, knowing the boys would perk up soon enough, "I need the boys to form a single line down the stairs, starting with William, and then number off, beginning with one. Be sure to remember your number!"

"What are you doing?" Sutton whispered behind her.

"I'm improvising," she whispered back as she distributed the unassembled kites and congratulated each girl.

"Why does that frighten me . . . ?"

Smirking, she pretended to ignore him. "Now, will the captain of the girls' team please join me here." The girl did as Claire bade. "And will the rest of the young ladies please make a line down the stairs as the boys have done?"

Claire glanced at William to see whether the boy had figured out what she was doing. His sullen expression said he hadn't, but she knew it wouldn't take long. "To your left are special tables with fresh pastries and punch set up for you young men and women. As you're enjoying your refreshments, I ask that each young lady seek out the young man who has her corresponding number. For instance, Miss Sally Forthright, captain of the girls' team is number one. Likewise, Mr. William Acklen"—Claire smiled as a light crept back into William's eyes—"is number one on the boys' team. So, Sally and William"—Sally and William sneaked bashful looks at each other—"after you've finished your pastries and punch, your next task will be to assemble Sally's kite and then take it for its first flight. Weather cooperating, of course."

She would've sworn the boys' chests puffed out a good three inches and that the girls' smiles widened the same. The slight bobbing of their heads told her both the boys and the girls were mentally counting down the lines, figuring out who their partner would be.

"Quite the improviser," Sutton whispered behind her.

She reached back and tried to swat him, and missed. But she heard him laugh.

The remainder of the afternoon's events progressed even better than she'd imagined, and as the last carriage pulled away from Belmont at nearly six o'clock, Claire found herself utterly exhausted, and pleased beyond expectation.

Claire chose to forego dinner and lay down for a nap instead. Still wearing her dress, she barely remembered her head touching the pillow. When she awakened some time later, her bedroom was awash in the glow of twilight.

A coolness layered the air.

She felt a hunger pang and squinted to see the clock on the mantel. Half past eight. Not as late as it felt. But as Sutton had said, it was getting dark earlier. She climbed from the bed, hoping Cordina's stash of day-old bread would yield a roll or two left from dinner. That would be enough to last her until breakfast.

The grand salon was quiet. A single lamp illuminated the room, its light swiftly surrendering to the shadows crowding the corners. Where was everyone? Voices drifted toward her, coming from the *tête-à-tête* room.

At first she thought it was Sutton and Mrs. Acklen, but as she picked her way into the dark entrance hall, she realized the man's voice wasn't Sutton's.

"Lucius . . ." Mrs. Acklen's lilting laughter carried through the closed door. "I don't know where you get your stories."

"They're not stories, Adelicia. They're just my life."

More soft laughter. "I guess it's the way you describe things that makes them so comical."

Claire smiled at the exchange, but . . . who was *Lucius*?

Not wishing to eavesdrop, she quickly turned to go when a darkened silhouette stepped from the shadows. She nearly jumped out of her skin. "Mrs. Routh!" Hand over her heart, Claire took several breaths. "You scared me to death, ma'am. What are you doing out here?"

"I was in the study making certain the windows were latched, Miss Laurent. What are *you* doing out here?"

"I just awakened from a nap. I was on my way to the kitchen when I heard voices, and—" Even without seeing the housekeeper's face, Claire could feel Mrs. Routh's disapproval. Would she never win this woman's favor? "I came in here to see if Sut—" She caught herself. "To see if Mr. Monroe was here. But he's not. And since I didn't wish to eavesdrop, I was leaving to—"

The door to the *tête-à-tête* room opened, and light poured into the entrance hall.

Mrs. Acklen emerged, oil lamp in hand. A gentleman followed, one Claire remembered having seen at the party earlier that day.

Mrs. Acklen paused in the doorway. "Mrs. Routh. Miss Laurent. Did I miss the notice for our gathering?" She smiled in an almost jovial manner.

"No, ma'am," Mrs. Routh answered, her tone having thawed by a degree. "I'm taking care of my nightly duties, and Miss Laurent was on her way to the kitchen, it would seem."

"Ah, yes, Miss Laurent." Mrs. Acklen shone the lamp in Claire's direction. "We missed you at dinner. Cordina said you'd gone to lie down. I hope you're feeling more rested?"

"Yes, ma'am. I am. Thank you." She sneaked a look at the gentleman who was watching Mrs. Acklen with rapt attention.

"Well, I'm glad to hear it. Because come Monday morning"—Mrs. Acklen gave her a pointed look—"we have much work to do."

Claire stared, wondering if Mrs. Acklen meant what she thought she meant. "A-are you saying that I—"

"Yes, Miss Laurent. Congratulations, I'm granting you the position."

Having hoped and prayed she would hear those words, Claire could hardly believe them. And judging from Mrs. Routh's stoic expression, neither could she. "Thank you, Mrs. Acklen. I promise, I'll work hard every day and do my very best."

"Yes, yes, Miss Laurent." Mrs. Acklen nodded. "And I'll accept nothing less. Now go get your dinner. Cordina said she was going to leave you a plate by the stove."

Claire fairly floated down to the kitchen and retrieved her plate and a glass of milk, then slipped back up to her room. Wishing she could tell Sutton the news, she guessed he probably knew already.

She made quick work of the pork chop, sweet potatoes, and black-eyed peas, and ate every crumb of the corn bread Cordina had slathered with butter. She licked the melted butter from her fingers, certain nothing had ever tasted so good.

Full as a tick, as she'd heard Eli say, she changed into her gown and blew out the light, wishing she could have talked to Sutton again before going to bed. As she turned back the sheets, she glanced out the window. And stilled.

Down below, in the same area where she'd seen Zeke digging, someone knelt in the dirt, digging just like Zeke had. She crept closer to the window, keeping her head down, glad her lamp was extinguished. She watched, and waited. For what, she didn't know.

Whoever was down there was taking their time digging and then smoothing the dirt out again. Then it occurred to her. They weren't digging. They were *burying.* The person stood and Claire's breath caught. *Sutton!* She recognized his stance, his walk.

He moved a few feet over and repeated the process she'd just witnessed, and her thoughts turned to Zeke and how the boy had told her he'd found coins buried down there, among other things.

She watched Sutton reach into his pocket, then drop something—a coin, she assumed—in the hole, then smooth the dirt over again, looking from side to side as he did. Who would have thought . . .

As it turned out, Sutton was the apparent inspiration behind *her* brilliant idea for the theme of William's party. Smiling, she shook her head to herself and crawled between the sheets, then rustled her legs beneath the covers, trying to get warm.

Silvered slats of moonlight fell across the room, moving with the tree limbs outside her window as they bent and swayed in the wind. She wished she could tell Sutton the truth. In the same breath, she also wished—as silly and as farfetched as it sounded, even to her—that he cared for her the way she was beginning to care for him. Even though she knew she shouldn't.

Because nothing would ever come of it. Because how could you love someone you didn't know? And Sutton didn't know her. Not really. And if he did, he wouldn't like what he saw. Because everything he stood for—integrity, honor, defending the law—she had smeared with disregard.

She hadn't blatantly lied. But she hadn't been truthful either. Was telling a lie and not telling the whole truth the same thing? She didn't think it was. But right now, in that moment, they felt the same.

Because if she were to tell Sutton the truth—about her past and the paintings she'd forged, and her family's gallery where they had sold them—she knew in her heart that he would believe she had lied to him, and to Mrs. Acklen. And he would be right. And she would be gone.

Away from Belmont. Away from him. Away from this fresh start at a new life.

No . . . telling the truth came at too great a cost. Besides, that life was behind her now. Wasn't her pledge to start over, to do better, never to steal or to lie or to forge anything else again . . . enough?

23

You're certain I'm not speaking too quickly this morning, Miss Laurent? You're keeping up?" Mrs. Acklen crossed the study to the secretary's desk and peered over Claire's shoulder.

"Yes, ma'am. I've written everything down. Including the Christmas menu, along with the amounts and what to order from which company." Claire offered her the pages for review, accustomed to Mrs. Acklen's perusal. Her hand ached from taking dictation all morning, no matter that the fountain pen was the nicest she'd ever used. The ink fairly glided onto the page.

A gentle rap sounded.

"Come in," Adelicia announced, turning as the door opened. "Ah! Miss Cenas, how are you this morning?"

Claire looked up to see the children's tutor smiling in her direction and returned the gesture, mouthing a quiet "Good morning." She'd met the teacher earlier in the week, and a more organized individual she'd never known.

Miss Heloise Cenas worked magic with the children and their studies. With never a cross word and never her voice raised, the eloquently spoken schoolmarm delivered the lessons in such a way that even Claire had found herself listening, on occasion, outside the classroom, which was conveniently located in a spare bedroom off the grand salon.

Miss Cenas paused inside the doorway. "I'm very well, Mrs. Acklen, thank you. And so happy to be back at Belmont. Forgive my interruption, ma'am, but I wanted to remind you that the children and I will be away for the day. We're venturing across town to see Joseph Jr. We'll have lunch with him and see his new quarters at school."

"Very good, Miss Cenas. Please be sure and take the basket of goodies Cordina made up for him this morning. And I wrote him a long letter before going to bed last evening. It's in the salon on the side table, unless Mrs. Routh has already tucked it . . ." Mrs. Acklen paused, and turned to Claire. "Excuse me for a moment, Miss Laurent. I need to make sure everything is as it should be for Joseph."

Mrs. Acklen swept from the room, intent on her mission. And with another quick dip of her head, Miss Cenas closed the door behind them. Claire welcomed the moment of quiet.

Stretching her back and shoulders, she peered out the window and saw Belmont's gardeners hard at work. The men toiled from dawn to dusk every day, it seemed. No wonder the gardens were always so pristine.

She claimed a spot on the settee and flipped through a back issue of *Godey's Lady's Book.*

Four out of the past five mornings, with the exception of Sunday, she and Mrs. Acklen had barricaded themselves in this room, Mrs. Acklen dictating, and her transcribing. Everything from letters to formal acquaintances, to responses to business owners, to list after list of projects to be completed, which included ordering fresh oysters from New Orleans for Christmas dinner.

On Sunday morning, the entire family had attended church services, Claire included. Apparently now that she was a more permanent employee, Mrs. Acklen expected her to attend, which was fine. Claire had enjoyed the service, especially Reverend Bunting's sermon, and though church meant going into town, church was also the last place Antoine DePaul would be.

The only part of the experience she hadn't been particularly fond of was when she'd discovered that the pew she'd spent the night on had been Mrs. Acklen's personal pew. She grew warm again remembering Sutton's hushed remark to her as they'd left the sanctuary. *"I've never noticed before, but that pew is almost comfortable enough to sleep on."*

She smiled to herself. *The scoundrel . . .*

Though he'd more than made up for the comment the following day when she'd discovered a bouquet of wildflowers by her bedroom door along with a note—*Congratulations on a job well done, Captain. Respectfully, Your Lowly Corporal.*

Not really reading the pages of *Godey's,* she returned the magazine to the table and noticed a newspaper tucked beneath a *Harper's Weekly.* The newspaper seemed vaguely familiar for some reason, and when she tugged it free of the magazine, she realized why.

Mrs. Acklen subscribed to the *New Orleans Picayune*? Not that hard to believe, she realized, considering Mrs. Acklen had plantations in—

A headline caught her eye, and her heart skipped a painful beat. MAN SLAIN IN ROBBERY ATTEMPT. Holding her breath, she scanned the article and—cruel though it seemed—she was relieved to discover it was about a man killed during an attempted robbery of a mercantile and wasn't about her father, as she'd feared.

Calming, she checked the date on the newspaper. September tenth. She counted back. The day she'd arrived in Nashville. Unable to resist scanning the rest of the paper, her gaze flew over the column headings on the front page. Then she moved to the second page, and the third. By the time she reached the back page, she was allowing herself to believe—

A headline at the very bottom siphoned the breath from her lungs even as the miles between her and her old life disappeared. The last column, the last article on the right. And so few words. She could almost read them at a glance.

GALLERY ROBBERY AND SLAYING

As previously reported, thieves robbed the European Masters Art Gallery in the French Quarter and absconded with an extensive art collection of undisclosed worth. Art dealer and part-owner, Bernard Gustave Laurent, first reported as being stabbed in the robbery, died Friday evening following complications from his injury. Private interment held Saturday.

Claire's eyes burned, a dozen different emotions roiling inside her. The greatest being panic! What if Mrs. Acklen or Sutton were to read this and see her father's name? Or what if they already had? Yet she knew if they'd read it, they would have said something to her by now. Neither were shy of confrontation. On the heels of panic came regret—that she hadn't been there to bury her father.

But what surprised her most was the pity she felt. *This* was her father's legacy. This brief newspaper article. So succinct, so impersonal. Like a footnote or an afterthought.

From nowhere, Antoine DePaul's deceivingly handsome face appeared in her mind. Nothing within her ever wanted to see that man again. Not after tasting what life was like beyond his and Papa's reach, beyond the walls of that gallery where she'd felt so—

The sound of a door closing somewhere beyond the small study bulleted Claire off the settee. She had to hide the newspaper before Mrs. Acklen—

The door to the small study opened.

"As usual, Mrs. Routh had everything in order," Mrs. Acklen said, turning to close the door behind her. "So Joseph will know with full assurance that his absence is greatly felt here at home. Now, where were we, Miss Laurent?"

Standing by the settee, Claire laid the *Godey's Lady's Book* atop the pile of magazines where she'd hidden the newspaper, for the time being. "You were reviewing the dictation from this morning, ma'am." She handed Mrs. Acklen the papers, her heart still pounding.

But Mrs. Acklen didn't start reading. "Miss Laurent, please do take extra care with where you place the fountain pen."

Claire quickly retrieved the pen from where she'd laid it on the desk.

"I'm overly protective of this secretary, I realize. But it's a treasured antique. A gift from my father." Mrs. Acklen smoothed a hand over the flawless rich cherrywood. "The desk came over on the *Mayflower*. My father had it restored for me upon the occasion of my eighteenth birthday. Remarkable to think that when the desk came into my possession, it was already well over two hundred years old."

"It's lovely," Claire said, checking to make sure none of the ink had leaked out.

"Yes, and I'd like to keep it that way." Mrs. Acklen perused the notes, nodding as she did so. "Your handwriting is impeccable, Miss Laurent. But I do believe a course in shorthand would be prudent. The skill would serve you well, and would save you a good deal of soreness."

Only then did Claire realize she was rubbing her right hand. "I'm fine, Mrs. Acklen, honestly. But I'd be happy to learn it if you think it's important."

"What I think, Miss Laurent . . ." With a sigh, Mrs. Acklen crossed the study and opened a window. A lusciously cool breeze wafted past the heavy brocade curtains. "I think we've been cooped up inside this room far too long this week. A taste of fall is in the air, and I'd very much like to take advantage of it." She turned back, a glimmer of challenge in her eyes. "By any chance . . . do you ride?"

Half an hour later—with the newspaper tucked in the bottom of the trash bin in the kitchen—Claire found herself seated sidesaddle on a beautiful little black mare named Athena. The spirited animal pranced beneath her, straining at the bit, but Claire managed to hold her steady.

Armstead, Mrs. Acklen's coachman, assisted Mrs. Acklen into the saddle of a magnificent bay stallion. The horse looked identical to one depicted in an oil painting in the central parlor, and also to a bronze replica in the small study. The painting was of Mrs. Acklen some years earlier, holding the reins of a stallion—a thoroughbred, she'd learned.

Mrs. Acklen skillfully prodded the massive brute up beside the pretty mare, and Athena snorted and tossed her head, as though challenging his superior breeding. The stallion, standing a good three hands taller than Athena, merely glanced over with passing interest.

Mrs. Acklen leaned forward and stroked the thoroughbred's neck. "How long has it been since you've ridden, Miss Laurent?"

Claire had to think. "Over two years, I'd say. But when we first came to this country, we lived near a horse farm. The owner was gracious enough to let me ride in the afternoons in exchange for giving his young daughters art lessons. So . . ." She dared let a touch of confidence slip through. "I'm a fairly good rider. Or at least I was."

"Is that so?" Mrs. Acklen's gaze moved over her as though she were evaluating Claire's equestrian skills. "Don't let Athena's size mislead you, Miss Laurent. She's a spirited little thing who flies across these meadows. But I'm afraid she *can* get rather ornery when she loses to Bucephalus."

Loses to Bucephalus? Who had said anything about racing? Claire ran her fingers through Athena's mane, debating whether or not to say what she was about to say. Prudence advised that she not, but friendly competitiveness won out. "In my limited experience, Mrs.

Acklen, I've noticed that sometimes the horse who's least favored ends up finishing first."

Athena whinnied as though in agreement, and Claire leaned forward to reward the mare with a quick rub behind the ears.

Unmistakable challenge brightened Mrs. Acklen's eyes. "*Hmmm* . . . look at that. I think she likes you."

"You sound surprised, ma'am."

"No, no. Not surprised." Mrs. Acklen's smile turned sugary sweet. "It's just that Athena usually prefers men. She threw her last two female riders. Shall we be off?" Without waiting for a response, she flicked the reins and Bucephalus started forward.

Staring slack-jawed, Claire felt the powerful ripple of Athena's rib muscles beneath her. She gave the mare a gentle prod, and Athena shot off at a trot.

Mrs. Acklen set a steady pace down through the meadow and across the creek to the valley beyond. Claire rode beside her, doing her best not to allow Athena to pass Bucephalus, which the mare seemed intent on doing. Claire wondered whether she should try to make conversation, but after listening to dictation for hours on end, she preferred the quiet and the rustle of the wind through the meadow grasses and figured Mrs. Acklen did too.

A touch of crimson edged the maples—the same ones Sutton had pointed out from her bedroom window. But that slightest hint of color was enough to prime her imagination. Mrs. Acklen had already paid her her first wages, more than Claire had expected to earn. So she planned on buying canvases and paints later in the week, and would be ready to capture nature's masterpiece when it was at its height.

"Beautiful, isn't it?" Mrs. Acklen said, her focus trained ahead.

Claire knew the question wasn't really a question, but neither was it rhetorical. "Belmont is one of the most beautiful places I've ever seen. The first time I saw it, I thought of it as a miniature American Versailles."

Mrs. Acklen laughed. "Having experienced the beauty of Versailles firsthand, as I'm assuming you have as well . . ."

Claire nodded.

". . . I'll take that as a compliment."

"As it was intended, ma'am."

Athena quickened her pace again, and Claire tugged the reins to keep the mare in step. Mrs. Acklen was right. The mare seemed bent on putting Bucephalus in his place.

Mrs. Acklen nudged Bucephalus to a faster trot, giving Athena a passing sideways glance. If Claire didn't know better, she might think Mrs. Acklen was taunting the animal. And *her*!

"Are you finding time for painting these days, Miss Laurent?"

Claire heard far more than simple inquiry in Mrs. Acklen's question. "No, ma'am, not yet. But I hope to in coming weeks."

Sutton had informed Mrs. Acklen about her desire to paint professionally, Claire felt certain, and about her reaction to learning of the auction for new artists come spring. He would have viewed the advisement as part of his job, which she understood. "I give you my word, Mrs. Acklen, my aspirations in that area won't interfere with my responsibilities to you."

"Thank you for that assurance, Miss Laurent. I'll be sure to hold you to it." Mrs. Acklen looked over at her. "And while I would venture to say that you do possess talent, it takes years of practice to perfect the expertise needed to garner any level of recognition at the new artists auction. I would hate for you to set your hopes too high."

Well, that answered the question of whether Sutton had told her. Feeling adequately warned, and humbled, Claire let the subject die.

As they rode on, she sneaked a look at Mrs. Acklen. Adelicia Acklen carried herself with such poise and confidence. Had the woman always possessed those attributes? While Claire still felt every bit the employee—as well she should—she'd also come to feel a certain intimacy with Mrs. Acklen, privy as she was to the woman's thoughts and preferences.

The amount of correspondence Mrs. Acklen received, and responded to, was dizzying. The woman's mind never seemed to stop. She'd set dates for dinners and afternoon teas for the next three months, rattling off guest lists and menus and verbiage for invitations, including what color stationery she preferred, and whether she wanted roses on the table because they were so-and-so's favorite, or whether gardenias or orchids. And the birthday party favors had been so well received, she wondered whether Claire would paint another set of the candy boxes for her next ladies' tea. And come spring, she wanted to host a ball "the likes of which Nashville has never seen."

Claire took a deep breath and tilted her face toward the sun, letting the warmth soothe her overfull mind. If a boy's birthday party had taken that much time and planning, she could only imagine the work it would take to orchestrate a ball. It was months away, of course, but there *was* another event quickly approaching.

The LeVert family's visit. Barely over a week away. She'd all but forgotten about it in the blur of party planning.

While Mrs. Acklen hadn't assigned her any official duties in regard to the LeVerts' upcoming visit, she had commented that Madame LeVert would have need of transcription. Claire had no idea how long the mother and daughters would stay. But according to Cordina, who knew everything, they had stayed a full *two months* on their last visit to Belmont. Cordina spoke very highly of the entire family, but it was Cara Netta—the young woman who had shared the onion soup with Sutton in Paris, per Mrs. Acklen—who Claire looked forward to meeting most.

And least, at the same time.

Mrs. Acklen guided Bucephalus left toward a treelined path, and the stallion snorted and sidestepped as though eager to be given free rein. But Mrs. Acklen held him on course. Claire admired her handling of the spirited stallion, just as she admired the stallion itself. Magnificent creature. Fit for a king. Or a queen, in this instance.

The trail grew narrower, and Claire guided Athena to fall in behind. The mare whinnied, apparently taking offense at being made to follow. "Bucephalus is a beautiful animal, Mrs. Acklen."

"He is, isn't he? I named him after Alexander the Great's horse. My father first read me the story of young Alexander when I was but seven years old. Even then, I found myself inspired. You're familiar with the account, I'm sure."

Claire's face heated, and she sat straighter in the saddle, glad Mrs. Acklen couldn't see her. "No, ma'am. I'm not."

"Oh . . . well, we'll have to rectify that. My father saw to it that I was schooled in the classics. He read them to me every night. He was such a gifted storyteller. After all these years, I can still remember how his voice sounded as I rested my head against his chest, curled up in his lap, listening as he read. His voice was so rich and deep. He captured all the characters so perfectly."

Mrs. Acklen's description painted a vivid picture, and Claire felt a disquieting envy creep up inside her. The narrow path opened into a vast meadow awash in golden rays, and Claire started to prod Athena into step beside Bucephalus again, but the mare needed no urging.

"Look! There!" Mrs. Acklen pointed.

On the horizon, far in the distance, Claire spotted the horse and rider, and she knew instantly who it was. Such fluid grace . . . "It looks like they're flying."

"Mr. Monroe is a fine horseman. And Truxton, his thoroughbred, is nearly Bucephalus's equal."

They watched until Sutton disappeared over the crest of a hill before continuing on.

Memories Mrs. Acklen had shared of her own father churned up memories of Claire's. She'd thought about Papa more in recent days, and almost wished for the harried stress of planning a party again. Sometimes the memories brought a sadness that moved her to tears. But most of the time, especially late at night, when the house was still and everyone else was asleep, the memories filled her with a regret that brought a different kind of sadness. One that left her tearless and guilt-ridden—and wondering if she'd tried harder with her father, if maybe, just maybe, they could have had the relationship she'd always wanted.

"I'm certain you hold fond memories of your father as well, Miss Laurent. God rest his soul . . ."

Gentle invitation colored Mrs. Acklen's tone, yet Claire wasn't about to admit that her relationship with her own father had been nothing like what Mrs. Acklen had experienced, especially after appearing so disadvantaged by her lack of training in the classics. "I'm sure you'll understand, Mrs. Acklen, but I find it . . . difficult to speak of my father at present." She'd tried to say it kindly, but even Claire heard the bitterness in her own voice.

And apparently, so had Mrs. Acklen, judging by her wary expression. "Yes, I do understand, Miss Laurent." Her voice held compassion. She reined in, and Claire followed suit. "But if you'll allow me a word intended to comfort . . . The passing of time *does* help. It eases the pain, however little solace that may offer at the moment."

Bristling, Claire looked away.

Mrs. Acklen meant well, she knew, but she couldn't help comparing the woman's privileged life and upbringing to her own lesser one. True, Mrs. Acklen had lost her husband and her father, but she was also well twice Claire's age. Death was part of life. But it was one thing to lose a parent when you had a family and children of your own. It was another to lose a parent when losing them meant losing everything—your family, your home, your place to belong. Every security in life.

"When did you lose your father, Mrs. Acklen?"

"Seven years ago," Mrs. Acklen said, looking out across the meadow.

"And of course your mother, Mrs. Hayes, you still have with you."

Mrs. Acklen slowly looked back. "Yes, Miss Laurent. As you well know. And I have sisters and brothers who live not far from here too." Mrs. Acklen stared, as though reading the threads of Claire's thoughts. "Is there something else you'd like to ask me, Miss Laurent? Or say to me?"

Claire swallowed, still tasting the bitterness of regret, but also feeling a twinge of caution. This was her employer, after all. She bowed her head. "No ma'am. There's not."

"Then let me say it for you."

Claire looked up.

"You don't believe I know what it feels like to lose a parent at your age. And you resent my insinuation that I do." She raised a brow. "Am I correct?"

Cheeks flaming, Claire could hardly hold up her head, ashamed now at being so easily read. And yet a part of her still felt justified. "Yes, ma'am. That . . . sums up my thoughts fairly well."

"Then your thoughts would be accurate, Miss Laurent."

Claire frowned, her grip tightening on the reins.

"I don't know what it's like to stand over the grave of my parents at the tender age of nineteen. I had the blessed privilege of a loving father for forty-one years of my life. And my mother is . . ." Mrs. Acklen blinked, and briefly firmed her jaw. "My mother is a blessing I treasure to still have with me." She took a breath and opened her mouth as though to continue, then closed it.

A painful moment of silence passed.

Claire was forming the words to an apology when Mrs. Acklen turned to her.

"Mr. Monroe shouldn't be the only one allowed to fly on this beautiful afternoon, Miss Laurent." She leaned forward in the saddle, a fire in her eyes. "You said you knew how to ride. Prove it!"

24

Winded from their ride, Sutton prodded Truxton up the last hill, appreciating the power and grace with which the thoroughbred ate up the ground, as if the ascent were nothing but flatland.

Muscles aching, in a good way, Sutton reined in, then leaned down to stroke Truxton's neck. "Good job, fella," he whispered. He never tired of this, and he'd needed this ride after his lengthy meeting with Bartholomew Holbrook that morning.

Holbrook seemed ten years younger these days, rattling off facts about dates and buyers of art pieces, how much was spent, which city a piece of art shipped from and to, and the name of the gallery. All part of reviewing the research the investigators had compiled thus far. The older man's enthusiasm was contagious, and Sutton found himself optimistic about the progress they'd made.

On the other hand, there'd been no word yet from the review board, and his hope was waning in that regard. The wheels of justice had been turning painfully slowly recently, and decidedly in the wrong direction. Daily, it seemed, both the *Republican Banner* and the *Union and American* newspapers reported verdicts in similar cases. And without exception, they all ruled in favor of the new Union.

But there was one bit of information the older man had given him today. Not meaning to, Sutton felt certain. A name. Colonel Wilmington.

Wilmington was the head of the review board, the man responsible for notifying Holbrook of the verdict. After leaving Mr. Holbrook, Sutton had headed straight to the government offices across town. He hadn't known exactly what he was going to say to Wilmington when he'd found him, only that he wouldn't reveal how he'd learned the man's name or position.

But Wilmington hadn't been in, and Sutton had decided not to leave a message with the man's secretary. He saw no point. The review board didn't welcome further input from him. Surprise was his best tactic. Not that he wanted to ambush the man. He simply wanted a chance to tell the truth about what had happened to his father. Reading it on a piece of paper was one thing, staring into the eyes of the murdered man's son was another.

Sutton stretched and rubbed the back of his neck, determined to put the issue from his mind, at least for a while.

He prodded Truxton closer to the point, willing the familiar view to lend him a slice of the peace it usually did. The vantage was one he'd appreciated since boyhood.

The rolling hills, lush and green with cedar, pine, oak, and poplar, swelled and dipped in a seamless rhythm that was as soothing to the eye as it was the soul. Then the view of Nashville, much changed since he was a boy. He couldn't imagine ever leaving Tennessee. Or ever wanting to.

The roofline of the mansion rose from among the treetops, the statues along the parapet a brilliant white in the afternoon sun. Adelicia's gardens boasted a riot of color, even at this distan—

Movement in the meadow below drew his attention.

He leaned forward in the saddle, squinting, unable to believe what he was seeing. It was both a premonition and nightmare—Adelicia and Claire bulleting across the meadow beneath him, their horses neck and neck, bodies angled forward, hair flying, stubborn wills on full display.

He exhaled. "You two women . . ."

Adelicia, he didn't worry about. She was a skilled rider on a well-trained thoroughbred. But Claire . . .

He wheeled Truxton around and barreled downhill, intending to meet them before they reached the mansion. He had no idea of Claire's experience with horses. Obviously, the woman could ride. But racing across meadows where summer grasses disguised rocks and gopher holes was worlds different than trotting down a city street or through a field. What had Adelicia been thinking to allow such carelessness?

He thought—and hoped—Claire was riding Athena, but he couldn't be sure. Feisty and fearless, the intelligent little mare was fleet and surefooted, and handled herself about as well with a rider as without.

Sutton reached the bottom of the hill and reined Truxton toward home. The stallion surged forward, responding to Sutton's slightest command with enthusiastic obedience, his hooves pounding, yet seeming as if they barely touched the earth. Sutton couldn't count the hours he'd spent training this animal. But every one of them—every last rewarding moment—had been worth it.

Crouched low, wind whipping his face, he knew with a certainty born of boyish dreams matured by manhood that that was what he really wanted to do with his life. Train horses—thoroughbreds—for racing.

With the ease of a blink, Truxton cleared the creek, and Sutton spotted the two riders as they crested the final hill toward Belmont. Unfortunately, the women were at least thirty yards in front of him. They approached the manor from the south, so the mansion lay between them and the stables.

Sutton knew which way Adelicia would take—he'd raced her before—and he could tell by the way Claire looked first to her left, then right, that she was weighing her options. At the last moment, Adelicia veered left and headed around the back of the mansion. Claire headed right, and so did Sutton.

To his relief, no carriages were parked in the front drive. Claire had a clear shot to the stables. Halfway down the road, when he was certain Claire thought she had it won, Adelicia and Bucephalus bolted through the trees. And again, the horses were neck and neck.

Just then a carriage appeared from around the corner, coming down the road at a healthy clip. Adelicia and Claire apparently saw it too because they adjusted course at the same time, and headed straight for the corral. Adelicia never slowed. She and Bucephalus scaled the split-rail fence in a perfect arc. And, to Sutton's amazement, it looked as though Claire and Athena would too.

Until the very last second. When Claire hesitated.

He read it in her body, in her hold on the reins, and he saw it in how Athena's confidence weakened beneath Claire's doubt. Athena skidded, her legs stiffening, and Claire went sailing, straight over the split-rail fence.

25

Claire!" Sutton leapt from his horse, vaulted the fence, and ran to where she'd landed on her side. He knelt, and careful not to jar her, tugged her skirt down over her legs and brushed the hair back from her face. "Claire . . ." He leaned close. Her gray dress was torn at the shoulder revealing a bloody scrape. "Are you all right?"

She blinked, and then her eyes slipped closed.

He checked her pulse on the underside of her throat the way he'd seen his father do. Her heartbeat was strong. Rapid, but that was to be expected.

"Miss Laurent!" Adelicia's panicked steps sounded behind them. "Is she hurt, Mr. Monroe? Is anything broken?" She knelt, her face ashen.

"I don't know yet." Keeping his own panic at bay, Sutton ran a hand over Claire's left arm and found it sound. Her right was still tucked beneath her.

"Zeke!" Adelicia called over her shoulder. "Ride for the doctor. *Immediately!*"

Sutton took Claire's hand in his. "Claire, I need for you to tell me where you hurt. I don't want to move you until we're sure nothing's broken."

Her eyes fluttered open. She turned her head and looked up at him, squinting as though trying to clear her vision. Adelicia smoothed a hand over Claire's forehead and cheek—a motherly instinct that Sutton appreciated. But what had the woman been thinking? Racing that way . . .

"Claire?" He spoke louder. "If you can hear me, I need to know where it hurts. That's all you need to do, Claire."

She took a breath. "I will"—she frowned as though in pain—"if you'll please just stop saying my name. . . ."

Her mouth tipped in a weak smile, and Sutton exhaled, cautious relief trickling through him. He wanted to take her and hug her tight but knew better. There'd be opportunity for that later. And if not, he'd make one.

Adelicia brushed a smear of dirt from her cheek. "Can you tell us if you're injured, Miss Laurent?"

Slowly, and with Sutton's assistance, Claire eased over onto her back. She took a deep breath and released it, her eyes looking more focused. "Mostly . . . it's my pride that's wounded."

Adelicia half laughed, half sighed, and bowed her head. "I never should have challenged you like that, Miss Laurent. I don't know what I was thinking. Will you please forgive me?"

Sutton glanced up. It wasn't the apology that surprised him so much. When proven wrong, Adelicia admitted it. She was a woman with fierce opinions but also a woman of fine character. It was the glistening in her eyes that took him aback.

Claire looked over at her. "Of course I'll forgive you, Mrs. Acklen . . ." She smiled. "If you'll just say that I won."

Sutton curbed a grin, seeing that the gleam in Adelicia's eyes was only exceeded by the one in Claire's.

By now, servants from inside the house and out had joined the stable hands and were watching at a distance. With Claire's permission and Adelicia's help, Sutton checked her arms and legs, then the curve of her neck and shoulders. Thank God, nothing was broken. He helped her to a sitting position, letting her rest against him until the dizziness passed.

Then at Adelicia's request, he gathered her in his arms and carried her inside, taking it slow so as not to jar her, all while trying to convince himself that what he felt for the woman cradled in his arms . . . was only friendship.

Mortified over what she'd done—not only in front of Adelicia, but also Sutton—Claire smoothed the bedcovers over her lap, careful not to move her head. The pounding was only now beginning to subside. Still, she wished they would stop making such a fuss. She felt like a complete fool.

Dr. James Denard returned his stethoscope to his leather satchel. "Miss Laurent needs bed rest, Mrs. Acklen. For a day or two, at least. But I see no sign of serious injury." He turned to Claire. "Which is a fairly remarkable feat, young lady, considering what Mr. Monroe described to me. Sounds like you took a nasty toss."

Claire felt Sutton staring at her from the foot of her bed but couldn't bring herself to look at him. "I'm sure it wasn't as dramatic a scene as what's been painted, Dr. Denard."

"Thrown over a fence"—Sutton's tone was matter-of-fact, if not bordering on sarcasm—"and landed a good fifteen feet away. You're right, Miss Laurent. It wasn't dramatic in the least."

Hearing concern in his voice, she chanced a look at him. And whether due to being beneath the bedcovers fully clothed or to the way he was looking at her, she grew overly warm, overly fast.

After being thrown, she'd attempted to make light of what had happened, wanting to save face. She alone was at fault, and she knew it. She'd been trying to impress her employer, prove that she could keep up. And at the last minute, she'd panicked. The accident was due to her lack of experience, plain and simple.

"Will she be all right, Doctor?" Sutton asked, inching closer to the bed.

"She'll be fine, I assure you." Dr. Denard slipped his suit jacket back on. "But no more riding for now, Miss Laurent. And with the size of that knot on the back of your head, I want you to stay awake for a while. At least until"—he checked his pocket watch—"around bedtime tonight. That's a good five or six hours from now. Understood?" He aimed an appraising gaze first at Mrs. Acklen and Sutton, who nodded, and then to Claire.

"Yes, sir." Claire managed a smile, but for reasons she couldn't explain, she questioned whether or not he was being honest with her about her injuries. Yet, other than her head hurting and her feeling achy, she felt normal. So why did staying awake seem like such an impossible feat? All she wanted to do was close her eyes and sleep for days.

Dr. Denard retrieved his medical bag. "Expect to be sore for a while, Miss Laurent. That bruise on your hip will turn several lovely shades of purple and black before it's healed." He gave her a quick smile. "But again, you'll be fine, I assure you."

Claire nodded, but still felt that niggle of doubt.

The doctor crossed to the bedroom door, then paused, peering over his spectacles at Mrs. Acklen. "If her headache worsens, Mrs. Acklen, or vomiting develops, send for me without delay."

"We will, doctor." Mrs. Acklen joined him. "Thank you so much for coming so quickly. I'll see you out." She left the door ajar.

Sutton retrieved the desk chair, thunked it down by Claire's bedside, and straddled it in a decidedly masculine way. "So . . . which will it be? Chess or checkers?"

"Neither, please. I just want to rest."

He leaned toward her. "It appears you're going to live after all."

"It would seem . . ." Claire forced a smile, but all she could think about was that last night in New Orleans when she'd asked the physician about her father's condition. *"He'll be fine, I assure you,"* had been his response too. And then her father had died.

She wasn't afraid of dying in that moment. She'd been thrown from a horse, not stabbed with a knife. It was the *thought* of dying—of this life ending and of coming face-to-face with God—that sent an unrelenting shiver through her. Because she wasn't ready. She didn't know why exactly—she only knew she wasn't. She wanted the peace her mother had somehow found toward the very end.

Only, she preferred to find it before the final hours of her life.

"Not yet, sleepyhead." Sutton gently squeezed Claire's shoulder, seeing her eyes drift shut again. "Doctor's orders. It's not even eight o'clock."

With eyes still closed, she frowned. "But I'm so tired, Sutton," she whispered. "And please, no more checkers. Just let me rest for a minute or two."

"Sorry, but I can't do that." He nudged her shoulder again. Nothing. So he dipped a damp cloth in water and wrung it out, then pressed it against her cheek.

She sucked in a breath, eyes going wide.

"I'm sorry, but you just can't go to sleep. Not yet." He smoothed her matted curls. "Does your head still hurt?"

"It's pounding . . ." She winced. "Like a drum."

"The doctor said you can have a half dose of laudanum. But only after you've eaten a few more bites of Cordina's soup."

"Cordina made soup?"

"Yes, she did, to answer that question for a third time." He smiled and helped her sit up a little straighter in the bed. Dr. Denard had told Adelicia on the way out that Claire's memory might be sketchy for the first few hours. Sutton wasn't surprised, not when remembering his father having treated patients with head injuries. And Claire had hit her head pretty hard. "It's potato soup. Your favorite. At least that's what you said thirty minutes ago when you ate some."

Claire gave him a look that said she wasn't sure whether to believe that or not, but apparently she decided not to argue the point.

Soup bowl in hand, he eased down onto the edge of the bed, ladled a spoonful of soup, and held it to her lips.

"I can feed myself." She reached for the spoon, but he pulled it back, shaking his head.

"There you go again, Miss Laurent, tryin' to steal my joy."

Sighing, she smirked—and opened her mouth. After a couple of bites, she looked up at him, a disconcerting vagueness in her eyes. "Do you ever think about dying, Sutton?"

He stilled. "Claire, honey, you're going to be fine. I know you probably feel otherwise right now, after that fall, but—"

"No . . . I realize that. What I'm asking is if *you've* ever thought about dying."

"Everyone thinks about dying. At some time or another."

Accepting another bite of soup, she looked up at him, her expression saying that she wanted—and frankly, expected—more of an answer.

"Yes." He scooped up a chunk of potato. "I've thought about it. Many times. Mostly during the war."

"You fought," she said softly, more a statement of fact than a question.

"Along with everyone else."

"Were you wounded?" She accepted another spoonful.

"I was shot. In the shoulder. I was lucky, though—the bullet went straight through."

The milky smoothness of her forehead crinkled. "Did it hurt?"

He laughed. "*Yes,* just a little."

She looked down. "I'm sorry. That was a silly question."

But thinking about lying in that church sanctuary, with Mark

Holbrook's blood as well as his own drenching his clothes, and with his father only days in the ground, Sutton's humor fell away. "Men were dying all around me. I thought I was going to die too." He dipped the spoon in the bowl again, but she shook her head, her eyes never leaving his. He laid the bowl aside.

"Were you scared?" she asked, her voice tentative.

He looked down at her, wondering where all her questions were coming from. But not minding them. "Yes . . . I was scared."

"Were you . . . ready?"

Sutton felt a tug inside him, like someone had looped a cord around his heart and pulled tight. Had he been ready to die was what she was asking. No one had ever asked him that question before. Not even Cara Netta when they'd spoken once, and ever so briefly, about that night.

He allowed a moment to pass. He had no choice. He couldn't speak past the thickness in his throat. "Yes," he whispered. "I was ready. And . . . no." He fingered the edge of the quilt. "I don't think there's a man alive who, once he knows he's going into battle . . . isn't forced to face the possibility that he might not come home. And I'd reconciled myself to whatever was going to come. If God chose to call me home . . ." He'd never forget the moment when the reality of that possibility became real—rifle aimed, bullets zipping by, cannon fire exploding all around him. "Then I knew He'd take me home. We all carried letters with us, just in case. I still have mine."

"Do you still carry it with you?"

The question warmed him, just like she did. She was one beautiful woman, inside and out. Though he tried not to focus on that. "No, I don't still carry it. Why?" He eyed her with suspicion, hoping to lighten the conversation. "Do you know something I don't?"

She smiled, but only for a second. "You said yes, you were ready. But then you also said no. Why *no*?"

The woman didn't give up easily. He liked that. But he was hesitant to answer in too much detail. He wasn't ashamed of his reasons for wanting to stay around a little longer. They simply weren't reasons he felt comfortable sharing with just anyone. Of course, Claire wasn't just anyone. "Because there were things I hadn't done yet with my life that I wanted to do. That I still want to do."

She perked up. "Like what?"

He shook his head, remembering Cara Netta's reaction when he'd shared his dream of raising thoroughbreds.

"I won't laugh, Sutton. I promise. And I won't tell anyone, if you say not to."

And looking at her, he believed her. "I enjoy practicing law and find it rewarding, and honestly, I don't ever see leaving that completely. But what I'd really like to do one day is . . . own my own thoroughbred farm."

Her eyes lit.

"But not just own the farm," he clarified. "I want to train the horses. Myself. For racing. I also want to mend the fences and help birth the foals in the spring. I want to be as involved in every detail as I can."

The look of delight on her face was like a gift. "That's a wonderful dream, Sutton. And you'll do it too."

How did she do it? Looking into her eyes, he really believed that one day, he *would* have his own farm. When he'd shared his dream with Cara Netta when they were traveling in Europe, she'd reacted with exuberance, and yet her very next question had been about the law firm, and when he might make partner, and wasn't that a more attractive opportunity to him than owning horses. But he couldn't completely fault her for that reaction. Not after he'd purposefully mentioned that Bartholomew Holbrook had confided that a future with him being made partner was a possibility.

Yet Cara Netta had never mentioned the thoroughbred farm to him again. And looking back, he knew now that her reaction had contributed to his hesitation in moving forward in their relationship. At least at first. Now there was a whole other reason for his hesitation. She was about five-foot-six, with auburn hair and blue-green eyes, and had a way of looking at him—like she was now—that made him think he could do just about anything.

Except tell her about Cara Netta. Which he had to do.

The LeVerts would be arriving within days. But how could he tell her without making it look as if he'd been hiding the truth from her all this time? Which he hadn't. It just hadn't seemed important at first. And then the more they'd gotten to know each other, he simply hadn't found the right opportunity.

Which meant he had to *make* that opportunity. Right now.

"Thank you, Claire, for that vote of confidence. And I'd ask you what your dream is, but I think I already know." He glanced at an extra *joujou* sitting on her mantel. "To paint. And to enter the art auction come spring?"

"Yes." She smoothed a hand over the bedcovers. "If I can paint something that's good enough."

"I'm sure you will. You're very talented. And whatever you decide to paint, I know it will be wonderful."

She held his gaze, looking as if she wanted to say more, so he waited.

When she didn't, he figured that was his cue. "Something I've—"

"It's nice to—"

They both laughed, having spoken at the same time.

"I'm sorry." He gestured. "You go first."

She dipped her head. "I was just going to say that it's nice to know you have something you want to do in your life that you haven't done yet. Even as accomplished as you are." She looked down for a second, and when she looked up again, her eyes glistened. "And the way you talk about it, the way your face lights up, I can tell it means a great deal to you."

Sutton studied her. "I could say the same of you when you were looking at the paintings in the gallery. Your love and appreciation for art radiates from you, Claire. And I'm guessing here . . ." He squinted as though evaluating her. "But I'm betting that difference comes through in your painting too. I look forward to seeing your work on something other than a *joujou* and a candy dish."

For an instant, she looked as if she might cry, then she leaned up and put her arms around his neck. "Thank you, Sutton."

Surprised at her reaction, but pleased, he slid an arm around her back, gently, not wanting to hurt her where she might have been bruised in the accident.

"May I ask you something?" she whispered, her breath warm on his neck. "For a favor, of sorts?"

More than a little distracted by her closeness and moved by the shyness in her voice, he drew back, not really wanting to. "Ask away, as long as it doesn't involve breaking any laws. The Tennessee courts—and Mrs. Acklen—might frown on that."

Her face when blank for an instant, then she gave a breathy laugh. "No, this doesn't break any laws."

He smiled, touched by the timid look on her face, and also by their close proximity to each other on the bed. The doctor had checked her heartbeat earlier, and the buttons at her neckline remained loosened, the collar hanging open. He didn't see anything he shouldn't, but what he saw inspired thoughts he knew he shouldn't have. Or, at least, shouldn't encourage.

The strong, steady beat of her heart was evidenced in the soft, inviting hollow at the base of her throat. And then there were those lips. Lips whose smile could lay him waste with the least little effort, and her eyes that—

Were reading every thought he was having at the moment. Or seemed to be.

Sutton took a breath even as a telling shyness came over her. If she hadn't known before how attracted he was to her—and he didn't think she had—the woman had to know now. Or at least suspect it. Should he say something or just let it pass? Never having been good at the latter, he reached for an apology. "I'm sorry," he whispered. "I didn't mean to stare."

She briefly looked down at her hands, an embarrassed smile playing at the corners of her mouth. "I don't mind the attention . . . coming from you."

A bolt of lightning coursing through his rain-drenched body would have had less effect on him than her soft admission. Watching her, a steady warmth built inside him, and as the seconds lengthened, he knew he needed to steer the conversation, and his thoughts, toward safer waters. "So . . ." He breathed out, breaking hold of her gaze and hoping his face didn't look as hot as it felt. "What is this favor you're wanting to ask me?"

He would've sworn he glimpsed a flicker of daring in her expression. Maybe from something she thought of saying and then thought better of it.

"What I was going to ask is . . . as soon as I'm well, and once Dr. Denard says it's all right for me to ride again, I'm wondering if—"

"I'd teach you to jump," he guessed, reading the answer in her eyes and already looking forward to that first lesson. "I'd be honored. And by the time I'm through with you, you'll be scaling every fence and creek east of the Mississippi."

Her smile was reward enough. "Thank you, Sutton. And now it's your turn. You had something you wanted to say?"

He tried to think of a way to tell her about Cara Netta. But no matter how he phrased—and rephrased—the words in his mind, he realized he couldn't say what he'd planned on saying a moment ago. Because—after what had just happened—how could he explain to her that he had an understanding with another woman? Which he did.

But how could he proceed in good faith into an engagement with Cara Netta, honestly pledging his affections and life to her, when Claire so obviously had a hold on his heart?

He rose from the bed, glancing back at the clock on the mantel. "I just wanted to say that it's almost nine thirty. And according to doctor's orders, you can go to sleep now." Unable to curb the desire, he leaned back down and kissed her forehead. "I'll be here when you wake up."

26

Did you give Cordina the list of special requests for this evening's dinner?"

"Yes, ma'am, I did." Claire smiled inwardly at the way her employer hovered near the front window and kept glancing out every so often. For the past few days, Mrs. Acklen had been intent on making certain everything was in order for the LeVerts' visit—and for the dinner party being held in their honor tonight. The entire Belmont household was atwitter with anticipation.

"I met with Cordina earlier this morning, Mrs. Acklen. We're having all of Madame LeVert's favorites, as you requested. Fresh coconut cake, warm pear and apple compote, Cordina's pork loin with rosemary and thyme . . ." Claire rattled off the menu by heart.

"And what of the guest list? No one has sent any last-minute regrets? Or acceptances?"

"No, ma'am. The guest list remains unchanged." Without being asked, Claire had made place cards for everyone who would be seated in the formal dining room—Mrs. Acklen, the LeVerts, Sutton, and Mrs. Hayes, Adelicia's mother. Along with Mrs. Acklen's brothers and sisters and their spouses. It would be a full table, and she was honored that Mrs. Acklen had stipulated she should sit in there too, instead of with Miss Cenas and the children in the family dining room.

"*Hmmm . . .*" Mrs. Acklen said nothing for a moment. "So . . . Mr. Polk wasn't able to alter his previous engagement?"

"I guess not, ma'am. He hasn't advised otherwise, so I'm assuming he won't be in attendance this evening."

Nodding, Mrs. Acklen turned back toward the window.

Though Claire would never have actually inquired about such a thing, she wondered what kind of relationship Mrs. Acklen and Lucius Polk shared. They'd seemed friendly with one another on the night of William's party, and Mr. Polk had been to dinner at Belmont twice since. But Mrs. Acklen was a very wealthy, attractive widow, and that combination was bound to attract a good amount of male interest.

Mrs. Acklen pressed closer to the window, and Claire leaned forward in her chair, sneaking a look out herself, eager for the LeVerts' arrival too. Though for far different reasons.

Following Mrs. Acklen's comment a few weeks back about Sutton and Cara Netta sharing onion soup in Paris, she hadn't heard Cara Netta's name mentioned again until this week. And never in the same sentence with Sutton's. So whatever relationship the young woman and Sutton shared—or *had* shared—apparently wasn't of a serious nature. He would have mentioned something to her by now if that were the case. Especially in light of what happened between them the evening following her accident.

Not that anything had *really* happened. Not outwardly, anyway. A warmth rose to her face. But the way he'd stared at her . . . She recognized that look.

She'd received it on occasion from men whose attention she didn't welcome. Sutton, however, was in a category all his own, and to think that he looked at her in *that* light seemed like too much to hope for. She appreciated how he'd sat with her that first evening, keeping her awake. Since then, he'd been working longer hours in town, leaving before breakfast and returning after dinner. Working on a lawsuit, he'd said. One that would keep him busy for several months. She was glad when she'd learned that. She'd begun to think that maybe he was trying to avoid her.

"*Be careful who you love . . .*"

The memory of her mother's words rose like a warning inside her, and her thoughts turned to her father. Had her mother's advice been more of a warning? Considering the kind of man Papa had been, Claire couldn't discount that. In the same breath, *if* Sutton did feel something more than friendship toward her—and she thought he did—she knew her mother's *warning* wasn't needed. Because Sutton was nothing like Papa.

Sutton was kind and honest and good, and he would never lie. And would certainly never try to coerce her to do something she didn't want to do. Much less, do something that was wrong.

His comment about not doing anything that broke the law had caught her off guard. She'd quickly realized he wasn't serious, but the casual remark had reminded her again of the barrier her past was between them. While he might find her attractive—which was a nice enough thought on its own—she knew better than to put more weight on that discovery than it could bear. Someone of Sutton's social status and upbringing would never seriously consider her, not if he really knew her.

Still, the way he'd acted tempted her to hope . . .

"You're looking in full health these days," Mrs. Acklen said, glancing back. "You're not experiencing any lingering pain from your fall?"

Your fall . . .

That's how everyone—even the servants—referred to her pitiful attempt to jump the corral fence. "No, ma'am. No pain whatsoever. The bruise on my hip is healing nicely and the headache is gone. Dr. Denard said I could commence riding again in a couple of weeks."

"Mr. Monroe is going to teach you to jump, I hear."

"He told you?"

"He mentioned it. Mr. Monroe's a skilled rider and an excellent teacher. He's trained several of my thoroughbreds. Which, when you consider that his formal training is in the law, makes for an interesting combination in a man."

Claire couldn't have agreed more.

"Mama?" Pauline peeked her head in the doorway. "Is Miss Tavie here yet?"

"Not yet, dear." Mrs. Acklen crossed the study and kissed her daughter on the forehead. "But soon. I'll have Mrs. Routh notify Miss Cenas after Miss Tavie arrives so you can give her and her daughters each a welcome hug. Now hurry on back to class. I look forward to hearing what you learned over dinner."

Pauline nodded, tossing Claire an excited grin before she skipped away.

Claire thought of the get-well drawings the children had given her just after her *fall.* Pauline's pastel-colored drawing featured a fairylike character clad in a pink dress who floated precipitously in the air.

Claude's picture, Claire decided, was far truer to form and depicted her soaring headfirst over the fence, mouth wide in a gaping scream.

William, *sans* picture—since he was "too old for such childish undertakings"—had simply asked if she would demonstrate to him how it happened again. She'd socked him playfully in the arm and had received a grin in return.

For feeling so out of place when she first arrived, Claire had to admit she felt more a part of things now. Certainly not like one of the family. Or even an *equal.* But accepted. As if she was beginning to belong. And it felt . . . wonderful.

"A new project for you, Miss Laurent . . ." Mrs. Acklen reached to straighten a lace doily draped over the back of the settee. "I want you to teach Pauline the basic skills of sketching and watercolors. I believe she possesses a giftedness for the creative arts, and while Miss Cenas's knowledge of art history is extensive, her skills at drawing are lacking."

"I'd be honored to teach Pauline, ma'am!" Claire thrilled at the prospect of having the girl as a pupil, and even more at Mrs. Acklen's trust in her.

"It will only be for a month or so, mind you—until master artist Giovanni Domenico from Italy takes guest residence at the gallery in town. Then Pauline will go there to be tutored in the techniques of oil on canvas. But I believe some helpful bits of instruction from you in the rudimentary aspects would be a worthwhile foundation to her lessons with him."

As the reality of Mrs. Acklen's request sank in, Claire worked to hide her disappointment. Mrs. Acklen wanted her to teach Pauline the *basic* skills—which clearly meant that her employer didn't consider her capable of teaching a six-year-old anything else.

But Giovanni Domenico, a *master artist,* giving instruction to a six-year-old? Wealth certainly did have its privileges. "Of course, Mrs. Acklen. I understand. I'll look forward to working with Pauline in that regard."

"Very good." Mrs. Acklen ran a hand over the bronze statue of Bucephalus on a side table, her expression growing pensive. "How many responses have we received to date for the tea in November?"

Claire glanced down at her notes, already knowing the answer, but not eager to relay the information. She'd sent out thirty invitations for the tea the Monday following William's party, and every other day, it seemed, Mrs. Acklen requested an update. "We've received four so far, ma'am. . . ." And those from Mrs. Acklen's mother, two sisters, and Mrs. James Polk, a close family friend, though she withheld that detail. "But it's still early yet. The tea is a full month away."

Mrs. Acklen said nothing, and Claire sensed she was more than a little hurt by the lack of timely replies. Frankly, Claire didn't understand it. What woman would turn down an invitation for tea from Mrs. Adelicia—

"A carriage!" Mrs. Acklen gave a tiny gasp. "They're here!" Smoothing the front of her dress, she exited the study without a backward glance.

Claire hurried to the open window and watched the driver of the carriage negotiate the winding path past rose gardens and between statues and fountains. The carriage came to a halt at the front steps, and not wishing to be seen, Claire took a step backward and peered around the draperies. Eli opened the carriage door and bowed low.

A gloved hand appeared, elegantly extended, and Claire leaned forward, waiting to see to whom it belonged.

With Eli's assistance, the woman stepped from the carriage, and Claire knew immediately that the woman was Madame Octavia LeVert—the Pride of Mobile, Alabama, and the granddaughter of George Walton, a member of the Second Continental Congress, one of the three Georgia signers of the Declaration of Independence, and . . . a former governor, if she remembered correctly.

Bless Cordina's heart . . . Knowing that woman provided all sorts of advantages.

Madame LeVert's dress was exquisite, reminiscent of a style Claire had seen in a recent issue of *Godey's.* She glanced down at her own *new* gray dress, mended as it was, and though it fit her station, she suddenly felt underdressed.

"Welcome to Belmont once again, Octavia dear . . ." Mrs. Acklen's voice drifted in through the open window. "Seeing you again does my heart such good."

"As seeing you does mine, Adelicia. Bless you for allowing us to break our journey here. The girls and I have been beyond ecstatic when thinking of seeing you and . . ."

As the two women embraced, a second woman exited the carriage with Eli's assistance. From what Cordina had shared, Claire guessed her to be the older of the two daughters. Then a third woman stepped from the conveyance and Claire sucked in a breath.

Cara Netta.

With thick tresses of rich black hair, dark as a raven's wing, and with eyes that—even at this distance—shone more violet than blue, the young woman was stunning. With such delicate features, and so tiny a waist. And her dress and . . . *décolletage.* Claire laid a hand to her own decidedly less bountiful bodice, and suddenly the onion soup comment made by Mrs. Acklen took on more meaning.

"Miss Laurent?"

Claire jumped, her heart catapulting to her throat. "Mrs. Routh!"

The head housekeeper approached. "Taken to lurking behind the draperies now, have we?"

Claire pushed back from the window. "No, ma'am . . . I simply heard the carriage and—"

"And now that you know the LeVerts have arrived, Mrs. Acklen would appreciate it if you would come out from hiding and be *properly* introduced."

Wishing again that she hadn't gotten off to such a poor start with the woman, Claire laid the papers in her hand on a side table. "Yes, ma'am."

Mrs. Routh promptly scooped the papers up, gave them a good stacking on the edge of the table, and placed them in perfect symmetry on the antique secretary. "Madame Octavia LeVert is not only a most beloved public figure, Miss Laurent, she's also Mrs. Acklen's dearest friend. And I trust you will do everything within your means to make the LeVerts' stay here at Belmont both enjoyable and . . . harmonious."

Wondering at the woman's choice of wording, Claire nodded. "Of course, I will, Mrs. Routh."

The head housekeeper led the way into the entrance hall. "Much like their mother, Madame LeVert's daughters are both delightful creatures," she continued. "So talented and refined. It's no wonder they've attracted the interest of some of Nashville's finest gentlemen."

Claire didn't find that statement surprising, not after seeing the sisters. And that they came from wealth—and would likely bring it *with* them when they married—would most certainly guarantee their prospects for a good match, especially in these difficult times. What she *did* find surprising, however, was Mrs. Routh's talkativeness. This was the most the woman had said to her since she'd arrived. And frankly, Claire decided she preferred the woman's stoic silence.

Mrs. Routh opened the front door, and Claire spotted Sutton riding up the road. Odd to see him home so early when he'd had to work so late recently. Then again, he knew the LeVerts were expected.

"Ah, Mr. Monroe, on time as always." Mrs. Routh smiled in a way that didn't quite reach her eyes. "He's long been a favorite of the LeVert family, and feels quite the same about them. As I'm sure you'll soon see."

Something in Mrs. Routh's tone gave Claire the feeling she was attempting to tell her something without saying it outright, which wasn't like Mrs. Routh at all.

Not nearly as eager to meet the LeVerts as she had been earlier, Claire checked her dress one last time and walked outside to the portico, shy of descending the stairs and entering the fray of hugs and familiarity.

Seeing the exchanges of affection should have warmed her heart. But instead they roused within her a yearning to belong that eclipsed everything else, and that edged up the veil on this precarious, make-believe existence she was living.

She didn't have anyone in her life who would greet her so warmly after an extended absence, nor anywhere she could go "to break her journey" should she travel. And standing here, at the top of the stairs, taking it all in, she felt alone and insignificant.

But not until she saw Cara Netta turn and see Sutton, then run to greet him, hug him, and give him a quick peck on the cheek—and watch Sutton return her embrace—did Mrs. Routh's comment begin to make sense.

27

The moment Sutton dreaded had arrived, and the fact that he dreaded it as much as he did—even as he hugged Cara Netta—only compounded his guilt. And that Claire stood watching from the front steps only made it worse.

He should have told her about Cara Netta. He'd known it that night following her accident and he knew it now. He'd spent the week contemplating, searching . . . But he hadn't been able to think of a way to explain to her what was going on inside him. Mainly because he was still sorting it out himself.

"Mr. Monroe!"

He turned to see Madame LeVert headed straight for him, arms outstretched, and he gladly surrendered daughter for mother. They embraced, and Sutton was reminded again of how important this woman and her family were to Adelicia. "What a pleasure to see you again, Madame LeVert. You're looking very well, ma'am." From his peripheral vision, he kept an eye on Claire—standing on the portico, off to one side. "I believe the extended stay in New York agreed with you, ma'am."

"My dear boy, it is not New York to which I owe any improvement in my countenance. It was my anticipation of seeing you, and Adelicia, and Belmont again that buoyed me on."

He still couldn't see her without thinking of her late husband. He missed Dr. LeVert's dry wit and knowledgeable insights, and knew that the three most important women to Henry LeVert were still grieving the man's passing these two years later.

"How is she?" Madame LeVert whispered. "She looks more rested and content than I've seen her in a long time."

Sutton kept his voice low. "She took your suggestion—along with my *strong* encouragement once we returned—to heart and hired a personal liaison."

Madame LeVert's eyes brightened, and Sutton nodded toward Claire, who was inching her way back toward the front door. Madame LeVert followed his gaze, and Claire froze as though having been caught in a crime.

Uncertainty clouded her expression, and Sutton sent her a smile, hoping to allay her nervousness. "She assists Mrs. Acklen with nearly everything now, and performs her duties with grace and efficiency." He leaned closer. "Adelicia's quite pleased."

"That's high praise, Mr. Monroe. I'm especially eager to meet this liaison now." She smiled and patted his arm. "Anyone who can please Adelicia Acklen is certain of pleasing me."

"Mother, would you please stop monopolizing the South's most handsome and eligible bachelor?"

Sutton had no trouble keeping a straight face with Madame LeVert's older daughter, Diddie. "I'm certain she would, Miss LeVert. If only that gentleman were present."

Everyone laughed. Everyone but Diddie.

"*Miss LeVert?* That's what you've taken to calling me now, young man?"

Sutton let his smile show. "Hello, Diddie. How are you?"

"I'm exhausted, Sutton, and my back aches." She grinned and rewarded him with a hug. "And I'm most grateful to be out of that carriage and onto solid ground again. And to the exquisite grounds of Belmont, no less. I almost feel as if I've come home."

Diddie—always unpretentious, speaking her mind, yet not without a certain charm. Sutton wondered, as he had before, why she'd not yet married. Surely it wasn't for lack of suitors. Only three or four years his senior, she always made a point of reminding him of his junior status.

Conversation around them fell away, and he looked toward the mansion to see Claire starting down the steps. Knowing she wouldn't have made that descent without being prompted, he caught Adelicia's discreet signal for her to join them—a quick flick of her wrist, a gesture she usually reserved for servants.

And the discovery that she used it with Claire . . . disturbed him.

"We've missed you, Sutton." Cara Netta wove her arm through the crook of his. "Very much." She pressed close.

Hearing what she was really saying, he caught the knowing smiles of the women around him and felt himself tense, grateful Claire was still some yards away. "You've all been missed very much too. I feared Mrs. Acklen might redecorate the entire mansion again while anticipating your visit."

While Adelicia laughed and shushed his comment away, Sutton attempted to introduce an inch of space between himself and Cara Netta, without success.

Cara Netta ran a hand along his upper arm, and squeezed. "The gardens are exquisite, Sutton. Perhaps you might show them to me following dinner."

Surprised at her forwardness—and at the generous display of bosom her dress permitted at this angle—Sutton nodded politely, then felt a none-too-subtle check in his spirit. He realized Cara Netta wasn't being overly forward, not when considering the understanding between them and those long months spent traveling together in Europe.

It was *his* behavior that was making him uncomfortable. The way he'd allowed himself to become too close to Claire. Encouraging the friendship beyond what was proper for a man in his situation, however innocently done at first. But this situation wasn't Cara Netta's fault. It was his own, and it was therefore up to him to rectify it.

Cara Netta gave his arm a tug, and he realized she was awaiting his response.

"Yes," he whispered down. "I'd be honored to show you the gardens later. That will give us a chance to talk."

"And . . ." She smiled. "To get reacquainted."

His collar tightened at the look in her eyes.

"Sutton . . ."

He turned, grateful for Diddie's interruption.

"You must ask Cara Netta about the sonata."

It took him a few seconds to place what she was referring to. Finally remembering, he covered the lapse of memory with a gentlemanly bow and used the opportunity to extract himself from Cara Netta's affections, mindful of Claire standing just behind Adelicia, waiting to be introduced. He would have made the introductions himself, but it was Adelicia's privilege as mistress of Belmont and Claire's employer. "I have no doubt that Cara Netta has mastered that Haydn sonata by now. Which one was it . . ."

"Number thirty-seven in D major," Diddie supplied, loving pride in her eyes. "And yes, she's mastered it. I don't see how she plays with such vivacity. And flawlessly!"

Cara Netta gave her sister a lighthearted frown. "You ought not tell such fabrications, Diddie." She glanced at Sutton. "Though I *can* get through it passably well now."

"Passably well?" Madame LeVert shook her head.

"Following dinner this evening"—Adelicia eyed Cara Netta, her gaze holding playful indulgence—"you shall play the sonata. I insist! And we will decide for ourselves whether *mastered* is an appropriate term."

Cara Netta curtsied. "As you wish, Mrs. Acklen. But I beg you, do not hold me responsible should any of your guests develop a sudden ache in their heads." Her comment drew muted laughter.

"Ah . . . Miss Laurent." Adelicia motioned for Claire to come closer.

Sutton tried to catch Claire's attention but to no avail. Her trepidation was understandable. The LeVert women were daunting enough each on their own terms. But taken together as a whole—*and* with Adelicia . . .

"Thank you for joining us, Miss Laurent." Adelicia gestured. "Allow me to introduce to you Madame Octavia Celeste Valentine Walton LeVert, the most accomplished woman of my acquaintance, and one whom I am deeply privileged to call my dear friend." Adelicia wordlessly took hold of Madame LeVert's hand, and the two exchanged a glance. "And these two lovely women are her daughters, Miss Octavia Walton LeVert, whom we affectionately call Diddie."

Diddie dipped her head, smiling.

"And this dark-haired beauty"—Adelicia slipped an arm around Cara Netta's shoulders—"is Miss Henrietta Caroline LeVert, whom we all know as Cara Netta. And in turn, ladies, may I present Miss Claire Elise Laurent, my personal liaison . . . and the talented and assiduous young woman who is bringing a wealth of much-needed order to my life again."

With aplomb and grace belying the nervousness Sutton knew she felt, Claire curtsied deep. "Madame LeVert, it is indeed an honor."

She smiled at Diddie and Cara Netta. "Ladies, my pleasure to meet you as well."

Madame LeVert extended her hand. "Miss Laurent, I'd not been here five minutes before I heard your abilities being praised to the utmost by Mr. Monroe."

Claire looked at Sutton then, and he smiled at her, happy to see a flicker of the same on her face, along with another emotion he couldn't define. And he usually read her so well. She was getting better at masking her feelings. The discovery wasn't welcome. Neither was the way Cara Netta wove her arm back through his and pressed close.

Claire's gaze dropped to where Cara Netta was touching him, then quickly skittered away.

"I would welcome your assistance," Madame LeVert continued, "in penning some overdue missives—with Adelicia's permission, of course."

Claire opened her mouth to respond, but Adelicia beat her to it.

"She would be thrilled to assist you, Octavia. Miss Laurent can begin whenever you wish. And likewise, if either of you girls needs anything, please don't hesitate to ask her. She will be at your disposal and will be happy to make your stay at Belmont as pleasant as possible. Won't you, Miss Laurent?"

"Yes, ma'am." Claire tilted her head in acknowledgment. "It would be my pleasure."

But pleasure was the last thing Sutton felt. That same disturbing feeling he'd experienced moments ago grated through him again. Maybe it was the way Adelicia had flicked her wrist at Claire moments earlier or how she'd answered for her just now that rubbed him the wrong way.

Or maybe, he sighed inwardly, it was his own frustration—and disappointment with himself—that he was feeling.

As dinner guests began arriving that evening, Claire worked in the formal dining room to finish the last-minute details, doing her best not to think about what she'd been trying not to think about ever since the LeVerts arrived—Cara Netta.

Or more to the point, Cara Netta and Sutton.

Friends didn't quite describe them, she'd swiftly concluded. Not with the way Cara Netta looked at him, touched him, laid almost tangible claim to him. Sutton had to be aware of Cara Netta's feelings for him. He'd have to be blind not to. And one thing Sutton Monroe wasn't was blind. The man noticed everything.

Well, almost everything.

She'd done her best to bury the hurt she'd felt when the LeVerts arrived, along with the twinge of jealousy that still twisted inside her. After all, she had no claim on Sutton, not when women like Cara Netta existed in the world. And, Claire knew, not when she'd done the things she'd done.

She smoothed a wrinkle from the tablecloth and turned the candelabra a fraction, an ache starting somewhere near the vicinity of her heart.

She straightened, determined to ignore it, and eyed the china and crystal stemware. If she'd *lost* Sutton, then she'd lost something—and someone—that was never hers to begin with. So really, she hadn't lost anything. At least that's what she kept telling herself. Over and over.

She'd gotten the impression from Sutton's occasional glances that he'd wanted to speak with her during the course of the afternoon. But between helping Madame LeVert with her letter writing and getting ready for the dinner party, she'd simply not had the time.

No . . . That wasn't true. She simply hadn't wanted to talk to him yet, not when she sensed what he was going to tell her—that he reciprocated Cara Netta's affections. What man wouldn't? So she'd managed to avoid being alone with him. Not a difficult thing to do at Belmont.

A clock chimed from the hallway, snapping her back to the moment, and she consulted her list again.

She checked the place cards—arranged according to Mrs. Acklen's instructions—then the flowers comprising the centerpiece and those on the antique sideboard, along with the gifts Mrs. Acklen had requested be placed at the top of each place setting. Boxes of cigars for the gentlemen and scented lace handkerchiefs for the ladies.

She stepped back to admire her efforts and took a cleansing breath. Five minutes before six. Hardly any time to spare. She looked at the place card with her name on it, near the foot of the table, and was grateful again to be included in the adult gathering rather than joining Miss Cenas and the children in the family dining room.

"Claire?"

She turned and, though she told herself not to, she found herself staring. "Sutton . . ." Dressed in a fitted black suit with waist-cut jacket and tails, he walked toward her adjusting his tie and wearing an expression that made her glad she was a woman. Even if not the *right* one for him.

"You're a difficult woman to catch alone."

Maybe it was her disappointment talking or the jealousy goading her, but she couldn't resist picking apart his phrasing. He was usually so well spoken. "I believe, *Counselor,* that what you mean to say is that I'm a woman who is difficult to be caught alone."

He tilted his head as if casually acknowledging his *faux pas.* "And yet, considering the woman in question, and her response just now, I think I'll let my statement stand, Your Honor."

She would've laughed if he'd said such a thing yesterday, but she couldn't today. Not with the telling tightness in her throat and with watching his own smile fade. He had such an ease about him. Such a way of just being himself that made her—and everyone else, apparently—want to be around him. To be *with* him.

"Claire . . ." He looked down for a second, his brow creasing, and she felt a sinking inside, dreading whatever words would accompany that look. "My timing in this is poor, I realize. But there's something I should have told you." He lifted his head, and the seriousness in his gaze wrenched the knot inside her even tighter. "Cara Netta LeVert and I—"

"Sutton! There you are." The young woman herself appeared in the doorway. "I've been looking for you." She floated toward them in a gauzy dress of pearl-colored satin, a sash the color of her eyes accenting her diminutive waist. She slipped her hand into the crook of Sutton's arm as if the gesture were more of a reflex than a conscious action. "Oh, how beautiful!" Her gaze swept the table. "And look . . ." She picked up one of the place cards—Madame LeVert's, which Claire had taken extra care with in sketching a street scene from Paris. "How exquisite. Mother is going to be ecstatic when she sees these! Where did Mrs. Acklen have them made?"

"Miss Laurent made them." Subtle pride layered Sutton's voice. "She's quite the artist, in addition to being a fine personal liaison."

Claire warmed at the compliment, especially when remembering his original opinion of her. The image of him falling backward out of the gazebo stirred up emotions she knew were best forgotten.

"Really, Miss Laurent?" Cara Netta stepped closer to Sutton. "You sketch and paint?"

"Yes, but not much lately, I'm afraid." Claire managed a smile. "Time hasn't been too plentiful in recent weeks."

"And are you enjoying serving as Mrs. Acklen's liaison? I imagine it to be a demanding position."

"I'm enjoying it very much, Miss LeVert. And I'm most grateful for the opportunity Mrs. Acklen is giving me."

"Yes, I would think so. And living here at Belmont must seem like a dream for you."

Claire felt an indistinct barb in the comment, yet detected nothing of the sort in Cara Netta's sweet expression. "Belmont is exquisite, yes, ma'am. A kind of American Versailles, if you will."

It felt odd referring to Cara Netta as *ma'am,* when the young woman seemed not that much older than she was. Yet the difference in their stations in life demanded it. A difference she had been reminded of more times today than in all her weeks at Belmont thus far.

"Miss Laurent is originally from Paris," Sutton offered, filling in the silence. "She and her parents came to the States when she was nine. She moved here from New Orleans earlier this fall."

"Well . . ." Cara Netta's smile broadened. "You're quite the expert on the subject, Sutton."

Claire was thinking the exact same thing, surprised he'd remembered those details so readily. And that he voiced them in light of present company. It was obvious—to her, at least—that Cara Netta wasn't happy with her presence.

"Mrs. Acklen informed me again, Miss Laurent, that your talents are at our disposal while we're here. I'd be most grateful if you'd agree to assist me with a certain . . . undertaking."

Not missing Sutton's sideways glance at Cara Netta, Claire wondered if that *undertaking* would involve cleaning something . . . like a chamber pot, perhaps? "Of course, Miss LeVert. I'd be happy to assist you. Simply let me know when you wish to meet."

Guests began entering the formal dining room, and Cara Netta glanced behind her before turning back. "I see it's time for dinner, Miss Laurent. It's been a pleasure."

Claire looked from her to Sutton, realizing Cara Netta's assumption, yet not feeling at liberty to correct her.

"Actually," Sutton said, his smile a little stiff. "Miss Laurent will be joining us for dinner, Cara Netta."

Cara Netta's countenance faltered only for an instant. "Well . . . how wonderful. Then I'll look forward to continuing our conversation over the meal."

Claire thanked her, then excused herself, wanting to believe the young woman's sentiment was genuine, but something inside told her otherwise.

Oohs and *ahs* issued from Mrs. Acklen's mother and sisters, and from Madame LeVert and Diddie as they found their places at the table. They commented on the place cards, then their gifts. The gentlemen expressed pleasure as well as they took a whiff of their cigars.

"Thank you, Adelicia, how gracious."

"The handkerchiefs are beautiful, Adelicia. So lovely, all of it!"

Mrs. Acklen fielded thank-yous with a queenly nod here and there, and Claire watched just in case Mrs. Acklen might nod her way. But she didn't. Soon conversation filled the corners of the room, and Claire had just taken her seat—on the opposite side of the table from Sutton and Cara Netta, and a few places down—when Mrs. Routh appeared in the doorway.

One look at the woman's face and Claire knew something was wrong.

28

Mrs. Routh strode past Claire to where Mrs. Acklen sat at the head of the table. She leaned down and whispered, and Mrs. Acklen's focus instantly connected with Claire's. With an almost imperceptible rise of her brow, Mrs. Acklen signaled Claire.

Claire scooted her chair back and started to rise, but her skirt caught beneath a chair leg and she bumped the table, causing the stemware and china to clink. Conversation in the dining room dipped to a hum as everyone turned to look. Her face hot, Claire indicated she was fine and kept her eyes down as the chorus of voices gradually regained volume.

"Yes, Mrs. Acklen?" Claire whispered, leaning close.

"There is a situation, Miss Laurent." Displeasure sharpened Mrs. Acklen's hushed voice, yet her hostess smile never wavered. "Mr. Polk has just arrived to join us for dinner. Did you not check the mail today to see if he had changed his response?"

"Yes, ma'am, I checked. He didn't send—"

"Well . . ." Mrs. Acklen smiled at her mother, Mrs. Hayes, seated two places down, then lifted her water glass to her lips but did not drink. "He is very much here now and waiting in the entrance hall."

"I see." Claire thought fast. "I'll go to the dish room and get another place setting immediately and then—"

"It would be far less obtrusive, Miss Laurent, if you would simply eat with Miss Cenas and the children in the family dining room."

Claire felt the prick of tears and hated herself for taking offense. "Yes, ma'am, of course."

"And you *did* think to get an extra box of cigars, I hope."

Claire winced. She'd almost bought an extra box but hadn't wanted to waste the money. How foolish. "I'm sorry, but . . ."

Just then she saw Sutton rise from his chair, his box of cigars in hand. Without knowing how he knew, *she* knew what he was doing.

"Yes, ma'am." She took a quick breath. "I have a box of cigars for Mr. Polk."

"Then arrange it, Miss Laurent. *Quickly!*"

Claire stood, biting back tears, and not daring to look in Cara Netta's direction. Not when she knew the young woman was surely watching her. With every step, Claire felt the awkward attention of people trying their best to appear as though they weren't staring, when they were—and as if they weren't thinking, just as she was, how much she did not fit in here.

When she reached her seat—or the seat that had been hers—a box of cigars lay by the place setting. The scented handkerchiefs were gone. As was Sutton. She was almost to the door when she remembered and stepped back to retrieve her place card, the one with her name on it. But it was gone as well. *Sutton.*

In the hallway, she met Cordina and a host of other servants coming up the stairs.

Dressed in black with a crisp, starched apron, Cordina carried a silver tray laden with her signature pork roast. Cordina puffed out her chest. "We got dinner all ready, Miss Laurent, and right on—" She frowned, pausing in the hall. "What's wrong, child?"

Claire shook her head. "I'm fine. Everything is fine. I just—" She spotted Mrs. Routh escorting Mr. Polk down the hallway, and she smiled, curtsying as he passed, a little longer than needed so he wouldn't see her face. She rose. "I'm fine, Cordina. Now, please, carry the food on in. Mrs. Acklen is ready."

With a look that said she knew better, Cordina continued, her entourage following. Claire glanced into the family dining room and saw Miss Cenas with William and Claude and Pauline, but she wasn't hungry anymore. She hurried across the grand salon, living only to hear her bedroom door latch behind her. And when she rounded the corner, she saw Sutton waiting in the darkened hallway, an unopened box of handkerchiefs in his hand.

She couldn't stem the tears any longer. He started to say something but she put up a hand. "Please, Sutton. Not now. I . . ." She took a breath. "I appreciate what you've done, but I just need to be by my—"

He drew her into a hug and held her, those powerful arms wrapping her in safety, shielding her. Her tears came in waves, and she shook against him. She had trouble drawing breath, her sobs came so hard. It scared her at first, how deep the well of hurt went inside. And she realized the tears weren't only because of Sutton and what had happened just then and earlier that day. It was as if every tear she'd held back and stuffed down for months—for years—was rebelling against the restraint.

She'd tried so hard to be strong for her mother throughout the illness and in those last days. Then afterward for Papa, and for herself. But a person could be strong for only so long. And then . . .

They broke. And something was breaking inside of her. Something she didn't think she would ever be able to put back together again. Not like it had been.

Embarrassed at Sutton seeing her like this, she made a halfhearted attempt to push away, but he only held her tighter. And she slipped her arms around him and held on as if he were the last solid thing in the world.

"Claire, I'm sorry," he whispered against her hair. "Cara Netta and I have known one another for a long time. Over the past few months, while we traveled in Europe, she and I became better acquainted. And we reached . . . an understanding between us. One I should have told you about before this." He pulled back slightly, looking at her in a way Claire knew she wouldn't soon forget. There was a finality in his eyes, and a sadness. "It was wrong of me not to say anything, and I apologize for that. But the reason I didn't was because—"

She briefly pressed a hand to his mouth. "You don't have to do this, Sutton. I know the reason," she whispered, her head beginning to throb. She just wanted to lie down and curl up into a ball . . . forever. "And believe me when I say . . . that I understand."

He searched her eyes. "You do?" he finally whispered.

"Yes." She drew in a shaky breath. "You and I are friends. *Good* friends, and I treasure that. But . . . I don't expect any more than that." Just as she knew he wasn't prepared to give it.

"Friends . . ." He said the word like he wasn't certain he could be that to her anymore. Which she doubted too—considering the way Cara Netta felt about her.

Slowly, he released her, a resolute set to his jaw. "Will you be all right?"

She dabbed at her cheeks. "Yes, I'll be fine. I'll join you all again, after dinner. I just . . . need a few minutes."

He looked down at the box of lace handkerchiefs in his hand and held them out to her. She took them, feeling her tears return. She walked to her bedroom door, then paused to look back. "Sutton?"

He stopped, and turned.

"Thank you," she whispered. "For . . . this. For . . . helping me."

The shadows in the hallway hid the precise definitions of his face, but she thought she saw him smile. "You're welcome, Claire. That's what friends do for each other. . . . Right?"

"If you will permit me, Mr. Monroe, I have a rather personal and . . . bold question to pose."

Sutton studied Adelicia sitting opposite him in the carriage, guessing what she was going to ask now that they were alone—a rarity since the LeVerts' arrival. "I'm accustomed to your boldness, Mrs. Acklen. And I sincerely doubt—once you've set your mind to it—that there's any question I could dissuade you from asking."

Her smile was instant. "I'll take that as a yes." She returned her attention to the window, and Sutton glimpsed the turnoff to Belmont ahead. "Have you and Cara Netta discussed plans for marriage yet, Mr. Monroe?"

It felt as if someone had punched him in the gut. "I beg your pardon?"

"I warned you it was a bold question."

"Bold, yes. Abandoning propriety, no."

A fine black brow rose ever so slightly. "Please understand the motivation behind my inquiry. You are not merely an employee to me, Mr. Monroe. You were my late husband's *protégé,* and you are courting the daughter of my dearest friend. I believe that gives me a bit of leeway in this respect."

Summoning patience he didn't feel, Sutton prayed for wisdom he sorely lacked. "To be clear, Mrs. Acklen, I'm not officially *courting* Cara Netta. We have an understanding of sorts between us, but we haven't—"

"Exactly what is your definition of courting, Mr. Monroe?"

Heat rose from his neck to his face. "But *no*," he continued undaunted, "we haven't spoken formally, or otherwise, about marriage plans. I . . ." He hesitated, wondering how much to tell her, and if she might already suspect the truth about his feelings for Claire. Adelicia was as perceptive a woman as she was persuasive, and considering that, he decided to approach her question from a different angle.

"I don't wish to rush Cara Netta into a decision. After all, Europe was . . ." He searched for the right words.

"Another world away?" she supplied.

"Yes," he said, aware of her close attention. "And while I have no doubts about her character or person, I believe she deserves more time to reflect upon my own situation."

Adelicia frowned. "Do not speak so meanly of yourself, Mr. Monroe. While it may be true that your financial standing is more precarious these days, the fine fabric of your character, the qualities that matter most, remain unchanged. The LeVerts are convinced of this, I know."

Her comment gave him the impression that she and Madame LeVert had been discussing the two of them behind closed doors. Which didn't surprise him but it aggravated him all the same.

The carriage rounded the corner, and Adelicia directed her attention out the window. Sutton did likewise. He'd been out of sorts lately—with Adelicia, with others, even with himself. The reasons were varied and mostly out of his control. Which only made it worse.

No word from the Federal Army's review board yet, but daily he waited. Earlier in the week, he'd ridden out to his family's land late one night, seeking comfort, he guessed. Or reassurance, maybe. But instead, the visit only stirred up painful memories best forgotten.

Regarding the report from New Orleans that he'd been waiting for, his colleague had sent a telegram . . . "Your request forthcoming. Pursuing additional information. Will post within a fortnight." He wasn't eager to wait another two weeks, but he'd appreciated the man's discreet wording. And though Adelicia's interest in the report's contents seemed to have waned, his hadn't.

Not that he expected to learn that Claire was a fugitive wanted for murder or some other outlandish possibility. He simply wanted to know more about her background, enough to satisfy the lawyer in him responsible for protecting Adelicia's interests.

And . . . to satisfy some of his own.

The carriage jostled over the rutted road, and he remembered how she'd cried the other night, and how he'd held her. He grimaced thinking of what a fool he'd been about to make of himself—on the brink of confessing to her how he felt about her, and why telling her about his understanding with Cara Netta had been so difficult.

Then she'd said the one thing he could have lived the rest of his life quite happily never having heard from her lips. "*You and I are friends.* Good *friends . . .*"

He clenched his jaw. But that's what they were. In her eyes. And what he knew he needed to start viewing her as . . . in his.

Cara Netta LeVert was awaiting a proposal of marriage from him, and he should be grateful to have her in his life. She was sweet and kind and possessed a tenderness of heart that appealed to a man's innate sense of wanting to protect. Cara Netta could be headstrong and opinionated when her wishes were crossed. But then who couldn't be, on occasion? She was fiercely loyal to family and had adored her father, doting on his every word. And Sutton knew she missed him. Conversation with Cara Netta came easily—it always had—and no matter the subject, he noticed, she always steered it back to him. What he'd been working on at the law firm. What he'd been doing that week for Mrs. Acklen.

But never did she mention the thoroughbred farm. Not once.

On two occasions in recent days, he'd attempted to speak with her about the future of their relationship. The first time, she'd deftly skirted the issue. The next, they'd been interrupted by Diddie, though he still wondered whether that had been an accident or more of a planned interruption.

The carriage passed the conservatory and water tower, and the mansion came into view.

Bathed in an October sun and set against a cloudless azure sky, the manor more closely resembled an oil on canvas than a real image, and it occurred to him then how easy it was to speak of "*the fine fabric of one's character and the qualities that mattered most*" when your financial standing was secure, unthreatened.

Adelicia shifted on the carriage seat opposite his and cut him a look. "Perhaps this is none of my business, Mr. Monroe, but from what little I've heard, the case on which you and Counselor Holbrook are collaborating could end up being one of a rather *lucrative* nature, should you succeed in winning. Which would dramatically alter your financial standing and therefore your ability to move forward with more . . . *personal* ventures." Adelicia's tone held encouragement, and hinted at her appetite for gossip.

Sutton leaned forward, trusting her but still mindful of what he said. "It could. If we win. Which is anyone's guess at this point." Local investigators were researching the sales and purchases of hundreds of works of art across the country. It was tedious work, and they had recovered fraudulent paintings. That wasn't the issue. It was identifying the forgers and, even more importantly for prosecution, finding the swindlers—those who had negotiated the exchange of goods in acceptance of payment, all under the guise that the art was original—that was proving to be next to impossible.

One would think that art dealers and collectors would keep more meticulous records. Then again, thinking of Adelicia, Sutton knew that wasn't true. How many times had he insisted that her art collection be properly cataloged? And yet, that still remained to be accomplished.

They rounded the last garden, and he counted the seconds, eager to be out of the confines of the carriage and of this conversation, and to go for a good long ride with Truxton.

"Marriages are built on many different foundations, Mr. Monroe."

Sutton looked across from him, expecting to see that arched brow of hers again. But Adelicia's expression was all sincerity.

"Some are more deliberate," she continued, "a choice made after thorough examination. Others involve far more of the heart. Make sure you choose wisely, for each has its rewards . . . and its costs."

The squeak of carriage wheels on packed dirt bracketed her counsel, and it occurred to him that she might be speaking of her own situation, and not him. He asked as much.

She hedged a smile. "I suppose you could say that I'm advising us both."

He stared. "You're contemplating a third marriage, ma'am?" His thoughts jumped to Lucius Polk.

She didn't answer.

"It's a bold question, I know, Mrs. Acklen. But I believe our relationship can sustain such."

Her eyes narrowed playfully. "I'm considering it, Mr. Monroe, and we'll leave it at that. But I do believe, with all my heart, that you and Cara Netta would make a handsome couple. Your strengths as individuals complement one another. You're dependable to a fault—she's spontaneous at heart. You analyze every decision before making a move—she acts in the moment and embraces life's joys." She raised a shoulder and let it fall. "In the event that you desired my opinion."

He merely nodded, listening, but his mind was already working through the financial ramifications should she seek matrimony for a third time. She'd required Joseph Acklen to sign an agreement prior to their marriage—which Joseph had readily done—stating that the property and holdings Adelicia brought into the marriage would remain her own. An astute businessman, Joseph had promptly tripled Adelicia's wealth after only a few years of marriage, so her fortune was never in peril.

Sutton would insist that her third husband sign a similar agreement. His loyalty to Joseph—and Adelicia—would brook nothing less. But there was another part of this puzzle. One that affected him personally.

If Adelicia married again, her husband would likely assume the management role he had been filling since Joseph's death. Not the legal side of Adelicia's business, of course, unless the man were an attorney—which Polk wasn't. But regarding the management of Belmont, Sutton's services would no longer be required.

Which, when considering he already stood to lose his family's land, made this case he was working on with Holbrook even more crucial. But even then, in one sense, that victory was only a means to an end. An opportunity that would give him the chance to do what he really wanted to do with his life.

But not if he had a wife beside him who didn't share his dream.

29

Late the next afternoon Sutton returned from the law offices to find Cara Netta waiting for him in the art gallery, eager to take the walk she'd requested.

As they strolled the grounds, she peppered him with questions about his day, and he answered, sneaking occasional glances up at the mansion. He wondered where Claire was. Whether she was peering out one of the curtained windows or perhaps giving Pauline another lesson in sketching.

When he'd seen her in recent days, she'd seemed fine. There was no awkwardness between them. But she was always running—fulfilling Mrs. Acklen's and Madame LeVert's requests, and now tutoring Pauline in sketching. He didn't know when she was going to have time to do her own painting. But the auction for new artists wasn't until March. She still had time.

After touring the gardens, he and Cara Netta made their way toward the stables. For October, the temperatures were still on the warmer side, and fall was still struggling to take firm hold.

"Mother and Diddie and I were discussing a return trip to Europe next summer, Sutton. But only for two or three months this time. Doesn't that sound divine?"

At the moment, he could think of little else he would've liked less. Last summer, he'd been eager to escape Nashville and the memories of war, and he'd welcomed the diversion of Europe—and of Cara Netta, he realized with discomfort. But the thought of repeating such a trip wasn't the least appealing.

Not wishing to hurt her, he knew it was best she realize his feelings on the subject. "Actually, making a trip like that again doesn't sound *divine* to me at all, Cara Netta." He smiled to soften the opinion. "My focus is far more . . . stateside at present."

"Well, of course it is," she said quickly. "With all the concerns you have pressing, that's understandable. Even . . . commendable." She smiled up at him. "I'm certain that any day now you'll receive word that your land is indeed still yours. Then you can start rebuilding your family home."

"I wish I shared your positive outlook. But I'm not anticipating the review board will decide in my favor. Not if their track record has any bearing."

"But your family name is so highly esteemed in Nashville, Sutton. Not to mention your own reputation. I'm certain they'll make allowances for that."

He gave a bitter laugh. "Those men care no more about my *esteemed* family name than I do about theirs. The same for my reputation." The thought of his father's name and honor being sullied—all because of him—sickened him.

Cara Netta didn't say anything for a moment, then gestured to the mares grazing in the pasture. "I know how you love horses, Sutton. I do too. That's yet another thing we have in common."

He nodded, hearing the forced brightness in her tone. "Yes, it is."

"I've been thinking"—she paused, looking up at him—"about what we discussed in the air balloon that day, floating above Paris. Do you remember?"

"Of course I remember. But I'm a little surprised you do. You were clinging to my arm so tightly." He gave his shoulder a slight rotation, as though it still ached, and she grinned. Sutton studied her, feeling genuine affection for her. But was it the strength of feeling a man should feel for his future wife?

Her smile faded. "You said you thought each man—and woman—ought to spend their life doing what God created them to do. That they should do no less, and *could* do no more."

He grew curious at the look in her eyes, and where she was headed. "You have a very good memory, Cara Netta."

"I agreed with what you said, and I know you'll be the most celebrated attorney in Nashville someday. And who knows where that will lead? You could become a judge or even a senator." She looked down and bit her lower lip, and only then did Sutton realize how nervous she was.

She didn't say anything for a moment, then moved closer and laid a hand on his arm. "I wish Father were here to deliver this news. He would have done better at it than I will, I'm sure. And I know it would have given him great pleasure because . . . he thought the world of you, Sutton."

Sutton looked at where she touched him, wondering at the nervous quality in her voice. "Your father was a fine man. I admired him a great deal."

"Which is only part of what makes all of this so perfect." She took a breath, held it, and then exhaled. "Mother has found a house here in Nashville. That she wants to buy us. As a gift."

He stiffened. "I beg your pardon?"

"I know it's a lot," she said, her words coming fast. "And I hope I'm not getting too far ahead of . . . where we are, but a man in your position needs a home of his own. In town. I know you want to rebuild on your family's land, and we'll do that too, but it makes so much sense to have a house in Nashville proper as well. And Mother knows—just as I do—what a success you'll be at the law firm when you make partner. Mrs. Acklen says you'll likely be the youngest partner they've ever had. And there'll be room enough for your mother to come and live with us, if you'd like."

"Cara Netta—"

"And there's a stable, Sutton. A small one, granted. But big enough for four horses, so you can dabble in your hobby in the evenings and on weekends when we're not"—her violet eyes sparkled—"out at the opera, or dining with heads of state, or entertaining dignitaries. And in time, if you still want to, we can purchase a larger estate, where you could own thoroughbreds like—"

"No . . . Cara Netta."

She blinked. "But . . . I thought you would be pleased."

"Pleased that I don't have the means to provide for you in the manner in which you're accustomed? And expect?"

A frown formed. "I never said that."

"I know you didn't. You're too good and fine a woman to do that. But that's what I hear in this . . . very generous offer from your mother. That I must flatly refuse."

Her mouth slipped open. "But why?"

"Because a man wants to provide for his wife and family himself, Cara Netta. *This* man, anyway."

"This would simply be Mother's wedding gift to us, Sutton. And it would be Father's too, if—" Her voice broke. "If he were still here." She looked away. "Most men of my acquaintance would be pleased at this offer, and frankly"—her expression lost a bit of its sparkle—"would accept it with gratitude."

"Then I'm sorry to disappoint. And regarding my *hobby* . . ." Hearing the defensiveness in his voice, he took care to soften its edge. "As I explained to you before, or tried to . . . When I shared with you about wanting to own a thoroughbred farm, I didn't simply mean I wanted to own it, Cara Netta. I want to run the farm, train the thoroughbreds myself."

Shades of understanding shadowed her features, and he realized she'd understood his aspiration from the start—she just didn't share it.

She stared at him for the longest time, then lowered her head. And in a blink, Sutton saw future years passing before him. He could almost feel the soft brush of yet-to-be-lived memories on his face. It would be so easy, in one sense, to follow this course—to marry Cara Netta, to become the wealthy son-in-law of Madame Octavia LeVert, to have a fine house in Mobile, and another in Nashville, and yet another on the coast. He would have his thoroughbred farm in no time, though it would never be the one he'd envisioned. Nor would it be the life Cara Netta had envisioned either. And he wouldn't be the husband she wanted. Not really.

What confounded him was why she seemed so *set* on him. Cara Netta LeVert could have her choice of so many other men. Wealthier, and from better families.

"*Marriages are built on many different foundations, Mr. Monroe.*"

Adelicia's comment returned on a dull echo. What kind of marriage would he and Cara Netta have if he were to proceed in seeking her hand? The question wasn't easily answered. But what bothered him far more—and what he couldn't deny, no matter how he tried—was knowing that if Claire *had* felt something more than friendship for him, he wouldn't be here right now, working so hard to justify his feelings for Cara Netta.

The truth was jarring.

"Cara Netta . . ." How could he share his hesitations without hurting her, without causing her to think it was her fault? "You and I have been friends for a very long time, and I'm not saying that we shouldn't—"

She took hold of his hand and squeezed tight. "Have I ever told you what my father said about you the night before he died?"

Wary, he shook his head.

"He told me that he thought you were one of the finest men he'd ever known. And that you were *just* the sort of young man he would have chosen for me."

Sutton blinked, feeling a veil being ripped away. And he heard the answer—at least in part—to his earlier question of why she'd set her cap on him. And the truth was—she hadn't. Henry LeVert had done that for her. Cara Netta was following her father's wishes, not those of her own heart.

And knowing that explained so much.

"I appreciate that, Cara Netta," he whispered. "I know you loved your father very much."

She nodded, her grip tightening on his hands.

"And you're doing what you believe he would have wanted you to do."

She nodded again, then stopped. Her gaze turned appraising.

Sutton touched her cheek, seeing awareness dawn in her eyes. "But you need to make your own choice in this. You need to listen to what your heart is telling you." Just as he did.

"I *am* listening. And it's telling me that we would make a grand couple, Sutton." Tears rose in her eyes. "And that we would have a good life together. A happy life."

Sutton considered the statement, and found truth in it. He and Cara Netta had their differences, but they were compatible in many ways. More so than many couples he'd known. He got along well with Madame LeVert, and Diddie was the sister he'd never had. Still, something inside him held back from agreeing.

A dinner bell rang in the distance, and they turned to see Cordina waving from up by the house. He offered Cara Netta his arm. She looped her hand through, and they started back.

"Cara Netta, about what we were discussing, I think it would be wise for us to give ourselves time to—"

She turned to him and pressed a hand to his chest. "Let's not talk about this now, Sutton. You've had a busy day and an even busier week. You have a lot on your mind right now. And I agree. . . . Let's give things some time." Her smile was almost convincing. "Let's simply enjoy each other, and . . . we'll talk about all this later."

He knew they needed to finish the discussion, but he needed time to sort things out. And he would do anything not to deliberately hurt her. He only wanted the best, for them both. Whatever that was.

When they reached the front door, she turned to him, her expression vibrant once again, as though their exchange by the stables had never taken place. "I'm so excited about tonight," she said, preceding him into the entrance hall.

"Tonight?"

She smiled and swatted his arm. "We're all going to the opera. Mother arranged everything. Did you forget?"

His stomach churned at the thought. "No," he said quickly. "Of course not."

She eyed him.

"All right, yes. I forgot."

Just before they entered the formal dining room, she slipped her hand into his. Everyone else was seated and turned their way, and he grew uncomfortable beneath the "happy couple" image they no doubt displayed.

Especially when he met Claire's gaze.

It wasn't until dinner was over that it occurred to him—had Claire been invited to the opera too? Sutton assumed she had. She'd joined them in the grand salon each evening as Cara Netta played and they enjoyed Cordina's desserts.

He stood and scooted his chair back beneath the table and tried to get Adelicia's attention. But she and Madame LeVert were in deep discussion about something. He couldn't very well ask Cara Netta, and asking Diddie—who'd been unusually quiet during dinner—didn't seem like a good idea either.

He spotted Claire speaking to Claude and Pauline while she slowly inched her way toward the dining room door.

"Claire?"

She turned, her features guarded. "Yes, Sutton?"

The formality of her tone almost made him bristle. "I was

wondering whether—" If she said no to his question, what was he going to do? He hadn't exactly thought that through. "Whether you're going to the opera with us tonight?"

Her smile was instant, and telling. "No, I'm not. I've got so much to do here. It's really best that I stay and get some work done."

He felt a stab of anger. How could Madame LeVert, or whoever had arranged for the tickets, not have thought to include her? "Why don't you take my ticket, Claire. You know how I feel about the opera, and—"

"No, Sutton." She shook her head, her voice firm. "No."

"Oh, Diddie, tell me it's not true!" Madame LeVert said behind them. "How disappointing. And you've been looking forward to this all week."

Sutton turned to see the women grouped together, little Pauline now with them. "What's wrong?" he asked.

"Diddie's not feeling well," Mrs. Acklen answered. "So she won't be joining us this evening."

Sutton glanced at Diddie, whose coloring did look rather greenish. But he saw the opportunity and seized it. "I'm sorry you don't feel well enough to go, Diddie. But, so your ticket won't go to waste, perhaps we could impose upon Miss Laurent to take your place. If she's agreeable."

He turned back and saw a light slip into Claire's eyes. She smiled and nodded, and for a second, everything in the world lined up in perfect order.

"Sutton," Cara Netta said sweetly from across the room. "That's so thoughtful of you, but . . . I've already asked Miss Cenas to go in Diddie's stead. She's getting her shawl and reticule right this moment."

Sutton's chest went tight, especially when he sensed that Cara Netta knew exactly what she was doing, or had done. She hadn't wanted Claire to go. Claire simply smiled, as if the mix-up were of little consequence to her, and a fierce protectiveness rose inside him.

But what galled him most was that *he* was the one who had placed Claire in such an embarrassing position. "I'm sorry, Claire," he whispered.

"There's nothing to be sorry about, Sutton. I honestly prefer to stay here." Her perfect smile would have convinced anyone else. But he knew better.

And he pledged to make it up to her somehow.

30

Claire gently rapped on the door of the *tête-à-tête* room. Hearing no response, she slipped inside and closed the door noiselessly behind her. She'd been sneaking into the room in the early mornings for the past couple of weeks to read, and if she hadn't been reading what she was reading, she might have felt a little guilty.

Since the night she'd come *undone* . . . at least that's how she thought of it—crying as she had, falling apart, and in front of Sutton, no less—she'd developed a thirst for the verses that had given her mother such comfort and hope in her final hours.

The Acklen family Bible lay on the table before the hearth, and Claire scooted a chair closer, mindful of the carpet. Mrs. Acklen had told her in passing that the Bible never left the room, but she hadn't said not to read it, so Claire assumed that was fine. After all, it was the Bible.

But knowing Mrs. Acklen, she'd gone a step further and never moved the Bible from the table. She simply opened the pages, read, and when she was done, made certain the large leather-bound book was exactly as it had been.

She checked her hands to be sure all traces of breakfast were gone. Since the LeVerts arrived, she'd begun taking the meal downstairs in the kitchen with Cordina and the other servants rather than in the dining room with the family and guests. It was simpler that way.

Claire leaned close to the book and breathed in the scent of hand-oiled leather and years-old paper and dust. The pages crinkled as she turned them.

Genesis, Exodus . . . She skimmed over the next few books, watching for the right name. Esther, Job, the Psalms . . .

The Psalms had been what Maman had requested that she read from most, and Claire had read all of those again last week before moving to other books. The next time she went into town, she planned on purchasing a Bible of her own. Not that she went into town that often. Though time had passed and the likelihood of crossing paths with Antoine DePaul was slim, she still held a dread of that happening. How quickly all she'd worked for—and had been given—at Belmont could be taken away.

There it was . . . the book of Isaiah.

She'd started reading from Isaiah because Reverend Bunting had quoted from it last Sunday, and she'd liked what she'd heard. But she'd soon discovered that the first five chapters of the book weren't nearly as uplifting as the part he'd quoted from.

Still, she was determined to give it a fair try.

"Chapter six . . ." She found the page and started to begin reading, then remembered and bowed her head. "Thank you, Lord, for being the Bread of Life, and for this . . . my daily bread." She lifted her eyes, feeling quite the poet. Only, the words weren't hers. Not originally. She'd borrowed them from a gentleman she'd heard pray aloud in church.

She kept her voice soft. " 'In the year that King' "—she studied the name before pronouncing it—" 'Uzziah died I saw also the Lord sitting upon a throne, high and lifted up, and his train filled the temple.' " *Very majestic, descriptive . . .* " 'Above it stood the seraphims . . .' "

As she read, images of angels and a temple took shape in her mind, and she pictured the scene as an oil on canvas. A scene she'd like to paint someday. " '. . . And the posts of the door moved at the voice of him that cried, and the house was filled with smoke. Then I said, Woe is me! for I am undone . . .' "

That word again . . . And a feeling she knew only too well.

" 'For I am undone,' " she repeated softly, " 'because I am a man of uncl—' " She frowned, familiar with the next term too, uncomfortably so. " 'Unclean lips,' " she finished, the words resonating inside her.

She read ahead, wincing slightly, as though the angel in the verses who had taken a live coal from the burning altar had touched *her* lips, instead of Isaiah's. " 'And he laid it upon my mouth,' " she read, "'and said, Lo, this hath touched thy lips; and thine iniquity is taken away, and thy sin purged.'"

Movement from outside the window drew her eye.

Diddie and Cara Netta passed. Coming for breakfast, no doubt.

Claire recalled the "undertaking" Cara Netta had requested her help with—making a scrapbook from bits of memorabilia and pamphlets from the family's tour of Europe. But Claire knew the real desire behind Cara Netta's request: to put her in her place as an employee of Belmont and to regale her with all that she and Sutton had experienced together.

Memories of the opera evening, over a week ago now, were still fresh too. She'd cried a few more tears that night after everyone had left. Then she had decided "No more." What was done was done, and she reconciled herself to change what she could. Instead of attempting to change the impossible.

She had work to do—projects for Mrs. Acklen, and now for Madame LeVert, and lessons with Pauline, which were coming along quite well. She hoped to have some time to sketch for herself this afternoon, to start narrowing down the choices of venue for her first painting for the auction.

She stared out the window, waiting to see if Sutton was accompanying the LeVert sisters. But apparently he wasn't.

He'd been scarce in recent days. Busy with the lawsuit he was working on, she guessed, and with business for Mrs. Acklen. She wondered how the relationship was between him and Cara Netta. She saw them walking together often enough, and saw them at dinner, of course, but other than that, she avoided them as much as possible.

It was her preference, but she also knew it was Cara Netta's. Not that she blamed the woman. She would feel the very same, if put in Cara Netta's position. Claire fingered the edge of the page. She imagined that—under different circumstances—she might have liked Cara Netta very much . . . if Cara Netta wasn't in love with Sutton. And he with her.

Drawing her thoughts back, she returned her attention to the page and soon lost herself in reading again.

"Good morning, Miss Laurent."

At the voice behind her, Claire stood and spun. "Mrs. Acklen!

Good morning, ma'am." Claire glanced at the open Bible, wishing now that she'd requested permission. "I didn't hear you come in."

"Yes, that's apparent." Mrs. Acklen looked from her to the Bible and back again. "What are you reading?"

Claire decided not to respond with the obvious. "Isaiah, ma'am."

"Have you read it before?"

She shook her head.

"Isaiah is one of my favorite books. Difficult to understand in places, granted. But well worth the effort." Mrs. Acklen's gaze narrowed. "Do you not have a Bible of your own, Miss Laurent?"

"No, ma'am. I . . ." Admitting to not owning a Bible made her sound like a heathen. But what could she say in response to the question? "My Bible was . . . to be packed in my trunks. So I decided to borrow yours. I hope you don't mind." There, that was the truth.

"Your trunks *still* haven't arrived, Miss Laurent?"

Claire bit the inside of her cheek. "Not to my knowledge, ma'am."

"Well, we'll remedy that immediately. Give your previous address to Mr. Monroe and he'll wire a colleague in New Orleans who will check on your trunks for you. We'll have them sent directly to Belmont."

"Please, Mrs. Acklen, I don't want you to go to any trouble."

"Those are your trunks, Miss Laurent. *Your* clothes. *Your* personal belongings. You have a right to have them back. You cannot simply allow someone—or in this instance, some incompetent railroad steward—to *take* them from you. Is that not clear to you?"

Claire held back a sigh. "Yes, ma'am. It's quite clear."

"Very good. And when you're done in here, please come to the library. I have several Bibles. I'll give you one. I also have a task for you today."

Thinking of giving Sutton her New Orleans address, Claire felt more undone by the second. "Yes, Mrs. Acklen. I'll be right there. And . . . thank you, ma'am."

Mrs. Acklen closed the door, and Claire sank back down in the chair. She stared at the open Bible. So much for finding hope and comfort.

"The Bible is there, Miss Laurent," Mrs. Acklen said, her back to Claire as she perused a bookshelf. "On the corner of the desk."

Claire reached for the Bible lying on a stack of mail. Somewhere toward the bottom, an issue of the *New Orleans Picayune* peeked out. She'd checked each issue since finding the article about her father, but to her relief, none of them had held further mention of Papa or the gallery.

"Do you see it, Miss Laurent?"

"Yes, ma'am, I do." Claire picked up the tan leather Bible and read the gold-embossed name on the cover—*Mrs. Joseph Acklen.* "Thank you, Mrs. Acklen." She fingered the pages edged in silver. Certainly a nicer edition than she would have purchased for herself. "I appreciate your sharing it with me. I'll take very good care and return it when I'm done."

"It's yours, Miss Laurent. As I said, I have several. I had an envelope here . . ." Mrs. Acklen searched through papers atop the library desk. Finally, she sighed. "Perhaps I left it in my bedroom. I'll find the envelope while you arrange with Eli for a carriage."

"A carriage, ma'am?"

"Yes." Mrs. Acklen started toward the door. "I need you to go into town for me this morning on an errand."

Claire started to object and yet knew better. But there went any extra time for sketching this afternoon.

Mrs. Acklen paused and looked back. "Perhaps you have another, more pressing engagement this morning, Miss Laurent?"

Claire felt herself blush. "Of course not, Mrs. Acklen. I'm happy to go."

She followed her into the entrance hall, where they met Diddie and Cara Netta coming from the grand salon.

"Good morning, Mrs. Acklen," they said, then sent nods Claire's way. "Miss Laurent."

Claire curtsied. "Good morning, ma'ams."

Mrs. Acklen hugged them both. "And what are you dear girls doing today?"

"Seeing that we're returning home in two days"—Diddie's smile temporarily waned—"we're going into town to shop! That will surely cheer us up." She grinned again. "Eli's bringing the carriage around now."

"That's wonderful!" Mrs. Acklen gestured to Claire. "Miss Laurent was leaving on an errand into town on my behalf. Would you mind if she accompanies you?"

Claire couldn't hold back. "Oh no, I don't want to intrude. I'm quite content to walk. It's a lovely day. Very dry at present," she added, directing the statement toward Mrs. Acklen. "And I'd appreciate the exercise."

Mrs. Acklen looked at her as if she'd grown a third eye. Diddie and Cara Netta merely stared.

"I am quite certain," Mrs. Acklen said, "that it's going to rain. And I'm sure Diddie and Cara Netta would be happy to share their carriage." She looked at the sisters.

"Of course we would, Mrs. Acklen," Cara Netta chimed in, her smile expectedly sweet. "We'll wait for you out front, Miss Laurent."

Claire returned to her room for her shawl. She hadn't been excited about the errand in the first place, but now she had to abide the trip with Cara Netta.

She slipped a few coins into her dress pocket, not having replaced her reticule she'd left behind at the shipping office. Mrs. Acklen was paying her very well, but recent expenditures had diminished her savings. First, the gray dress, then the canvases and tubes of paint she'd ordered two weeks ago. And Dr. Denard's fees had been more than she'd imagined too. Mrs. Acklen had offered to pay the physician, but Claire had insisted. It was her own fault, and therefore her responsibility.

Knowing the sisters were waiting, she hurried back to the grand salon. Mrs. Acklen had agreed to meet her there with the envelope, but it was Mrs. Routh descending the staircase, and wearing her usual dour expression.

Determined not to be intimidated this time, Claire forced a smile. "How are you this morning, Mrs. Routh?"

"I'm well, Miss Laurent. And you?"

"Quite well. Thank you." Claire glanced at the envelope in her hand. "Is that from Mrs. Acklen?"

Mouth firm, the head housekeeper held it out. "You're to deliver this to Mrs. Perry at the dress shop straightaway this morning. And you're to await a reply."

Claire studied the envelope. The front bore Mrs. Perry's name in Mrs. Acklen's impeccable handwriting. She turned the envelope over. "It's sealed," she said, wondering why Mrs. Acklen had penned the letter herself instead of asking her to do it.

"Yes, it's sealed, Miss Laurent. Which would lead one to think that its contents are intended for Mrs. Perry's eyes alone."

Realizing Mrs. Routh's insinuation, Claire's face heated. "I understand that, Mrs. Routh. I was simply wondering why—" Seeing the distrust in the head housekeeper's eyes, Claire knew that no matter what she said, it would make no difference. "I'll give Mrs. Perry the envelope. Good day, Mrs. Routh."

Claire hurried out to the carriage, wondering again why the woman seemed so bent on distrusting her. Mrs. Routh's dislike was palpable, and it bothered her more than she cared to admit.

The two-mile ride into town seemed twice as long as usual. Diddie did most of the talking and was very kind, but Claire didn't doubt for a second that the older sister knew how the younger felt about her.

When the carriage pulled up to the dress shop, Claire climbed out with Armstead's assistance and was surprised when the sisters followed.

"Mrs. Perry's was at the top of our list of places to visit today," Diddie explained. "After all, she has the nicest dresses in town."

And the most expensive, Claire wanted to add but didn't. She smiled and allowed the women to precede her into the shop, hoping that Mrs. Acklen's errand wouldn't take too long. She was already looking forward to returning to Belmont. On foot. And alone. As long as the gray clouds held.

When they entered the store, they found Mrs. Perry assisting a patron, so Claire waited off to the side as Diddie and Cara Netta browsed the dresses. Over half the dresses in the shop were darker in color—grays, like the one she had bought, and midnight blacks, and darker blues. Colors of mourning. The colors of war.

"I'm sorry to keep you ladies waiting." Mrs. Perry joined them and greeted Diddie and Cara Netta by name. "And Miss Laurent, a pleasure again, and so soon. Are you here for another dress? A style came in yesterday that would be lovely on you."

"Good morning, Mrs. Perry, and I'm afraid not." Claire handed her the envelope. "I'm here on behalf of Mrs. Acklen. She asked me to deliver this, and I'm to wait for your reply."

Mrs. Perry read the note, then peered up. "You've not read this, I take it?"

Claire eyed her, thinking again about Mrs. Routh's insinuation. "No, ma'am, of course not. It was sealed."

Mrs. Perry tucked the note back inside the envelope, her face practically glowing. "Then, may I be the bearer of good news, Miss Laurent. I believe it would be appropriate to say that Christmas has come early for you this year, my dear."

31

Claire could scarcely believe what Mrs. Acklen had done for her. Six dresses! *Six!* And all of them lovelier than any she'd owned before. Mrs. Perry had also included an assortment of lacy undergarments—chemises, underskirts and pantalets, stockings—all in a separate pink paper-lined box. Along with a woolen coat for coming winter and a pair of shiny black boots in another.

Claire had never owned such fine things, nor had she been treated so royally. She stood at the door of the dress shop, peering out at the steady downpour but determined not to let it dampen her spirits. Not after such a wonderfully unexpected surprise.

The fittings had taken longer than she imagined, and Mrs. Perry had generously provided lunch for her. Diddie and Cara Netta had left two hours earlier with the promise of returning for her in "the Clarence," as Diddie called their leased carriage, and so she waited.

It occurred to her then that perhaps she should have felt insulted by what Mrs. Acklen had done—because apparently Mrs. Acklen didn't feel as though she dressed appropriately for her station. Yet she wasn't insulted in the least. She was grateful beyond imagining, and could hardly wait to get back to Belmont to thank her employer properly. Mrs. Perry said the alterations would be completed within a few days and she would have the dresses delivered to Belmont.

Claire spotted the LeVerts' carriage coming down the street. She could hardly miss it. The Clarence had a circular front with glass—very stylish, and no doubt very expensive, even leased. She made a dash for the carriage and climbed in with Armstead's assistance, not surprised to see ribboned boxes stacked on the seat beside her.

Diddie and Cara Netta occupied the seat encased by glass, which suited her fine. Whoever sat there was on display, something she preferred not to be. Aware of Cara Netta watching, Claire brushed drops of rain from her skirt and willed a cheerful tone to her voice. "Did you two have a successful shopping trip?"

"Yes, we did." Cara Netta's smile looked mildly convincing. "Though not as successful as yours, I wager."

Diddie shot her younger sister a look, then checked the gold ladies' watch pinned to her own bodice. "It's a quarter 'til one. Shall we see if Sutton is still at the law office? I told him we might stop by."

Cara Netta nodded, but Claire looked between the two sisters. "We're not going back to Belmont?"

"Soon," Diddie said, tapping on the window. Armstead appeared and she gave him instructions, then leaned back again. "We won't be long, Miss Laurent. I promise. And I feel certain, after seeing how much Mrs. Acklen appreciates you, she won't begrudge you an hour or two more."

"Oh!" Cara Netta perked up. "We could visit that wonderful little pie shop where Sutton took us last time. They have the most divine coconut cream."

Diddie agreed, and the two sisters began talking, finishing each other sentences as they usually did.

Resigned, Claire eased back in the seat. And as the carriage rumbled past shops and office buildings, she began to get a familiar feeling. When the driver stopped in front of a redbrick building with a brass placard reading *Holbrook and Wickliffe Law Offices,* she realized why.

She looked out, remembering the older man she'd seen at Broderick Shipping and Freight, and then again, entering this building. "*This* is where Sutton works?"

Diddie nodded. "Holbrook and Wickliffe is the most prestigious law firm in town. Sutton was employed here exclusively . . . before Mr. Acklen passed away. Following that he moved to Belmont to help Mrs. Acklen manage things there."

"I'd have thought you would've known that," Cara Netta said, "since you and Sutton are such . . . *good friends.*"

Claire didn't quite know how to respond to that. It was the first time Cara Netta had said anything directly to her about Sutton. Much less about her *and* Sutton. And the tone she'd used . . . as if she questioned whether they were only *good friends*.

"I knew Sutton worked at a law firm here in town . . ." Claire glanced back at the building to see Sutton exiting the front door. The rain had let up, and the hope of sunlight was peeking through the clouds. "I simply didn't realize he was connected with *this* law office." And with that older gentleman she'd met.

"Mrs. Acklen told Mother he'll be a full partner one day." Possessiveness colored Cara Netta's voice. "One day not far off, I'm guessing."

Diddie's soft smile held agreement. "Mr. Acklen thought very highly of him, as do the current partners in the firm."

Claire watched Sutton jog down the front steps, leather satchel in hand, and she felt a stir of desire for him. A lock of dark hair fell across his forehead, and even this early in the day, the shadow of tomorrow's beard and a smile that could melt snow in winter gave him an almost roguish quality.

He appeared every bit the future young law partner—and deserved a wife equal to that status. Claire glanced again at Cara Netta and the word *thoroughbred* came to mind. Sutton appreciated the finer things in life, and he deserved them too.

At the last minute, Diddie deftly stood and switched to sit on Claire's side of the carriage, scooting the boxes to one side and leaving the space beside Cara Netta available for Sutton. It was a calculated move but not meanly meant, Claire knew. It was simply what one did when knowing the heart of a beloved sister. Just as summer followed spring, and winter followed fall, it was understood that Sutton and Cara Netta belonged together. Anyone looking on would know that.

Claire felt a telling tug of jealousy. So why was she having such a hard time accepting that fact?

"Hello, ladies . . ." Sutton opened the door and started to climb in. "Miss Laurent!" He paused, and Claire would've sworn she saw a light come into his eyes. "I didn't realize you would be shopping with the LeVerts today."

"Actually, I didn't either." Claire stole a look at Cara Netta, who was looking back at her—not in a happy way. "Mrs. Acklen asked me to come into town this morning on an errand, and the LeVerts were kind enough to let me share their carriage."

Sutton claimed the seat next to Cara Netta, and seconds later the carriage lurched forward. He raised one of the windows and Claire welcomed the breeze in the close quarters. With no prompting, Diddie and Cara Netta proceeded to give him a full accounting of everything they'd purchased that morning.

The carriage stopped briefly at a thoroughfare, and Claire noticed passersby looking their way. No doubt, looking at the Clarence. Or at the handsome couple seated behind its glass partition.

The carriage continued on, and Diddie and Cara Netta showered Sutton with questions about his day. Claire listened with interest as he responded. But when the conversation turned to the pie shop, she focused out the window at the steady stream of pedestrians.

Businessmen hurrying to their next appointments, women clutching infants while Negro nannies followed, baskets and toddlers draped over their arms. Negro men swept front porches and hefted crates of dry goods into wagon beds, their muscular forearms rippling and glistening in the sun. Boys squared off on street corners, hawking newspapers and soggy sacks of boiled peanuts, while still others dogged the heels of suited men, begging to shine their shoes for a penny.

And yet here she sat in a fine carriage because of her position as Mrs. Adelicia Acklen's liaison, with new dresses enough to fill a wardrobe, and with her dreams of painting on the horizon. Life didn't seem fair sometimes, all the sudden twists and turns it could take. Even when those turns were working in her favor. Especially then . . .

Because she knew she wasn't deserving.

The carriage slowed again, and she leaned forward to catch a bit of breeze. A man crossing the street caught her eye. His clothes so stylish, the manner in which he carried himself so proper. His back was to her, but he paused and turned in her direction, and stilled.

His face suddenly registered, and Claire felt herself falling forward, even as she pressed her body back against the cushioned seat.

32

Antoine DePaul! Heart in her throat, Claire told herself to breathe. She could hear Diddie talking beside her but couldn't make out the words over the roar in her own ears. Sutton was focused on Cara Netta, who was focused on him, all while her own world spiraled downward.

Please, God, please . . . Don't let him approach the carriage. She gritted her teeth and willed the carriage to move. *Just move!* She didn't dare look out the window again. She just kept praying, over and over—pulse racing—that Antoine hadn't seen her.

"Miss Laurent?"

Claire turned to see Diddie staring. As were Sutton and Cara Netta.

A keenness slipped into Sutton's expression. "Are you unwell, Miss Laurent?"

She heard the question but couldn't respond. Because at any second, the life she'd found at Belmont would be over. Antoine DePaul would see to that with swift and vicious resolve.

Just as Sutton leaned toward her, the carriage moved forward, and the viselike grip on Claire's throat lessened its hold.

She took a breath. "I'm . . . fine, Mr. Monroe. Thank you." Beyond the window, storefronts and pedestrians swept blissfully by. "I simply . . . grew a little warm, I think."

"Miss Laurent," Diddie said, casting her sister a look, "if you'd rather go on home, we can. I know for a fact that Cordina was baking tea cakes earlier."

Claire could have hugged her. "I would prefer that, Miss LeVert. If it's all right."

More than once on the way back to Belmont, Claire discreetly glanced behind them to make certain no one was following. The image of Antoine DePaul was locked in her mind, as was the reality of how swiftly her circumstances could change. She told herself that perhaps Antoine had only been looking at the Clarence. After all, his tastes ran toward the most expensive and extravagant. Belmont was the last place he would ever think of to look for her. She was safe there. She was certain of it.

Now if she could only convince the tremor inside her.

When they arrived at Belmont, Claire sought out Mrs. Acklen and conveyed her gratitude for the generous gift of the dresses. Then at dinner in the formal dining room, she tried to be attentive as Diddie and Cara Netta regaled everyone with the day's events.

She smiled on cue and commented when necessary, but inwardly she kept reliving the moment she'd seen Antoine—when he'd turned on the street and had gone so very still. She shuddered again just thinking about it.

Mrs. Acklen rose from the head of the table. "Shall we move all this gaiety to the grand salon?" She tilted her head in Cara Netta's direction. "After much persuasion, Miss LeVert has graciously agreed to play for us again."

Cara Netta dipped her head as though acquiescing to her hostess's wishes.

Claire stood, aware of Sutton looking her way. He silently mouthed, "Are you all right?" She smiled, but only a little, and nodded once, then looked away, wary of Cara Netta's misinterpretation of the exchange should she notice.

But that Sutton cared enough to inquire meant everything.

Cara Netta played beautifully, as usual, her fingers flying over the ivories, even at the most difficult parts. Claire longed to paint like Cara Netta played. She wanted to create something that would resonate with people. That would make them stop and take notice of the portrait or landscape, a scene that would so capture their emotions they would pause and search the lower right-hand corner of the canvas and say, "Ah, yes . . . *Claire Elise Laurent.*"

Claire studied the remnants of coffee in her china cup, thinking of her *Versailles* and wondering where the painting was. Even more, she wished she could see it again. See her mother standing there at the edge of the garden path, half hidden behind the lilacs. *Maman . . . I miss you. So very much.*

"Do you have a request, Miss Laurent?"

Claire blinked and raised her head. Mrs. Acklen was looking at her, as was everyone else. "I-I'm sorry, ma'am?"

"Do you have a particular piece you'd like for Cara Netta to play?"

"She's taking requests," Diddie added. "And we're doing our best to stump her!"

One composition immediately came to Claire's mind, and the title was out of her mouth before she'd thought it through.

" 'Moonlight Sonata'?" Cara Netta repeated, eyeing Claire over her shoulder. "By that I presume you mean the first movement of Beethoven's Sonata in C-sharp Minor. A beautiful piece, to be sure. But . . . it's hardly a challenge, Miss Laurent."

"No, I suppose not," Claire said softly, feeling stares from around the room. "But perhaps the true test of a pianist's ability lies not only in mastering the difficult, but the simpler as well."

Cara Netta chuckled. "And why would that be, Miss Laurent?"

Claire weighed her response. "Simpler music can prove as complex, perhaps more so, because one must work harder to capture the intended emotion. After all, as Beethoven said, 'Playing without passion—' "

" 'Is inexcusable,' " Cara Netta finished for her, her expression inscrutable. Then with a look, she turned and began playing. Softly at first, then building, each arpeggio so sweet, the melancholic chords so perfectly succinct. And the tempo . . . masterful. Claire closed her eyes and let the music—and the memories the music summoned—wash over her. Tears slipped down her cheeks, and she did nothing to stop them. Cara Netta finished and the last chord hung, somber and still, sustained in the silence like a prayer.

The final note faded and quiet blanketed the room.

"That piece," Mrs. Acklen finally said, "holds special meaning to you, Miss Laurent."

Claire nodded. "Yes, ma'am," she whispered, wiping her cheeks. "It was my mother's favorite." Claire looked back at Cara Netta and with far less effort than she would have imagined in recent days, she formed a smile, one not the least bit false. "Thank you, Miss LeVert. That was *exquisite.*"

For a long moment, Cara Netta held her gaze, then inclined her head. "My pleasure, Miss Laurent. Thank you for requesting it. It's long been a favorite of mine as well. Simple though it is."

Seconds passed.

Cara Netta cleared her throat, an obvious attempt to lighten the mood. "And now," she said, addressing everyone, "it's *my* turn to see if I can stump you!" She turned back to the piano and began playing again. A lighter tune with a livelier tempo.

Claude jumped up from the settee, followed by his younger sister. "That's easy!" he said. "'*Wait for the Wagon!*' Miss Cenas plays that one!" Claude and Pauline crowded around the piano bench along with Diddie. Even William sidled up to listen.

Seizing the opportunity, Claire rose as well. The evening was young, and it was still light out. She needed a walk. Maybe she would take a pad of paper along and do some sketching. The idea held appeal.

Madame LeVert bid everyone good evening, and Claire thanked Mrs. Acklen again for the dresses, aware of Sutton coming alongside her.

"Your generosity is overwhelming, Mrs. Acklen. The dresses are the most beautiful I've ever owned, ma'am. I'm very grateful to you."

"And you're most welcome, Miss Laurent." Mrs. Acklen seemed genuinely pleased. "As my personal liaison, you are now an extension of me. Therefore, there are certain . . . expectations that accompany that role, as I'm sure you're aware. Since William's birthday party, when people see you, they also see me."

Claire hadn't thought of herself in that light before. As an employee, yes. But as an *extension* of Adelicia Acklen? She was honored by the comment. And terrified.

"When you were in town recently," Mrs. Acklen continued, "and you were ordering painting supplies . . ."

Claire fished back through her memory, wondering if she should be worried.

". . . Mrs. Worthington overheard your conversation with the clerk and commented to me and Madame LeVert at tea last week how very kind and polite you were to the young girl. Even when the girl had difficulty taking your order and then proceeded to charge you the wrong amount."

Claire hadn't even known Mrs. Worthington was in the store, much less listening.

"Not many people will correct a clerk's miscalculation when the error is in the *customer's* favor."

Claire studied the black-and-white-checked floor beneath her feet, uncomfortable with the integrity their comments assigned her. "It was the girl's first day. She was flustered and nervous and—"

"Yes, yes, I'm sure she was." Mrs. Acklen tented her hands. "The point is, I appreciate your honesty and the decorum with which you conduct yourself, Miss Laurent. Your behavior, your decisions, your slightest comment all reflect greatly upon me. Upon the whole of Belmont."

Claire could barely manage a nod as the far-reaching implications of Mrs. Acklen's words took hold. Especially in light of what had nearly happened that afternoon. Needing that walk now just to calm her nerves, she bid everyone good night, excused herself, and headed to her room to retrieve her shawl.

Footsteps sounded in the hallway behind her.

"Claire?"

She turned at Sutton's voice, surprised he'd followed. But even more surprised by the somber set of his features.

His steps slowed as he came toward her. "Be careful, *Miss Laurent*. You're treading on very dangerous ground here."

Nerves cording tighter, Claire tried to think of something to say, a question to ask that would give her some idea of what he—

A slow smile tipped one side of his mouth. "Because I don't think I've ever seen Adelicia Acklen so pleased with anyone before. Which means you're setting the bar awfully high for the rest of us."

Wanting to smack him and hug him at the same time, Claire settled for replenishing the air in her lungs. "Well, I'm pleased that *she's* pleased."

"She informed me she'll be hosting a ball in the spring." His brow rose. "I'm assuming she's discussed that with you?"

She nodded. "We've been discussing May of next year, maybe even June. So that gives me at least seven months. Plenty of time to prepare, which I'll need. She's thinking of inviting as many as five hundred people!"

He smiled. "Her guest lists can be extensive."

The piano music coming from the grand salon faded, and they both turned and looked down the hallway. The music started again and they turned back to each other. Claire wondered if he was thinking the same thing she was—that it was *safe* to keep talking as long as Cara Netta was playing. As observant as he was, surely he'd noticed her and Cara Netta's truncated exchanges.

"What happened this afternoon, Claire? In town . . ."

His question caught her off guard. But only a little. She was growing more accustomed to his direct nature and also—much to her discomfort—to *creatively* circumventing his questions. "I think perhaps it was a combination of things. Trying on dress after dress, then the warmth of the carriage . . ."

"You're sure? Because you seemed . . . flustered."

"*For I am a man of unclean lips* . . ." Claire glanced to the side. Telling him about Antoine DePaul was out of the question. That would be like lying down in front of an oncoming train. Yet how could she answer him and still be honest? And then it came. How often had she witnessed Mrs. Acklen use the tactic . . . "You're right, Sutton. I *was* flustered about something. At the time." She met his gaze full on. "But I'm fine now. Thank you for asking."

A humorous glint slid into his eyes. He started to speak again, but she silenced him with a look, seeing who was standing at the end of the hallway.

Sutton turned.

"Excuse me, Mr. Monroe." Mrs. Routh took a purposeful step forward. "Miss Cara Netta is looking for you, sir. She requested that I let you know she's waiting for you in the central parlor."

Claire hadn't noticed, but sure enough, the piano music had fallen silent.

A muscle flinched in Sutton's jaw. "Thank you . . . Mrs. Routh. Please tell Miss Cara Netta I'll be there in a moment."

"Very good, sir. And shall I send Eli for a carriage? Miss LeVert thought the two of you might venture over to Laurel Bend this evening. It's so lovely out. I'd be most happy to—"

"No, Mrs. Routh. Miss LeVert was mistaken. No carriage is required." His voice gained a flat edge. "But thank you."

Mrs. Routh merely bowed her head in Sutton's direction, then aimed a fleeting but satisfied look in Claire's.

With Mrs. Routh's retreat, Sutton turned back, his expression devoid of humor. For a moment, he said nothing, only stared at some point beyond Claire's shoulder.

Claire told herself it would be wiser not to ask, but she couldn't help herself. "What is Laurel Bend?"

With blinkless efficiency, his gaze connected with hers. "It's the Monroe family estate. At least for now." A shadow moved across his face, chased by a lostness that seemed more fitting for a boy of seven than a man of Sutton's stature and strength. He bowed his head.

Claire wanted to inquire further—to know what he meant by "*at least for now*"—but she got the distinct feeling he didn't want to discuss the topic.

"One more thing, Claire." He looked up. "Then I'll leave you to enjoy your evening. What you said this evening to Cara Netta, about the music . . . That was very gracious. Especially in light of her . . . cool behavior toward you."

So he *had* noticed . . . She wondered whether he'd noticed *her* behavior toward Cara Netta. She hadn't exactly gone out of her way to be kind to her. Not until tonight. "I meant every word, Sutton. Cara Netta is exceptionally talented. And she's . . ." Claire believed what she was about to say, but still found it difficult to voice. "She's also a very lovely young woman."

"Yes, she is," he said, but didn't sound happy about it. "Well, I should let you go."

But he didn't move. His gaze moved over her face in a way that made Claire's mouth go dry. And if she hadn't known better, she might have thought he wanted to lean down and kiss her cheek. But she did know better, and he didn't lean down.

"Good night, Claire." He turned and strode down the hallway, not looking back.

Claire watched him until he disappeared around the corner. "Good night, Sutton," she whispered, wishing now more than ever that she'd taken her mother's final words of advice to heart.

"I thought riding out to Laurel Bend might be a nice way to spend the evening, Sutton. A welcome diversion for you." Cara Netta peered up at him as he entered the parlor. "You've seemed so . . . burdened lately. We could talk about the house, about your plans to rebuild."

Going out to Laurel Bend was the last thing Sutton wanted to do, and it hardly represented a welcome diversion. Each visit stirred up the same old bitterness. The waiting, the not knowing, was taking its toll. "Actually, I'd rather stay here, if you don't mind. We could walk, if you'd like. It would give us the chance to talk."

"Of course I don't mind." She reached for her wrap, holding his gaze as if trying to read what was on his mind.

Sutton held her arm as they descended the front steps of the mansion, the weight of what he had to tell her bearing down hard. His decision was made. He knew what he had to do. He'd felt the confirmation inside him moments ago when he'd stood in the hallway with Claire. Now he just needed to do it.

Cara Netta slipped her hand through the crook of his arm and smiled up, and the weight inside him increased a hundredfold.

"I enjoy being with you, Sutton. Wherever we are. I was telling Diddie earlier today that it's wonderful how close you and I are. And how well we get along." She squeezed his arm. "Do you remember that afternoon in Paris when we spent the day wandering the city, going from bakery to bakery, and then from museum to museum . . ."

Sutton listened, nodding at appropriate intervals, as she recounted experiences from their trip. He almost got the feeling she was retelling the memories for his sake, in case he'd forgotten. He directed their course away from the mansion and downhill toward the conservatory, not wanting to risk being interrupted.

With each step, her grip tightened on his arm, and he wondered whether she sensed what he had to tell her.

"And then there was that time in Rome when we went to that little café on the corner. Do you remember the one? It was—"

"Cara Netta . . ."

He stopped, took her hands in his, and felt a stablike pain in his chest when he saw the fragile look slip into her eyes. She knew. Or at least she suspected. "I would do almost anything not to hurt you. I hope you know that."

She shook her head. Her gaze grew watery. "Whatever it is, Sutton, we can work it through. That's what couples do."

"I wish it were that simple, Cara Netta. But if I were to allow our relationship to continue . . . if we were to marry . . . that's exactly what I would be doing—*hurting* you."

Her grip tightened. "How can you say that? We'll be the most splendid couple in Nashville. In all of Dixie. I know it."

"You're an extraordinary woman, but—"

She gave a humorless laugh. "Nothing good ever comes from a sentence that starts that way." She withdrew her hands and moved to a nearby bench.

Sutton claimed the place beside her, and she looked over at him.

"Is it because of the house Mother wanted to buy us?"

"No."

"Is it because I want to go to Europe again?"

"No," he said, praying for the right words. "It's none of those things. And yet . . . it is, in a way." How to be honest with her without shattering everything they had? He owed her the truth, and yet the truth seemed so painful and would drive such a wedge between them. "You're a beautiful young woman. Kind and caring, generous and intelligent—"

"And yet, apparently, those attributes aren't enough." She bowed her head. "Because somehow I've fallen out of favor."

He leaned down in an attempt to regain her attention. "You didn't fall out of favor, Cara Netta. I'm simply not the man you should be marrying. And if you'll only look at me closely enough, you'll see that. You could have your choice of so many other men. Men who—"

"I don't want any of them."

"But that's only because you haven't looked. You've been so . . . *decided* on me. And frankly, I never understood why—until you told me what your father said."

She huffed. "That again."

"During the past year, and specifically on our trip, I think we were both hurting and lonely, and we confused friendship for something more. I hold myself largely responsible for that too. I shouldn't have allowed our understanding to continue for as long as it has."

Her gaze rose sharply. "So you decided a while back that you didn't love me. And yet you said nothing."

His neck and shoulder muscles tensed. "Cara Netta, it wasn't a decision I made. It was—" He was making a mess of the whole thing. "It simply took time to sort out my feelings. To see things more clearly."

She angled herself away from him, and he couldn't blame her.

"Would you look at me, Cara Netta?"

She didn't move.

"Please?" he whispered.

Reluctantly, she turned.

"I'm not a wealthy man, by any means. And what little land I have, I stand to lose. I don't care for the opera, and that one trip to Europe will last me for a lifetime." He sighed. "Not that I could have afforded to make the first one on my own. And yes, I'm an attorney at a prestigious law firm, but . . ." He searched for the simplest term for his dream that he could find. "What I really want to do is to run a horse farm."

She blinked, and the indignity in her expression, though subtle, spoke volumes.

"And my wife," he continued, gently as he could, "should I ever be blessed to marry, needs to want that too. As much as I do."

Cara Netta looked at him, and he could almost see the layers of *might have been*s shedding away, one by one. Along with his appeal in her eyes.

She stood, and he joined her. Wordless, they walked back toward the manor, not touching, not speaking. When they reached the art gallery, she turned, her face awash in emotion.

"For what it's worth, Sutton . . ." Tears slipped down her cheeks. "I think you're making a mistake. I think we could have a good life together. I've seen a lot of fine marriages that have far less affection between partners than we have for one another."

Her words pained him. Not because they weren't true but because she had somehow convinced herself that a marriage like that should be enough. "What you're saying is true, Cara Netta. But you deserve so much more."

Chin trembling, she stared at him through fresh tears. Movement at the edge of his eye begged his attention, but he didn't look until Cara Netta did.

Claire was walking back toward the mansion from the fields. If she saw them, she made no indication that she did.

"I wonder," Cara Netta said, her voice soft but not the least delicate. "How does *Miss Laurent* feel about horse farms? Have you ascertained her thoughts on the subject yet?"

She spun on her heel and walked back inside.

Stunned, but knowing he was guilty as charged, Sutton waited outside, giving her time to get to her suite.

And later, as he lay in bed, thinking back through their painful exchange, he knew he'd done the right thing, for them both. While they might have had a *good* life together, he would have been robbing Cara Netta of the life—and love—she deserved.

Because she deserved a man who felt a thrill every time she walked into the room, a man whose pulse skipped a beat when she raised a stubborn brow in challenge. A man who wanted to shield and protect her, who would fight to fulfill every one of her dreams. A man who could hardly wait to touch her again, even if it was only by accident as they walked side by side. A man who lay awake at night, dreaming of ways to woo her and win her heart, of taking her in his arms and kissing her until she was breathless.

She deserved a man who felt about her the way he felt about Claire.

33

The next morning, Claire awakened late. She'd slept fitfully, dreaming about Papa and Antoine, and about a boat they were on that was sinking. No matter what she did, she couldn't find a way off. And the most gruesome part—just as the water was reaching her neck, alligators appeared in the murkiness, swimming straight for her.

By the time she dressed and left her room, it was a little past eight. She wished she could take a long walk and chase away the darkness of dreams with cool morning air and sunshine, but the buzz of conversation coming from the family dining room told her that would have been considered rude.

She rounded the corner and conversation at the breakfast table fell silent.

Even before she took her seat, she sensed an air of anticipation in the room. "Good morning," she said quietly, seeing breakfast hadn't yet been served.

Good-mornings echoed around the table. Mrs. Acklen and Madame LeVert sat at one end, both of them beaming. Diddie wore a similar expression, as did the children. Cara Netta, however, had dark circles under her eyes and looked as if she'd slept about as fitfully as Claire had, or worse. Sutton, like Cara Netta, lacked the others' exuberance too.

He smiled, but in a way that made Claire wary. She unfolded her napkin, draped it across her lap, and scanned the faces around the table, growing more nervous by the second.

Finally, Mrs. Acklen leaned forward. "I've concocted the most marvelous plan, Miss Laurent! And I think you're going to love it!"

Diddie wriggled in her seat, and Madame LeVert looked about ready to burst. Cara Netta glanced at Sutton with a look Claire couldn't interpret.

"It's a party!" Pauline blurted, then clasped a pudgy little hand over her mouth as her brothers frowned in her direction.

"A *reception*, actually." Mrs. Acklen tossed her daughter a playfully stern smile. "In honor of Madame LeVert, and we'll host it right here at Belmont. It will be the social event of the season! I stayed up late last night working on the guest list and the menu. And I'm eager for your ideas, Miss Laurent, on invitations and decorations and centerpieces. And then there's the music, of course, and party favors, and . . ."

As Mrs. Acklen continued to speak, Claire listened, her mind already churning. Maybe it was because she'd slept so little and so ill, but she couldn't get excited about planning another huge event. Not when she needed to be painting. Yet she didn't *dare* let her reaction show. After all, meeting Mrs. Acklen's every need was her job.

She'd barely had two weeks to plan the birthday party for forty-seven children and their parents, and the party preparations had consumed nearly every waking minute. But with the proper time to plan the reception, to choose and coordinate details—

Claire's thoughts screeched to a halt. She'd heard Mrs. Acklen mention a number but was certain she'd misunderstood. "Pardon me, Mrs. Acklen, but . . . *how* many guests did you say?"

Mrs. Acklen tilted her head to one side as though communicating her displeasure at being interrupted. "I said one thousand, Miss Laurent. Perhaps a few more than that. . . . I'll let you know."

Claire could scarcely wrap her mind around that number of people in one place. Much less in a house. And with tables and favors and centerpieces and invitations. And the cost! She looked across the table at Sutton, who gave her an almost imperceptible nod of his head, as though to say, "Stay calm."

"But not to worry, Miss Laurent"—Mrs. Acklen gestured to Cordina and two other women who came from the kitchen bearing breakfast—"the reception isn't until December eighteenth. So that gives you a good seven weeks to get everything in order!"

Seven weeks! Seated sidesaddle on Athena, Claire prodded the feisty black mare uphill, her mind churning. Seven weeks to plan a reception for over one thousand guests! "The social event of the season," Mrs. Acklen had said.

Claire's head felt ready to explode.

She'd masked her frustration well, she thought, but the moment breakfast was over, she'd made a beeline for the stables. Until Mrs. Acklen caught her in the entrance hall. "Mrs. Worthington has invited us to coffee this morning, Miss Laurent, and I felt we needed to accept, seeing as the LeVerts are leaving Belmont in the morning . . ."

As soon as Claire heard the words, she'd begun formulating an excuse as to why she couldn't attend. But as it turned out, *she* hadn't been included. The invitation was extended to Mrs. Acklen and the LeVerts only.

Athena bounded over the crest of the hill, and Claire reined in, breathing hard but welcoming the exertion. She hadn't wanted to go to the silly coffee anyway. It would have meant making polite conversation on topics of no interest that she knew little to nothing about, and sipping too-weak coffee when she preferred the richness of *café au lait*. . . .

She sighed. So if she hadn't wanted to go, why was it bothering her that she'd not been invited?

She prodded Athena forward through stands of pine and white birch, hoping the path led where she thought it would. She leaned forward and gave Athena's neck a rub, appreciating the animal's speed and strength, as well as Mrs. Acklen's permission to ride the mare whenever she desired. Never in all her days could Claire have afforded such a fine mount.

That last thought lingered, settled, and the reason for her frustration became clearer, and reached far deeper than disappointment over not being invited to coffee. She didn't belong in Adelicia's world of wealth and privilege. She had no right to be there. The world of afternoon teas, fancy silk dresses, and evenings at the opera was as foreign to her as racing thoroughbreds at Nashville's Burns Island track was to Athena.

The pretty black mare tossed her head as though voicing her disagreement at the thought. Claire ran her fingers through Athena's mane. "It doesn't make you any less a fine horse, pretty girl," she whispered. "It just makes you"—she thought of Sutton and Cara Netta—"different from them."

Seeing Antoine DePaul had done more than frighten her. It had forced her to see herself again for who she really was—Claire Elise Laurent, daughter of Gustave and Abella Laurent. Her father, an art dealer who had made his living selling fraudulent paintings from a second-rate gallery. And her *maman,* the gifted, but misguided, artist who had painted them.

But even more than showing her who she was—Claire's throat thickened with unshed tears—seeing him had revealed who she wanted to be. Herself, only, truer. More honest. Without the past dogging her heels and without the feeling that, at any moment, her old self could show up and wreak havoc. But how did she become that person she wanted to be without sacrificing everything she now enjoyed?

The path ahead opened as she'd hoped it would. She dismounted and stood close to Athena, holding the mare's bridle and looking out across the valley, feeling small and insignificant. And yet, strangely, not as alone as she'd once felt.

Belmont sprawled below, the mansion and grounds professing a different kind of splendor when viewed from this height. The flourish of fall was only days away and she wished the canvases and paints she'd ordered would hurry up and arrive. Not that she would have time to paint now.

Bitter irony tinged her tongue. She was in the perfect place to create, literally surrounded by beauty and where she had the opportunity for her work to be seen by people of influence, and yet she had no supplies. And even when they did finally arrive, she would have no time to paint. She had the *social event of the season* to plan!

She half laughed, half sighed.

She still believed God had led her to Belmont, and was grateful to Him for that. But why lead her to a place with such opportunity, and then keep her so busy she couldn't pursue her painting? She wanted to create something that would last. That would stir people's emotions so they would feel the passion she poured into her work and would recognize her giftedness.

She reached up and scratched Athena behind the ears. Not only did she see little evidence of God's plan for her painting, she also didn't think His timing was very—

The distinct thud of hoofbeats sounded, and Claire turned toward the treelined path to see a horse and rider cresting the hilltop. Recognizing both, she smiled.

Sutton reined in beside her, out of breath. "You're a hard woman to catch."

She peered up, shading her eyes from the sun. "You followed me?"

"I tried." He leaned forward and rested his arm on the saddle horn. "You and Athena tore out of there pretty fast."

"I did not. I waited until after Mrs. Acklen and the LeVerts left to go to coffee." Hearing a hint of defensiveness in her tone, she smiled and glanced at Athena. "This pretty little girl just needed to work off some frustration."

Sutton dismounted, his hair windblown. "And what about *this* pretty little girl . . ." He reached up and tugged a curl at her temple. "Has she worked off her frustration too?"

Claire's heart did a little flip. *He's a friend. He's only a friend.* Remembering the *stay calm* look he'd given her at breakfast, she shook her head. "I hope my feelings weren't too obvious."

"Only to me. But I know what to look for."

She narrowed her eyes, pretending to be offended. "And just what does that mean?"

"I'm not about to tell you my secrets. Let's just say you covered your lack of enthusiasm fairly well."

"Except to you."

He winked. "Except to me." He looped Truxton's reins over a branch, and Claire did the same with Athena's. Sutton took a few steps forward. "Pretty up here, isn't it? Prettiest view in all of Nashville."

Maybe it was the softness in his voice or the way he looked out over the countryside as she'd done earlier, but Claire didn't get the sense he was intentionally trying to change the subject. "Yes, it is. I'd love to paint it. Someday."

"Which reminds me . . . Your canvases and paints were just delivered. That's what I came to tell you. I told Eli and Zeke to put everything in your room. I thought you'd want to know."

"Thank you, Sutton. I was hoping they would arrive soon." She could hardly wait to open up everything. And how thoughtful of him to ride to tell her. His gaze settled on a point in the distance, and she wondered . . . "What are you looking at?"

He inched back toward her, pointing. "See that rise just there to the left? Near where that bird's flying right now?"

She moved closer and peered down the line of his arm. "Yes, I see it."

"That's Laurel Bend, my family's land. Our house stood just over that hill there. My grandfather built it in 1817, when my father was a boy."

"Our house stood," he'd said. Past tense. She sneaked a look at him, remembering his comments from last night and hearing the same subtle hurt in his voice now that she had then.

"My grandparents raised seven children in that house."

She felt herself responding to his sad smile. "And how many did *your* parents raise?"

He turned to her, his face close. "Only one. They wanted more, but . . . it never happened." He lowered his arm, studying her with an intensity that sent a shiver through her.

"I don't know whether my parents wanted any more children or not," she whispered, thinking it strange now that she didn't know that. Yet being this close to him, seeing the tiny flecks of gold in his eyes, she felt no interest in exploring the question. "But regardless, I was it."

He smiled. "And I'm betting you were more than enough for them both. For your father especially, when it came to fending off interested young men."

His words wounded in a way she knew he couldn't fathom, nor had intended, and she turned away.

"Claire . . ." He urged her back, but she resisted. "Claire," he whispered again, closing what little distance there was between them. His hands on her face were her undoing. "I'm sorry. I shouldn't have spoken about your father with such casualness. I'm—"

"No, Sutton. It's . . . not that." She tried to smile and brush it off, but a tear slipped from the corner of her eye. "It's nothing."

He wiped it away with his thumb. "It doesn't look like nothing."

She shook her head, unwilling to tell him more.

He leaned closer, his features tensing, as though he were wrestling with something, and losing. "I need to tell you something," he whispered, his voice husky. "About . . . me and Cara Netta."

Cara Netta. The name made her pull back an inch or two.

The lines at the corners of his eyes grew more pronounced. "Cara

Netta and I . . . We've spoken and . . ." Certainty deepened his gaze. "I want you to know that the understanding between us has changed."

"Changed?" Claire whispered.

He looked at her long and steady. "She and I have been friends for many years. And, somewhere along the way, we confused our friendship for . . . something more."

Something more. That was a good term for what she felt for him. Something more than friendship. Far more . . . Whatever conversation he'd had with Cara Netta, it had pained him. Claire could tell by the regret shading his expression. And no doubt, that conversation had hurt Cara Netta too. Which explained her reticence that morning at breakfast. "Does Cara Netta agree with your conclusion? About . . . your friendship?"

He didn't answer immediately. "Maybe not right now. But I have no doubt she will, given time."

Knowing Cara Netta what little she did and how much she seemed to care for Sutton, Claire questioned how soon that would happen. Yet she couldn't deny a sense of relief at the news. Even hopefulness.

"I'm sorry, Claire, again, if my not telling you about her earlier on hurt you in any way." He cradled her face, stroking the curve of her cheek with his thumb, and unknowingly fanning the spark inside her into a flame. "I promise you, that was never my intention. Your . . . friendship is very important to me."

"And yours is the most important of my life, Sutton." His thumb stilled on her cheek. Claire read surprise in his eyes, and for an instant, she wished she could take back the words.

Then he smiled, only the tiniest bit, and more with his eyes than with his lips. Oh, but those lips . . .

He got that look about him again, as though wrestling with something, and the sea blue of his eyes darkened. His thumb slid from her cheek to her mouth, and he traced a feather-soft path over her lower lip. She closed her eyes, thinking that maybe if she didn't look at him, she wouldn't be so moved.

But the lack of sight only made her that much more aware of his touch.

His hands, so strong, so warm . . . One of them edged down her neck, and she tilted her head, certain the hillside moved beneath them. And then, his lips on her cheek. Oh, how was she still standing?

His breath was warm and minty. And his hand, inching up her arm only added to the weakness in the hollow backs of her knees.

"Open your eyes," he whispered.

But she didn't want to. She didn't want it to end.

"Claire . . ." He sighed, a smile somehow wrapped up in the sound.

Reluctantly, she did as he asked, and what she saw in his eyes took her breath away. It was then that she realized he was holding her in his arms, and her arms were around his neck. And that he intended to—

His lips brushed hers, softly at first, as though she might break, then grew more confident, and eager. He tasted like peppermint and sunshine, and somewhere deep inside, long cordoned off and forgotten, a place slowly began to open again.

Or maybe it was opening for the first time. *Yes* . . . that was it. Because never had anyone touched her there before.

Sutton deepened the kiss, and her willing response sent a bolt of lightning through him. With determination he knew was right but was already regretting, he drew back. He wasn't sure who was more breathless, him or her.

Seeing her eyes still closed, her lips full and parted, any question in his mind about whether this woman felt more than mere friendship for him, vanished. He kissed her cheek, and she slowly opened her eyes. His chest tightened at the mixture of innocence and desire he saw there.

On impulse, he drew her to him again and held her, tracing the small of her back, then the curve of her spine, admiring how well they fit together, her head tucked beneath his chin, her arms around his waist. If he had to choose between kissing her and holding her, he would definitely choose the kissing. But the holding wasn't too bad either.

"My father and I," she said softly, her cheek against his chest. "We weren't close."

We weren't close. Only three words. Yet they said so much, and helped to explain her reaction from moments earlier. "I'm sorry," he whispered.

"My mother and I were, though."

He felt her quick intake of breath and tightened his arms around her, wishing he could take away the pain in her voice. "And she passed away how long ago?"

"Almost eight months." She exhaled. "Tuberculosis."

"I'm so sorry."

She gradually looked up at him. "A moment ago you said that your family house *stood.* Meaning it's not there anymore?"

He looked back in the direction of Laurel Bend. "The house is gone. The Federal Army burned it—and everything else—to the ground. . . . The same day they killed my father."

Questions flitted across her face, and yet she said nothing, only waited, her gaze patient.

"Federal officers had been out to the house, more than once, demanding that he sign the Oath of Allegiance. That he and I both sign it."

"But you both refused?"

He nodded. "My father served in the hospitals and cared for the wounded. His family, patients, and friends were fighting for the Confederacy, but he refused to take up arms against his fellow countrymen." Sutton stared out across the valley toward home, or what was once his home, and told her about finding his father's bloodied body, and of his mother collapsing in his arms. "The reason my father refused to sign the oath was because of me. I told him that he would be a—" The words caught. "That he would be a traitor to me and to our family name if he signed."

Claire winced, as though sharing the weight of his regret.

"Not a day goes by that I don't wish I'd been there. That I could've intervened. That I could tell him that no matter what he did, he could never have been a traitor in my eyes." Sutton bowed his head. If he could turn back the clock and do things over again, he would. It wasn't right for a father to pay the price for his son's pride. He took a breath and lifted his eyes. "Now the government's laid claim to my land and is trying to brand my father as a traitor to his country."

Claire drew back, fire in her eyes. "But they can't do that! The war is over. They have no right to take something that's not theirs."

He felt the hint of a smile, able to envision her in a court of law. Heaven help the judge who riled this woman. "I've made an appeal to the Federal Army's review board, but it's a long shot. And the longer it drags out, the less hopeful I am. So . . . I'm preparing myself to lose it all."

She reached for his hands, raised them to her lips, and kissed them. Her gentleness, the way she held his hands between hers, caused a knot to form at the base of his throat.

"My *maman* used to say that things happen for a reason." Her smile came slowly, sweetly, and shone in her eyes with a strength that belied the quiver in her voice. "I haven't always believed that in the past. But I do now . . . believe that God has a plan for me. I don't know what it is . . ." She laughed, squeezing his hands. "But I'm choosing to believe He does. And I'm going to believe that for you too."

With effort, he swallowed. "Thank you, Claire." He knew she had no idea what that meant to him. Or what *she* meant to him. "I'm going to do better at believing that too. For us both."

He glanced over her shoulder and saw Truxton and Athena standing side by side, munching on field grass, and an idea came. Though he'd not seen the bruise on Claire's hip after her fall, he'd known from Dr. Denard that it had been bad. And while he didn't want to push her before she was ready, he was eager to get started on their jumping lessons.

He looked back at her. "How's your hip feeling these days?"

Confusion clouded her expression.

"I'm just wondering if you're healed up enough to start those—"

"Yes!" Her face lit and she gave a little squeal. "I'm completely healed. When can we start?"

34

Standing between Sutton and Mrs. Acklen on the front portico the following morning, Claire raised a hand in farewell as the LeVerts' carriage pulled away. Diddie and Cara Netta, seated by open windows, reached gloved hands through and waved. Cara Netta had barely met her gaze when they'd said good-bye a moment earlier. Diddie, too, had seemed slightly less cordial.

But under the circumstances, Claire understood. She assumed Cara Netta had told Diddie about the change in relationship with Sutton, but she guessed from Madame LeVert's unaffected behavior that Cara Netta hadn't told her mother yet.

She'd seen Sutton and Cara Netta walking the gardens earlier that morning, but no longer arm in arm. Anyone seeing the sheen of emotion in Cara Netta's eyes as she and Sutton had said good-bye would have attributed her tears to those of parting, but Claire knew better.

And she felt for Cara Netta. Even as she felt relief at her departure.

She welcomed the familiarity of routine again. She had a reception to plan, after all, and also needed to work in time to paint. And guilty though she felt, when thinking of Cara Netta, she welcomed time with Sutton again. Especially after yesterday's meeting on the ridge.

She glanced at him and discovered his gaze fixed on the carriage as it rounded the last garden at the bottom of the hill and disappeared from sight. She would have given more than a penny for his thoughts.

As though aware of her staring at him, a slow smile turned his mouth. But he took his own sweet time before peering over at her. His smile took a more intimate turn, and Claire would've sworn he'd reached over and touched her. But he hadn't.

He could do all that with a single look . . .

Not wanting to give him the satisfaction of the last word, as it were, she raised an eyebrow as though finding his actions *blasé*. To which he responded by dropping his gaze ever so slowly to her mouth, where his focus lingered. Then he looked up at her again, his thoughts easily read. Claire reached out to a nearby urn to steady herself.

Mrs. Acklen sighed, her mood of a sadder nature this morning. "'Friendship is a single soul dwelling in two bodies.'" She turned back toward the mansion, and Claire did likewise, wondering if her employer's tender emotions were due to the LeVerts' departure, or to something else.

Sutton offered them each an arm as they climbed the steps. "I've no doubt, Mrs. Acklen, that Aristotle had you and Madame LeVert in mind when he penned that notion."

Mrs. Acklen smiled. "Thank you, Mr. Monroe. But I'm not quite that old. Yet."

He laughed. "You know that wasn't what I meant to imply."

"Of course I do, sir. Because, as we all know, you *imply* nothing, Mr. Monroe. You state it forthrightly and for all to hear." Mrs. Acklen glanced over at Claire, her countenance growing a touch brighter. "Miss Laurent is improving her skill in that area. You must be giving her private instruction."

Claire felt Sutton's nudge and her face went warm.

"Yes, ma'am," he said, hardly missing a beat. "I've been working with Miss Laurent on a private basis for some time now. She can be a challenge, as you're aware. But overall I've found the experience to be very . . . gratifying."

Her hand tucked into the crook of his arm, Claire pinched him through his suit jacket. He smiled as he reached to open the door.

"Mr. Monroe, will you be going into the office today?"

"Yes, Mrs. Acklen, I will. I need to get some files, as well as stop by the telegraph office."

"I have a letter on my desk for Mrs. Holbrook, regarding a committee we're on together. Would you take it to her husband, please?"

Sutton closed the door behind them. "With pleasure, ma'am."

Once inside, Mrs. Acklen paused in the entrance hall and looked up at the picture of her late husband. She said nothing. Only stood and stared, as though no one else were in the room.

Claire shot a look at Sutton, who was gazing at the painting as well. He seemed unbothered by Mrs. Acklen's sudden reticence, and not the least surprised by it.

"Miss Laurent?" Her voice soft, Mrs. Acklen's focus remained unchanged.

Claire took a tiny step forward. "Yes, ma'am?"

"We'll be working in my personal quarters today. We have boxes of letters and cards to go through. I want your assistance in creating something special for Octavia. To present to her at the reception. A book of memories, perhaps, of . . . happier days gone by."

Claire curtsied, bowing her head. "Yes, ma'am. Of course." She looked at Sutton, who gave her a silent nod. "But first, ma'am, why don't I go down to the kitchen and get you a cup of Cordina's tea? I'll bring it up shortly."

Mrs. Acklen turned, her eyes glistening with unshed tears. "That would be lovely, Miss Laurent. Thank you. But wait an hour, perhaps two. I'd appreciate time to rest." She reached the doorway and looked back. "And do remember to bring a cup of tea for yourself too, when you come."

"I'm glad you stopped in, Mr. Monroe."

Sutton turned at hearing Bartholomew Holbrook's voice. "I just came by to get some files and check my mail, sir. I left an envelope from Mrs. Acklen for your wife with the receptionist. But she told me you were out for the afternoon."

Holbrook waved for Sutton to join him in his office, then for him to close the door. Sutton did and claimed one of the two leather chairs opposite the senior law partner's desk.

"I'm doing my best," Holbrook said, "to stay out of sight and get some work done." He held out a file. "An investigator hired by our client dropped this by earlier today."

Sutton flipped through the folder that contained another list of cities and dates with titles of art pieces listed beside them. Some, but not all, of the titles had dollar amounts by them. "I don't want to be pessimistic, sir, but we already have lists like this. We need to identify the people involved."

"Yes, Mr. Monroe, but each time they turn up a *new* city and a *new* piece of art, that gives the investigators another opportunity to uncover another shred of truth. And it increases their chances of finding this . . . invisible partner who's coordinating the sales of all these fraudulent paintings, and who knows the people painting them. These are small steps, I grant you. But it's in the tiny details that people make mistakes. A name written in a guest register, a cross word spoken to a concierge who has a very good memory." Holbrook tapped his temple. "Something will turn up. And very soon. I can feel it!"

Sutton wished he shared Holbrook's enthusiasm. The whole case was moving too slowly for him. What they needed were names. Mainly that of the man pulling the strings at the top. The rest would follow. *If* they could only learn his identity . . .

After their meeting, Sutton retrieved the files he needed and checked the mail on his desk. Nothing from the colleague in New Orleans. What was taking the man so long? But there was a letter from his mother. Her shaky handwriting told him much.

Checking the time, he tore open the envelope.

He smiled at her descriptions of what it was like living with her older sister, Lorena, and at how she accused his aunt of limiting the number of cookies she ate after dinner to two, though his mother had made them herself. She described how the wind blew louder in North Carolina than in Nashville, and contained a funny odor. And how the women at church were ignorant of appropriate hat attire and how ostrich feathers would never go out of fashion, no matter what the preacher's wife said.

He shook his head. *Oh, Mother . . .*

He knew to take her descriptions and divide their seriousness by half, if not more. His mother had always been given to exaggeration and moments of eccentricity, but following his father's death, those tendencies had greatly worsened. He read on . . .

Then suddenly came to his feet. "No," he whispered, reading the last sentences to himself aloud. " 'So I have told Lorena that if she dares look at me again in that insolent fashion, I shall move back to Nashville straightaway. If you have not yet finished rebuilding our new house, then I shall beg shelter from Mrs. Acklen. As you know, she and I were once the dearest and best of friends, and I am certain she would welcome me to her bosom with great sisterly affection and kindness. With all my love, dearest Willister, Mother.' "

He groaned and dropped back into his chair.

His mother—God love her, and so did he—had almost driven Mrs. Acklen to drink the short time she had visited before. And Mrs. Acklen customarily abstained from alcohol. The two women never had been close. They'd hardly known one another. It was his father who had known the Acklens and who had spoken of them at dinner so often, which is where he guessed his mother was somehow forming the opinion that she and Adelicia were friends.

But that, too, was a figment of his mother's innocent, but overwrought, imagination.

Sutton checked the date on the letter written almost a week ago. He reached for pen and paper and authored a kind but hurried reply.

An hour later, hoping his mother wasn't already on her way to Nashville, Sutton stood in line at the post office. He handed the clerk his letter and she handed him an envelope.

"This just arrived for you, Mr. Monroe."

"Thank you, Mrs. Prescott." He checked the return address—New Orleans. *Finally* . . . But he didn't want to read the contents in a crowded lobby. He slipped the envelope inside the pocket of his suit coat.

He started down the street toward the law office, where he'd left the carriage, then paused for a moment, contemplating what he'd been thinking about doing for some time now. Everything he owned, or had once owned, rested on the review board's decision, and he was weary of waiting. Of lying awake at night and wondering, worrying.

Jaw clenched tight, he turned and strode toward Colonel Wilmington's office.

The New Orleans hand stamp on the envelope in his suit pocket, along with the name included in the return address, left no question about the contents. The only question . . . Was he prepared to learn his colleague's findings about Claire?

When he reached the end of the street, he turned right and kept walking. He and Adelicia had done the right thing in requesting the report. Still, he felt as if he'd gone behind Claire's back to do it. Especially after their time together on the ridge.

To say he was *taken with* her was putting it lightly. Earlier that morning, when the LeVerts were leaving, and she'd raised that haughty little eyebrow at him. . . .

He smiled to himself, certain the woman had no idea what effect she had on him. Which was a good thing. Especially considering that his primary obligation in this instance—understanding they were both Mrs. Acklen's employees—was to Adelicia, and to protecting her interests.

He thought of the contents of the envelope again.

Whether Claire was aware of it or not, of all the employees who worked at Belmont, she was in a position to do Adelicia the most harm. As Adelicia's liaison, Claire was privy to information—both personal and business—that no one else was. Besides him. And Claire had the added insight of reading and responding to Adelicia's private and social correspondence, as well as managing her personal calendar.

But most importantly, she had won Adelicia's trust. Completely. That had been clear to him today. What had also been clear was that Adelicia's motivation behind hosting the upcoming reception was twofold.

He didn't doubt Adelicia's sincere desire to honor Madame LeVert. But he had an inkling of how the woman's mind worked. Octavia LeVert was the most beloved belle in all of Dixie, and Adelicia's own reputation had suffered in the past couple of years. First due to the cotton fiasco, then when news of her European travels became widespread. And having the mansion redecorated while on the trip hadn't helped matters either.

He slowed his steps as he approached the next intersection. He waited for a carriage to pass, then continued on to the left. What concerned him most was that while Adelicia was working to repair her reputation—utilizing Claire's skills to accomplish that—Claire was, in turn, hoping to benefit from Adelicia's *fine standing* in the community to achieve her personal goals. Each woman was, in effect, using the other.

And here he was, wedged right in the middle of them both. He glanced up.

The government building loomed ahead, appearing more ominous than the last time he'd visited—the only other time. His stomach knotted.

Inside, the lobby bustled with employees and patrons, the air stagnant and stale. Sutton made his way to the staircase and to the second floor. He approached Colonel Wilmington's secretary, certain she wouldn't remem—

"Mr. Monroe." She smiled. "You're back."

Sutton cleared his throat, surprised. "Yes, ma'am, I am. And I'd like to see Colonel Wilmington, if he's available."

"He's in his office, Mr. Monroe, but . . ." She glanced behind her at a closed door that bore a placard with the colonel's name. "He's with someone right now. Would you like to wait? It shouldn't be too long."

With everything in him, he wanted to leave. "Yes, ma'am. I'll wait."

"May I inquire as to what you're seeing the Colonel about?"

"A legal matter. I'm . . . with *Holbrook and Wickliffe*." Which he was, in a way. Just not in relation to this particular visit.

He declined the secretary's offer of coffee or tea and took a seat. His mind raced even as his heart beat heavy and sluggish in his chest.

Ten minutes passed, then twenty.

Becoming more tense by the second and needing to occupy his mind, he pulled the envelope from his pocket and opened it. If there was something he needed to know about Claire, he decided he wanted to know sooner rather than later. For Adelicia's sake, as well as his own.

The report, written in letter style, was surprisingly brief for having taken so long to compile. He scanned it. Claire's parents, Gustave and Abella Laurent, were originally from France. He'd already known that. About two years ago, they'd moved to New Orleans and had operated a local—he frowned—art gallery.

An art gallery . . . That was something he hadn't known. And that Claire had failed to mention. He read on. . . .

The gallery was occupied by a gift shop now, the building space having only been leased by the Laurents. The gallery had been one of "lesser consequence," the report read. Sutton would check with his colleague to be sure, but he guessed that meant it had associated with lesser-known artists, a fact which would have limited Gustave Laurent's ability to trade stock with the larger galleries, as Sutton had recently learned while preparing for the upcoming trial.

But her association with the art gallery explained where Claire had learned how to paint. At least in part. Her mother, Bella Laurent, died of tuberculosis eight months ago. Claire had told him that.

And—Sutton smiled to himself—Bella Laurent had been an artist. *Of course she had.* Another reason why Claire was so gifted. Gustave Laurent died of—Sutton stumbled over the next words—"an injury resulting from a knife wound sustained during a robbery." And the robbery of the gallery, no less.

Claire definitely hadn't mentioned either of those facts.

He'd never asked her about how her father had died, so she hadn't purposefully hidden anything from him. Still, that seemed like a detail one might mention. Then again, when people inquired about his father, did he willingly offer the details surrounding his death?

Swiftly laying that question to rest, Sutton retraced his memory about Claire's arrival at Belmont.

She arrived around the second week of September, which was about when her father had died, according to the report. And which also coincided with what she'd told them. She'd been forthcoming about her father's death during the interview, and about his death being unexpected too.

He mulled that over, reading on through the last paragraph.

Claire had attended boarding school for several years. His colleague had actually traveled to the most recently attended school to speak with the headmistress. The woman had described Claire as "a quiet, shy sort of girl, exceptionally gifted in the arts but lacking in self-confidence." He couldn't believe it. That was exactly what Adelicia had said about Claire following their first meeting. "*It's belief in herself that she lacks.*"

That didn't seem to fit the Claire he knew now, and yet . . .

Upon first meeting her, he might have described her in terms somewhat similar to those. He turned the page over, but that was the end of the report. It definitely left some loose ends that needed tying up. But his biggest concern was, why would Claire have failed to say anything about her parents owning an art gallery?

He scanned the report again, his attention snagging on a possibility. *Of lesser consequence* . . . Perhaps in light of Belmont's elegance and Adelicia's own extensive art collection, she'd been ashamed to reveal her own lesser connection with art. That possibility fit with her behavior the evening he'd inquired about the dinner with the Worthingtons, but still . . .

A pang of guilt hit him, and he stared at the letter in his hand.

If he were going to be completely forthcoming with Claire, he would need to tell her about inquiring into her background. Not that other employees had been told. But this was different. Claire wasn't like any other employee. But surely she would understand. It was his job, after all. He'd made it clear to her from the very beginning that part of his responsibilities at Belmont centered around protecting Adelicia's interests. But . . .

That was before they'd grown as close as they had, and before he'd kissed her. The mere memory of that kiss riled emotions that sent heat skimming to his collar.

Corralling his thoughts, he mentally circled the parts of the letter that needed further answers—if only to satisfy his own curiosity—but decided that nothing within the report's contents even came close to confirming Mrs. Routh's suspicions about Claire. So the chances of Claire Laurent absconding with *Ruth Gleaning* during the dark of night still remained in the category of humorous.

He checked his pocket watch and had all but decided to leave when the office door opened. A man exited, nodding to the secretary as he left.

The secretary rose and held up a hand, indicating to Sutton to please continue waiting. She stepped inside the colonel's office and returned a moment later, looking at him, and yet not, at the same time. "Colonel Wilmington will see you now, Mr. Monroe."

Sutton knew it could be his imagination, but he got the feeling she knew something about him now that she hadn't only seconds before.

Each step forced, he walked into the colonel's office.

"Mr. Monroe." Colonel Wilmington met him a few steps inside the office. He gave a short nod, arm extended. "I'm Colonel Wilmington, and I can guess why you're here, sir."

Gripping the man's hand, Sutton thought of something his father had told him when he was still a boy. "*It's not just how firm a man's handshake is that defines him, son. Any fool can have a strong grip. It's the way a man meets your eyes, or doesn't, that tells you who he is. That says whether he's dealing with you honestly or not.*"

And the earnestness in the colonel's face, the solid grip of his fingers that hung on to Sutton's just a tad too long, hinting at reluctance and regret, told Sutton everything he didn't want to know.

35

Claire climbed the staircase leading from the grand salon to the second floor, one eye focused on the heavy silver service weighting the tray in her hands, the other on her footing on the plush red carpet. And all beneath Queen Victoria's regal gaze.

Halfway up, where the staircase divided and branched to the left and right, the portrait of England's monarch loomed larger than life, as though the queen herself were waiting to see which direction Claire would choose. Claire wished she could stop and examine the painting. She'd never seen it up close before. But the tea service grew heavier by the second, and Mrs. Acklen was waiting.

The split staircases were works of art in themselves—rich mahogany woodwork and intricately carved white spindles. Twin alcoves tucked into the curve of the walls, one on either side, boasted a marble bust of a man, and the other, a vase of freshly cut shrub roses.

Choosing the left staircase, she continued to the second-floor gallery and found it quiet. Rows of narrow rectangular windows below the ceiling line ran the length of the gallery, allowing ample sunlight. Another staircase, smaller, continued upward. To the cupola, she guessed. Oh, how she would love to go up there too. She could only imagine the view . . .

But would be able to imagine it a lot better if her arms weren't *aching*!

She carefully lowered the tray onto a side table, mindful to keep it level. No wonder Cordina had eyed her when she'd volunteered to carry the tray up herself. The heavy silver teapot, filled to the brim with steaming water, probably weighed ten pounds by itself. Not to mention the tray, the cups and saucers, sugar and milk, and the plateful of fresh tea cakes.

Looking both ways, making sure the hallway was empty, Claire popped one of the tea cakes into her mouth. Not a very ladylike thing to do, but oh . . . Cordina's tea cakes were delectable. Tiny little cakelike cookies covered in powdered sugar. Like Southern beignets. How the woman managed to get them so moist and all the same—

"May I help you, Miss Laurent?"

Nearly choking, Claire turned.

Standing in a doorway a short distance down the hall was Mrs. Routh. Claire would've sworn the woman could walk through walls. Frantically chewing, her cheeks packed, she held up a forefinger, embarrassed, trying to swallow, wishing for tea but knowing if she stopped to pour herself a cup that would only make matters worse.

Finally, she managed to choke down the cake. "Mrs. Routh . . ." Breathing as if she'd run a footrace, she wiped the corners of her mouth, aware of the suspicion in Mrs. Routh's stare. "Mrs. Acklen requested that I meet her in her personal quarters, and"—Claire glanced around—"I was just looking for her bedroom."

"Really?" Mrs. Routh closed the distance between them. "Because it appeared as though you were consuming a tea cake, Miss Laurent."

Instinctively, Claire started to apologize, then caught herself. She had done absolutely nothing wrong. *Why* did she always kowtow to this woman? But she knew why—because she didn't have the courage to stand up to her. Like the sliding of a bolt into a latch, something shifted inside her.

She squared her shoulders and her gaze. "Mrs. Acklen *requested* that I meet her in her private quarters, Mrs. Routh. I offered to bring her tea, and yes, I helped myself to a tea cake just now. Which, I am certain, is not a sin." Claire blinked, not believing she'd actually said the words aloud. And without a single stutter. More than a little proud, she tried not to show it.

Mrs. Routh stared, her expression revealing nothing. "Your flippancy, while not at all surprising to me, Miss Laurent, is not the least bit becoming." She spoke softly, evenly, not a hint of sarcasm in her voice. "Especially when considering your *position* here at Belmont."

Hearing that one word, Claire's briefly lived pride faded, and the words she feared would haunt her for as long as she worked for Mrs. Acklen returned. "*You are an extension of me. . . .*"

Feeling as though she'd faced a test and failed miserably, she bowed her head. She was weary of these tense, abbreviated exchanges with Belmont's head housekeeper, and she knew that if she didn't do this now, she would lose her nerve. "Mrs. Routh, I realize that from the first time we met, your estimation of me has been less than stellar. You've been brutally honest in conveying that to me, on a near daily basis. But I've done my best since coming to Belmont. I work hard. Every day. I perform every task Mrs. Acklen asks of me, and then look for ways to help her more. Yet you seem determined to think the worst of me, and"—a traitorous sting of emotion burned her eyes—"for the life of me, I don't know why."

Mrs. Routh's eyes fluttered closed, and she sighed, as though tired of their conversations too. "I'm well aware of the job you're doing for Mrs. Acklen. And contrary to what you may believe, Miss Laurent, I do not *seek* to think the worst of you. I simply do not trust you."

Feeling as if the floor had disappeared beneath her, Claire searched Mrs. Routh's face. "But I . . ." She exhaled. "Why? I don't underst—"

A door squeaked opened in the hallway behind her. Soft footsteps . . .

"Ah . . . there you are, Miss Laurent," Mrs. Acklen said. "I was beginning to wonder. Oh, good, you brought our tea. Good afternoon to you, Mrs. Routh."

Mrs. Routh looked past Claire. "Good afternoon, Mrs. Acklen. You're looking more rested, ma'am. Is there anything I can get you or that I can do to . . ."

As the two women spoke, Claire turned to pick up the tray, sensing a fierce loyalty in Mrs. Routh's manner and in the way she addressed Mrs. Acklen. And the discovery shed new light on the confrontation of moments earlier. Mrs. Routh was like a mama bear protecting her cub. Which, while sweet, in a way, was also amusing. Adelicia Acklen was hardly a defenseless cub. She was an assertive, powerful woman of enormous wealth and far-reaching influence.

From what, or whom, could she possibly need protection?

Crossing the threshold into Mrs. Acklen's private quarters was like stepping into another world. Claire deposited the tray on the table Mrs. Acklen indicated, unable to keep from staring at her surroundings.

She felt as though she'd walked into a land of make-believe, of far-off places and ancient times—and she didn't know where to look first. From baseboard to crown molding, two murals flowed from scene to scene to scene around the room, separated by a decorative chair rail. Every inch of wall space in the spacious room was covered.

Brilliant blues and reds and mossy greens enhanced the renderings of scenes from a story Claire knew only too well.

"It's not your customary decor," Mrs. Acklen said. "But I like it. It's from—"

"*Les Aventures de Télémaque,*" Claire whispered.

"*Oui, mademoiselle! Très bonne!*" Surprise lit Mrs. Acklen's expression. "I wondered if you might recognize it. You've read the novel, then?"

"A number of times. It was a favorite of my *maman*. And mine." Along with everyone else in France, and the greater part of Europe. And apparently America.

Mrs. Acklen poured a cup of tea for Claire and then for herself. "This very wallpaper hangs in the Hermitage, the late President Andrew Jackson's home not far from here."

Claire nodded, finding the rendering of a temple in the mural—specifically the rows of Corinthian columns situated along its front—strangely reminiscent of Belmont. She turned slowly, looking at the scenes. "Remarkable," she whispered, speaking not only of the mural, but also of the room itself.

A bed of gleaming rosewood in a style reminiscent of a sleigh set the tone for the bedroom, and the matching side tables, bureau, and wardrobe only enhanced the beauty, as did the marble fireplace and gilded mirror hanging above. Velvet draperies framed the windows, and the patterned wall-to-wall carpet—Claire blinked—was almost dizzying.

"Shall we begin, Miss Laurent? We have much to do." Mrs. Acklen nodded toward hatboxes stacked in the corner. Seven boxes in all, various sizes, dusty from disuse. "Move them over here, if you would. Closer to the windows."

Claire did as she bade, discovering the boxes were heavier than she'd imagined. She followed Mrs. Acklen's lead and opened one, and found it full to the brim with what appeared to be newspaper clippings. Same as the box Mrs. Acklen had opened.

After a brief discussion they decided that Claire would begin organizing the articles by newspaper first, and Mrs. Acklen would follow behind to review them and decide which ones to include in Madame LeVert's memory book.

Claire briefly scanned the articles as she sorted, not wanting to appear as if she were trying to read them. Which of course, she was. But she didn't want Mrs. Acklen to think she was prying. Which was a little comical, because, after all, what she was reading had been published in a newspaper.

Many of the clippings were from the local *Republican Banner* and the *Union and American*. But there were also articles from the *New York Herald* and the *New Orleans Picayune*, as well as papers from Atlanta, Mobile, and even Paris, Rome, and London.

They worked through the afternoon, falling into a quiet rhythm, only commenting on occasion.

The other boxes contained cards and letters, not only those from Madame LeVert to Mrs. Acklen but from other family members as well. Hundreds of them—perhaps more. Some bundled with ribbon and string, but apparently—like the clippings—grouped with no apparent attention to date or year. As thorough as Mrs. Acklen was in other areas of her life, her correspondence, while painfully plentiful, lacked proper organization.

Amidst the boxes of letters and cards were party invitations and wedding and funeral announcements. Claire quickly grew familiar with the various family members' handwriting and could fairly well place the author of any given missive based solely on the handwriting on the front of the envelope.

"I believe, Miss Laurent"—Mrs. Acklen rubbed the back of her neck, then covered her mouth when she yawned—"that we have additional folders available in the library. If not, Mr. Monroe has a supply in the art gallery. Which reminds me . . ."

Claire sensed another project on the horizon.

"I've been meaning to speak to you about the art gallery."

Claire stopped sorting the letters in her hand and offered her full attention.

"I've never had all the art at Belmont—both in the house and the art gallery—properly cataloged. Mr. Monroe's been after me to do that for some time, but"—Mrs. Acklen rubbed her temples, squinting—"I never seem to make it a priority. However, with your assistance . . ." She lowered her head into her hands.

"Mrs. Acklen, are you all right?"

She didn't look up. "I'm fine. This happens on occasion."

"This?"

"An ache in my head." She sighed. "It starts here"—she rubbed the front of her forehead—"and then continues to the back."

Claire winced. "Too much reading, perhaps?"

"Dr. Denard refers to it as neuralgia." She slowly raised her head. Her eyes appeared fatigued, and she kept squinting, as if the late-afternoon light, though soft in the room, was painful. "Miss Laurent, would you please take all this to your room and finish there? I think we have enough for Madame LeVert's book, don't you?"

"Yes, ma'am. More than enough." Claire rose and gathered the numerous stacks sitting about the room, careful not to mix them as she placed them in the boxes and carried them into the hallway. "Is there anything I can get you, ma'am . . . before I leave?"

Mrs. Acklen had moved to the bed and lain down. "I have some powders Dr. Denard left for me. They're in a bowl on my dressing table, right through there."

Claire opened a door into what she might have called a closet, if not for the room's ample size. Gowns and trunks abounded. She crossed to the dressing table and spotted a crystal bowl containing folded medicinal papers, similar to those that had packaged her mother's medicine. She withdrew a translucent sleeve from the batch and felt the slight bulge of powder within.

Careful to keep it level, she'd turned to go when a portrait on the wall stopped her in her tracks.

36

Three angelic faces stared back at Claire, their soft expressions so sweet, so full of hope and promise. Dressed all in white and with the same dark hair, the girls shared the identical shade of chocolate brown eyes. Similar smiles tipped their rosy little lips and lit a kindred spark of mischief in their precious heart-shaped faces. There was no question in Claire's mind.

Sisters.

As if prompted by some unseen hand, Claire looked back at the doorway leading to the bedroom, then slowly to the painting again, and a knifelike pain stabbed her chest. She placed a hand over her heart as memory forced her back to the day she and Mrs. Acklen had gone riding. Bits and pieces of their conversations returned on a terrible wave. "*You don't believe I know what it feels like to lose a parent at your age. And you resent my insinuation that I do.*"

Claire squeezed her eyes tight, recalling her own bitter, self-centered response to Mrs. Acklen's statement, her all-too-clear insinuation that Mrs. Acklen didn't understand the depth of her loss. How Mrs. Acklen had looked at her . . . Claire sensed she'd wanted to say something else that day, but now she *knew* it with certainty.

Because she was staring at what Mrs. Acklen hadn't said.

That in addition to losing her father and husband, Mrs. Acklen had lost two daughters as well, leaving pretty little Pauline as the only girl. Death was no respecter of age, Claire knew. Children died. Parents died. Loss was all too commonplace, especially these days. Until it happened to you. And then it was different.

For some reason, she'd simply assumed that Mrs. Acklen's wealth had insulated her from loss.

She moved closer to the portrait, close enough to see the brushstrokes of oil paints on canvas. *Masterful,* how tiny little dots of color—artful smears blended with the bristles of a brush—once combined, could evoke such powerful emotion. And such powerful regret.

"Miss Laurent . . . did you find the powders?"

"Yes, ma'am," Claire answered quickly. "I have one right here."

She kept her eyes averted as she retrieved Mrs. Acklen's teacup and filled it halfway with tepid water from the teapot. She added the powder and stirred until the granules dissolved. She assisted Mrs. Acklen as she drank, the scene feeling all too familiar for her.

Mrs. Acklen reclined on a bolster of pillows. "Is something wrong, Miss Laurent?"

Claire shook her head. "No, ma'am. Nothing's wrong."

Lines furrowed Mrs. Acklen's brow. "Your *maman*?" she whispered, a trace of question in her voice.

Knowing that was only part of her struggle, Claire nodded.

"I'm *so* sorry for your loss, Miss Laurent."

Claire bit her lip again, trying to stave off words that seemed to have a life of their own. "I'm sorry too . . ." She glanced briefly toward the closet, unable to get the image of the angelic faces from her mind. "About your daughters."

Mrs. Acklen's expression clouded briefly. "Ah . . ." She sighed. "The portrait."

Claire exhaled a shaky breath. "And I'm sorry I said what I did to you . . . that day we went riding. The way I acted . . ." She shook her head. "I didn't know," she whispered, tears rising. "I just didn't know."

Mrs. Acklen's own eyes glistened. "It's all right, Miss Laurent. It was a long time ago."

Claire nodded once, then thought of Pauline. "But not so long. Pauline's not that old."

Mrs. Acklen briefly closed her eyes. "Pauline isn't in that portrait, Miss Laurent. The painting is of my daughters Victoria . . . Adelicia . . . and Emma." It seemed as if the very act of speaking their names was painful. "The portrait was painted over twenty years ago." She managed a tremulous smile. "Before you were even born. But granted, there are days"—she took a sharp breath—"when those years feel like mere moments."

Claire stared. *Three* daughters. All passed. "They were so beautiful."

"And they were angels, all of them. Victoria was six and Adelicia four, when they died. Three days apart. From bronchitis and croup. Emma was only a year and a half old at the time." Mrs. Acklen briefly closed her eyes, and Claire wondered if it was the medicine taking effect, or if it was the wash of memories. "Emma died from diphtheria nine years later."

"You must have grieved for them so. And your husband . . ."

Mrs. Acklen looked over at her. "Yes, Joseph grieved with me. He loved Emma, very much. And Emma loved him. But he wasn't her father, nor was he Victoria's or Adelicia's." She gestured to a side table.

Claire picked up the framed miniature painting of an older man. A man she didn't recognize and who certainly wasn't the same man as in the portrait in the entrance hall.

"That was my first husband, Isaac Franklin. We married when I was twenty-two." She reached for the photograph and smoothed her fingertips over the frame. "We were quite the talk at the time. He was twenty-eight years my senior."

Claire quickly did the math.

"We had four beautiful children together, and seven wonderful years. Our third child, a son, lived only a few hours." She gazed at Mr. Franklin's face, a quiet, distant love in her expression. "Mr. Franklin passed away . . . six weeks *before* Victoria and Adelicia died."

Claire tried to think of something suitable to say. But everything fell so far short of the weight of loss.

"Oftentimes, through the years, Miss Laurent . . ." Mrs. Acklen's voice was barely a whisper now. "I've pondered how much is provided for us by God's goodness. So many sources of enjoyment, and how thankful we should be. And even if afflictions come . . . we should know that they are of the hand of God." She sighed, the semblance of a smile gracing the edges of her mouth. "We should not expect to have all the blessings of life and none of its trials. It would make this world too delightful a dwelling place, and I fear we would never care to leave it." Her eyes slipped closed. "As it is . . . I have come to believe that it's only by taking some of those objects from us to which our hearts so closely cling that He endeavors . . . in His kindness, to draw us from this world to one of greater happiness."

Claire sat perfectly still, not daring to make the slightest sound, feeling as if a veil had been lifted ever so briefly between her and this woman. And she feared the slightest movement or merest breath would dispel the solemnity of the moment.

The silence lengthened and finally Mrs. Acklen opened her eyes and returned the framed daguerreotype.

Claire set it back in its place on the side table and helped situate the pillows behind Mrs. Acklen's head. "Is there anything else I can get you before I leave, ma'am?"

Mrs. Acklen gave the tiniest shake of her head, her eyes closing again.

Claire had all but shut the door when Mrs. Acklen whispered her name.

Claire peered back inside, the creak of the door overloud in the quiet.

"Thank you, Miss Laurent, for allowing me . . . to remember."

That evening, Claire arrived a few minutes late for dinner. She'd lost track of time reading through a few more of the newspaper articles, and contemplating what Mrs. Acklen had said. She paused inside the family dining room, finding the table empty . . . but for one place setting.

A fire burned low in the hearth, its woodsy smell lending the room a cozy feel. Wondering if she'd missed some special instruction, Claire took her seat and draped her napkin across her lap.

Scarcely a minute later, Cordina bustled up the stairs from the kitchen carrying a covered plate and a tall glass of lemonade, filled with ice, as usual. "Evenin', Miss Laurent." Her smile ever present, she gave Claire a wink. "From what I hear, ma'am, you's the only one eatin' in here tonight. Gots it all to yourself."

Claire glanced at the empty chairs. "Where is everyone else?"

Cordina set the plate, piled high with food enough for two, before her. "The Lady's feelin' poorly, as you already know. Them head pains she gets from time to time. And Miss Cenas and the children, they's gone into town for dinner. Special treat for the younguns since they's doin' good in their studies, Miss Cenas said." Cordina gestured to Claire's plate. "You want some of my squash relish tonight, ma'am? I run fetch it for you. It be good with them pork chops."

Not overly hungry, Claire shook her head. "No, thank you. This will be more than enough." She tried for a casual tone. "By chance, do you know where Mr. Monroe is?"

"No, ma'am. I haven't seen him since breakfast. Mrs. Routh just said you'd be the only one eatin'. You can come on down to the kitchen, if you want. But I gots to warn you, we been bakin' bread all day and it's hot as blazes down there tonight."

Claire returned her smile. "I think I'll stay here, if that's all right."

"Sure it is, honey." Cordina patted her shoulder. "Might be kinda nice just to sit and enjoy the quiet. You ring that bell there if you need somethin'. I'll hear you and come right up."

Knowing she'd never use the bell, Claire nodded. "Thank you, Cordina."

She ate a bite of pork chop with mashed potatoes, then tasted Cordina's sweet creamed peas and corn, and by the time she took her first sip of lemonade, her appetite had returned. Still, she couldn't finish half of the food on her plate.

The fire in the hearth crackled and popped, and the clock on the mantel ticked off the seconds. Claire drank in the solitude—until her thirst for silence was slaked, and then some. She carried her plate and glass downstairs to the kitchen, smelling the yeasty aroma of fresh bread even before she pushed open the door.

"Good evening, Miss Laurent!" Eli greeted her by taking her plate. And when he reached for her glass, Claire playfully held it back from him.

"I'll only give it to you if I can have some more of your wife's lemonade. If there's enough to spare."

He grinned, glancing across the kitchen at his wife, who was visiting with three other women. "We always have sweet lemonade at the ready, Miss Laurent. Mrs. Acklen's orders." He leaned closer. "And my dear wife's as well."

Claire grinned. Surprised as she'd been when learning that Eli and Cordina were married, now that she'd gotten to know them better, she couldn't imagine them apart.

He returned with her glass filled, his shaved head boasting a sheen of sweat. True to Cordina's word, the kitchen was overly warm. Claire thanked him and took a good long drink, then gestured to the crusted loaves lining the wooden tables. Enough for a small army. "What's all this for?"

"It's going to an orphanage across town. Mrs. Acklen provides food for the children there every month. Cordina suggested we take some of her bread with us this time, and Mrs. Acklen was pleased with the idea."

An orphanage. Claire couldn't remember Mrs. Acklen ever mentioning anything about an orphanage. And before this afternoon, she would've said she knew her employer quite well.

She retreated back upstairs and outside to the front gardens, where she was greeted by a late October breeze—cool, but not chilling—and she welcomed it after the heat of the kitchen. The leaves on the maples atop the hills were turning. Within days the foliage would be ablaze with color. She thought of her newly arrived canvases and tubes of paint in her room, and her right hand itched to hold a paintbrush again. *Soon* . . .

She walked down the hill as far as the third tiered garden, and paused to look back, picturing the evening of the LeVert reception with over a thousand people arriving in all their finery, milling about the gardens and grounds before crowding into the grand salon and other rooms. The event would begin at eight in the evening. They'd decided that much, at least. And though a waning yellow sun still hovered over the countryside this evening, she knew it would be a different story come mid-December.

She continued on downhill, wishing now that she'd brought a wrap, but not enough to turn back.

In her mind's eye, she could see lanterns draped at even intervals along the curving road toward the mansion, golden light blanketing the path, welcoming visitors. And perhaps a brass ensemble situated in the gazebo nearest the house so that guests would arrive amidst the melodies of chamber music and—

She spotted a rider coming up the road. Not needing to look twice, she walked to the edge of the path to greet him.

"Finally," she said, smiling up as Sutton reined in beside her. "The prodigal has returned." She'd been waiting all week to use the term she'd learned from Reverend Bunting's sermon last Sunday.

"Good evening, Claire."

Good evening, Claire? That was hardly the teasing response she'd hoped for. And so formal. She noted the firm set of his jaw, despite the coerced smile, and his eyes lacked their usual warmth. "Is everything all right, Sutton?"

He looked away. “Yes, it’s just been a long day.”

She stepped closer. “If you’d like dinner, I’d be happy to fix you a plate and bring it to the—”

“No . . . thank you. I ate in town.”

“Oh . . .” She nodded. “Good.” The breeze that had brought cooling relief moments earlier gave her a chill now, and she rubbed her arms.

He gestured behind him. “A statue Mrs. Acklen ordered while in Europe arrived today. A wagon is bringing it right behind me.”

A statue! Claire peered down the road, seeing no wagon yet. And in light of Sutton’s present mood, she tried not to appear too excited. “Who is the sculptor?”

He eyed her, then laughed, a sharp, humorless sound. “Nice attempt at indifference, but unconvincing.”

She made a pouting face. “I’m sorry. But I love statues, and paintings, and . . . all of that.”

“I know,” he said quietly. “I know you do.”

His melancholy tone stirred her concern. “Are you sure you’re all right?”

The distant squeak of wooden wheels on hard-packed dirt announced the wagon’s arrival.

Truxton whinnied and pranced, but Sutton held the stallion steady. “I need to unlock the gallery so the men can carry the crate inside. I’m not sure where Mrs. Acklen wants this one. I haven’t even told her it’s arrived.”

Claire nodded, wanting to go with him. But if he wanted her company, he would invite her. Which, at the moment, seemed doubtful. She smiled and stepped back off the road.

But Sutton didn’t move. Holding Truxton in check, he looked down at her and sighed. “Would you like to come along?”

Hardly the invitation she’d hoped for . . . Claire started to decline, but she’d been looking forward to seeing him all day. And it *was* an invitation, however wanting. “I’d love to!”

He scooted back in the saddle, removed his boot from the stirrup and reached down for her. Claire slid her foot into the stirrup and gripped his arm. He lifted her up beside him and held her steady as she situated her dress over her lacy underskirts.

With his solid chest at her back and his arm around her waist, she kept her balance, even when he urged Truxton to a canter. The stallion moved with grace and power that was almost heady. What would it be like to fly across open fields on this animal? Much less over a fence? She could hardly wait for Sutton to teach her how to jump.

As they drew closer to the art gallery, Sutton slowed the stallion's gait, and withdrew his arm from around her waist.

She glanced back. "Are we still having my first jumping lesson this weekend?"

His delayed response caused her hopes to slip.

"I . . . won't be able to keep our appointment this weekend, I'm sorry. Maybe there'll be time next week, or . . . sometime soon."

She kept her focus forward, glad he couldn't see her face. "I understand. And actually"—she was determined to sound convincing—"that works out better for my schedule too. I have a lot of work to do with Mrs. Acklen on the reception. A lot of planning with the menus and flowers and invitations."

Sutton reined in behind the gallery but didn't dismount.

She felt his warm breath on the back of her neck, and the longer they sat there—not speaking—the more aware she became of him behind her. She felt something on her waist and looked down. His hand . . .

His fingers gently tightened on the curve of her hip, and Claire closed her eyes, her pulse edging up a notch. Slowly, his hand moved up her side, to her back, tenderly, as if tracing its course, memorizing as it went. She could feel the warmth of his palm through her dress.

"Claire," he whispered, "I . . ."

She shivered and leaned back into him, certain the air had grown thinner. Being this close to him brought a distinct kind of pleasure. And longing. Especially remembering his kiss. The way he'd held her.

His hand stilled on her back, then was gone, and her skin suddenly felt cool at its absence. Only then did she see the wagon circling around the back of the building.

Wordlessly, he dismounted, assisted her with the same, looped Truxton's reins at the post, and went to unlock the gallery.

37

"Thank you, gentlemen." Sutton shook the workers' hands, pressing a gratuity into each of their palms in the process. "I appreciate your careful attention to the freight."

They thanked him for his generosity as they left the gallery.

Watching by the door, Sutton waited for the wagon to round the corner of the building, then returned to the storage room. This statue was one Adelicia was especially partial to and had been waiting impatiently for. He was no connoisseur of art, but in his opinion, the piece was the most exquisite of her collection. And not only because of the statue's personal meaning for her.

He reached the doorway of the storage room . . . and paused to take in the view.

Claire was on her hands and knees, peeking through the slats of the crate, apparently still trying to determine the sculptor, and all of this while being remarkably unaware of his presence.

He wanted so badly to say something aloud that would make her jump. Yet the delight he got from watching her far outweighed his desire for the other. Her single-mindedness was intriguing. Everything about her was intriguing. He had half a mind to walk across the room and take her in his arms again.

Why, after the news he'd gotten from Colonel Wilmington, had he thought about Claire nearly every other minute? And not just thought about her. But *thought* about her. About holding her again, about the softness of her mouth, and about how her laughter—spontaneous and rich—had the power to draw him in like no other.

Moments earlier, he'd come close to kissing one luscious-looking little place on her neck but knew she would've knocked him off the horse if he did. And rightly so. But looking at her now, at her shapely little *derrière* stuck up in the air—he shook his head—it would've been worth the fall.

His humor faded as he realized she'd done it again—lifted his spirits, without even knowing it.

Colonel Wilmington had been compassionately direct in delivering the review board's verdict, which they'd arrived at late last evening. And in the course of five minutes, the man had not only stripped him of the land he should have inherited—land his grandfather had purchased and deeded to his father, and that his father would have deeded to him—but had forever tarnished the honor of his family name.

The official record of the incident, as submitted by the Federal captain and purportedly substantiated by soldiers with him that day, indicted his father as a traitor to his country. Sutton bowed his head. His father, one of the gentlest, kindest, most godly men he'd ever known. And all because his father had refused to sign a piece of paper.

And as Holbrook had informed early on, just or not, what the review board decided stood as law.

Sutton thought again of what Claire had said when he'd ridden up earlier. "*The prodigal has returned. . . .*" He guessed that was fitting, in a way. Because like the son in Scripture who returned home broken and empty-handed, so had he returned to Belmont. Only, his father hadn't been waiting to greet him.

But Claire had.

She sighed, drawing his attention back. She was still intent on her task.

"Drop something, Claire?"

She scrambled to her feet, her eyes wide. "How long have you been standing there?"

He managed a smile. "Not terribly long." Aware of her frown, he crossed to a workbench and retrieved a crowbar.

"Oh! We're going to open it tonight?" Her expression brightened, then just as quickly clouded. "But shouldn't we wait for Mrs. Acklen?"

Sutton fit the flat end of the crowbar beneath a board. "I always inspect the statues before she sees them. And usually before the freighters leave. But this one"—he applied pressure, and the board loosened with a crack—"is very special. Plus"—he repositioned the crowbar—"you're here."

She smiled, and Sutton felt an odd little tug in his chest.

The next few slats came off the top of the crate with little complaint. One by one, he removed them, then set the crowbar aside. They knelt and together began removing the straw and other packing materials that encased the statue. When he felt the cool of the smooth marble, he quietly held back and let her finish the job.

She was like a child at Christmas—a very reverent child—and the joy he received from watching her face was gift enough for him. She removed the last layer of straw and went perfectly still. He remembered well what he'd felt the first time he saw the statue of the two children. He was more interested in watching Claire see the statue for the first time.

Her lower lip trembled, and she put a hand to her mouth—exactly as Adelicia had done when she'd first seen it.

"It's entitled *Sleeping Children,*" he said softly, on his knees beside her. "By William Rinehart. Adelicia purchased it in Rome, in memory of her daughters."

Claire reached out her hand, then paused and looked over at him, as if asking for his permission. He nodded, and she cradled the smooth stone cheek of one of the children's faces.

She let out a breath. "It's one of the most beautiful things I've ever seen. They're so . . . lifelike."

Sculpted of white marble, the statue portrayed two children lying in sweet repose—*asleep in death,* Sutton remembered Rinehart telling them—and was so realistic in its detail. One of the infant's chubby little arms was lovingly draped across the other's chest, and their heads were propped on a pillow that—even chiseled from stone—bore the soft folds and texture of a pillow fashioned from satin. Same as the blanket covering the infants.

Claire covered the child's little hand that lay on the other one's chest. "Just today, Mrs. Acklen told me about Victoria, Adelicia, and Emma. And about the son she lost too." She sniffed. "Four children." She exhaled. "I can't imagine what that feels like."

Touched by her response, Sutton withdrew his handkerchief from his pocket and handed it to her. "This statue isn't in memory of those children, Claire."

She turned and looked at him, confusion in her expression.

"Joseph and Adelicia had twin girls. Born to them in"—he thought back, remembering he was around twelve at the time—"about fifty-two, I think . . . at Angola Plantation in Louisiana. The twins were just two years old when they died. Both from scarlet fever. And only a couple of weeks apart."

Remembering Adelicia's special request of the sculptor, Sutton leaned forward to see the front of the statue. And sure enough, there were the girls' first names. He pointed.

"Laura and Corinne," Claire whispered, running her finger over the engraving.

"And on the back—" He looked to be sure. "She asked him to inscribe 'Twin Sisters.' Which he did."

Claire moved to see, wiping moisture from her cheeks. "You said Mrs. Acklen doesn't know this has arrived yet."

"No, I haven't told her. I didn't know until after I left the—" He caught himself in time. "The office in town."

Claire nodded. "Do you know if she has a place in mind for it?"

"I have no idea."

"Well, I have one," she said softly, smoothing her palm over the *Sleeping Children* again. "Do you have a base built for this yet?"

He shook his head. "Why?"

"Because I'd like to do something special for Mrs. Acklen, Sutton. To show her my appreciation." She half laughed, half sighed. "I can't buy the woman anything she can't buy for herself a thousand times over."

Sutton understood that only too well.

"But I can do this for her, if you'll let me. All I need is a few days."

38

"Are you certain you have time for this?"

Hearing the excitement in Claire's voice, Sutton adjusted a stirrup to accommodate her stature, admiring the glimpse of her lovely calf before she smoothed her skirts. "I should be asking you that question. Seems you're as busy as I am these days, if not more so."

She shifted in the saddle. "I could hardly sleep last night for thinking about this!"

He'd been looking forward to their first lesson too, and had ridden out to the meadow late yesterday evening to set up various-sized stacks of logs. And this after telling Claire, not five days ago, that he wouldn't have time for a lesson this week, or anytime soon. He'd responded to her in a moment of frustration and had since apologized. Twice.

He needed this time with her. Conflict seemed to be hitting on all sides these days, and she helped to balance the parts of his life that were coming apart.

He hadn't told her about the review board's decision yet. He hadn't told anyone. Not even Bartholomew Holbrook. He knew he needed to, but he'd also needed time to accept this new reality. Not that he had a choice. The loss of his family's land had hit him harder than he thought it would.

In a way, it felt as if he were losing his father all over again. With the sadness and grief came renewed anger—and a profound sense of disappointment in himself.

He hadn't decided yet whether to tell her about the report from his colleague. Adelicia had read the findings and was satisfied—as was he—and said she saw no need to tell Claire about it. "This is a procedure that we insist every employee undergo, Mr. Monroe. We've not yet felt a need to tell an employee prior to this. Why should you feel a compulsion to do so now?"

The way Adelicia had looked at him, the smartness in her tone, had told him she knew—or at least suspected—about his feelings for Claire. He'd told her about his and Cara Netta's *decision* to rescind their understanding, and she'd been disappointed. But to Adelicia's credit, she hadn't broached the subject again.

"*Oh* . . . you're such a handsome fella," Claire cooed in a sultry voice.

Sutton looked up to see her stroking Truxton's neck and running her fingers through his mane. He exhaled. All that woman . . . wasted on a horse.

"All right, Captain Laurent. Just a few reminders . . ." Truxton whinnied and tossed his head, and Sutton held him by the bridle. "Truxton's experienced at jumping, so he already knows what to do. That's the beauty of learning to jump on a horse that's trained. But when they have a rider—"

"Like *moi,*" Claire said, grinning.

Sutton gave her a look that said to *please pay attention.* "Their training has taught them to follow your lead. So if you're unsure, the horse will be too." He checked her stirrups again, the image of her being thrown over that fence returning with striking clarity. She looked so tiny atop Truxton, and had insisted on riding sidesaddle. He understood but would've preferred that she jump astride.

"I want you to take this first jump"—he pointed to the shortest stack of logs, barely a foot high—"at an easy canter. Head out over there, like I showed you, and then come around. And remember to—"

"I know, Sutton. I was listening." With a tiny flick of the reins, she prompted Truxton to sidestep, then laughed. "He's so smart!"

Sutton gripped the reins. "If you want me to teach you, Claire, then you're going to have to *listen.*"

She looked down, the tiniest smirk on her face. "Yes, sir . . . Corporal."

Sutton wanted to yank her down and . . . He sighed. And do what, he didn't know. He just couldn't erase the image of her being thrown. He released the reins. "I simply don't want you to get hurt again."

"I know," she said softly. "I'll be careful. Now"—she smiled, the morning sun at her back setting her hair to shining—"what else did you want to tell me?"

"Just before you jump, make sure you give him as much rein as possible. Grab his mane or the neck strap if you need to. And keep your shoulders open. Don't lean down his neck." He looked back. "And *never* rein in, Claire. If you do, he'll stop short and you'll go flying. That's what happened with Athena."

She nodded, her expression attentive.

"And this may sound simple"—he smiled in hopes of lightening the mood—"but remember to breathe. Always look ahead. Never look down or to the side. That ruins your balance. Fix your gaze on something past the jump, not on it. Push your heels in hard too, just before he takes off. You'll feel the timing, I know you will." He ran a hand over Truxton's sinewy withers, willing his trusted mount to carry this lady well.

"Is there anything else?" Claire tossed him a flirty little gaze.

"Yes, ma'am, there is." He smacked Truxton solidly on the rump. "Enjoy the ride!"

With a grin, Claire flicked the reins and Truxton took off. Sutton watched as she circled wide just as he'd told her.

On Sunday following church, he'd overheard a group of ladies talking about "Miss Laurent." Claire was becoming quite the popular topic of discussion among the social elite. At least half a dozen women among Adelicia's peers had now hired their own personal liaisons. And at least that many men—all Adelicia's age, or older—had made discreet inquiries about Claire to Adelicia, having seen Claire in church or "having heard about her through various sources."

And whether *he* liked it or not—and he most certainly did not—the upcoming reception for Madame LeVert would be an unofficial *coming out,* as it were, for Claire. Her first introduction to Nashville's society. And though he knew she would shy away from the attention, if aware of it, he also had no doubt that she would shine.

Claire made the turn and leaned slightly forward, lining up with the jump, then urged Truxton to a canter.

"Keep your heels down," he whispered, feeling himself tense. *Eyes forward, straight ahead . . .* One of the hardest things about jumping was learning the horse's rhythm. Sometimes the jump came up faster than you thought.

Twelve feet away, eight . . .

Good girl . . .

Claire's hand disappeared into the mane, her body in perfect line.

Now give him the reins—

The second Sutton thought it, the reins went slack in Claire's hand, just as he'd taught her, and she and Truxton flew over the jump, clearing its height by a good two feet. Sutton heard Claire's laughter from where he stood.

"I did it!" She squealed as she rode up, her eyes sparkling.

He laughed. "Yes, you did. I'm so proud of you. You did everything perfectly." The sparkle in her eyes deepened, and it took him a few seconds to realize she was tearing up. "Claire . . ." He reached up and took her hand. "Is something wrong?"

"No . . . nothing's wrong. Everything's"—her fingers tightened around his—"very right." She exhaled a quick breath, her exuberance reviving. "May I try it again?"

"Will I be able to stop you?"

Her cloud of dust told him no.

Following dinner two evenings later, Sutton knocked on the door of the winter parlor. "Mrs. Acklen?"

"Please come in."

Seeing her seated on one of the two settees pulled him back to the day he'd entered the room to find her interviewing Claire. The memory brought a smile, as did thinking of what Claire had waiting for Mrs. Acklen in the entrance hall. "May I join you for a moment, ma'am?"

"Please do, Mr. Monroe." Adelicia laid aside the book she'd been reading. "I've been . . . reflecting."

He took a seat on the settee opposite her. "On?"

"Life, Mr. Monroe, and how it all fits together. And on why things happen the way they do. Or don't."

Sutton looked over at her, wondering if she'd heard about the review board's decision. Doubtful, seeing as he'd only discussed it with Bartholomew Holbrook, who had received the board's written notification yesterday. Sutton knew the senior attorney wouldn't reveal its contents until he gave the go-ahead.

He leaned back, trying to appear comfortable. "As soon as you piece it all together, Mrs. Acklen, would you please explain it to me?"

Her laughter was immediate. "You, and everyone else in the world."

He smiled, satisfied that she didn't know, yet knowing he needed to tell her. Soon. His losing his family's land wouldn't change her opinion of him or endanger his position at Belmont, however temporary that position may be should she decide to marry again. He also wasn't concerned about her offering him the money to start a thoroughbred farm. In the past two years, he'd helped Adelicia develop a method of weeding out which investments were sound and which were not. And according to his own criteria, his would definitely fall in the "were not" category.

Besides, he wanted, needed, to achieve his dream on his own.

The crackle of the fire in the hearth filled the silence. West-facing windows invited the last vestiges of a waning November sun peering around the corners of the art gallery. Fall had been ushered in, and Christmas and the New Year would arrive in a breath.

He rose. "Would you do me the honor, Mrs. Acklen, of accompanying me into the entrance hall?"

Her eyes narrowed, but she rose and slipped her hand into the crook of his arm.

Sutton paused in the grand salon, just before they reached the staircase. "The statue you've been waiting for arrived two days ago."

Question marked her expression. "It fared the journey well, I hope?"

"It did, ma'am." He glanced toward the entrance hall. "Miss Laurent was with me when I opened it." He covered Adelicia's hand on his arm. "Her response at first seeing it," he whispered, remembering, "was identical to your own."

Adelicia briefly closed her eyes, as though she were back in the sculptor's studio, halfway around the world. "Seeing that statue for the first time is a moment I'll never forget, Mr. Monroe. It felt as though God himself had carved it especially for me. Like a gift . . ." She sighed. "A tender reminder that He's holding my precious children . . . until I can hold them again too."

Sutton smiled, grateful Claire had insisted they wait until after dinner, when the house was quiet and the children were upstairs for the night. He led Adelicia into the entrance hall, where Claire stood waiting, and though Claire had shared with him what she intended to do, seeing her handiwork had a powerful effect.

The moment was perfect.

Gas flames flickered overhead in the bronze chandelier, and fading daylight shone through the ruby-red Venetian glass of the front door and side windows to cast the room in a rosy hue. Nestled beneath the portrait of Adelicia and Emma, the *Sleeping Children* lay perched on a pedestal artfully draped in forest-green velvet, the white marble almost glowing in the soft light.

"Oh . . ." With a barely audible cry, Adelicia released his arm and moved closer. "It's more beautiful than I remembered." She ran a hand over the marble blanket covering the children. "I shall go to them, but they shall not return to me," she whispered, her voice fragile.

Sutton recognized the Scripture she paraphrased—words King David had uttered upon the loss of his own son, and he admired how Adelicia had made the verse her own.

Adelicia looked over. "Thank you, Mr. Monroe. The placement, the display . . . I couldn't have done better my—"

Sutton shook his head. "It was all Miss Laurent's doing, ma'am. Not mine. She gave Eli the measurements for the stand and made the table skirt herself."

Adelicia turned to Claire, her tears falling freely, just as Claire's were. "With all my heart, Miss Laurent . . . thank you. As long as I am at Belmont, I shall never move it from this place."

39

Claire had finished adding the column in the ledger book when a knock sounded on the library door. She quickly made note of the final tally, not at all confident in the number. "Come in . . ."

"Good afternoon, Miss Laurent."

Recognizing Eli's voice, she glanced up, and a shooting pain burned the back of her neck. It took her a moment to focus. Too many hours spent poring over figures and sums, along with late nights of planning with Mrs. Acklen, working on Madame LeVert's memory book, arranging for not only a brass ensemble, but an orchestra as well, along with omnibuses to transport guests to and from the reception, and painting party favors—one hundred fourteen Belmont *bombonnières* for Mrs. Acklen's most honored guests, filled with assorted sugar candies this time—along with myriad other tasks on the ever-growing list.

Recent days were a blur, and she had no idea how she would get everything done in time.

Rubbing her neck, Claire lifted her gaze. "Good afternoon, Mr. Eli."

He held up a cotton sack. "More responses for the reception came in the mail, ma'am."

"Thank you." She gestured to a table in the corner. "Would you set them over there, please?" Five weeks ago, she'd addressed and mailed five hundred seven invitations, the majority to couples. As of yesterday, the twenty-ninth of November, eight hundred forty-six guests had sent acceptances.

Eyeing the sack in Eli's hand, she somehow knew that not a single one of those envelopes would contain a declination. Which pleased her, for Mrs. Acklen. But it puzzled her too.

Without exception, the women who had declined Mrs. Acklen's invitation to tea earlier in the month had swiftly accepted the invitation to the LeVert reception. And Claire wondered why they'd said no then but yes now. It seemed too much of a coincidence that their calendars would have all been full that day. Could it be that Madame LeVert's presence was the swaying factor? And if that were true, did Mrs. Acklen realize it?

Claire knew that if the answer to the first question was yes, the answer to the second had to be as well. Because Adelicia Acklen was as intelligent and discerning an individual as she'd ever met. Yet to think that Mrs. Acklen was *intentionally* hosting this reception for Madame LeVert only to ingratiate herself to her peers seemed beneath the woman. Furthermore, it felt . . . self-serving.

No sooner came that thought than Claire felt as though she were looking into a mirror, and she didn't like what she saw. But her situation was different—at least that's what she told herself—yet she still didn't like the comparisons her conscience was drawing.

"Excuse me, Miss Laurent, I don't mean to take you from your work"—Eli laid a copy of the *Banner* on the desk and pointed—"but Mrs. Acklen's party got another mention today, ma'am."

Welcoming the interruption, Claire picked up the paper. "Thank you, Eli." An article had appeared in this same newspaper four weeks earlier announcing the "By Invitation Only" event being coordinated by "Mrs. Acklen's personal liaison." At first, Claire had been a little miffed that the newspaper hadn't included her by name—she would have enjoyed seeing her name in print.

Then thoughts of Antoine swiftly resurfaced, and she was grateful for the journalist's oversight.

Eli paused by the desk. "Is there anything I can get you, Miss Laurent?"

Claire glanced at the ledger book, then massaged her forehead, sighing. "Another pair of eyes to check these numbers, perhaps?" As soon as the words were out, she wished she could recall them. Eli was well spoken and could read and write, which was uncommon enough for a Negro, illegal as it was, or had been. But she had no idea about the extent of his education. And the thought of offending the dear man made her want to—

"I'd be obliged to work the sums for you, if you'd like, Miss Laurent."

Claire nudged the ledger book toward him, and in a fraction of the time it had taken her to add the numbers, Eli reached for the pencil and made a correction. "You can check me, ma'am, but I'm fairly sure this is right."

Claire counted the column again, aware of her lips moving as she did and of the slow *ticktock-ticktock* of the clock on the mantel. She finally peered up. "Thank you, Eli. And you did it so quickly."

He smiled and offered a bow.

"Have you always been gifted with numbers?"

He shrugged. "I guess you could say that. It comes naturally to me."

She looked at the columns and rows of figures. "I wish it came naturally to me."

"I'd be happy to work those sums for you later, Miss Laurent. If you wish."

Claire lifted her head. "Truly? You wouldn't mind?"

A smile spread across his face. "No, ma'am. I wouldn't mind at all. I used to keep the office records for Mr. Franklin over in Gallatin. But that was a long time ago."

"Mr. Franklin," Claire said. "Mrs. Acklen's first husband?"

Eli nodded.

"I didn't realize you'd been with Mrs. Acklen that long."

"Yes, ma'am. Her first husband bought me before they were married."

Bought me . . . The very term made her cringe.

"Miss Laurent?"

Claire turned to see Sutton in the doorway. "Mr. Monroe, come in." She stood and smoothed a hand over her skirt.

"Am I interrupting something?"

"Of course not. Eli and I were just talking."

"If you'll excuse me, ma'am," Eli said, "I think I'll take myself on downstairs and see if Cordina needs my help."

"Yes, that's fine. And thank you, Eli, for volunteering to work these sums for me. I appreciate your help."

"Work these sums?" Sutton asked.

Eli stopped in his tracks.

"Yes." Claire gestured, detecting censure in Sutton's brief question. "Eli volunteered to help me with my expense records for the reception. I'm not sure if you're aware, Mr. Monroe, but Eli once kept the office records for the late Mr. Franklin."

Sutton looked at Eli, whose gaze was considerably lowered. "I didn't realize you performed that task for Mr. Franklin, Eli."

"Yes, sir, Mr. Monroe." He peered up. "For the better part of eight years, sir."

Surprise heightened Sutton's expression, followed by a flicker of admiration. Eli must have glimpsed it too, because the man's chin lifted ever so slightly.

Sutton looked at Claire as though seeking to explain. "I audited the Gallatin records when I first came to work for Mrs. Acklen. Those records . . ." The words seemed to stick in his throat. "Those records were the best organized and most accurate I've ever seen."

Eli's chin raised another good inch. "Thank you, Mr. Monroe. I appreciate that, sir."

A moment passed before Sutton looked at the man beside him, and finally he answered. "You're welcome, Eli."

With a dip of his head, Eli left, and Sutton closed the door behind him. Hand on the door latch, Sutton stared at her.

"What is it?" Claire asked.

"Don't tell me you've forgotten your next appointment."

She glanced at the clock, scanning her memory, then shook her head. "I'm sorry but—"

He walked to the desk, picked up the leather portfolio Mrs. Acklen had given her at Thanksgiving, and opened it. "November thirtieth." He peered over the book as if the date should have special meaning.

"I *know* what day it is, Sutton. But I—"

"At twelve thirty sharp."

She knew full well there was nothing written on her calendar for twelve thirty today. Her next appointment was at half past one with a company specializing in decorative lanterns and other illumination devices for gardens. But still, she played along. "And what, pray tell, does this twelve-thirty appointment involve?"

"Lunch, Miss Laurent." He snapped the portfolio shut. "With me."

Claire walked with him outside to the gazebo nearest the house, the one he'd "fallen" out of. Inside was a patchwork quilt, spread on the floor, and a basket set off to one side. Filled with picnic food, she guessed by the loaf of fresh bread peeking out. What she noticed next warmed her heart. Dotting the blanket were red and orangey-yellow maple leaves.

"You haven't had much time to paint," he said. "Not like you've wanted to. So I thought I'd bring some remnants of fall color to you. I caught a glimpse of the paintings in your room." He got a shy look about him. "I came looking for you the other day, but you weren't there and your door was open. The one of the hillside all ablaze is especially beautiful."

Claire shook her head, knowing it was far from her best work. "Thank you, Sutton, but . . . it didn't turn out as I'd hoped."

The painting of the hillside lacked something. As did the ones of the rose garden and the statues she'd painted in the garden. Maybe it had been the flat afternoon light—early morning was better, but her mornings had all been scheduled. Maybe it was her texturing or color choice. She wasn't sure. She only knew she wasn't pleased. With any of them. And none of them would garner serious interest at the auction, much less make a name for her.

She required more time to paint well. She was a fairly quick sketcher, but painting a portrait or landscape took her hours, if not days, and grueling repetition. She thought of her *Versailles.* How much time had she spent studying Brissaud's style, his technique, until she'd mastered it.

Until she'd made it her own.

Sutton tipped her chin upward. "The time to paint more often will come, I promise. But I want you to know that you're doing an excellent job with the reception. This event promises to be the grandest Nashville has ever witnessed." He lifted a curl from her shoulder. "And you've probably been too busy to notice, but Mrs. Acklen is starting to receive invitations again. She's visiting friends in town. She's taking flowers and food to people at church. I haven't seen her so happy or so . . . *hopeful* in a very long time."

Claire appreciated the compliment, but her attention honed in on one thing only. "She's starting to receive invitations *again*? What do you mean by that?"

Sutton looked away, as if realizing he'd misspoken. "I didn't mean anything by it, necessarily. Only that . . ." A seriousness moved over him. "Sometimes people in positions of wealth and influence such as Mrs. Acklen can become the object of gossip and ridicule, whether it's warranted or not. As you can well see"—he motioned to their surroundings—"Mrs. Acklen came through the war rather well, compared to others. And some people begrudge her that."

Claire wanted to ask him if he begrudged her resilience but couldn't bring herself to voice the words.

"My point," he continued, "was that you're making such a difference here. One for which I'm personally most thankful."

Standing on tiptoe, she kissed his cheek, half wishing at the last second that he would turn his mouth toward hers. But he didn't. And she told herself she was fine with that.

They made quick work of the bread, sliced ham, and cheese, talking as they ate. For dessert—which Cordina insisted be part of every meal—they each had one of Cordina's tea cakes. A third tea cake remained, and they both eyed it.

"We could Indian-wrestle for it," he said, giving her a look that made her grateful for the cool breeze.

Claire scooted to the bench on the side of the gazebo and positioned her elbow on the edge.

He smiled. "Like those tea cakes, do you?"

Familiar with the children's game, she grinned. "If you're not over here by the count of three, you forfeit the tea cake. One-two-three," she said quickly.

But he was beside her in a flash. He positioned his elbow by hers and gripped her hand. "I see you Indian-wrestle about as honestly as you play checkers."

"I did not cheat at checkers! I won fair and square."

"Cajun checkers? *Cajun* checkers?" He eyed her. "There's no such thing."

She bit her lower lip so she wouldn't smile. "It's just the way we play checkers in Louisiana."

He nodded. "Well, let me show you how we Indian-wrestle in Tennessee." He slid his other hand between their elbows, and following his lead, she grasped his forearm as he did hers. Then he pulled her arm a little closer, and the rest of her had no choice but to follow.

40

Claire was grateful for every point and curve where their bodies touched—their hands, their arms, their knees—and she was especially grateful for the privacy of the vine-laced gazebo. "Would you like for me to count again?" She didn't wait for an answer. "One-two-three!" She pushed against his arm—to no avail. She couldn't help laughing, which didn't help her goal.

His smile broadened. "That's the most pitiful attempt at cheating I've ever seen, Miss Laurent."

Claire giggled but continued to push, wanting to win and knowing that her time and strength were limited. Already, she could feel the pressure of exertion in her head, while Sutton seemed completely at ease, his arm totally immovable.

She rose up on her knees for better leverage, and he effortlessly pulled her closer. He brushed his lips across her knuckles, slow and patient, and her body lost its strength by a third. His mouth moved and teased as he kissed her hand, then her wrist, his eyes taunting her.

"What you're doing, Mr. Monroe"—she sucked in a breath—"would be considered cheating in Louisiana."

His laughter was warm against her skin and sent shivers from her shoulders to her toes. "Aw, shucks, ma'am, it's just the way we country boys Indian-wrestle here in Tennessee."

Surprising herself, she leaned forward and kissed him, feeling their tangle of arms between them, and she did to his mouth what he'd just done to the back of her hand.

"This," he whispered in the midst of their kiss, "is most definitely cheating . . . in any state."

Claire smiled and drew back slightly, loving the dazed look in his eyes, and the fact that his forearm lay decidedly beneath hers on the ledge. He hadn't even noticed. "Thank you for the tea cake, Sutton," she whispered.

He frowned, then looked down. "I don't believe it."

Laughing, she reached for the last tea cake, took a big bite, and fed him the rest.

They packed up their picnic, and he walked her back inside with ample time to spare. Her next appointment hadn't arrived yet. She would have seen the carriage coming up the long drive.

In the library, Sutton picked up one of the *bombonnières* she'd painted, and he studied the decorative candy box. "You have such a gift, Claire. Where did you learn to paint?"

"From my mother. But her giftedness far exceeded my own." She searched the folders on the desk for the one she needed for her next meeting. "As my father said often enough, there's nothing unique about my talent." As soon as she said it, she gritted her teeth. Seconds passed, and she finally looked up, hoping Sutton hadn't taken notice.

He was watching her. "Your father said that to you?"

"Sutton, I'm . . . I'm sorry. That was wrong of me to speak ill of those passed."

He returned the *bombonnière* to the shelf with the others. "Obviously, I can't judge your mother's talent, Claire, but looking at these, and having seen the paintings in your room . . ." He shook his head. "Your talent is anything but ordinary. And, forgive me, but . . . I can't imagine a father saying that to his daughter."

Claire looked back down at the desk and began riffling through the files, not even knowing what she was looking for anymore. She just didn't want him to see her tears. Tears for a father she was certain had never loved her. Not really. Not when remembering her mother's love. And not after having seen the love in this household—that Mrs. Acklen had for her children, and they for her, that Eli and Cordina shared, and that the servants, many of whom were family, had between them.

"Claire?"

"Yes?" She didn't look up.

"Are you all right?"

"I'm fine . . . Ah!" Forcing a smile, she pulled a file from the stack. "I knew it was here somewhere." Emotions patched back together, she lifted her gaze, and the tenderness in Sutton's eyes nearly dismantled her again. Seeing him about to speak, she shook her head. "Don't, please," she whispered, wishing her next appointment would arrive or that Eli would knock on the door—anything to avoid this conversation right now.

"Claire . . ." Sutton's voice was soft, so safe sounding. "You can tell me anything."

Claire exhaled, wishing that were true. "My father and I . . . As I told you before, we weren't close. But it was more than that. He had a temper, and sometimes he—"

"Did he *hurt* you?"

"No," she said, seeing a fierceness in his eyes. "He never hit me, if that's what you mean." *He saved that for Antoine DePaul.* "Looking back, I just don't think he was a very happy man. Or . . . maybe he just wasn't happy with me. Or with my mother." She shook her head. "I don't really know. But it's not important anymore. Because he's gone. And I'm fine." She put on her bravest face.

He moved closer. "Your mother, being so talented, was obviously involved in art. Was your father too?"

Claire found herself filtering her response, not with encumbered lies, but not with the ease of truth either. "My mother was an artist, and my father . . ." She glanced down as though searching for another file. "He was an art broker. He"—she forced herself to look up—"bought and sold art."

Sutton smiled. "That's a good thing for an art broker to do, I guess."

"Yes." She smiled too, but it didn't feel natural. She didn't want to tell him about her parents operating the gallery. That would be too specific a piece of information to share for her ever-shrinking comfort. But if he were to ask directly, though the chances of that were slim—*Oh please, God, let them be slim*—she would tell him.

"Did your parents work together?"

Sending up another prayer, she nodded.

"And where did they work?"

Claire turned as though reaching for something behind her and squeezed her eyes tight, feeling herself start to shake. It was as if he knew the exact questions she didn't want him to ask. She took a breath, hoping she wouldn't stammer. "They worked in an art gallery."

"I bet you loved that. Being around all that art."

She shook her head. "It wasn't like that, Sutton. Not like Belmont, I mean. All of this . . ." She indicated the home around them. "The art Mrs. Acklen has collected . . . is *far* beyond the pieces my father worked with and anything I've ever been around."

He moved around to her side of the desk. "You told me about your mother's passing. But I'm wondering, if it's not overstepping my bounds and isn't too painful for you . . ." His voice was gentle, just above a whisper. "You've never told me how your father died."

She told herself to breathe. "My father passed away unexpectedly after I left New Orleans. I didn't even learn of his death until after I arrived in Nashville." She looked for something to occupy her hands and found nothing.

"So . . . your father didn't die of an extended illness, then. It was more . . . sudden."

It wasn't a question, and if she hadn't known better, she would have thought he already knew what had happened the night she left New Orleans. But that was absurd. As determined as she was to put her past behind her, she also felt another determination rising up inside—she would not lie, not again. And not to this man.

"There was a robbery. At the gallery." It was surreal, hearing the words come from her mouth, and with the scene still so vivid in her mind. Kneeling over her father, the blood staining her hands. "My father was injured. The doctor told me he would be all right. That his injuries weren't"—she took a steadying breath and met Sutton's gaze—"a threat at all to his life. But . . . the doctor was wrong."

Sutton reached over and touched her cheek. "And that's the last time you saw him, that night you left?"

She nodded, her eyes watering.

The clomp of horses' hooves and the squeak of a buggy announced the arrival of her next appointment. Claire reached to gather the items she needed, but Sutton took hold of her hand, surprising her.

"I'm glad you eavesdropped on those women in church the morning we met," he whispered, pressing a kiss into the palm of her hand.

Claire felt the sensation all the way through her. "And I'm glad you *coerced* me into confessing." *Both then, and now* . . . But part of her still wished he knew the whole truth, so she could stop worrying, fearing he would find out. And there was a way for that to happen, she knew. But the cost . . .

The cost grew higher every day.

Sutton pulled her close, and she pressed her head against his chest, hearing the solid beat of his heart. And she would've sworn his sigh held as much relief as her own.

The carriage came to a stop in front of Belmont, and Claire waited as Eli assisted Mrs. Acklen's exit before her. It was overwhelming . . . how much work had been done to prepare for the reception in recent weeks, and yet how much remained to be done in the next two days.

Pauline and Claude raced out the front door to greet their mother. Claire had come to enjoy her sketching lessons with Pauline very much. Claude and William even took part on occasion. True to Mrs. Acklen's word, the young girl showed surprising talent for being only six.

"You two ladies have a nice outing, Mrs. Acklen?" Eli offered Claire his hand as she stepped down.

"Yes, Eli," Mrs. Acklen answered, hugging her children. "We most certainly did. Miss Laurent and I personally confirmed every confectionary centerpiece, every potted plant, and every flowering camellia."

"I'm sure that kept you busy, ma'am." Eli tossed Claire a wink and leaned closer once Mrs. Acklen was a few feet away. "Are you feeling well this afternoon, Miss Laurent?"

"Yes, I'm fine, Eli. Just a little tired." Which wasn't the full truth. She was exhausted. More tired than she could remember.

Mrs. Acklen hadn't told her until that morning that she required her assistance in town today. Who would've guessed giving final approvals would take so long? Claire only hoped the repairs to the floor of the grand salon had been completed as Sutton promised.

Only the day before, they'd discovered a weakening in the floor joists beneath the salon. Workmen had been in the basement all yesterday afternoon and were back this morning when they left, pounding and hammering, carrying in reinforcement beams. Mrs.

Acklen had shown surprising restraint at the news, but Claire had about come apart. And yet, she couldn't complain.

Even with all she had left to do in the next forty-eight hours, she was living in a dream compared to most people. It was easy to forget that, living at Belmont. But outside these grounds . . .

While driving through the city of Nashville in a carriage that probably cost more than the majority of people made in a lifetime, it had been impossible for her not to realize how much God had given her since her arrival at Belmont. And her deserving none of it.

"All this party hubbub will be over soon, Miss Laurent. Then you can get back to your normal work." Eli's brow wrinkled. "And to your painting."

Claire nodded, wondering if the time to truly paint again would ever come. Especially with the LeVerts arriving tomorrow. She dreaded seeing Cara Netta again.

"You have a gift from God, ma'am," Eli continued. "And it's not right to hide something like that away. People need to see it. What you did for Cordina and the ladies in the kitchen . . ." He shook his head and made a sound as if he'd just tasted one of his wife's tea cakes fresh from the oven. "It's like they've got windows down there now. You don't even feel like you're under the earth."

Social etiquette forbade it, but Claire wished she could hug the man. She'd had such fun painting those white plaster walls. She'd done it late at night by lantern light when she was so tired but couldn't sleep, and when she wanted so badly to paint but lacked the concentration to create something of real worth.

She'd painted scenes of rose gardens with gazebos, and of statues and fountains. She even painted a scene of the servants' brick houses all clustered together. It had been good practice for her, painting them in the style of François-Narcisse Brissaud. The paintings wouldn't garner any prizes, by any means. Yet the smiles the women gave her each time she entered the kitchen did her heart good.

But come March, she needed to have painted something worthy of entering into the art auction.

"Thank you, Eli." She covered his hand with hers, smiling when his eyes widened. "It was my pleasure. You and your wife have made me feel so welcome here. Almost like I belong."

He squeezed her hand right back. "The way I see things, Miss

Laurent, you *do* belong here at Belmont, ma'am. Because if you didn't, the good Lord wouldn't have brought you here. He knows what you're doing here, even if you don't."

"Miss Laurent?"

Claire looked up to see Sutton standing on the portico by the front door, and her heart did a funny little flip. Mrs. Acklen stood with him. "Yes, Mr. Monroe?"

"Your attention, along with Mrs. Acklen's, is required in the grand salon. We're still having . . ." His gaze cut away from hers. "Well, you'd best come and see."

Her heart fell. He'd assured her at breakfast that they would get it fixed in time. But, oh, if they didn't . . .

She raced up the stairs, out of breath, and followed him and Mrs. Acklen through the entrance hall. The house was strangely quiet compared to the recent flurry of preparation. Bracing herself, she rounded the corner into the grand salon, and came to an immediate halt.

41

In the center of the room stood a statue of an angel—at least five feet tall—situated atop a polished marble platform. Her delicate-looking wings, carved from white marble like the rest of her nude body, hung folded elegantly down her back. Claire could only stare, wordless.

"You may hold me personally responsible, Miss Laurent," Mrs. Acklen said beside her, "for any anxiety that Mr. Monroe's *fabrication* of a problem with the floor caused you. I wanted to surprise *you* this time, knowing how deep an appreciation you have for such things."

With boyish charm, Sutton gestured toward the statue. "I'm sorry if I worried you, Miss Laurent. We had to reinforce the floor beneath the grand salon to support the weight."

All worry fading, Claire beamed. That the two of them would even think of wanting to surprise her like this. . . "You're completely forgiven. Thank you both, so very much."

Mrs. Acklen motioned her closer. "I purchased it on my return from Europe, in New York. It's called *The Peri,* taken from a poem by Thomas Moore, *Paradise and the Peri.* I'm so pleased it arrived in time for the reception."

Claire studied the faultless sample of the human form. The angel was a female, judging by her flowing hair and the gentle swell of her breasts. The artist had tastefully left the rest to the imagination. "Who is the sculptor?"

"Joseph Mozier, an American. And as he explained to me," Mrs. Acklen continued, "the angel is standing at the gates of Paradise. In her right hand she holds the tears of the penitent sinner—"

Claire looked closer at the angel's right hand resting at her side, palm extended outward. And true to Mrs. Acklen's word, three tears lay tucked in the heart of the angel's palm.

"—and in her left hand, she holds one of the bowls found on the shore of the lake from which the redeemed penitent drinks."

The angel cradled the bowl close to her heart. "Beautiful," Claire whispered, marveling at the emotion the sculpture evoked. She'd never even heard of Joseph Mozier, and yet, he had created *this.*

"Yes . . . she is that." Mrs. Acklen's eyes were moist with emotion. "I especially liked the inscription on the back of the pedestal."

Claire bent to read it. " 'Joy, joy forever, my task is done. The gates are passed, and heaven is won.' "

"Isn't that an encouraging thought?" Mrs. Acklen smoothed a hand over the tears in the angel's palm. "No more sadness or loss, only joy."

"Yes, ma'am," Claire whispered. And while she did find that thought lovely, she found her focus centered on the bowl the angel held. "*One of the bowls found on the shore of the lake from which the redeemed penitent drinks . . .*"

In her morning readings, she'd come across a passage about a woman who was thirsty and who was coming to draw water from a well. Jesus had been resting there, and He told the woman that He could give her living water. Claire swallowed, wondering if the water Jesus had offered the woman back then was the same water represented in the angel's cup.

And if it was, how she could get some.

The next night, Claire climbed into bed, hardly believing the day of the reception had almost arrived. In less than twenty-four hours "the grandest party Nashville has ever seen"—according to the newspaper's account—would be under way, and all the weeks of preparation and work would come to fruition.

It wasn't late, only a little past nine, but everyone had retired early in anticipation of the party. Shivering between the cool sheets, Claire pulled the covers up to her chin, her eyes so heavy she could barely keep them open.

A knock sounded on the door.

Chilled in the bed but knowing she'd be even more so out of it, she debated, then called out, "Yes?"

"It's Mrs. Acklen. May I have a word with you, Miss Laurent?"

Claire shot out of bed. A fire burned low in the hearth, but the wooden floor, absent of rugs except for a thin one by the fireplace, held the December chill. Goose bumps rose on her arms as she grabbed her coat and draped it around her shoulders.

She opened the door to see Mrs. Acklen dressed in her wrapper, standing off to the side, oil lamp in hand.

"I'm sorry, Miss Laurent. Were you already in bed?"

"No. I mean . . . yes, ma'am, I was. But I wasn't asleep."

"May I come in, please?"

"Of course." Claire opened the door wider. "Is something wrong, ma'am?" Only then did she see the dress bag draped over Mrs. Acklen's arm.

Mrs. Acklen entered and looked about. She scrunched her shoulders. "It's chilly in here, Miss Laurent. Why didn't you say something? See that rugs are ordered and installed by the end of the week."

Claire started to say that wasn't necessary, then realized she could hardly feel her toes. "Yes, ma'am. Thank you, ma'am."

"What do you plan to wear to the reception, Miss Laurent?"

The question was unexpected. Claire crossed to the small wardrobe and withdrew one of her new dresses. A dark gray one that Sutton had complimented her on more than once. "I brushed it earlier this evening and shined my boots, so I'm all ready." She presented the dress for inspection, knowing what a stickler Mrs. Acklen was for being well groomed.

"While that's very nice, Miss Laurent, I think I have something that might suit you—and the event—a little better. But first . . ." Mrs. Acklen draped the dress bag across the bed. "I want to remind you that I'm a stickler for adhering to propriety. You know that."

Claire nodded.

"However, there are times in life when I believe that conforming to society's expectations can be . . . confining. Even suffocating. And unnecessary."

Though tempted to nod, Claire wasn't sure what she would be agreeing to, so she raised her eyebrows instead and tilted her head slightly. A gesture she'd learned from Mrs. Acklen. One indicating attentiveness without committing to agreement.

Mrs. Acklen chuckled. "You have mastered that response quite well, Miss Laurent." She ran a finger along the edge of the dress bag. "Allow me to speak in plainer terms. I've spent the greater part of my life dressed in black. And as I face my latter years, I've begun to wonder if the length of time associated with this tradition is ill-conceived. When I'm gone, do I want Pauline to be draped in the memory of my passing for a full year? Or two? Do I want her to continually focus on the fact that I'm no longer with her? Or would I prefer for her to mourn me, yes, but then to move on with her life and live—and dress—in such a way that would celebrate my eternal inheritance?"

Claire sensed the question was rhetorical. But if she'd had to give answer, she would have easily chosen the latter.

"By no means, Miss Laurent, are you under obligation to wear this dress to the reception. But I think it would be stunning on you." She withdrew the garment from the bag. "And I sincerely hope you will."

42

Rest assured, Mr. Monroe, we'll make certain everything is kept safe. The guests won't even know we're here."

"Thank you, Matthews." Sutton gripped the man's hand and took a last look around the art gallery. All doors were locked except for the main entrance, through which a steady tide of reception guests were already coming and going. A recent theft from a home in town, and during a social gathering no less, prompted Sutton to be more vigilant than usual. "I'll check back with you later this evening."

"Very good, sir."

Sutton stepped out into the brisk December evening and felt as though he'd walked into a fairy-tale world. Belmont was awash in a cascade of twinkling lights, and the chilly night air thrummed with anticipation. He'd been at the estate while the luminary company had installed hundreds of oil lanterns and candlelit contraptions all across the grounds—hanging them throughout the gardens, over trellises, and lining the pathways, starting at the gated entrance to Belmont and leading all the way to the front step—but the sight of them lit was overwhelming.

It was nothing short of magical. Otherworldly.

He made his way toward the mansion, dodging the carriages and omnibuses as they deposited guests along the front circular drive. Nashville's finest in all their finery. He was careful where he stepped. The animals were leaving deposits faster than Zeke and the other stable hands could collect them.

Huge cast-iron sugar kettles dotted the grounds, nestling fires to coddle guests in warmth while they strolled the garden paths or awaited entrance into the main house. Or, later, to warm them when they traded the crowded rooms and hallways of the mansion for a moment of cool night air. He took it all in. Claire Laurent was brilliant. And Adelicia Acklen would be the talk of the town for months—if not years—to come. Whatever walls she'd erected between her and her peers in the past, tonight would go far in tearing them down.

Just as Claire had instructed, every window in the main house was awash in candlelight, and the stately harmonies of a brass ensemble—the lead trumpet's trills clear and strong, not missing a beat—drifted toward him.

He'd last seen her a couple of hours ago, relatively calm and making certain everything was carried out to the last detail. When she'd excused herself to get ready, she'd looked as excited as Adelicia and the LeVerts, who had been holed up in the second-floor bedrooms of the mansion all afternoon.

He'd seen Cara Netta briefly last night at dinner, after their arrival, and relations between the two of them had been strained. Even Madame LeVert and Diddie had acted a little cool toward him. He understood, but he still held that he'd made the right decision.

For everyone.

Seeing Claire's handiwork at every turn, he thought again of his conversation with her in the library, and of what her father had said to her. He had trouble believing it. He believed *her*. His difficulty came in understanding *how* a father could say such a thing to his daughter. And judging from the pain in Claire's eyes, he would wager that Gustave Laurent's words had hurt her more often than not.

In light of that discovery, he'd decided not to tell her about the report on her background. All of his questions had been answered, and his concerns—like Mrs. Acklen's—were laid to rest.

"Monroe!"

Sutton turned and spotted Mr. Holbrook strolling up the drive with his wife, Mildred, on his arm. "Good evening, sir, Mrs. Holbrook." He fell into step beside them.

Mildred's eyes twinkled in the golden glow of lantern light. "I've never seen anything so beautiful in all my life. Mrs. Acklen has truly outdone herself this time. None of us will ever dare throw a party in Nashville again!"

Sutton felt a swell of pride. "Mrs. Acklen's personal liaison, Miss

Claire Laurent, arranged everything this evening, down to the last detail. I'll be sure to pass along your compliments to her, Mrs. Holbrook."

"I'd appreciate a personal introduction to this Miss Laurent, if that's possible. To tell her myself."

Sutton nodded. "I believe I can arrange that."

"Any word from your dear mother recently?" Holbrook asked.

"I received a letter two days ago." Sutton heard his name across the way and nodded a greeting to arriving guests. "She's doing well. And, at least for now"—he gave them a look, knowing they understood his mother's eccentric nature—"she says she's contented there with her sister and won't contemplate a visit to Nashville until next fall." To his immense relief.

The entrance to the mansion was crowded, but they eventually made their way inside, and as the music from the brass ensemble on the front lawn fell away, the sweet strains of the stringed orchestra in the grand salon reached out to greet them.

Cinnamon sachets and pillows adorned the tables and chairs, lending a homey scent. Potted camellias and confectionary centerpieces accented the tables, and poinsettias added splashes of color to every room.

Guests clustered around *Ruth Gleaning,* their murmurs and raised eyebrows abounding. Mr. and Mrs. Holbrook stopped to admire the *Sleeping Children,* but Sutton continued on. He caught a glimpse of Adelicia and Mrs. LeVert on a raised dais on one end of the grand salon, where they greeted guests. Beside them, Diddie and Cara Netta did likewise. Adelicia looked radiant in the dress she'd worn when presented at Napoleon's court.

The women looked like royalty, which, in Nashville society, he guessed they almost were. They were engulfed by guests, and he was pleased to notice the number of men already pressing for Cara Netta's attention.

Pausing, he peered over the crowd, searching for Claire. Then like the parting of the Red Sea, the crush of guests dispersed into various other rooms, emptying the hallway. And there she stood—

At the entry to the grand salon, dressed in an opalescent blue dress, looking back at him over her shoulder. Her *bare* shoulder.

Sutton's breath seeped from his lungs. For as long as he lived—and at the moment he prayed that would be a very, very long time—he would never forget how beautiful she looked tonight. And that inviting look on her face . . . Playful, enticing, as if she had a secret she shouldn't tell, but would—with coaxing—to him.

In six long strides, he was beside her, wishing he could nuzzle the soft column of her neck or the creamy curves of her shoulders. As it was, he lifted her hand to his mouth. "You . . . are . . . radiant," he whispered, and bestowed a soft kiss.

A blush crept into her cheeks. "And you . . . are right on time." She lowered her voice. "I'm scared to death. I don't know anyone in this room."

"Sure you do. You know me."

She tilted her head to one side and smiled, but he sensed her nervousness. He offered his arm and she accepted, moving to stand closer beside him.

He made a show of looking at her. "That dress is stunning on you."

She swayed from side to side, causing the beaded tassels on her bodice and sleeves to dance. "Isn't it pretty? It was a gift from Mrs. Acklen last night."

Sutton did his best not to stare where he shouldn't. He'd seen a woman's bare shoulders before. The grand salon was full of them. But he'd never seen Claire's. Not with her being in mourning. It surprised him a little that Adelicia would encourage her to wear such a dress. Then again, he doubted anyone outside this household knew about her parents' deaths, and no one inside would begrudge her this night, and this dress. Not after all she'd done since coming to Belmont.

He leaned closer and caught a whiff of lilac in her hair. She'd gathered up her curls for the most part, but some hung loose, framing her face and falling down her back. The effect was intoxicating.

"Mr. Monroe?"

He turned. "Mrs. Holbrook . . ." He quickly made introductions between her and Claire, wondering where her husband had drifted off to. He wanted to introduce him to Claire as well.

Claire curtsied. "It's a pleasure to meet you, Mrs. Holbrook."

"The pleasure is all mine, Miss Laurent. When Mr. Monroe told us you were responsible for all of this, I knew I needed to meet you. I'm in charge of the Nashville Women's League, and we're having our annual spring tea this coming—"

"Mrs. Holbrook." Sutton shook his head, halfway curbing a grin. "How often have you reprimanded your husband and me for conducting business at these events? And here you go—"

"I was simply making a connection, Mr. Monroe." Mrs. Holbrook batted her eyes. "So just you never mind and let us ladies talk for a minute. Go find my husband and keep him out of mischief."

"I'll do that, ma'am. But first, may I have a private word with Miss Laurent?" At her consenting nod, he drew Claire off to the side. "Would you give me the honor of saving the first dance for me, *mademoiselle*?"

"Oh . . ." Claire pouted. "I'm sorry, *monsieur*." Then she smiled. "I saved you the first two."

This woman . . . "Do you know the meaning of the word *throttle*, Claire?"

"I do. It's what I'd like to do to you nearly every other day, Willister."

Sutton delivered her back to Mrs. Holbrook and walked away with a grin.

Cup of cider in hand, Sutton found Bartholomew Holbrook occupying a prime corner in the grand salon—a raised stair that provided a perfect view of the dance floor. The man had a glass of champagne in one hand and two of Cordina's tea cakes in the other. Lemon, from the looks of them.

Mr. Holbrook sipped the champagne, his attention on the guests. "You haven't told Mrs. Acklen yet, have you?" His deep voice was a whisper.

"No, I haven't." Sutton didn't have to ask what he meant, and he, too, kept his focus on the room, mindful of who was standing within earshot.

Holbrook lifted his glass in silent greeting to a gentleman walking by. "The review board's decision will be public record soon, Mr. Monroe. Possibly as early as next week. And as we both know, news travels fast."

"I'll tell her soon. I didn't want anything to spoil this evening for her." *Or for Claire*, he thought, dreading having to tell her the news even more than telling Adelicia. He hoped it wouldn't make him appear lesser in her eyes, as it did in his own.

Mr. Holbrook looked over at him. "Forgive my wife for wading into the pool of gossip, and me for splashing in her puddles, but she told me she learned that you and Miss Henrietta Caroline LeVert have dissolved your understanding."

Sutton nodded, not surprised that word had spread. "It was for the best."

"Would that acknowledgment be shared by both parties?"

Coming from anyone else, the question would have seemed like prying. But this man was as close to a father as Sutton had. "Yes, sir. Or it will be, given time."

Holbrook merely nodded, swirling the champagne in his glass. "Any news on the cotton fiasco?"

Sutton took a sip of the cider, tasting something a little stronger than *spice* in the brew. "We should know something by March. I'm traveling to New Orleans at the first of the year to check on things."

"If you need assistance, I'm available. I always enjoy a warm beignet." With a grin, Holbrook bit into a tea cake.

Sutton smiled and looked about for Claire. He spotted her across the room, and his senses heightened. So much for her being nervous about not knowing anyone. Five—no, make that six—men swarmed around her, their infatuated grins better suited to a schoolyard than a grand salon. Claire said something, and all the men laughed. She shook her head at one of them in particular, then glanced in Sutton's direction, and Sutton gathered the man had asked for either her first—or second—dance.

He didn't want to admit it, but he was jealous. All but one of the men was old enough to be her father, yet he knew that didn't matter in the least. Two of them were widowers. And all of them, without exception, were wealthy.

He spotted Lucius Polk speaking with Adelicia, and though he hadn't planned on broaching this subject with Holbrook tonight, he decided the timing was right. Because *should* Adelicia marry again, his managerial position at Belmont would come to a swift end. "Sir, a while back you mentioned you were fairly certain you could make a position for me at the law offices. Do you think that opportunity might still be available . . . sometime in the near future?"

Mr. Holbrook shifted his weight. "In the future, yes. In the near future, unfortunately . . . no."

Sutton looked over at him.

"With the exception of the lawsuit we're working on together," he said low, "the number of cases in the firm has dwindled in recent months. It's just a sign of the times. Same for everyone. But something happened that, frankly, I didn't see coming. Wickliffe's son-in-law will be starting at the firm within the week. The young man is an accountant by trade but couldn't find work. New wife and a baby on the way . . ." Holbrook shook his head. "Jobs are scarce, and family takes care of family, you know." He stopped, as though just realizing what he'd said. "I'm sorry, son, I didn't mean for that to sound—"

"Don't, sir. Please. I understand."

"Your position here at Belmont hasn't altered, has it?"

Knowing he couldn't very well tell him about Adelicia contemplating a third marriage, Sutton shook his head. "No, sir. My position hasn't changed."

"Good, good." Holbrook gripped his shoulder. "I'm glad to hear it. Because I think it might be a while before our offices can bring anyone else in on a primary basis. There may be work from time to time, mind you. And if we win this case we're working on, that could also change the landscape considerably."

"Thank you, sir. I appreciate your consideration." And he did, but Sutton couldn't shake the feeling that he was balancing on a three-legged stool, with two legs already kicked out from underneath him, and the remaining leg cracked and held together with string.

"Is the name Samuel Broderick familiar to you, Mr. Monroe?"

"No, sir. Should it be?"

"He runs a shipping company here in town. Took it over from his father a few years back. I knew Samuel the first quite well. Fine man. Served on several city committees with him. But his son . . ."

"Fell far from the tree?"

Sutton caught the way Holbrook's eyes narrowed.

"The jury within me is still deliberating that point. But if I were to wager a gamble, not only would Mildred have my wrinkled old hide, but I'd put everything I have on Broderick being rotten to the core."

"And your basis for that wager would be . . . ?"

"Hunch, mostly."

Sutton laughed, assuming this exchange dealt with their current case. "Which will hold up well in court, sir."

"You'd be surprised how many cases I've won through the years with only a hunch to go on at first." Holbrook started on his second tea cake.

Sutton continued to watch Claire from across the room. "Can you tell me about this hunch of yours?"

"I believe"—Holbrook's voice lowered—"that Samuel Broderick is partnered with someone in the shipping of fraudulent art. And that the man he's partnered with could well be associated with the gallery in New York that sold our client the fake Raphael."

Sutton turned to look beside him. "All that, from a hunch?"

"Yes, but mind you, Mr. Monroe"—Holbrook winked—"we have no solid evidence. Yet." He bit into his tea cake and turned back to watch the crowd.

But Sutton could only stare. If what Bartholomew Holbrook just told him proved true, that could be the lead the investigators had been searching for. Which could provide the evidence he and Holbrook needed in order to proceed with their case.

Holbrook stopped chewing. "That young woman there . . ." He indicated with a discreet nod. "The pretty one flanked by admirers. Do you know who she is?"

Mind churning, Sutton trailed his gaze, then smiled. "In fact, I do. That's Miss Claire Laurent, Mrs. Acklen's personal liaison. She's the young woman your wife requested to meet." Claire looked at him then and gave him a playful look, and Sutton could hardly wait for the music to start.

Seconds passed, and he felt the older gentleman's stare.

"If I were blind, Mr. Monroe, I might inquire as to whether you knew that young woman well."

Sutton couldn't hide his grin. "Miss Laurent and I are . . . close acquaintances."

"Ah . . ." Holbrook nodded.

"What's the *ah* for, sir?"

"No reason. I was merely wondering."

"You never *merely* wonder about anything, sir."

"On occasion, Mr. Monroe, with someone that pretty . . . I actually do." Smiling, Mr. Holbrook popped the last bite of tea cake into his mouth.

The orchestra music faded, and the director turned and announced for guests to find their partners for the first dance. The traditional waltz.

Sutton maneuvered through the crowd easily enough. It was fighting his way through the wall of Claire's enthusiasts that proved most difficult. But the second his eyes met hers, she cut a path toward him. He escorted her to the dance floor and bowed to her. She curtsied and gave him a smile he tucked away for later.

And though he'd never been overly fond of receptions or balls, tonight he welcomed the music, and the dance, and the chance to hold this woman in his arms.

43

For weeks, Claire had imagined this moment. The never-ending list of tasks behind her, save one—not to step on Sutton's foot as they danced. Her left hand on his right shoulder, she looked up at him, silently counting. *One-two-three, two-two-three, three-two-three, four-two three.*

"Stop counting," he whispered.

"I'm not counting."

"Your lips were moving."

She gave him a look, and he smiled.

His fingers tightened around hers. "Just follow my lead."

The pressure of his hand on her back increased and he drew her closer. Their bodies weren't touching, but on occasion, as they turned, his thigh brushed against hers. He was so handsome in his black cutaway and paisley ascot, a dark lock of hair falling across his forehead. And those eyes . . .

"You . . . look . . . divine," she whispered.

He laughed softly. "I can safely tell you that no one has ever said that to me before."

"Well, it's true. You're the most handsome man in the room."

Again, that smile. "What about the men in the central parlor? Or those outside?"

She feigned contemplation. "I haven't had opportunity to give them study. I'll do that and let you know once I have."

The waltz ended and the quadrille began. And by the time the last chord of the livelier music had ended, Claire had found her rhythm and wasn't eager to relinquish Sutton. But not changing partners would have been considered rude. Of them both.

Her dance card was almost full, and after four more dances, with four different men, she was ready for some fresh air and a cool drink. She bowed and thanked her dance partner, Mr. Waverly, an older gentleman who smelled of hair tonic and mothballs and who gained enormous pleasure from telling her about the many lucrative businesses he owned.

Claire discreetly took her leave of him and picked up a cup of cranberry punch on her way outside. The night air was heavenly, and she paused on the front steps to take in the view.

The effect of lantern light on the estate grounds was mesmerizing, prettier than she'd imagined it would be. Everything had come together beautifully. She'd sampled delicious tea cakes, meatballs, stuffed mushrooms, and other appetizers until it was a wonder she still fit in her dress. And the midnight supper Cordina was preparing with the extra hired help would be every bit as delectable.

Claire took a breath and exhaled, stretching her shoulders. Mrs. Acklen had told her not to worry about the expense, and she hadn't. She'd observed Mrs. Acklen throughout the evening, and she seemed pleased enough. Claire had seen her and Lucius Polk dancing together earlier, but surprisingly, only once. And come to think of it, Mr. Polk hadn't been invited to dinner at Belmont in recent weeks. . . .

Another swell of guests arrived, and Claire moved off to the side. She stood in the darkness, shielded from the glow of coach lamps, not ready to go back inside.

"I was shocked too, when I learned the news." A woman's voice drifted upward from the lawn below. "And now he's left with nothing, I hear. Which I'm certain is why *she* put a hasty end to it. As well she should have, considering her wealth. He's far below her station now."

"But did you hear about his father?" a man replied, his tone a husky whisper. "He was a traitor to the Confederacy. True, he might have refused to sign The Oath, but he was a *sympathizer.*" The man said the word as though it were vulgar. "He doctored the Acklens' Negroes, right here at Belmont, is what I hear. I wager Mrs. Acklen didn't know that. And here she is, still harboring the man's son beneath her roof. He's reaping the sins of his father, if you ask me. . . ."

The voices faded and the breath in Claire's lungs went flat. She tried to see the couple below, but darkness obscured their retreat. *Sutton.* It had to be him they were talking about. But what they'd said didn't make sense. Unless . . . He'd gotten word from the review board and hadn't told her yet.

But he'd promised to tell her once he heard.

Realizing how long she'd been gone, she walked back inside only to find Cordina and the servers carrying platters of food up from the kitchen to the formal dining room. Savory aromas of roasted beef and turkey wafted toward her. She checked a nearby clock. Almost midnight. Cordina was never late.

"Miss Laurent?"

"Mr. Stanton!" Her second dance partner that evening, Andrew Stanton was smooth on his feet, especially for his age. Not that he was old, but Claire guessed he was forty-five, at least. She smiled, having enjoyed his company earlier and remembering how she'd heard his prayer in church and had then taken it for her own. "I hope you're having an enjoyable evening, sir."

"Yes, I am. And largely due to your talents, Mrs. Acklen informs me."

"Not at all." She gave a dismissive shake of her head. "I've merely learned that one of the secrets to being successful lies in knowing which person to ask for what advice."

He laughed. "It took me nearly forty-eight years to learn that, Miss Laurent. Which means you're far ahead of me."

Forty-eight. She hadn't been off by much.

He gestured. "I was thinking of getting something to drink and wondered—"

"Oh! Of course, Mr. Stanton." She should have already offered. Not only was he one of Adelicia's honored guests, he was one of the wealthiest men in Nashville. "I'd be happy to get you something. Would you prefer a cold drink or perhaps some warm cider?"

His smile came slowly, shyly. "Actually, Miss Laurent, I would be honored if you would allow me to get a drink for *you*. Then perhaps we could find a quiet corner to visit. If your dance card and responsibilities allow, of course."

His request slowly sank in, and Claire didn't know what to say. She didn't really want to accept, yet she couldn't exactly say no. "I would like that very much. Thank you."

"Hot or cold?" he asked.

"Cold, please. Most definitely."

Claire watched him walk away and gradually grew aware of stares from guests standing close by. She wondered what they were thinking.

"Here you are, Mademoiselle Laurent." Sutton appeared at her side, a glass of champagne in each hand. He held one out. "I hope you're thirsty."

"Sutton, I—" She started to take it from him, then saw Mr. Stanton returning. With a glass of champagne in each hand.

Sutton moved closer. "Are you feeling all right, Claire? You look a little—"

"Here you are, Miss Laurent!" Mr. Stanton handed her the drink. "Mr. Monroe, how are you this evening?"

Relieved they already knew each other, Claire took a long sip from the stemmed glass, uncomfortable in the moment.

"I'm well, Mr. Stanton. It's nice to see you again, sir." Sutton stealthily slipped one of the glasses onto the table behind him.

"Likewise." Mr. Stanton sipped his champagne, not seeming to notice anything out of the ordinary. "I was complimenting Miss Laurent a moment ago on the reception. It's magnificent. And I've heard some telling reports on you this evening as well."

Sutton's expression sobered. "Is that right, sir?"

Seeing Sutton's reaction left no doubt in Claire's mind that what she'd overheard earlier was true. Wondering why he'd kept the news from her, she scrambled to fill the void in conversation. But Mr. Stanton beat her to it.

"Mrs. Acklen speaks very highly of your services too, Mr. Monroe." Andrew Stanton raised his glass. "No wonder she's doing so well with you two at the helm beside her."

Sutton's laugh came out tight. "And you well know, Mr. Stanton, the only one at the helm around here is Mrs. Acklen. I merely hoist the sails when she tells me to."

"And I merely swab the deck," Claire added, raising her glass.

They all three laughed.

"Well . . ." Sutton bowed. "If you'll both excuse me." He shifted his focus to Mr. Stanton. "Your kind indulgence of my company has been appreciated, sir."

Mr. Stanton shook his hand. "Good to see you again, Monroe."

Sutton left without a backward glance, and Claire felt an odd sense of separation in the pit of her stomach.

"Shall we?" Mr. Stanton gestured toward the small study.

They visited together over champagne and then over dinner until the orchestra signaled a toast. Along with the other guests, Claire and Mr. Stanton crowded into the grand salon as Mrs. Acklen thanked everyone for their attendance and for their repeated compliments on the "wonderland of lights" in the gardens.

"And now," Mrs. Acklen continued, "I'd like to present our most esteemed guest of honor, Madame Octavia Walton LeVert"—applause rose from those gathered—"with a token of my deep appreciation for her personal friendship and for all she's done for the city of Nashville."

Claire felt a flush of pride as Mrs. Acklen presented Madame LeVert with her memory book. Madame LeVert flipped through the pages, tearing up, then expressed an emotional thanks.

Mrs. Acklen held up the book and described what was inside, then looked in Claire's direction. "I'd like to thank my trusted personal liaison, Miss Claire Laurent, for crafting this extraordinary gift for my dear friend, and for her ingenuity in coordinating this grand event for us this evening."

Applause sounded, and Claire curtsied, appreciating Mrs. Acklen's public acknowledgment of all she'd done. She caught Mr. Stanton's quiet "Here, here" as well as the kind nods around her, and she drank in the moment.

Mrs. Acklen proceeded to call for the toast in honor of Madame LeVert, and glasses of champagne were distributed. Along with everyone else, Claire lifted her glass in salute, searching the crowd for Sutton, wanting to share the moment with him.

Sensing someone's attention, she turned and met the gaze of an older gentleman standing across the salon. It took her a moment to place him without the tall black hat, but—in a flash—she remembered where she'd seen him. And the joy inside her evaporated.

He raised his glass, his smile friendly, not the least bit menacing, and yet she felt a quiver of warning, remembering the day she'd seen him at Broderick Shipping and Freight. Then again on the steps of Holbrook and Wickliffe Law Offices. Claire saw Mildred Holbrook standing close beside him and like a precarious line of dominoes, snippets of seemingly unrelated bits of information fell into place, and she was reminded again of how tenuous her situation was.

Why, if God had brought her to Belmont, as Eli said, was she constantly reminded that she didn't belong?

At a quarter past five in the morning, following the last waltz, the crowd of guests had thinned, but only barely. Claire tucked her hand into the crook of Sutton's arm. "I don't think anyone wants to leave," she whispered, so no one else could hear.

"You have only yourself to blame. You threw too grand a party."

She smiled, wishing she could pull him aside and tell him what she'd overheard about him earlier that evening. Not only so they could talk about it, but so he would know that the review board's decision was public knowledge, or soon would be.

And yet, she realized it was *his* right to tell her when he was ready.

She glanced around, keeping watch for the older gentleman she'd seen during the toast—Mr. Holbrook, she assumed. With any luck, they wouldn't meet again. And if they did, he might not remember where he'd seen her. But even if he did remember, she told herself, it was no crime to visit a shipping company.

Sutton touched her arm. "Would you excuse me for a moment?"

"Certainly." She watched him disappear into the central parlor.

"Miss Laurent, you organize a wonderful party."

Claire turned to see Mildred Holbrook—and the man beside her—and felt herself tense. "Thank you, Mrs. Holbrook. I hope you both had a wonderful time."

"Oh, we did, my dear. As I told Adelicia earlier, this reception will be remembered for years to come." Mrs. Holbrook gestured beside her. "I don't believe you and my husband have met yet." She made the introductions.

Mr. Holbrook bowed. "A pleasure to make your acquaintance, Miss Laurent."

"And you as well, sir." Claire curtsied, wanting to believe he didn't remember her, and yet the keenness in his eyes hinted otherwise.

"Oh!" Mrs. Holbrook gave a little gasp. "I need to get my coat."

"Please . . ." Claire said, welcoming the excuse to leave. "Let me get it for you. It's no trouble."

"Nonsense." The older woman patted Claire's hand. "I know right where it is."

With a sinking feeling, Claire watched Mrs. Holbrook go.

"So, Miss Laurent"—Mr. Holbrook studied her—"how are you enjoying being Adelicia Acklen's personal liaison?"

"Very much, sir." Claire briefly met his gaze. "I appreciate the opportunities she's given me."

"I've heard from a very reliable source that you're doing a splendid job."

"Thank you, sir. It certainly is keeping me busy." Claire assumed the "very reliable source" was Sutton, knowing they worked in the same law firm.

Mrs. Holbrook rejoined them, coat buttoned up and with her husband's black hat in hand. "I'm ready to go, dear, if you are."

Mr. Holbrook donned his hat. "Perhaps we'll see one another again soon, Miss Laurent." He turned to follow his wife, then looked back and gave her a grandfatherly wink. "Say, perhaps, if we both have something to ship."

Claire's heart dropped to her stomach. She laughed and forced a smile as the couple left, but any question in her mind about the man remembering—or about the sharpness of his mind—vanished.

She made her way toward the entrance hall, bidding guests good night. Through the open doorway into the central parlor, she spotted Sutton, and moved slightly to the left so she could see whom he was speaking with.

Mr. Stanton.

Sutton glanced in her direction, and Claire quickly looked away. But she looked back again in time to see the two men shaking hands. Sutton returned to her side, but something was different about him.

"You look as if you're planning your escape," he whispered.

"And you look as if you're upset about something."

He shook his head. "I'm fine."

Across the salon, Cara Netta was surrounded by a host of admirers, as she'd been all evening, and she didn't look the least bit tired. Spotting Mrs. Acklen, Claire nudged Sutton. "Who is that gentleman with Mrs. Acklen? She danced at least three times with him this evening."

He looked over. "That's Dr. William Cheatham. He and Adelicia have been acquaintances for years. He's a physician in town . . . and a widower. Much like your Mr. Stanton."

Claire caught the off note in his tone. "*My* Mr. Stanton? You're quite the humorist, Willister." Her use of his first name didn't earn her the smile it usually did.

"You shouldn't be surprised at the attention, Claire. You're a vivacious, beautiful young woman. Men would have to be blind not to notice."

She knew he meant it as a compliment, but it didn't sound like one.

As dawn splashed pink across the eastern horizon, the remaining guests climbed into carriages and omnibuses, and Claire could hardly wait to fall into bed.

Sutton gestured. "I believe one—or both—of us is being summoned to the helm."

She turned to see Mrs. Acklen making her way toward them.

"I'm glad to find you together." Mrs. Acklen motioned them to a private corner. "Madame LeVert and I have been speaking, and I have the most wonderful news. It simply won't wait!"

Claire felt a dread. If her *wonderful* news involved planning another reception anytime soon . . .

"I've decided to take us all to New Orleans!" Mrs. Acklen clasped her hands at her bodice. "The entire family. It will be the first time we've all been there since before the war. And I desire for you to come too, of course, Miss Laurent. We'll have much work to do there. The LeVerts are leaving Belmont day after tomorrow, but Octavia informs me that they would love nothing more than to join us while we're there. We'll stay at the St. Charles Hotel and enjoy the delights of the city before retiring to the plantation for a few weeks. Does that not sound divine?"

Claire actually thought she might cry. Right there. In front of Sutton, the orchestra members packing up their instruments, and the servants gathering soiled dishes. Yet she knew she couldn't. Feeling the keen awareness of Mrs. Acklen's watchful gaze, she knew she'd best choose her next words with care.

44

Claire worked to keep the disappointment from her voice. "When do you think we would leave, Mrs. Acklen? Not straightaway, I hope."

"No, no, Miss Laurent. Not straightaway. We'll enjoy a quiet Christmas at Belmont before we leave. And we'll be back no later than mid-March."

Claire could feel the blood pooling in her feet. "But . . . that's a long time."

Mrs. Acklen's smile drained of pleasure. "New Orleans was your home, Miss Laurent. The Café du Monde, the French Quarter . . . I would think you would be pleased to visit again. And grateful for the opportunity."

Claire smarted at the reprimand. Still, she'd worked so hard for the reception tonight. Going without sleep, working to live up to Mrs. Acklen's stringent expectations. She needed time to paint! Hadn't she earned that much? She had scarcely three months until the artists' auction in March. Never mind the fact that she didn't welcome returning to the French Quarter, where ghosts of her past loitered around each corner.

"I *am* grateful to you, Mrs. Acklen. Truly. Please don't hear my hesitance as a sign of ingratitude. It's simply that—"

"Miss Laurent is being modest, Adelicia."

Claire glanced at Sutton beside her.

"What she's not telling you"—he cast a gently scolding look in her direction—"is that Mrs. Holbrook has requested that she organize the annual spring tea for the Nashville Women's League in early March. Isn't that right, Miss Laurent?"

Feeling Mrs. Acklen's scrutiny, Claire wondered whether Sutton was trying to help her, or get her summarily dismissed. "Yes, it's true, Mrs. Holbrook did ask me to meet with her to discuss that possibility. But I told her that I would need to seek your permission first, Mrs. Acklen. I would never undertake such an obligation without your consent."

Sutton nodded. "And you know how grateful the Nashville Women's League would be for your *lending* Claire to them. The women would be greatly indebted to you, in a manner of speaking."

Mrs. Acklen and Sutton exchanged a look.

"Also, ma'am," Sutton continued, "if you were to decide for Miss Laurent to stay here, she could catalog all of the art pieces. I've been after you for years to have that done. Not only for insurance purposes, but for posterity's sake."

Watching Mrs. Acklen's expression, Claire felt her decision being swayed. "If I *were* to stay, ma'am, that would also give me time to get all of your files in order. And to finish going through all those boxes of newspaper clippings and family mementoes. I could even make a memory book for you!"

Mrs. Acklen started nodding. "Madame LeVert has asked me to write an article for *Queens of American Society,* a book being published next year. It seems the author would like to include a chapter on me. A biography, of sorts."

Claire smiled. "Congratulations, Mrs. Acklen. I could write the first draft for you, if you'd like. Then I could post it to you for your review."

Mrs. Acklen paused, eyeing them both. "Don't think that I don't realize what you're both doing—because I do."

Claire swallowed. Sutton laughed beneath his breath.

"You, Miss Laurent, have your heart set on entering the auction for new artists. And you, Mr. Monroe, seem bent on helping her to do just that. And while I am the first person to encourage someone to pursue their aspirations, I don't relish the thought of one of my employees being made the object of others' criticism and judgment. Especially someone who works so closely with me."

Mrs. Acklen honed her focus on Claire. "The world of art, with which you're somewhat familiar, Miss Laurent, is fickle and subjective, and oftentimes cruel. One need only listen to my guests' overloud whispers tonight to realize that. And while you do have talent, I would loathe to see you set your sights on so high an ambition, only to have your dreams dashed."

Claire didn't know how the woman did it. In the same breath, she built up and tore down. "I assure you, M—"

Mrs. Acklen held up a hand. "I'll take everything into consideration and will let you know my decision by Christmas."

From habit, Claire curtsied. "Thank you, Mrs. Acklen."

Sutton bowed, a smile ghosting his lips. "Thank you, ma'am."

Mrs. Acklen strode down the hallway.

"Thank you, Sutton," Claire whispered. "She always heeds your advice."

"Not always."

"She would have said no to me outright."

He looked down. "That's because she doesn't want you to get hurt." Tenderness filled his eyes. "Something I don't relish happening either."

Claire shook the box. "Do you want to go first, or should I?"

Sutton eyed her over the rim of the *café au lait* she'd made him. "Ladies first. As always."

Grinning, she gave the beribboned package a shake, then tore into the wrapping. He was glad they'd waited to exchange Christmas presents until after everyone else had retired for the evening. They'd moved into the small study, where a fragrant evergreen swag hung from the mantel, and a fire burning in the hearth gave the room a cozy feel.

Kris Kringle, as Acklen family tradition called him, had visited the children that morning, and while Adelicia had been all smiles through the presents, then the dinner of fresh oysters, fish, and fruits shipped from New Orleans, he knew she was eager for the day to be over. As was he. For some reason, memories of departed loved ones always pressed closer on Christmas Day.

The holiday itself had been enjoyable and the house quiet, but it was nice to finally be alone with Claire. Especially since their days together were numbered.

Adelicia had said yes that morning to Claire staying behind, much to Claire's delight. And while he was happy for her, he wasn't for himself. He'd planned on going down to New Orleans for two weeks on business anyway, but he'd come to the decision that it would be best if he stayed there for a while. To give Claire time to paint, to document the art, to accomplish the growing list of projects Adelicia was continually dreaming up . . .

And also to give her the time and the freedom she needed . . . to choose.

Since the reception a week ago, a deluge of gentleman admirers had sent her flowers, confections, and notes. Just as he'd known they would. Almost daily something new arrived. He merely had to look over his shoulder—which he refused to do—to see the flowers Mr. Stanton had sent that morning.

Stanton had pulled him aside the night of the reception and inquired, most confidentially, whether he knew if any gentleman had previous designs on Miss Laurent's affections. Andrew Stanton was a gentleman and a senior officer he'd served with in the war, and Sutton knew him well enough to know that Stanton would never have pursued Claire if he'd simply answered, "Why, yes, sir. I happen to love the young woman myself. More than I care to admit. So if you don't mind, would you take your stellar reputation, fine estate, all your money, and your family's good name and just trot on along. . . ."

But of course he hadn't said that. He couldn't. He didn't feel at liberty to close such a door for Claire. That door was hers to close, not his.

And no matter how he tried, he couldn't stop comparing Andrew Stanton and Claire . . . to Isaac Franklin and Adelicia. A similar age difference, both men successful and wealthy. And from what little Adelicia had said of Isaac Franklin through the years—and the picture she kept of him in her bedroom, even after all this time—theirs had been a marriage of the heart.

"Oh, Sutton!" Claire stood and held up the painting smock against her. "It's perfect! Thank you!" She leaned down and kissed his cheek—lingering long enough for him to get other ideas—then she slipped the smock on. He'd had it made especially for her. Mrs. Perry at the dress shop had helped him with the sizing. "I'll wear it every time I paint." She sashayed to the center of the small study and struck a pose.

He knew the image would stay with him. "I wish you could paint me a picture of that."

They both laughed, and she sat back down beside him.

She nudged the present at his feet closer. "Now it's your turn."

He picked up the box, acting as if he might buckle beneath the weight. "I already know what it is."

Her eyes narrowed.

"It's a twenty-four-volume set on how to cheat at checkers."

She giggled, her gaze moving from his face to the package, then back again.

He removed the wrapping and lifted the lid from the box—and couldn't believe it. He looked at her, then back down. It was a coat, but not just any coat. He stood and pulled the long leather duster from the box. He held it up to him, staring at it, feeling like a little boy again. The duster was exactly what he and Mark used to pretend they were wearing when they played at fighting wild Indians.

"If you're going to run a thoroughbred farm, Sutton, I thought you should have the right coat."

Embarrassed at the tightening in his throat and wishing he'd told Andrew Stanton that Claire's heart was spoken for, he shook his head. "Claire, this is too much."

"Try it on!" She jumped up and held it for him as he slipped his arms inside. "Now turn around." He did, and she backed up a step. Her gaze moved over him. "Oh, Sutton . . ." She pressed a hand to her mouth. "I knew it would look good on you, but . . ." Her expression turned decidedly more intimate, in a most approving way.

With his left arm hanging loose at his side, he edged the duster back on his right, acting as if he wore a gun belt slung low around his hips, the way he and Mark used to make believe.

He rested his hand on his imaginary Colt revolver, narrowed his eyes, and reached for his deepest western drawl. "Howdy, ma'am." He tugged the rim of an imaginary Stetson. "I'm sheriff of these parts, and I can see you're new in town."

They laughed together, and he sank back down on the settee beside her, grateful for once that the furniture in the room was so compact.

He smoothed a hand over the fine leather, not wanting to think about how much this coat had cost her. Much more than his gift to her. With the future of his job and earnings so unknown, he'd gone a more conservative route on her gift. Now he wished he hadn't. "This is the best Christmas present I've had in twenty years . . . since my buddy and I both got wooden rifles." He remembered as if it were yesterday.

Of all the material possessions he'd lost when the Federals burned his family home, that toy rifle was at the top of the list of things he wished he still had.

"Let me guess," she said. "You used to play cowboys and Indians."

"Sometimes. Mostly Mark and I took turns being either the sheriff or the outlaw. It was more fun to be the outlaw, though."

"But the sheriff was always a better shot."

He peered over at her. "You've played before?"

"No, but I've read enough dime novels to know what happens."

He leaned his head back on the settee. "Mark and I used to read those over and over again, then we'd grab our rifles and head outside. We had a friend, Danny Ranslett, who used to play with us. Except Danny got a *real* rifle when he was about seven or so, and"—he whistled low—"could that boy ever shoot."

"Do you all still see each other?"

"Daniel moved out west shortly after the war. And Mark . . ." Sutton let his eyes drift shut. "He died not far from here, at the battle in Franklin. Daniel lost his youngest brother that night too. Not far from where Mark fell."

She rested her head on his shoulder. "I'm sorry," she whispered. "Is that when you were wounded?"

He nodded. "I took a minié ball in the shoulder." He reached up instinctively. "I didn't even feel it at first. I was holding Mark . . . trying to stop the blood, trying to hear what he was telling me. But . . ." He took a shaky breath. "I couldn't. It felt like the whole world was coming apart." Emotion cinched a knot in his throat. He didn't want to talk about it. Not on Christmas night.

She wove her arm through his and scooted closer. He wiped his eyes, glad she couldn't see his face. The fire in the hearth burned low, casting a mesmerizing cadence of shadows on the walls.

She traced a forefinger over his open palm. It tickled, but he didn't want her to stop.

He waited until he was sure his voice would hold. "You met Mark's mother the other night at the reception. Mrs. Holbrook. Did you ever meet her husband?"

Her finger stilled on his hand. "Yes, I did. Briefly."

"You'll like Bartholomew Holbrook. He's been like a father to me since my own father died."

"Really? You're that close?"

He nodded. "He and I are working on a case together right now. I'm learning so much from him. Don't let that grandfatherly exterior fool you. He's a fine attorney. And relentless when it comes to getting at the truth."

She said nothing. After a moment, she leaned forward. "Sutton . . . there's something I need to tell you. Something . . . I overheard. About you."

She looked over at him, and he saw it in her face. The disappointment he felt in himself was magnified. "How long have you known?"

She bowed her head. "I heard some people talking—the night of the reception. And Sutton, I've come close to telling you so many times, but then I put myself in your place and I feel—"

"Sorry for me?" He stood and shrugged off the duster. "You should have told me you knew, Claire."

She rose. "I know I should have. But I knew it would hurt you for me to know." She stepped closer. "It doesn't matter to me, Sutton . . . what the review board decided. It makes no difference whether you have land or don't."

"It does to me."

Her sigh held understanding. She reached for his hand and brought it to her face. Closing her eyes, she pressed her cheek into his palm, then pressed a kiss where her cheek had been. Fire raced through his veins and only gained momentum when she looked up at him. He struggled to hold his desires in check.

She was radiant. Captivating. Intelligent. Witty. And *good,* in every way that mattered. No wonder she'd captured the attention of Adelicia's wealthy male counterparts. All of whom were rich beyond what he could ever hope to be—even if his land had been returned. Claire deserved all the grand things that a man of means could give her.

Everything he . . . could not. He'd been given the chance to make his choice between marrying for wealth or marrying from the heart. He'd made his decision and had no regrets, and Claire deserved the opportunity to do the same.

Now to have the strength to let her.

"I made more notes in your portfolio last night, Miss Laurent."

"Yes, ma'am." Claire opened the front door. "I've already read them, and everything is clear." Claire followed her down the front steps, carrying Mrs. Acklen's satchel to the carriage where the children and Miss Cenas sat waiting. She glanced behind her, wondering where Sutton was.

She'd hugged him good-bye a moment earlier when she bid the family a formal farewell, but it hadn't been the good-bye she'd wanted to give him.

"Why aren't you going with us, Miss Claire?" young Claude asked, his brow furrowing.

Claire rubbed her arms. She should have slipped her coat on. "Because I need to stay here and do some work for your mother. But I want you to be sure and eat two beignets for me at Café du Monde. And Pauline, practice your sketching while you're gone. Understood?" When Claire met William's gaze, she merely winked, and the I'm-not-a-child-anymore young man grinned in return.

With Eli's assistance, Mrs. Acklen climbed into the carriage, then looked down at Claire. "Do be careful, Miss Laurent, in your goings about. If you need anything, look to Eli or Cordina. They'll instruct you well."

"We'll keep her in line, Mrs. Acklen." Eli gave a mock salute. "Don't you worry, ma'am. And please give our best to everyone at Angola."

"Miss Laurent?"

Claire turned to see Sutton standing on the portico.

"I need to go over one more thing with you, please." He disappeared back inside.

Mrs. Acklen exhaled. "We need to be on our way, Miss Laurent. Please tell him to hurry!"

Claire raced up the steps, having seen the flash of impatience in her employer's eyes. "Sutton?" He wasn't in the entrance hall.

"I'm in the study."

She rounded the corner and saw him standing by the window. She was pleased to see that he was wearing the coat she'd given him for Christmas. "If you're worried that I won't record the art properly, I promise, Sutton, I'll do it just like you showed—"

He strode past her, closed the door, and pulled her to him. He dug his hands into her hair, angled her face to meet his mouth fully, and kissed her, long and slow, taking his time. Time they didn't have, but at the moment, Claire didn't care. Oh, how she'd wanted to kiss him at the reception, and then when they'd exchanged presents, and then when . . .

She slipped her arms around his neck, loving the feel of him against her, and in his sheriff's duster, no less.

All too soon, his mouth relinquished hers. He held her tight, tighter than she could remember. "You take care of yourself while I'm gone," he said, his voice hoarse.

"I'll be fine. You're the one traveling. *You* be careful."

He drew back slightly, and tenderly traced his thumb along her lower lip. "That wasn't fair, I know. Surprising you like that."

"That's all right. I cheat at checkers."

He laughed. "Yes, you do. Among other things."

She walked with him into the entrance hall. "I'll see you in two weeks."

"About that . . ." He paused by the front door, looking down. "I might be gone a little longer than I first thought."

"Why?"

"I've got work to do for Adelicia, plus some business to conduct for the firm." His gaze met hers but fleetingly. "And you need time to catalog the art and to do everything on the forty-seven lists Mrs. Acklen has left you."

Claire smiled, but only because she told herself to.

"I want you to have time to paint too, Claire. Time for yourself." He looked at her then. "You haven't had much of that lately. Time to think, to do what *you'd* like to do."

"That's very generous of you, Sutton, but quite frankly . . . I'd rather have time with you."

His smile gained longing, but his eyes . . . His eyes spoke of something different. With a brief smile, he reached for his satchel, and Claire instinctively reached for him. He dropped the satchel and his arms came around her. She held him as tight as she could, pressing herself into him, wanting him to remember what she felt like—what they felt like together.

The front door opened. Eli quickly lowered his eyes. "Excuse me,

Mr. Monroe, but the Lady's asking for you, sir." He closed the door, not waiting for a response.

Claire let go first, pleased that Sutton seemed reluctant to. "How long do you think you'll be gone?"

"I'm not sure." He picked up his satchel again.

"Can we write?"

Opening the door, he smiled a little. "Yes, we can write."

"Every day?"

His smile deepened, but in a sad way. "I'm going to miss you," he whispered, then tucked a curl behind her ear and pressed a hard, quick kiss to her forehead. "I'll see you soon."

And he was gone.

45

Feeling a little awkward, Claire stood outside Sutton's room in the art gallery, hand on the doorknob. Two weeks had passed since he'd left, yet it felt like much longer. He'd written, requesting she retrieve a file from his desk, and informing that a courier would come by for it. But even with his permission, she felt a sense of trespass.

The knob turned easily in her grip. Sutton had said it wouldn't be locked. Not with the main doors to the gallery kept locked at all times, something he'd stressed when he'd entrusted her with the key.

The door creaked as she opened it.

His room was cast in shadows, but she quickly remedied that by pulling the curtains back from the windows. Afternoon light poured in. The first thing that struck her was how sparsely decorated the quarters felt. Then she realized it wasn't the absence of furniture or necessities she was noticing. She was simply comparing it to the mansion's decor where crystal vases, miniature statuary, and bric-a-brac decorated every tabletop and mantel.

The simplicity and organization of Sutton's bedroom suited him.

The file was atop the desk, exactly as he'd said. She turned to leave, then caught the faintest scent and paused. She breathed in again, but it was gone. On a whim, needing a tangible reminder of him, she crossed to the wardrobe, opened it, and held one of his shirts to her face. She inhaled the hint of bayberry and spice, of sunshine and meadow, and something else decidedly male—and closed her eyes, memorizing it.

He'd written her twice since he'd left. She'd written him nearly every day. At night before she went to bed. He'd written her once from Café du Monde in New Orleans, and she'd found it more than a little unnerving to think of him being so close to where her family's gallery had been. But his next letter had reported them departing for Angola Plantation, some one hundred thirty miles from New Orleans, and she'd rested easier.

She smiled thinking of the postscript he'd included in his last letter. "*Try not to nod off during Pastor Bunting's sermons. Though, from what I hear, the pews are quite comfortable.*"

Reading his letters was like sitting next to him, conversing. And more than once she'd found herself laughing or responding aloud to something he'd written. Between managing Mrs. Acklen's business interests and working on the lawsuit with Mr. Holbrook—whatever that entailed—his days sounded overfull.

But her favorite part of the letter was his closing, where he told her he was praying for her, which had prompted her to do the same for him even more faithfully.

Two miniature framed portraits of a man and woman graced his bedside table. His parents, she presumed. The drawing of the man could well have been an artist's rendering of Sutton in future years. The resemblance was striking. *Delicate* best described the woman's likeness, the features of her face all softness and curves, no sharpness whatsoever. Beautiful . . .

Claire smoothed a hand over Sutton's pillow, wondering again if there was a reason beyond extended business that was keeping him away. Of one thing she was certain—leaving had been difficult for him. She'd seen it in his face, felt it in his manner.

Which, strangely, made being apart from him more bearable.

The rendering of the review board's verdict regarding his family's land had appeared in the *Nashville Banner* shortly after he'd left. On the front page. And it hadn't been complimentary to his father. Quite disparaging, in fact. For that reason alone, she'd been glad Sutton had been away. Though he'd no doubt read the article by now. Mrs. Acklen had the newspapers mailed to her at Angola.

Claire completed cataloging the pieces of art for that day, then retrieved her sketching pad and pencils and headed in the direction of the meadow. She pulled her coat collar closer about her neck, her breath fogging white in the January chill as she trod the well-worn path.

Recent days had found a steady rhythm. Awakening before sunrise, she read in the *tête-à-tête* room, enjoying it when she happened across Scriptures Mrs. Acklen had underlined in the Bible she'd given her. What insight that gave into a person—reading verses they'd found especially meaningful. After breakfasting with Eli and Cordina in the kitchen, she painted until midmorning, always searching for that one perfect venue to paint for the upcoming auction. The rest of the day was spent working on Mrs. Acklen's various projects and cataloging the woman's priceless collection of art. But the evening hours . . . those were by far the loneliest.

She'd already finished *Alexander the Great* and Thomas Moore's *Paradise and the Peri,* among other selections, but reading books and writing Sutton could only fill up so much time.

The cold air stinging her lungs, Claire followed the trail alongside the creek until she came to her favorite slab of limestone that jutted out from a hillside. She settled onto nature's bench, the bubbling harmony of water over rock speaking an ancient tongue. She drank it in, drawn to its peaceful tranquility.

A flutter of color drew her attention a short ways downstream, and she spotted a cardinal, the bright red of its feathers brilliant against the winter dull. The bird swooped and settled by the near bank, where a pool of water ran tranquil and deep. The bird drank its fill and fluttered off.

Claire stared at the spot where the bird had been, remembering her mother's last request—how she'd poured the water over her mother's body—and still seeing the scene so clearly in her memory. An image of the *The Peri* rose in her mind, the angel cradling the bowl of water against her chest, and Claire instinctively swallowed. *Father God, would you quench this thirst inside me . . .*

She sat for a while longer, until the sun began its evening journey, then she made her way back to the mansion, her limbs stiff with cold. Cordina greeted her inside the entrance hall.

"Land's sake, child, look at your cheeks. You're frozen through." She cupped Claire's face in her warm hands, and Claire shivered. "I'll be bringin' your dinner up shortly, Miss Laurent. A package came for you. It's on the table in the small study."

"Thank you, Cordina." Keeping her coat on, Claire hurried into the study, but her heart fell when she saw the fancy wrapping and ribbon. If the package had been from Sutton, it would have been wrapped suitably for posting.

As it was, she could easily guess who had sent it.

She'd had dinner twice now with Andrew Stanton, in addition to the first afternoon he'd come to visit. The man had sent her flowers following the reception—three times—along with chocolates and other confections. She opened the package.

A book. But not just any book. She ran a hand over the cover, then opened it. A first-edition copy of *Les Aventures de Télémaque,* published . . . *in 1699!* She opened the enclosed card. "*For you, Miss Laurent, in appreciation of our friendship and in loving memory of your dear mother. Most warmly and in anticipation for our next dinner, Andrew Stanton.*"

She shook her head, both at the book's antiquity and at Mr. Stanton's generosity. Such a kind man, honorable and genuine. She'd mentioned the book to him only once as being a favorite of hers and of her *maman.*

The other men who, to her great surprise, had sent gifts following the reception, had ceased their efforts to gain her attention, but Mr. Stanton was different. He was humble and unassuming, and easy to converse with. Widowed four years now, he had surprised her with his candor.

"When my dear Libba died," he'd confided, "the thought of ever remarrying seemed foreign. But as the years have passed and my grief has eased, I'm finding myself more open to that possibility."

Just as he'd been honest with her, so she had been with him, sharing that while she appreciated their friendship, she had no immediate aspirations toward that goal. She'd worded the sentence with careful emphasis and had taken his slow, understanding nod as a sign he understood.

Now she wondered.

Following dinner that night, Claire carefully turned the pages of the treasured copy of *Les Aventures de Télémaque,* rereading her favorite parts, and thinking of the mural in Adelicia's bedroom while knowing she couldn't—and wouldn't—keep the book. She would return it to Mr. Stanton the next time she saw him, along with her heartfelt thanks and an explanation as to why she couldn't see him again. Flowers and candy were one thing. But a gift of this magnitude constituted something far more.

And *more* with anyone other than Sutton wasn't a *more* she welcomed.

Early one morning the following week, as a late-January sun played coy with the coming dawn, Claire bundled up warm and snug and set out for the stables. Zeke had agreed to have Athena saddled and ready. But when she rounded the corner, it wasn't Athena Zeke held by the reins.

"Mornin', Miss Claire." The boy smiled big, his ears wiggling. "How are you, ma'am?"

Claire eyed him, then Truxton, not about to ride Sutton's horse without permission. "I asked you to saddle Athena, Zeke."

"Yes, ma'am. But Mr. Monroe, he told me different 'fore he left. He said to surprise you. So . . ." The boy glanced at the stallion and then back at her. "Surprise!"

She giggled, a thrill working through her. No offense to Athena, but riding Truxton was like riding a four-legged locomotive. And to think that Sutton trusted her so much. Remembering, she reached into her coat pocket. "Cordina sent you a little something."

Zeke took the cloth-covered offering and held it to his nose. "Smells like one of her biscuits." He sniffed again. "With fried chicken!"

Claire accepted his help into the saddle and felt the power of the thoroughbred beneath her. She did her best to make her next question sound unrehearsed. "Have you found anything new recently, in your digging out back?"

Grinning, he dug into his pocket and pulled out a quarter, along with several metal buttons and a dented lid from a tin of chewing tobacco. "I'm findin' new stuff all the time. Like I always tell Mr. Monroe, there's treasure buried there. But he just keeps on shakin' his head." Zeke stuffed the items back into his pocket. "When you think he'll be back, ma'am?"

Claire looked down, feeling a twisting inside her chest. "I'm not sure." And despite her asking Sutton in nearly every other letter, he'd given no indication about his return.

Truxton responded to her slightest command with agility and speed, and he flew across the meadow. The cold wind bit Claire's cheeks and burned her lungs. And the thought of Sutton's dream set her heart on fire. The thoroughbred scaled the stream as if it was a mere crack in the dirt, and she soared right with him just as Sutton had taught her.

She couldn't explain it, but she felt closer to Sutton in that moment than she ever had.

She guided the thoroughbred to the top of the ridge and reined in, out of breath. Seeing Belmont below and the city of Nashville in the distance, she ached to capture the beauty on canvas. She'd painted four landscapes so far, of different views in the meadow.

Her work was coming along—but slowly.

She would retire at night thinking a particular painting held promise, only to awaken the next morning and see it for what it was. Something any tourist wandering the French Quarter could buy from a street artist. Good, but not nearly good enough for the auction just over a month away.

"*Your talent simply lacks any unique quality. . . .*" Though she tried to shut it out, her father's opinion of her work rose from the grave and condemned her efforts even before the palette was wet. And a part of her wondered if maybe he'd been right.

Maybe she *was* just a mediocre painter—and a copyist—after all.

As the sun spread golden fingers over the vistas below, Claire closed her eyes tight, still seeing the views but as a concert of brushstrokes on canvas. *Father, help me create something worthy. Worthy of the auction and worthy in the eyes of the critics. . . .*

But even as the words left her heart and rose upward, they fell flat. She wished Sutton was at her side. He would know what words to pray, even if she didn't.

Two days later saw February ushered in and the gardens of Belmont blanketed in four inches of snow. Claire brought the last two hatboxes filled with letters and mementos into the small study, determined to get through them so she could begin the memory book for Mrs. Acklen. Not to mention finish writing the biography she'd started for Mrs. Acklen's chapter in *Queens of American Society.*

On the settee before the fire, cup of Cordina's tea at hand, she opened the first box—and saw the invitation she'd designed for Madame LeVert's reception on top. She smiled. Mrs. Acklen must have slipped it inside before she left for New Orleans.

Reception.

Mrs. Acklen

Will receive on Tuesday Evening, December 18th,

at 8 o'clock

Complimentary to Madame LeVert.

Mrs. Acklen had instructed her to keep the invitation brief and elegant. Claire had shown her the draft, fully expecting her to mark it up with suggestions. But Mrs. Acklen had approved it without the slightest alteration. Reliving that sense of satisfaction, Claire set the invitation in the stack of items slated for the memory book.

She ran across so many things that touched her heart. The funeral announcement for Emma Franklin, letters from various family members to Adelicia . . . Then her gaze fell to a newspaper clipping next in the stack. The title drew her eye—FRANCIS ROUTH ACQUITTED.

Francis *Routh*? As in . . . related to Belmont's Mrs. Routh?

Claire checked the date. July 18, 1842. Front page of the *Nashville Banner*. She skimmed the first paragraph and a flush of awareness moved through her, heavy and uncomfortable, as if she were reading a diary that wasn't hers.

46

Claire read the article, feeling as though she shouldn't, and yet reminding herself—as she had before when reading these clippings—that this had been public news. Granted, over twenty years ago now.

> Following a second appeal, Francis Routh of Nashville has been acquitted of a conviction in a Louisiana land fraud case that sent him to prison over two years ago. Routh was released from the Louisiana State Penitentiary on the second of this month after serving twenty-six months of a three-year sentence.

Claire's gaze hovered over the next paragraph, the words revealing, and starting to blur in her vision.

> Having suffered from declining health since entering prison, Routh died of pneumonia last week at the home of his close associate and former business partner, Isaac Franklin. Since Routh's incarceration, and the loss of his home and business, his wife has taken residence with Mr. and Mrs. Isaac Franklin of Fairview in Gallatin.
>
> From the outset, Routh maintained his innocence. He is predeceased by two sons, and leaves behind his wife, Mrs. Abigail Routh of Nashville.

The remainder of the article dealt with the alleged charges from years prior, and Claire dragged her gaze from the newsprint and stared ahead, focusing on nothing.

Mrs. Routh's husband. It had to be. . . .

A knock on the partially opened door brought her head up. Claire quickly buried the article in the stack of clippings. "Mrs. Routh." She forced a smile.

The head housekeeper stepped inside the study, envelopes in her hand. Her attention flitted to the pile of newspaper clippings, and lingered. "The mail arrived, Miss Laurent."

"Thank you." Claire stood and met her halfway. "I appreciate your bringing it to me." Mrs. Routh turned to leave. She'd seemed quieter, almost distant, lately, but Claire hadn't questioned it. Up until now, she'd simply been grateful for the reprieve.

Claire returned to the settee and absently flipped through the envelopes, hoping Mrs. Routh hadn't seen what she'd been reading. There was an envelope from Mrs. Holbrook—about the upcoming Women's League annual tea, no doubt. And Claire recognized Mr. Stanton's handwriting on another. But no letter from Sutton.

Gradually becoming aware of Mrs. Routh still standing in the doorway, Claire tried for a normal tone. "Is there something else you need, Mrs. Routh?"

Her expression stoic, the head housekeeper appeared as though she wanted to say something, and yet didn't at the same time. She stood a little straighter. "I wish to convey to you, Miss Laurent, that . . ." Mrs. Routh looked as if she'd just bitten into a sour lemon. "What you did . . . for Mrs. Acklen"—she said the name with such reverence—"with the statue of the children . . ." She gestured toward the entrance hall and glanced away.

Then, as if realizing she'd broken her own cardinal rule about needing to look at the person to whom she was speaking, she looked back. "It was a most gracious gesture, Miss Laurent." She spoke the last words quickly, as if gritting her teeth and hoping the doctor's needle would be swift.

Claire was certain her surprise shown in her face. "Thank you . . . Mrs. Routh. That's *very* kind of you to say. It was my pleasure to do it. I'm most grateful for all that Mrs. Acklen has done for me."

Mrs. Routh's hint of a smile was almost jarring. "As am I, Miss Laurent, for her great generosity to me." She promptly turned to close the door behind her, but not before casting one last look at the pile of articles on the settee and then at Claire.

For several seconds, Claire stared at the closed door, having the distinct feeling that she'd sorely misjudged the woman.

On Thursday evening, the carriage turned off the main road and Mr. Stanton's home came into view. Claire told herself she ought not be surprised at the manor's size and elegance. She'd known Andrew Stanton was wealthy.

She stepped from the carriage, assisted by Mr. Stanton's footman and with the wrapped copy of *Les Aventures de Télémaque* tucked in her coat pocket. A servant greeted her at the door, and Mr. Stanton met her inside the drawing room.

He kissed her hand. "Miss Laurent, thank you for agreeing to join me here this evening. I thought it might be a nice change to have dinner at home rather than in town."

Claire accepted his help with her coat. "Of course. I appreciated receiving your invitation." He'd asked to have dinner last week, but she'd been busy working to finish cataloging the pieces in the art gallery and painting every minute she could. Her gaze was immediately drawn to the paintings on the walls. All originals, as far as she could tell, and all artists she recognized. "You and Mrs. Acklen share a common love for art."

"More than once, she and I have found ourselves bidding against one another in an auction. She has exquisite taste."

"As do you, sir."

Andrew Stanton was a handsome man with silvering hair at his temples and a kind, open face, and conversation with him over dinner came easily. Following the meal, they retired into the drawing room for coffee where a fire burned warm in the hearth.

She sat on the settee, and he beside her. "You have a lovely home here."

"Even lovelier with you in it." He glanced away as though surprised he'd given the thought voice, and Claire felt her guard rise.

"Miss Laurent . . ." His smile was tentative. "Claire," he said, question in his tone.

She gave a single nod.

"I realize that you must look upon me as quite the older man. Which I am, compared to your youthfulness. But I believe that age and youth can sometimes complement one another. And I believe they would . . . in our situation."

"Mr. Stanton, I . . ."

"I would be honored if you would call me Andrew."

Biting the tip of her tongue, she nodded. "Andrew . . . I truly enjoy your company but"—she took a deep breath, recalling what she'd rehearsed—"at present, I'm not at all in a position to consider a relationship of the nature I believe you're wanting. In fact, I . . ." She didn't want to hurt him. "I think it would be best if we didn't see one another again."

To her surprise, he smiled. "That was a carefully worded—and well-rehearsed—response, Claire." Understanding softened his expression. "From the moment you misunderstood and thought I wanted *you* to get *me* a drink at the reception, you've been transparent with me. I appreciate that about you. And while I appreciate your friendship, it would be remiss of me to let you think that is all I feel for you. Or all that I hope you might one day feel for me."

The crackle of the fire ate up the silence, and the only word Claire could hear in her mind was *transparent.* That's the last thing she'd been. With him. With Sutton. With everyone. But it's what she now wanted to be more than anything in her life.

"Andrew—"

He held up a hand. "No need to say anything else tonight. I hadn't planned on broaching this subject, although I am glad it came up." In true gentlemanly form, he kissed her hand, then rose and called for the carriage. "I'll see you back to Belmont."

Andrew helped her with her coat, and the weight in the pocket served as a reminder.

She withdrew the book. "I appreciate it very much, but I can't." She laid it on a side table.

He promptly handed it back. "It was a gift, Claire. Between friends. With no expectations beyond that."

Seeing his determination, she didn't argue as he turned for his coat and gloves. The carriage ride back to Belmont was quiet, and when they rounded the corner and the moonlit silhouette of the darkened mansion came into view, Claire felt a homesickness inside her. One she hadn't felt in a long time.

Only it wasn't for a place. It was for a person.

The carriage stopped by the front steps just as Eli descended them, lantern in hand. He assisted her from the coach, and Andrew escorted her to the door. "Do you have any idea when Mrs. Acklen will be returning?"

"In a couple of weeks, I believe. But no later than March, for the art auction."

"She told me you were planning on submitting an entry for the auction for new artists this year. I'm looking forward to seeing that. Mr. Monroe also sings your praises in that regard. And in every other as well."

Claire perked up. "*Mr. Monroe* commented to you about me?"

Andrew's expression grew timid. "Yes, though . . . I somewhat imposed myself upon him. I pulled him aside at the reception and told him I was interested in getting to know you better. And I inquired whether any gentleman had previous designs on your affections."

Claire's heart skipped an odd beat. She remembered seeing them in the central parlor, speaking, shaking hands. "If it's not too forward of me, what was Mr. Monroe's response, exactly?"

Andrew took a moment to answer. "He said that you were the finest young woman he'd ever met and that he knew of no firm reason why I shouldn't pursue a friendship with you." He studied her beneath the single portico lantern Eli had lit. "However . . . I can clearly see one. Right now. In your eyes."

Claire lowered her gaze, but he tilted her chin back up.

A slow, somewhat resigned smile moved over his face. "Sutton Monroe is a very lucky man, Claire. Does he know?"

"Know?" she whispered.

"That you love him."

Tears tightened her throat. She shook her head, then shrugged.

He said nothing for a moment, then brushed a chaste kiss on her forehead. "Thank you, Claire, for a beautiful evening. And for the gift of your friendship."

Claire stood inside the entrance hall, a hand raised in parting as Andrew's carriage pulled away. She slipped her gloves into her empty pockets, the copy of *Les Aventures de Télémaque* safely tucked on the side table in Andrew's foyer.

Then she went straight to her room and wrote Sutton, and told him she and Mr. Stanton had "compared notes," and that she wanted him to come home.

And not just to come home, but to come home to her.

Claire slipped through the doors of the church and made her way down the aisle toward Mrs. Acklen's pew.

"Greetings, church." Reverend Bunting took his place behind the pulpit. "Let's all rise for the opening prayer and the first hymn."

Claire scooted into the pew and retrieved a hymnal, not knowing the words to all the hymns yet. As the prayer ended and the organ music began to swell, she joined in singing with the other parishioners, missing Sutton's rich tenor.

She'd mailed her letter to him on Friday, the morning following her dinner with Andrew Stanton, so she knew he hadn't received it yet. It took almost a week for letters to travel between them—sometimes longer, depending on the weather.

"Please open your Bibles to the book of Jeremiah, chapter eighteen. And remain standing for the reading of God's Holy Word."

Claire opened her Bible. Jeremiah came right after Isaiah, which she'd been studying, so she had no trouble finding the book.

She followed along as Reverend Bunting read aloud.

" 'Then I went down to the potter's house, and behold, he wrought a work on the wheels. And the vessel that he made of clay was marred in the hand of the potter. So he made it again another vessel, as seemed good to the potter to make it.' "

A vessel of clay? A potter? Her interest piqued, Claire continued to follow along.

"Then the word of the Lord came to me, saying, 'O house of Israel, cannot I do with you as this potter?' saith the Lord. 'Behold as the clay is in the potter's hand, so are ye in mine hand, O house of Israel.' " Reverend Bunting paused. "Blessed be this reading of the Lord's Word, and our adherence to it."

A hush of whispered *amens* filled the sanctuary as the congregation sat. Claire reviewed the passage as Reverend Bunting began to speak. This was something she understood. This struggle with the clay. Repeatedly in recent weeks, she'd tried to create something of worth. Something that would cause people to sit up and take notice. Like her *Versailles* surely would have done. She exhaled a slow breath.

In a way, it was comforting to know the Lord understood her frustration. Only, *she* was the clay in this instance, she realized. And looking at it from that perspective made her slightly ill at ease.

"You may be here this morning, pondering the Lord's goodness in your life," the reverend continued. "Or you may be wondering why He's allowed the hard times that He has. When afflictions come—and they will—we should determine to accept them as being from the hand of God. For either God is sovereign, or He is not. He is either Lord of all, or He is not. There is no in between."

That same theme again . . . What Mrs. Acklen had said that afternoon in her bedroom weeks ago. But Claire was coming to believe that Mrs. Acklen and the reverend were right. Though it was hardly encouraging to think about a sovereign God intentionally bringing both joy—and pain. Something about it seemed false.

When the reverend invited everyone to stand and sing, Claire was glad the song was one she knew by heart. She laid the hymnal aside and joined in. The pipe organ's rich tones rose and swelled, and she closed her eyes, swept up in the music and lyrics.

Would you paint if you knew you were painting only for me?

Claire opened her eyes, certain she'd heard a whisper, only not knowing whether it came from the pew in front of her, or behind. The people seated in front of her weren't looking her way, and neither were the people behind her—until she started looking at them. She quickly turned around, then casually glanced from side to side to see who was seeking her attention.

But she saw no one.

The organ music grew softer, and Reverend Bunting began to pray. Finally deciding she must have imagined it, she bowed her head and, in her mind's eye, the image of a pot on a potter's wheel came vividly into view.

She could see the wheel spinning, and the artist's hands—strong, and long-stained brownish-red—molding and shaping the clay pot as he saw fit.

Would you paint if you knew you were painting only for me?

Claire drew in a breath, hearing the infinite whisper with uncanny clarity this time. Only not with her ears but in her heart. Her scalp tingled, she gripped the pew in front of her, and yet she wasn't afraid. On the contrary. She'd never felt such peace, or such love.

She didn't open her eyes. She didn't have to. She only put a hand to her mouth to keep from saying aloud the name that was on her lips. . . .

Jesus.

Later that night in bed, she lay awake in the darkness, wishing Sutton were there, wishing she could talk to him, tell him what had happened that morning while the details were still fresh inside her.

But she *could* tell him. . . .

She climbed from the warmth of the covers, lit the oil lamp on the side table, and hurried to her desk for pen and paper. Then she scurried back, grateful for the thick rugs covering the wooden floor. Nestled beneath the bedcovers again, she pulled down the sleeves of her gown as far as they would go.

And she wrote.

She wrote until well after midnight, the words pouring from her like the rain splattering her windowsill outside. When the question had come the first time that morning, she'd missed it, not knowing what—or who—it was. *His* inaudible voice. But when she'd heard it the second time, she knew what He was asking. Even though a small part of her wished she didn't.

Because she wasn't completely sure of her answer yet.

When she finished writing Sutton, she'd filled seven pages. She stacked those aside and started on a fresh page, this time writing to *Him*. The one who had whispered. She wrote until her hand cramped and her neck and shoulder muscles burned. She wrote thoughts she'd never shared with anyone, and would be embarrassed if others read. She asked questions about Maman. About her father. And about why—if God had given her this gift of painting, however slight—He wasn't doing anything with it?

When she extinguished the oil lamp at half past three, she pressed her cheek into the cool of the pillow, exhausted, clinging to the memory of His voice, and praying she would never forget what she'd felt that morning. Such perfect, boundless love. Beyond anything she'd ever known. And yet she still wondered at the implications of His question—*would you paint if you knew you were painting only for me?*

Did that mean that her canvas for the auction—the painting she'd been working on and planned to enter—wouldn't be well received? Or maybe wouldn't be accepted at all? Did it mean her work would never achieve the acclaim she wanted? Or did it mean something else entirely? She didn't know.

She only knew that she wanted that love in her life. And that no matter what it cost her, the answer to Jesus's inaudible question . . . was *yes.*

47

Monday morning, the rhythm of steel wheels over miles of iron ribbon companioned the steady *tick-tick-tick* of Sutton's internal clock. He willed the train to travel faster. He'd left Angola Plantation within an hour of receiving Bartholomew Holbrook's telegram on Saturday morning. Finally, a major stride in their case.

Investigators had learned the name of an art dealer involved in the sale of two forged paintings they now had in their possession. And that man had been traced to Nashville. They didn't have him in custody yet, and Holbrook hadn't shared the man's name in the telegram. But it didn't matter. That they'd gotten this far was enough.

If they could only win this case. . . .

Holbrook was right—what doors it would open. And he needed an open door because it was becoming more and more likely that his days of working in a management capacity at Belmont were swiftly coming to an end. Dr. William Cheatham had visited Angola three times in the past two months, and the physician's relationship with Adelicia had definitely taken a more personal turn.

The match wasn't a surprise to him—the two had been friends for years—and Dr. Cheatham certainly seemed capable of assuming the managerial aspects of the estate. To Sutton's great relief, Adelicia had agreed that *should* she and William decide to marry, she would protect her financial interests with a premarriage contract, as she'd done with Joseph Acklen.

Sutton would continue to serve as her personal attorney, but there'd be no need for him to live at Belmont anymore. So where would he live? He had no family land. No home of his own. And while he had *some* money saved, the amount seemed inconsequential compared to what he needed to properly establish himself again.

But if they were to win this lawsuit . . .

He checked his pocket watch, already knowing the minute hand would read about ten minutes later than the last time he checked. The train was about a half hour or so from Nashville—he recognized the terrain—and he was itching to get back. To work on their case, but also . . .

To see Claire.

Nearly two months he'd been gone, and she'd mentioned Andrew Stanton only twice in their exchange of letters, and then only in passing. He'd tried to read between the lines of those mentions, wondering if Stanton had managed to make an impression on her or not.

As fine a man as Stanton was, Sutton prayed he hadn't.

Because after having only her letters to look forward to, he'd decided that he'd been a fool to leave her the way he did. Yes, she'd needed time, he knew, to learn her own heart. But he'd had time to learn his too, and his heart wanted *her.*

Now if he could only find a way to provide for her. If love were enough, he was convinced he had a lifetime of that to lavish upon her. But she was worthy of far more, and he wanted to give her everything she deserved.

He rested a hand on the artist's case he'd made for her in recent weeks. Nothing fancy. Just something she could store her canvases in as she trekked back and forth to paint. He hadn't worked with wood like that in years, and he'd enjoyed every minute of it. Just as he enjoyed anticipating the look on her face when he gave it to her.

The train whistle blew, signaling their approach into Nashville. But it couldn't come fast enough for him.

Satchel slung over her shoulder, and easel and white umbrella tucked under her arm, Claire started back down the ridge with the still-wet canvas in her grip. Perhaps it was the sun's brilliance overhead or the unexpected hint of spring, but she couldn't deny the sense of possibility filling her.

Or the fact that she was perspiring beneath her chemise.

At the foot of the ridge she paused and took off her coat, then lifted her hair from her neck. Oh, the breeze felt heavenly. And this after it had snowed only days earlier. Tennessee weather . . .

Since she'd gone to bed so late last night, staying up to write, she'd thought she might sleep later than she had. But she'd awakened at a quarter past seven, refreshed and eager to paint. Wishing she had a glass of Cordina's sweet iced lemonade, she heard something that sounded almost as refreshing.

Shouldering her load again, she gripped the canvas by its edge and started across the meadow for the creek.

Atop the ridge that morning, she'd stood staring out over the meadow at the Belmont estate and had felt her gaze being drawn to the hill in the distance where Sutton's family home had once stood. It was then she'd finally realized what view she wanted to capture and she'd painted it. An umbrella had helped to diffuse the bright sunlight and show the paint's true colors, but she looked forward to painting the view again, until she got it right.

She glanced down at the canvas, mindful to keep the winter grasses from brushing the oils still tacky to the touch. And with growing certainty, she heard the response inside her gaining strength. *I'll paint as if I'm painting only for You.*

She expected Sutton would receive her letter in a few days, and she prayed her plea would spur him to come home. She pictured him again at the LeVert reception, speaking with Andrew Stanton, and while she thought she understood the motivation behind what he'd done, she still wanted to shake the man senseless.

Yet she could hardly wait to be with him again.

Seeing the slab of limestone jutting out from the hillside, she felt as if she were seeing an old friend. She set the canvas in a protected cleft of the rock and deposited her belongings beside it. Then she knelt by the creek and dipped her hand in. The icy chill felt like a touch of heaven, and she drank until she'd slaked her thirst.

On a whim, she removed her boots and stockings and slid her feet in. She leaned back, face tilted toward the sun, and let out a sigh—one that felt as if it had been building inside her for months, if not years. As she lay there, her mother's face came to mind. She wished she still had her mother's locket watch, yet even without it, she could still picture her *maman*'s smile.

Knowing the day was slipping by and that work awaited, Claire rose and reached for her boots and stockings but paused when she saw the deep pool of water downstream. She glanced behind her, then around. The spot was secluded. She was alone.

By the time she reached the edge of the creek, she'd unbuttoned the front of her dress. Laying it aside, next came her crinoline and underskirts, until she stood in only her chemise and pantalets. She waded in, sucking in a breath as the water swirled around her ankles, then, as she got closer to the deeper pool, around her calves and waist. By the time the water reached her chest, she knew she couldn't—and wouldn't—turn back, but oh . . . it was cold.

Taking a deep breath, she closed her eyes and submerged herself beneath the surface, and for a few brief seconds, the world above faded from view. It was the desire to be clean, and the longing to bury her old life in exchange for the promise of a new one that permeated every corner of her heart, that crowded out every last doubt.

She didn't know how to go about reshaping this world she'd created without destroying it completely, but she trusted the Potter to know, to show her, and to mold her. Into whatever He wanted her to be.

Belmont came into view and Sutton reined in, as much to give the mare from the livery in town a chance to rest, as to give himself a moment to rehearse, again, what he was going to say to Claire when he saw her. *Forgive me for being such a fool* didn't seem like enough, yet that's the first thing that came to him.

In nearly every letter she'd written, she'd asked when he would be returning, so he felt sure she'd missed him. But being back now, coming in unannounced, and not knowing what the situation was between her and Andrew Stanton, he suddenly felt out of place, and it wasn't a comfortable feeling.

The mare pranced beneath him, and he urged her on uphill toward the mansion. He'd stopped briefly by the law office in town to speak to Holbrook, but he had been out on an appointment. Sutton hadn't been too disappointed. The person he really wanted to see was at Belmont. Or he hoped she was.

He spotted Eli on the front portico. Already the old man had an arm raised in greeting.

Eli met him at the front steps. "Welcome back, Mr. Monroe. We didn't know you were returning today, sir. I would have sent a carriage into town for you."

Sutton dismounted and handed him the reins. "Hello, Eli. And it's no bother. I left Angola sooner than planned."

"Nothing's amiss, I hope? Mrs. Acklen and the children are all right?"

"Everything's fine, and the Acklens are well. I simply had business to tend to. My trunks should be arriving from the station soon."

"I'll see to them, sir."

Sutton started toward the house. "Is Miss Laurent inside?"

"No, sir. She left earlier this morning. I'm sure she's fine, but I was about to send Zeke out to make sure she was all right."

"All right? Where did she go?"

Eli motioned. "Out across the meadow, sir, toward the creek, like she usually does. She had all of her painting things with her, sir. She's usually back by now for lunch, that's all."

Sutton reclaimed the mare's reins. "I'll ride out and find her." Astride the mare, he glanced down. "If she shows up without me, tell her I'm back and that I need to speak with her."

A hint of a smile tipped the old man's mouth. "Yes, sir, Mr. Monroe. I'll do that. And, sir . . . ?"

Sutton held the mare steady as Eli stepped closer.

"If I might be permitted to say something to you, sir . . ."

Sutton nodded but got the distinct feeling the older man was set on saying it either way.

"Your father was among the finest of men, Mr. Monroe. It doesn't matter what others might say about him now—or *write* about him, sir. Those of us at Belmont who knew Dr. Monroe still hold him in great honor. *I* hold him in great honor, sir." Eli's head dipped the slightest bit. "Just as I do his son."

Sutton looked away. Obviously Eli had read the article in the *Banner.* But why this man's opinion of his father—and of *him*—should move him to such a degree made no sense. Sutton worked to loosen the tightness in his throat. "Thank you, Eli. I appreciate that."

The old man held up his right hand and pointed to a raised scar that extended from the base of his thumb clear across the top of his wrist to the other side. "I would've lost my hand years ago, sir, had your father not doctored me. He came back every day for a month, then every week for several months after. He was out here the day before he—" Eli bowed his head. "Before they killed him, sir. He told me then, like he always did, how proud he was of you. And he'd be proud of you now too, sir, with how you're handling all this."

Sutton knew better than to try to speak again. It was all he could do to nod an acknowledgment. He rode out toward the creek, the breeze cool on his cheeks. Since the day his father had been killed, he'd carried the memory of the man close to his heart, as he had his own regret.

He'd always been proud to be Dr. Stephen Monroe's son. But never more so than in that moment. And what he couldn't explain, but knew without question, was that somehow, his father knew that too.

Sutton checked the meadow first, then looked up toward the ridge, but he doubted Claire would have gone that far on foot. He followed the path down toward the creek, and that's when he heard it. Singing.

He recognized her voice from having stood beside her in church, and it was a pretty sound. Prettier now after not having heard it for so long. He dismounted, looped the mare's reins around a pine branch, and followed the sound of her voice.

He saw her a split instant before she saw him, and his eyes went wide. She squealed and ducked behind a rock.

He couldn't keep from laughing, appreciating what he'd seen but not understanding why she was running around in her undergarments. And wet, no less. "What are you doing down here?"

"What are *you* doing back?"

He held his ground, still laughing. Especially when she peered up at him over the rock. "It's a little early yet to go swimming, Claire."

"I wasn't going swimming, *Sutton*. I was . . ." She smiled at him then, but held up a hand. "Do not come any closer."

He started forward just to see what she would do.

"Sutton!" She ducked back down, but he could hear her giggling.

"I'm only joking with you. I won't come any closer. Unless . . . I can help with something."

"You could have helped by letting me know you were coming home."

"It was kind of an . . . impromptu decision." She was adorable, peeking over the rock at him like that. "Seriously, Claire, what can I do to help you?"

"You can turn around and wait for me back over the hill."

He turned to go, then couldn't resist one last nudge. "I sure was looking forward to a hug."

"Sutton!"

Laughing, he retreated and did as he was told.

Minutes later she appeared over the hill. Seeing all that she was carrying, he hurried to help. He took the satchel and easel and tried to take the canvas, catching a quick glimpse of it. "Claire, that's absolutely—"

She turned the painting so he couldn't see it. "I can do better. I know I can."

"From what I saw, I'm impressed." And he was. But still she kept a firm grip on it, so he didn't force the issue.

A shyness came over her. "I'd rather you wait and see it when I'm finished, if you don't mind."

"Fair enough." He laid her belongings by a rock. "But would you mind propping it over there for a second?" He pointed, pleased when she complied without question. When she turned back around, he closed the distance between them and framed her face with his hands. Her pert look gave him hope. She laid her hand over his heart, and Sutton felt a rightness inside he'd never felt before. If Andrew Stanton had made any headway with her, it sure wasn't showing.

"Hello, Claire," he whispered.

Her eyes bright, her lower lip trembled with a smile. "Hello, Sutton."

He lowered his mouth to hers and kissed her, slowly, taking his time, just as he'd contemplated doing far too many times over the past two months. He savored the way she moved closer to him and tilted her head so her lips met his more fully.

"I'm sorry for staying away for so long," he whispered against her mouth, drawing back slightly. "I know I need to explain. And I will, more fully, later. But please know that I was simply trying to give you—"

"I know what you were doing . . . you silly, foolish man."

He stared.

"Mr. Stanton told me about your conversation the night of the reception." She ran a teasing forefinger along his jawline. Then over his lips. "I take it you didn't get my letter?"

"No, no letter." He kissed her again, not nearly so gently, but when she wove her fingers through his hair, he broke the kiss, trembling.

"I've missed you," she whispered.

"And I you." He reached up and tugged a damp curl, a weak effort to lighten the moment. He motioned back toward the creek. "What were you doing down there?"

"I was praying . . . and listening. Or trying to." Smiling, she searched his gaze, then lowered her head. When she finally looked up again, her eyes were moist but her expression was resolute. "I've done things in my life, especially in recent years, Sutton, that I'm not proud of."

He waited, weighing the earnestness in her gaze. "There's not a person living who hasn't done something they regret, Claire."

"I know. But I want to bury those things, put them behind me, once and for all." She part laughed, part sighed. "If that makes any sense."

He reached up and touched her face, the blue of her eyes drawing him in. "It does," he whispered, having felt that same need so many times. "I often come here to pray, and to work things through."

Her eyes lit as a tear slipped down her cheek.

He wiped it with his thumb. "Of course, I usually wear clothes."

Laughing together, they walked back to the mansion, and she talked the entire way. She told him how she was nearly finished cataloging Mrs. Acklen's art, how much she'd been painting, and how she wasn't sure if she had anything good enough for the art auction—which he knew wasn't true.

He drank in every last detail. Just like he'd read her letters over and over again before going to sleep.

"Speaking of the art auction," he slipped in as she took a breath, "you've already been approved by the committee to submit a canvas. "

"Thank you, Sutton, for arranging that for me."

He shook his head. "You only have yourself to thank. Members of the committee were at the LeVert reception, and your party favors alone convinced them of your talent." He decided not to say anything about the fee to enter. He'd filled out the application and paid the entry fee on her behalf. "There will be sessions occurring all week long, including the two auctions—the auction for the newer talent, and then a separate auction later in the week for the established artists."

She nodded, stealthily keeping the canvas turned away from him. "I get nervous just thinking about it."

"You'll do well, Claire. I have no doubt whatsoever." Another thought occurred to him, something he hadn't wanted to share with her in a letter. Not considering what had happened there. "While we were in New Orleans, I visited the art gallery that your parents owned and . . . where you used to live."

Her steps slowed as they approached the mansion. "You did?"

"I hope you don't mind. I'd been to the Café du Monde one afternoon, and my curiosity got the best of me."

Eli wasn't out front, so Sutton tied the mare to a hitching post and followed Claire inside. They got as far as the grand salon when she turned, that same resolute look on her face.

"Sutton, could we . . . talk for a while?"

He reached over and squeezed her hand. "I thought that's what we've been doing."

"I know but . . . there are some things I'd like to say to you. That I . . . need to say."

He kissed the worried lines of her forehead, lingering just long enough to catch the scent of lavender in her hair. "Of course we can talk. Why don't we tell Cordina to serve us dinner in the—"

"Sutton," she whispered and, with a brief nod, indicated the staircase behind him.

He turned.

"Willister? Is that you?"

The voice registered with him the instant before he recognized her descending the stairs. "*Mother?*"

48

Sutton met his mother at the bottom of the staircase and hugged her, still not believing she was standing in front of him. And that she was as thin as she was. "Mother, what are you doing here?"

She kissed his cheek and patted it softly. "Look at you, Willister. Handsome, as always." Emotion pooled in her pale blue eyes. "Just like your precious father—God rest him." Her gaze moved decidedly beyond him, and her expression gained a keen quality Sutton knew only too well. "And I might well guess who this lovely young lady is. . . ." She gave him an exaggerated grin and swept past him.

Seeing where things were headed, Sutton followed. "Mother, you don't underst—"

"You must be Cara Netta." His mother captured Claire in a tight embrace.

Wide-eyed, Claire said nothing, but Sutton sensed her waiting for him to explain.

"Oh, my darling"—his mother stepped back to look at her—"you . . . are . . . stunning. Let me take a good long look at my future daughter-in-law." She made a twirling gesture with her hand, and Claire obediently turned in a circle, her gaze connecting with Sutton's as she rotated his way.

"Mother," he said more forcefully. "This isn't—"

"You are *absolutely* breathtaking, my dear. And I've learned from my son's letters that you're quite an accomplished pianist as well. And so well traveled. And your mother, Madame LeVert! I can hardly wait to make her acquaintance. So fine a family my son is marrying into. I'm sure your mother and I will be the *very* best of friends, just as Adelicia and I have shared a close connection for so many—"

Gently, but firmly, Sutton took hold of his mother's hand. "This isn't Cara Netta, Mother. This is Miss Claire Laurent. She's Mrs. Acklen's personal liaison, and she's my"—he stumbled over what to call her—"*very* dear friend. More than that, actually. Far more," he added, seeing the tiniest light in Claire's eyes, which vanished when his mother looked at her with suspicion.

Claire offered a brief curtsy. "Mrs. Monroe, it's indeed a pleasure, ma'am, to make—"

"She's not Cara Netta?"

"*No,* Mother," Sutton answered, struggling to keep the frustration from his voice. The doctors had said normalcy and lack of agitation were best for her tenuous emotional state. But he'd forgotten how stubborn-minded she could be.

"But . . . I saw you kissing her."

"Yes, you did."

"But what are you doing kissing *her* when you're engaged to Cara Netta?"

"Sutton, perhaps I should excuse myself and—"

"Why, young woman, do you address *my* son, Mr. Willister Sutton Monroe, in so informal a manner?" His mother turned to him. "Did you not say she was Mrs. Acklen's liaison? Therefore an employee of this household? Her rank demands that she—"

"Mother! Your behavior is out of line." Sutton saw the telling tremble in her chin and regretted the harshness in his voice.

"Well . . ." She pressed a hand to her bodice. "I'm sorry my presence brings such displeasure to you, son."

"I didn't say that. It's *good* to see you again." And he meant it, for the most part. But in another . . . "I was simply surprised. I would have thought you might have written to inform me you were coming."

"I did write you, son. I told you that if your aunt Lorena ever looked at me in that haughty manner again, I was leaving." She squared her frail shoulders. "So I did. I packed up my things, bought my train ticket, and came home. For good."

"For good?" he repeated.

"Yes." She looked in Claire's direction, scowled, and promptly dismissed her presence with a turn of her head. "And now that you're here, Willister, I'd like to know when you'll be taking me to my home. I know you've been busy, as I read in your letters, but I'm sure you've rebuilt the family house by now."

Sutton didn't know where to begin to answer that question, and he certainly didn't want to do so in front of Claire. Even though she already knew the story. "We can talk about all this later, Mother. For now, let me help you get settled into a guest room."

"I'm happily ensconced in a room upstairs. Thank you, son." She started toward the staircase, then turned an austere look at Claire. "I'd like a pot of tea brought to my room, along with something to eat, please."

"Mother, Miss Laur—"

"It would be my pleasure, Mrs. Monroe," Claire said, her voice sweet.

Sutton waited until his mother's footsteps sounded on the second-floor gallery. "Claire . . ." He sighed, knowing he needed to check on his mother, but he also couldn't leave Claire without an explanation. "I don't know what to say. I apologize for all of that. I had no idea she was coming."

"That's all right, Sutton. Honestly. I understand."

But he could see that she didn't. "I think I told you before that my mother has a delicate emotional nature. But she also has a rather eccentric side to her as well." He glanced toward the stairs. "One that has apparently worsened. She does fairly well when everything goes according to her expectations. But she doesn't do well with change."

"Or"—Claire smiled—"with servants of lesser ranking taking liberties with her son."

He smiled in return, knowing she wasn't serious. But what had just happened wasn't the least bit humorous to him. "I didn't tell my mother about the change in my relationship with Cara Netta because I knew it would upset her. And I honestly didn't think it mattered—for the short term. Because she wasn't here. But . . ." He exhaled. "She is now. And if my guess is right, she's just ensconced herself in Adelicia Acklen's personal quarters."

Claire balanced the tray as she started up the stairs from the kitchen. Mrs. Monroe had been here for a week and the woman had yet to say anything other than "Yes, please," or "No, thank you" to her, unless she was asking for something. And then—Claire smiled to herself—Eugenia Monroe's vocabulary increased significantly.

Sutton felt terrible about the situation, but she really didn't mind that much. Mrs. Monroe could be demanding, even harsh at times, and the woman obviously didn't like her. But Claire sensed that the woman's dislike stemmed more from Mrs. Monroe's disapproval of her relationship with *Willister* than from a personal aversion.

Once Claire reached the main level, she headed toward the guest room at the end of the hallway, passing the formal dining room. She sensed a loneliness from Mrs. Monroe, and knowing all she'd been through, felt compassion for her. Just as hundreds of brushstrokes comprised a finished canvas, people were made up of a lifetime of experiences, both good and bad. And without knowing what someone had endured, it was impossible to truly know them—and accept them—for who they were.

That took time. And patience. And a forgiving heart, which she prayed Sutton would have with her once she told him the truth. Which she was going to do. Tonight. But she knew only too well that you could forgive someone and still decide you didn't want to be with them.

She'd forgiven Antoine DePaul everything, yet prayed she would never see the man again.

She didn't know what Sutton had planned for their evening tonight. He wouldn't tell her. He'd only instructed her to be ready by five thirty and to wear the dress she'd worn to the LeVert reception—which had been enough of a hint to have her flying high for the past five days.

Balancing the tray, she knocked on the guest room door.

"Enter."

She turned the knob, and saw Mrs. Monroe standing by the window. "Good afternoon, ma'am. Cordina made her famous chicken and dumplings for lunch. Would you like the tray on the table?"

"Yes, please." Mrs. Monroe's gaze stayed fixed on some point beyond the glass pane.

"Are you certain you wouldn't like to enjoy your meal on one of the front porches? It's lovely outside."

"No, thank you."

Claire arranged the tray on the table, sneaking glances. Sutton's mother was her height but much thinner, frailer, with hair the color of spun gold. And she bore an elegance about her that bespoke breeding and a manner accustomed to the finer things of life.

"Will there be anything else, Mrs. Monroe?"

"No, thank you."

Claire curtsied. "Good day, then." She picked up the breakfast tray she'd brought earlier that morning and smiled as she closed the door.

"What is it that you do when you leave here in the mornings, Miss Laurent?"

Claire stuck her hand out to stop the door from closing and nearly dropped the tray, shocked at hearing more than three words in a row from the woman. "I paint, ma'am. Landscapes. Oil on canvas." She righted an empty china cup on the tray. "Sometimes I go to the gardens out front. Sometimes to the meadow. Other times, like this morning, I walk to the ridge." She nodded in the direction of the conservatory on the opposite side of the estate. "There's a beautiful view from that hill." She decided not to add that a person could see the Monroe family land from that vantage point.

"Do you possess any talent?"

Claire smiled, knowing she shouldn't be surprised at the woman's bluntness. "It depends on whom you ask, ma'am. Some people find beauty in what I paint and seem to enjoy it."

"Given we are out of time, it will have to do . . ." Her smile faded as her father's criticism returned. Would his judgment always be a mere thought away? "But I'm certain there are others whose opinions would differ. I simply try to paint the very best that I can." *And paint as if I'm painting only for Him,* she wanted to add aloud but didn't.

Mrs. Monroe said nothing.

Claire thought of Mrs. Broderick, the elderly woman at the shipping company, and of her frailty and forgetfulness. But this seemed different. Mrs. Monroe wasn't that far along in years. Assuming their conversation was over, she turned to go.

"I used to draw," Mrs. Monroe said quietly, still staring outside. "I was quite good, actually. My husband told me so . . . many times. I lost all of my drawings in the fire."

Unprepared for such honesty, Claire didn't know how to respond at first. But she knew how much *losing* her *Versailles* had hurt. "Perhaps,

Mrs. Monroe, when your schedule allows . . . you might consider going with me one morning."

Eugenia Monroe turned a doubtful eye in her direction.

"I would welcome your company, ma'am. And the perspective of a fellow artist."

Mrs. Monroe didn't so much as bat an eyelash as she turned back to the window. "Good day, Miss Laurent. Thank you for lunch."

Claire felt as though she were living in a fairy tale.

She peered across the white-clothed table at Sutton—so handsome in his black cutaway coat and white tie—then around the elegant Creole restaurant where they'd enjoyed dinner. Their table overlooked the Cumberland River, and as the sun sank lower, it left a golden trail of light rippling across the water's surface.

She leaned forward, lowering her voice. "I'm afraid this is too expensive."

He mimicked her posture. "And I'm afraid that's none of your concern," he whispered back.

She smiled, but at the same time she felt a nervous knot in the pit of her stomach. The same knot she felt each time she thought about what his reaction would be when she told him the truth about her parents' art gallery, and how she'd forged the paintings. She would need to confess everything to Mrs. Acklen too, and planned on asking Sutton to accompany her, if he would.

When the *maître d'* presented the dessert menu, she almost declined, until she saw their house specialty. "Beignets, please."

"The same for me," Sutton said.

She waited for the server to leave. "This has been such a wonderful evening, Sutton. And such a nice surprise. Thank you."

He winked and sipped his water. "Only two days until the auction."

She made a panicked face, then grinned. She was disappointed that Mrs. Acklen hadn't returned from Angola yet and therefore wouldn't be bidding on her painting—a silly dream she'd somehow allowed herself to entertain. "Even if nothing comes from this opportunity for me, Sutton, I want you to know how much I appreciate your belief in me. And in my painting. How much I appreciate everything you've done for me while I've been here."

His eyes narrowed playfully. "Are you planning on going somewhere?"

"No." She laughed softly, that nervous knot twisting a half turn.

A server poured their after-dinner coffee, and Claire sipped hers slowly, savoring the rich chicory taste. So like Café du Monde.

"I don't typically discuss business over dinner, but . . ." Sutton pulled an envelope from his pocket and handed it to her. "I received this today."

Claire pulled a single sheet of stationery from the envelope. A legal document with the heading, *The State of Louisiana v. Mrs. Adelicia Franklin Acklen.* She didn't comprehend all of the legal terminology, but she caught words here and there, and when she reached the final paragraph, she began to smile. She kept her voice soft, mindful of patrons at nearby tables. "You won the cotton case!" She raised her coffee cup in salute. "Congratulations, Counselor."

He touched his cup to hers. "We won for now, at least. I'm sure the plaintiff will appeal. But . . . thank you for celebrating with me."

Watching him, she saw in his eyes at least a portion of what she was already thinking. That while he was very good at what he did, practicing law wasn't what he most wanted to do with his life, and she prayed again that God would open a door for Sutton to have his dream.

She slid the envelope back to him, wanting to ask some questions about the case. But not in the middle of the restaurant, with listening ears close by.

The server returned with dessert and Claire enjoyed every bite, resisting the urge to lick the powdered sugar from her fingers. Outside the restaurant, they discovered that Armstead hadn't returned with the carriage yet.

Sutton checked his pocket watch, then offered his arm. "Shall we walk for a while? Armstead will find us."

Claire accepted and fell into step beside him. "About the case you won, something I've wondered since reading about it in a newspaper article Mrs. Acklen saved . . ." She looked over at him. "Were *you* there with her? In Louisiana?"

His smile came slowly. "I was, for some of it, and the woman was a sight to behold. After seeing her manage those negotiations . . ." He shook his head. "It wasn't an easy time in her life either. She'd just lost Mr. Acklen. And at the time he died, she hadn't seen him in over a year and a half."

"Why so long?" Claire nodded to a couple who strolled past.

"The war. When Fort Donelson fell, we all knew it was only a matter of time before Nashville would fall too. Adelicia encouraged him to leave before that happened. She thought he was needed more at their Louisiana plantations and that he'd be safer there. Sure enough, a week after he left, the Federals occupied Nashville, and they began identifying *hearty secessionists.*" He said it with a note of bitterness, and Claire understood why. "Adelicia was named, and most certainly Joseph would have been as well. Like my father was."

Claire slowed her pace to match his.

"The last letter she received from Joseph was in late summer of sixty-three. He wrote telling her that the Confederates had confiscated all the mules and horses, and that he was afraid they were going to burn almost three thousand bales of cotton to keep it from falling into enemy hands. Joseph died about a month later from malaria, which left Adelicia in Nashville with a fortune in cotton about to be burned in Louisiana."

They reached the corner and he headed toward the right.

Claire glanced back in the direction they'd come. "Are you sure Armstead will be able to find us? Maybe we ought to head back."

"I told him we might go for a walk." He checked his pocket watch again. "We have some time yet."

They resumed their pace, and Claire found herself picturing Mrs. Acklen hearing the news about her second husband's death, after everyone else she'd already lost. "So you escorted her to Louisiana?"

He nodded. "I got special leave from my unit and took her and her cousin Sarah to the plantation, where Adelicia somehow convinced the Confederates to guard the cotton for her. She promised them she was going to ship it to England and sell it there, which she did. But she needed a way to transport it to New Orleans, and the Confederates didn't have any wagons. So—in the middle of a war, mind you—she managed to persuade some *Federal* officers to loan her their teams and wagons to move the cotton to the river."

"Where the cotton"—Claire continued for him—"was then loaded and sent to Europe and sold for a small fortune." She leaned close. "I read that part in the newspaper article."

They walked for a while, his hand covering hers on his arm, until finally they came to a corner. He stopped and turned to her. "I know this past week hasn't been an easy one for you . . . with my mother here. I want to thank you for how patient you've been with her."

"You don't have to keep saying that, Sutton. She's your mother, and I'm happy to do it."

He touched a curl at her forehead. "She told me you invited her to join you one morning, when you paint."

"She said she used to draw. I thought she might enjoy doing it again."

"I think I was still a boy the last time I saw her sketch. She drew the framed pictures you saw on my bedside table."

"Really? I'm impressed." She had confessed to him about visiting his room more than just that once while he was gone to Louisiana. At which time he had confessed to taking the *joujou* on the mantel in her bedroom the morning he left. She hadn't even noticed it missing.

"Thank you for having dinner with me tonight, Claire, and I'm sorry I made you walk all the way here, but . . ." He led her around the corner and gestured down the street. "I wanted you to be surprised."

Seeing what lay ahead, Claire let out a little squeal and threw her arms around his neck.

49

Opera patrons lined the walkway leading into the Adelphi Theater, and Claire couldn't have been more proud to be escorted by Sutton. Though she didn't remember most of the couples' names, she recognized many of them from the LeVert reception and nodded a silent greeting when they looked her way.

"What opera are we seeing?" she whispered.

Nearing the doorway, he nodded toward the billboard, and she felt a thrill. *Faust.*

She squeezed his arm. "I'll understand every word!"

"I know." He pressed his hand against the small of her back as they entered. "So you can explain the parts to me that I've never understood."

Once inside the foyer, an attendant led them up a winding staircase and down a narrow corridor lined with doors. Near the end of the hallway, the young man paused and opened a door to reveal a secluded balcony overlooking the stage. "Will Mrs. Acklen be joining you tonight, Mr. Monroe?"

"No, she won't. It's just the two of us this evening."

"Very good, sir. And do you desire the usual refreshments at intermission?"

Sutton nodded and slipped the man a bill.

Claire stood inside the doorway and drank in the scene. Swags of gold-brocaded curtains framed either side of the stage, bronze chandeliers twinkled above, the orchestra tuned their instruments, and the dissonant chords from horns and strings competed with the hushed conversation of a full house.

Sutton came behind her and caressed her shoulders. "Promise me you'll wear this dress at least once a week."

She wove her fingers through his and squeezed. "Sutton, this is all so . . ." She couldn't find the words.

He escorted her to her chair, then claimed his own beside her and scooted closer.

Claire saw movement below, on the floor level. Someone waving at them. "Oh!" She nudged Sutton. "There's Mrs. Holbrook." She gave a discreet wave in return.

Sutton nodded a greeting. "Her husband told me she was very pleased with what you did for the Women's League annual tea. They'd like to have dinner with us, incidentally."

"Mr. and Mrs. Holbrook?" Claire asked, remembering what Mr. Holbrook had said to her at the reception.

"No . . . President and Mrs. Johnson." Sutton glanced over at her and grinned. "Of course, Mr. and Mrs. Holbrook."

She managed a smile, glad when the house lamps were extinguished, but feeling that knot of tension inside her again, reminding her that she needed to tell him. But she couldn't tell him now, or it would ruin their evening. "Sutton," she whispered.

He turned to her.

"Could you set aside some time tomorrow so that I could speak with you? It's about something *very* important."

He pressed a kiss to her hand. "Of course. I'll look forward to it."

As the curtain rose moments later, with tears in her eyes Claire leaned over, intending to kiss him on the cheek. But at the last second, he turned his head and captured her mouth. "I love you, Claire," he whispered against her lips.

But she almost couldn't answer, wondering if he would still feel this way tomorrow. "I love you too, Sutton," she whispered, praying for the strength to accept whatever came, while thanking God for this man she loved, and for the seclusion of the private balcony.

With her painting satchel slung over one shoulder and the artist's case Sutton had made for her in her grip, Claire picked her way back down the ridge, humming an aria from *Faust*. The opera last evening had plucked every heartstring of human emotion. She'd laughed, she'd cried, she'd held her breath—and Sutton's hand until it ached, he'd told her later.

The artist's case he'd made her was ingenious. It contained a special mechanism to hold the canvas in place so she could transport it with greater ease, and less chance for damage. Which was especially important today because the canvas within was the one she would send to the auction hall tomorrow, via courier.

Seven times, she'd painted this particular scene, and each time something different came from her brush. But the landscape she'd most recently finished was without a doubt the one she was supposed to enter. She knew with a certainty, because—even though it frightened her—this was the only canvas of the seven that she'd *not* painted in the style of François-Narcisse Brissaud. But rather, in her own.

She hurried back to the mansion and saw gardeners tending the grounds, primping the winter garden—dormant though it was—to look its best for Mrs. Acklen's return at the end of the week, in time for the auction for established artists.

Though ready for her return, Claire couldn't imagine standing before Adelicia Acklen and telling her the truth. Telling Sutton today was going to be hard enough. . . .

She deposited her case and satchel in a corner of the entrance hall by the *Sleeping Children,* as muted conversation drifted toward her.

"Miss Laurent? Is that you?"

Recognizing Mrs. Monroe's voice, Claire walked around the corner to the *tête-à-tête* room. And when she saw who was seated beside Sutton's mother, her blood ran cold. "Uncle Antoine . . ." Of its own volition, the name left her lips.

"*Bonjour, ma petite!*" Antoine rose from the settee, looking elegant and far too much at home in his surroundings.

Mrs. Monroe scrunched her shoulders. "I love it when he talks that way. He's so charming!"

Claire stared, too stunned to speak.

Antoine DePaul crossed the room and leaned in as though to kiss her cheek. But Claire turned her head. His smile never broke.

"It's been too long, Claire. How are you, dear?"

She kept her voice low. "What are you doing here?"

"I'm visiting my niece," he said, loud enough for anyone in the hall outside to hear him. "After all, we're family, you and I."

Heart pounding, she gestured. "I'd like to see you privately, please."

Antoine returned to the settee and took his place beside Mrs. Monroe. "I think I prefer this room, Claire. It's so"—he glanced about—"*rich* looking."

The thud of horse's hooves sounded through the open window, and Claire's heart dropped to her stomach. She looked out, relieved to see it was Zeke and not Sutton. If Sutton were to find out about her this way, he would think she was only telling him because she was being forced to.

"Expecting someone, Claire? Perhaps the gentleman I saw you with last night?"

Claire looked back at him.

"Did you enjoy the opera? It looked as though you did from where I was seated. Below you, toward the back. Then again, the private balcony where *you* were seated was rather dark, and you did seem . . ." He gave her a knowing look. "Well, shall we say *preoccupied* at times?"

Claire's face heated.

"Miss Laurent," Mrs. Monroe said, apparently having missed what Antoine had hinted at, "tell Cordina to set another place so your uncle can join us for lunch."

"I wish that were possible, Mrs. Monroe, but"—she leveled a stare at Antoine—"he's unable to stay for lunch. He has an appointment in town. Don't you, *Uncle*?"

He met her eyes, seemed to debate his choices, then stood. "I guess I do need to be on my way. Madame Monroe—" He bowed and kissed her hand. "*Au revoir,* my dear. It was a pleasure meeting you and hearing all about life here at Belmont. Pity I wasn't able to meet Mrs. Acklen. Perhaps I'll come back some other day."

"Oh yes, do." Mrs. Monroe patted his hand. "She's the loveliest woman. She and I are the dearest of friends."

Shaking on the inside, Claire followed him into the entrance hall, closing the door to the *tête-à-tête* room behind them. She opened the front door and gestured him through it, but he paid her no mind.

He studied *Ruth Gleaning,* then made a show of looking around the room. "You land on your feet well, Claire."

"You need to leave."

"I will. Once I get what I came for."

"I'm not giving you anything. And you're not taking anything from here either."

He inhaled. "On second thought, lunch does smell delicious."

"Please," she said, hating the pleading quality of her voice. She closed the front door so no one could walk up on them unannounced. "You have no right to be here."

He raised a brow. "And you do?"

Her grip tightened on the door handle. How many times had she asked herself that question? And she knew the answer, only too well.

She felt so helpless, at his mercy. Was this what everything was coming down to? After she'd finally committed to telling the truth. After she'd begged God to make something more of herself than she ever could. She breathed deep, trying to still the trembling inside her. "I'm not painting for you anymore. Like I told Papa, I won't do it."

He looked at her for a moment, then scoffed. "Of course you will. Unless you want me to speak with your employer—" he glanced at the portrait—"Mrs. Adelicia Franklin Acklen." He spoke the name slowly, each syllable accentuated. "I'm guessing she doesn't know yet about the family business we had in New Orleans."

"*Your* business—and Papa's. Not mine."

"You were just as much a part of things as we were, Claire Elise. You knew it then. And you know it now. I can see it in your eyes." He shook his head as though pitying her. "You never were good at lying."

"Unlike you and Papa," she said, fearing at any minute that someone would walk around a corner.

He took a step toward her. "Mrs. Acklen is a very wealthy woman, and I would imagine that as her personal liaison—as the dear Mrs. Monroe informed me that you are—you have access to her *personal* accounts. And judging by the loathing in your eyes at the moment, I'm convinced you would pay a handsome sum to be rid of me. Am I correct?"

"I don't have access to Mrs. Acklen's money, and even if I did, I wouldn't—"

"*Get* access to it, Claire. Because if you don't, your part in our arrangement back in New Orleans will come to light in a most unflattering manner, and the world you've created for yourself here will come to a very hasty end. And I'm not simply referring to the loss of your job. They prosecute forgers, just like they prosecute the dealers who sell their work. Or haven't you considered that?"

Claire didn't know how to respond. She'd known what she'd done was wrong, and she was ready to admit that and accept the consequences. Or so she'd thought. But . . . *prosecution*? As in . . . the possibility of going to jail? That was a cost she hadn't calculated.

Sensing movement at the corner of her eye, she tensed. But when she looked, no one was there. It was only Mrs. Acklen's likeness staring down at her from the portrait. She thought of what Sutton had told her about Adelicia braving two armies, fighting to keep what was hers, and she prayed for a measure of that same strength and courage. What would Adelicia Acklen have done if they'd threatened her with arrest? With going to jail? Claire could only imagine. . . .

The door handle turned beneath her grip. Panicking, yet having no choice, she pulled the door open.

Eli looked at her, then at Antoine. "Is everything all right, Miss Laurent?"

"Yes," she forced out, her voice tight. "Everything is fine. But . . . my guest is ready to leave. He needs his horse."

Eli gave Antoine a thorough study. "Yes, ma'am. I'll get it right away."

"Thank you, Eli."

She turned back to see Antoine running a finger along the line of *Ruth*'s shoulder, then down her arm to the fragile right hand, where delicately carved fingers extended outward. Claire stepped forward, fearing he intended to do the statue damage.

Antoine crossed to the door and paused beside her. "I think five hundred dollars would tide me over for now, Claire. I'll contact you at the end of the week and we'll arrange to meet."

"I've told you, I won't do it."

He smiled. "You have until Friday. Use the time wisely. And remember, I'm neither as patient—nor as stupid—a man as was your father." He touched her face, but she pulled away. "While you may have your mother's beauty, Claire, you'll never have her talent. Yours was, and always will be, a cheap imitation." He gave her chin a hard pinch. "*À bientôt, ma petite.*"

He strode past her. Claire held on to the door, and not until he'd rounded the final bend toward the main gate did she draw a full breath again. *"See you soon,"* he'd said in farewell.

And God help her, she believed him.

50

The next morning, Claire read the note Sutton had slipped beneath her door sometime during the night, and she knew she was reaping what she'd sown.

Dearest Claire,

Forgive me for not being here when you awaken. Mr. Holbrook and I have meetings with the authorities first thing in the morning. I'll fill you in this evening, but suffice it to say . . . those prayers you're praying for me—and this lawsuit—are proving most powerful. I'll see you at the auction tonight and will be searching the crowds for your smile.

Always your faithful corporal,

Sutton

Claire rubbed the sleep—or lack thereof—from her eyes. Not only had he been unable to keep yesterday's lunch appointment due to his case with Mr. Holbrook, but he'd already left for the day. She sighed. This was her punishment for not having told him the truth sooner.

She'd awakened during the night, thinking about Antoine's visit and what he'd said. At first she'd worried what would happen if he returned to Belmont. But he wouldn't return. Because with a word, she could do to him what he was threatening to do to her. No, he would contact her, as he said he would, learn she wasn't going to give him the money, then ruin her from afar. All very safe, clean, and simple for him.

But in truth, could he hurt her any more than her own admission was going to hurt her? Yes, but only in one way—if he somehow contacted Sutton first. Which she couldn't let him do.

"May I help you, ma'am?" the clerk behind the desk asked.

"Yes, please." Claire's nerves were stretched taut. "I'm entered in the auction for new artists and was told to come here to check in."

"And your name?"

"Miss Claire Elise Laurent."

As the young woman skimmed her pen along the side of the page, Claire turned and scanned the lobby of the Worthington Art Center in search of Sutton. The hall was a sea of faces—but none of them his.

She'd gone by the law office on her way to the art center, hoping to find him. But the receptionist had said he was out of the office for the afternoon. He wouldn't forget the auction. At least she didn't think he would. But he'd been so preoccupied with his mother being here, and then with the lawsuit . . .

"Here you are, Miss Laurent."

Claire looked back.

"All of your information appears to be in order, ma'am, except for one item. I need for you to complete and sign this certificate of authenticity. It confirms that you are indeed the artist of the canvas you submitted and that it is an original work of your own design."

Claire stared at the form for a moment, the full weight of what it represented sinking in. Perhaps for the first time. This truly was *her* painting, for better or worse. It wasn't a copy. Or a fake. Or a forgery. She completed the form and signed her name at the bottom.

The clerk checked her information. "You're all ready, Miss Laurent. Best of luck to you!"

"Luck has nothing to do with it."

Claire spun around and, to her relief, saw Sutton—but with Mr. and Mrs. Holbrook beside him.

His smile turned sheepish. "Were you worried I wouldn't make it?"

"No, of course not," she said, then saw the way he looked at her. "Well, maybe I was a little worried."

Mrs. Holbrook gave her a quick hug. "This is so exciting, Miss

Laurent. Your first auction. I can hardly wait to see your painting. I'm sure it will do very well."

"And afterward," Mr. Holbrook chimed in, "we're taking you and Mr. Monroe out for dinner to celebrate. Our treat!"

Claire smiled, the evening already not unfolding as she'd planned. "How kind. Thank you."

Sutton offered his arm, and Claire slipped her hand through. He gestured for Mr. and Mrs. Holbrook to precede them into the auditorium, then leaned down. "Mr. Holbrook insisted they come with us to support you tonight. I hope you don't mind too much. I promise I'll make it up to you."

Seeing the sincerity in his eyes, Claire felt ashamed. "No, Sutton, it's fine. You're here and that's all that matters." Already, some of the framed paintings were being brought to the stage, but hers wasn't among them.

At the door a young man handed them each a program.

It was more crowded than Claire expected. They chose four chairs together near the middle and crowded in, and as Sutton visited with Mr. and Mrs. Holbrook, Claire read through the program, noting the artists' names. Seeing her own name near the bottom of the first column, she ran a finger across the printed type, a sense of satisfaction welling up inside her.

Conversation in the hall quieted as a gentleman on the stage took the podium.

"Welcome, everyone, to the Worthington Art Center and to Nashville's twenty-second annual auction for new artists. First, we want to thank Mr. and Mrs. Worthington for their generous contribution to the arts, which enables us to be sitting in this lovely building today. A portion of today's proceeds will benefit the Tennessee Endowment of . . ."

Claire searched the crowd until she located Mrs. Worthington. At that moment, Mrs. Worthington looked back at her and smiled. Claire did likewise—then jumped when the gavel came down, signaling the start of the auction.

The auctioneer stood behind the podium. "First up for bid is an oil on canvas entitled *Cherished Dawn*. The artist is Mr. Adam Marcus Avery of Gallatin, Tennessee."

Claire peered over heads in front of her to better see the framed landscape. *Stunning.* She leaned back in her seat, knowing her chances were doomed.

"As with all of our new-artist submissions," the auctioneer continued, "we'll start the bid at two dollars. And remember, folks, half of the winning bid goes to the artist and the other half to charity. So bid high and bid often."

Laughter skirted across the auditorium.

The auctioneer started the bidding, and paddles appeared from nowhere, popping up and down so fast Claire didn't know where to look next, what the bid was, or how on earth the auctioneer was keeping track of everything. It was all so exciting.

Only then did she see the bid paddle balanced on Sutton's knee. On the back of the paddle was written the name *Acklen.* "Is Mrs. Acklen bidding on some of these?" she whispered.

Sutton just looked over at her and smiled, and Claire felt her hopes rise.

"Thirty-two dollars going once, thirty-two going twice . . ." The gavel sounded. "*Cherished Dream . . . sold* for thirty-two to Mrs. Daniel Worthington."

Mrs. Worthington beamed and nodded to those around her as though she'd painted the oil on canvas herself.

The next several paintings didn't go for nearly what *Cherished Dream* had, and Claire's expectation for her own entry began to fall. But the next few auction items generated a flurry of bidding and she grew encouraged again. *I'll paint as if I'm painting only for You. I'll paint as if I'm painting only for You. . . .*

She repeated it over and over, reminding herself that no matter what came, she'd painted this canvas with that as her goal and she'd done her very best. And that was the most she could do.

Finally, hers was brought to the stage.

"The final item up for bid is an oil on canvas entitled . . . *An American Versailles.* The artist is Miss Claire Elise Laurent of Nashville, Tennessee."

Seeing her painting up there and hearing her name read aloud caused her to tear up. Sutton reached over and squeezed her hand.

The auctioneer started the bid at two dollars, and paddles flew. Claire felt as if she were on a carriage careening out of control. Her heart raced. She gripped the edge of her seat, not knowing where to look next.

"The bid stands at thirteen dollars. Do I hear fourteen?"

Thirteen dollars already! She got so excited.

The bidding started again and, feeling someone watching her, Claire looked over to see Mrs. Worthington looking their way. She smiled but the woman quickly turned around. And yet when the bid increased again, Mrs. Worthington glanced back. Claire looked at Mrs. Acklen's paddle resting on Sutton's leg and she gradually realized that Mrs. Worthington was waiting to see if Sutton was going to bid on the painting for Mrs. Acklen—before she bid herself.

"The bid for *An American Versailles* stands at thirty-two dollars. Do I hear thirty-three? Because if I do, *An American Versailles* will be the top-bidding item for a new-artist entry in this year's auction."

A paddle flew up. And another. And another. But Sutton's paddle stayed still and unused on his leg.

Claire bowed her head, trying to simply focus on the moment. Her first auction. And the painting was *hers*. Under *her* name. She thought of her mother and wished she could have seen this moment. But maybe, just maybe, she could.

"The bid stands at thirty-nine dollars, folks. Do I hear forty?"

Sutton raised Adelicia's paddle.

Claire turned to look at him, but he faced forward, smiling. Adelicia Acklen was bidding on *her* landscape! She could hardly sit still. Then she felt the stare again. She looked to see Mrs. Worthington bidding now too.

"The bid stands at forty-one dollars. Do I hear forty-two?"

Sutton raised the paddle again, and Claire wondered what bid limit Mrs. Acklen had set.

"We have forty-two dollars—forty-*three* over here on my left!"

Claire looked across the aisle. Mrs. Worthington's paddle kept popping up in the air.

"Forty-seven dollars. Forty-eight." The auctioneer gestured first with one hand, then the other. "Forty-nine. Fifty! Do I hear fifty-one?"

Sutton raised the paddle again, and Claire started thinking of all the kind things she could do for Mrs. Acklen. She would organize the woman's dresser drawers. She would calligraphy labels of every Latin name for every flower, plant, shrub, and bush in Mrs. Acklen's two-thousand-square-foot conservatory.

Only two paddles vied for the winning bid now. Acklen and Worthington. Back and forth. Back and forth.

"I have a bid, ladies and gentlemen, of sixty-one dollars. Do I hear sixty-two?"

Without hesitation, Sutton raised his paddle, intent on the auctioneer.

"I have sixty-two dollars. Do I hear sixty-three?"

Mrs. Worthington's faithful paddle went up.

The auctioneer smiled. "Looks like we could be here all night, folks."

Everyone laughed. The hall was standing-room only now and had grown warm.

"And to keep that from happening," the auctioneer continued. "I'm going to give each bidder a piece of paper and I want them to write down their highest bid. And make it a good one, friends, because you won't get another chance. Whoever wins this bid will be the proud owner of *An American Versailles.*"

Two young men made their way down the aisle with pen and paper. One to Sutton. One to Mrs. Worthington. They wrote their bids—Sutton writing Adelicia's where Claire couldn't see—and the young men took the bids to the auctioneer, who peered at them with a grin, then raised his gavel and slammed it down.

"*An American Versailles* . . . sold for ninety-four dollars, the highest bid *any* new artist has garnered in the history of this auction, to . . . Mr. Sutton Monroe."

Wordless, Claire turned.

But Sutton just smiled and winked. "You don't need to know everything, Miss Laurent."

51

Sutton . . ." Claire turned in her chair and hugged him tight, still not believing what he'd done. How could her heart be so full and yet be breaking at the same time? "That was money for your thoroughbreds," she whispered.

"That money was an investment"—he pressed a quick kiss into her hair—"in someone very, very important to me."

"Forgive my interruption . . ." Mrs. Holbrook leaned over, pointing discreetly. "But I think people are waiting to offer their congratulations. To you both."

Claire turned, and sure enough, a line was forming. For the next few moments, she and Sutton accepted people's felicitations—until Mr. and Mrs. Worthington approached.

Claire curtsied to the couple, noting the woman's dour expression. "Mr. and Mrs. Worthington, please let me offer my gratitude to you for bidding on my landscape. I'm deeply honored."

Mr. Worthington gave an acknowledging tilt of his head. "You're most welcome, Miss Laurent. Although I must say"—he glanced at his wife—"living with Mrs. Worthington for the next few days is going to be quite uncomfortable for me. She'd already chosen a place in the central parlor for your canvas."

Claire could hardly believe that.

"May I offer my thanks too," Sutton said, "for such a spirited bidding session, Mrs. Worthington."

"You may, Mr. Monroe." The tiniest smile shown through Mrs. Worthington's obvious irritation at having lost. "And may I offer a well-meant warning in return. . . . The next time, I'll bid *much* higher."

Sutton smiled, bowing slightly. "I'll take that under advisement, ma'am."

"And you may pass that along to Adelicia, as well," she added, her tone holding subtle challenge. "*If* she's planning to attend the auction later this week?"

"She is indeed, ma'am. Mrs. Acklen returns to Belmont day after tomorrow, in fact. I received a telegram from her this morning."

Claire accompanied Sutton and Mr. and Mrs. Holbrook to the cashier's office in a hallway off the main lobby. Sutton pulled his bank book from his inner coat pocket, and Claire thought again of how much he was paying for her painting.

"I would have painted you one for free," she whispered.

"Now you tell me." He sneaked her a wink, then handed the young woman behind the counter his check.

The pretty clerk smiled—more at Sutton, Claire noticed, than at her—and returned moments later with another check. "Here you are, Miss Laurent. Your portion of the proceeds. And"—she handed Claire the check while focusing back on Sutton—"Mr. Brownley, the curator, has invited you, Mr. Monroe, and your guests, to the private showing of art scheduled for auction later this week. The showing is under way right now, down the hallway. Refreshments are being served."

Sutton looked at Claire, then at Mr. and Mrs. Holbrook. "Are we interested?"

Claire glanced at Mrs. Holbrook, hopeful she would be, and smiled when the woman nodded enthusiastically.

"I believe the ladies say yes, Mr. Monroe." Mr. Holbrook gestured down the hallway.

Inside the gallery, Claire pulled Sutton aside and held out the check. "Here . . . I want you to have this. It's yours, after all."

He held up his hands. "That's your money, Claire. Yours to do with as you wish."

"But I don't feel comfortable taking it, Sutton. Please, just—"

"Lawd, help me," he said softly. "There you go again, tryin' to steal my joy."

Claire smiled, still able to hear Cordina when she'd caught them having breakfast in *her* kitchen. That morning seemed like forever ago, and she felt like such a different person inside now. Never could she have imagined that circumstances would turn out the way they had. She was so grateful for this man and for the fresh start God had given her at a new life.

But as grateful as she was, she knew there was something she still needed to do.

Sutton brought her hand to her lips. "Put that check in your skirt pocket where it belongs. I have a feeling you're going to need those funds for more canvases and paints."

She did as he asked, but touched his arm when he turned to rejoin the Holbrooks. "Sutton . . . there's something I need to talk to you about. Could we go somewhere, please . . . just the two of us?"

He touched her cheek. "Is everything all right?"

The tenderness in his voice cut through her. "Yes," she whispered, then shook her head. "And no."

Concern clouded his features. He glanced across the gallery. "We'll view the art with the Holbrooks for a moment, and then I'll make our excuses about dinner and we'll go straight home."

She nodded. "Thank you."

The gallery was larger than she'd expected, a maze of rooms, and by the time they made it back toward the entrance, the crowd had increased considerably.

Mrs. Holbrook slipped an arm around her shoulders. "Dear, are you feeling all right? You've grown awfully quiet."

"I think I'm just overtired, Mrs. Holbrook." Claire glanced at Sutton, who jumped right in.

"We appreciate the offer of dinner, but I think we'll make this an early evening, if that won't offend."

Mr. and Mrs. Holbrook assured them it wouldn't.

As they were leaving the gallery, a silver-haired gentleman approached their party. "Mr. Monroe, may I extend my gratitude for your most generous bid this evening, sir."

"It was my pleasure, Mr. Brownley." Sutton shook his hand, then gestured. "Mr. Brownley has been the art center curator for several years. Allow me to make introductions. . . ."

Claire curtsied when Sutton came to her. "A pleasure to meet you, Mr. Brownley."

"The pleasure is all mine, Miss Laurent. My congratulations in your success this evening. And forgive me, but having seen your *An*

American Versailles, you hardly strike me as being a new artist. My father and grandfather were both curators, so I've been around art all my life. And the elegance of style, the emotion in your painting, your execution of brushstroke . . ." He shook his head. "You're extraordinarily accomplished for one so young, Miss Laurent."

Claire grew uncomfortable beneath his praise. "I appreciate that, sir. Thank you." She glanced at Sutton, who seemed to sense her discomfort. Then she looked anywhere but back at Mr. Brownley—

And that's when she saw it—displayed on an easel in the far corner of the final room. "W-where did you get that canvas?" she whispered, a viselike grip squeezing the air from her lungs.

"Oh . . ." Mr. Brownley's sigh held reverence. "The auction of this landscape is quite a coup for our gallery, Miss Laurent. It's a François-Narcisse Brissaud original. *Jardins—*"

"*—de Versailles,*" she finished, walking toward it, drawn to the image of her mother standing at the edge of the garden, half hidden behind the lilacs.

Just as quickly, she stilled and turned, and searched the faces around her, certain one of them would be Antoine's. But she didn't see him. Then she remembered the newspaper article—all of the art had been stolen from the gallery in New Orleans that night. She slowly looked back at her *Versailles.* Or had it?

Mr. Brownley joined her. "Are you familiar with Brissaud's work, Miss Laurent?"

Her smile felt brittle, as false as the canvas before her. As false as she felt at that moment. And yet, she knew she was no longer the woman who had painted it. *God* had changed her. She still wanted to paint, more than anything she could imagine doing with her life. But she wanted to paint in such a way that when others saw her work, they would somehow see Him instead.

Feeling Mr. Brownley's attention, she turned and let out a held breath. "Yes, sir. I'm actually quite familiar with Brissaud's work." Sensing Sutton's presence, she looked over at him. "But . . ." She softened her voice so only he could hear. "This isn't an original Brissaud."

Frowning, Sutton shot a look at the curator, then at Mr. Holbrook, before coming back to her again. "Of course it's an original, Claire." His guarded expression told her to lower her voice even further. "The gallery has a certificate of authenticity."

Claire shook her head. "Whatever papers there are, Sutton, were forged. Just like this canvas."

"How do you know that?"

"I know because . . ." Seeing the question in his eyes and knowing how dedicated to the truth he was, she had no doubt what telling him the truth would cost her. She also knew it was a price she had to pay. Tears tightened her throat, all but cutting off the words. "I know because . . . I painted it."

52

Sutton took hold of Claire's arm and gently pulled her off to the side, hoping the curator hadn't heard. "What do you mean you painted it?" he whispered, aware of Holbrook's stern expression and the plainclothes investigator glaring at him from across the room.

Tears brimmed in her eyes. "That's what I've been trying to tell you." She looked down, hands knotted at her waist. "Before I came to Belmont, I . . ." She pressed her lips tight, glancing around them. "I painted forgeries," she whispered, her voice barely audible. "For my father, in our gallery. The same as my mother before me."

Sutton could've sworn the floor shifted beneath him. *She'd* painted forgeries? He looked at the Brissaud, then back at her. The idea was absurd. Part of him wanted to laugh, but he couldn't. Not with her looking at him like that. Like she was breaking inside. He kept his voice low. "Claire . . . you can't be serious."

Tears slipped down her cheeks. "I'm sorry, Sutton. I'm so sorry."

The idea that she'd painted forgeries was absurd enough. But that she'd painted *this* particular painting—after all they'd gone through to arrange for this landscape to be here, in this gallery, at this particular time—was almost more than he could take in.

"Mr. Monroe . . ." Mr. Brownley approached, concern in his expression. "Is there a problem, sir? Miss Laurent seems upset, and I fear we're drawing attention."

Sutton grew aware of patrons staring. "My apologies, Mr. Brownley." Knowing what was at stake in the upcoming auction, and thinking of the months of work both the investigators—and he and Holbrook—had invested to get to this point, he knew he had to make up something.

And fast. "The fault is completely mine, sir." He spoke loudly enough that those closest could hear. "I said something that upset Miss Laurent. It was callous of me, and I offer my apologies." He turned back to Claire and took her hand, giving it a quick squeeze. "Would you please forgive me, Miss Laurent?"

Her frown lasted for only an instant. Then she nodded, confusion still clouding her eyes.

He turned back to the curator. "Would you mind escorting my party to a more private venue, Mr. Brownley? Where I might make amends?"

Brownley looked at the two of them, then smiled back at the patrons as though to say, "*Ah . . . young love!*" "Of course, Mr. Monroe. Follow me."

The curator led the four of them through a side door into a meeting room, then closed the door behind him. Sutton urged Claire to sit, then claimed the chair beside her. He felt almost as shaken as she looked. Thoughts bombarded him. One, above all—if Claire really had forged the painting, what else might she have done? It was his responsibility to keep Adelicia Acklen's estate protected, and yet he'd missed the truth about her. Completely.

The Holbrooks sat opposite them on the other side of the table.

"Would you care to explain what just happened out there, Mr. Monroe?"

Sutton looked up. Irritation darkened Bartholomew Holbrook's features. "I'm sorry, sir. I didn't handle the situation very—"

"It wasn't Sutton's fault, Mr. Holbrook. It's mine." Claire took a shaky breath. "It's all my fault."

"All right, Miss Laurent"—Mr. Holbrook turned to her, looking and sounding every bit the senior attorney that he was—"you do the honors, then."

Sutton listened as she told Mr. and Mrs. Holbrook exactly what she'd told him moments earlier. The same brokenness etched her voice, and something twisted inside him again at hearing it.

Mrs. Holbrook paled a shade. "*You* forged that painting? A Brissaud?" She glanced at her husband. "That doesn't seem possible."

But Mr. Holbrook said nothing.

Claire's tears renewed. "Our gallery's main business was selling 'originals.'" She all but flinched at the word. "From European master artists. Which my mother and, later, I painted there in our gallery in New Orleans. Then my father would purchase forged certificates of authenticity and either sell them there or ship them to various galleries throughout the country. And sometimes overseas. My mother painted many artists in recent years, but her specialty—and mine—was François-Narcisse Brissaud."

Sutton angled his chair away from hers so he could watch her as she spoke. She told them in detail about the gallery, her parents, and when she'd first learned about what they did. Then she described her years at boarding school before she returned to work in the "family business."

"How many paintings did you personally forge, Miss Laurent?" Holbrook asked.

Sutton could see her lips moving the way they always did when she counted to herself.

"I've painted *Jardins de Versailles* five times, including this one. And maybe another twenty, perhaps twenty-five, canvases over the course of the last two years. That doesn't count the paintings I copied for people who knew they were buying a copy."

"Did you ever sell these paintings yourself?" Sutton asked, hoping what her answer would be.

"No, Papa always did that. And he made me leave the gallery when he was hosting those clients."

"So you never saw those patrons?" he followed up. "Or would be able to identify them?" *Or they you*, he thought.

"No."

"So you forged paintings over the last two years?" Holbrook continued.

"I started once my mother became ill, shortly after I finished boarding school." She spoke of the closeness with her mother, and the absence of comment about her father spoke even louder. "The doctors' fees and the medicine were expensive. I told Papa that I thought she would get better if we sent her to a sanitarium. He said those cost a lot of money, so I worked harder and painted faster. But . . ." She shook her head. "He refused to send her."

"And she died?" Mrs. Holbrook asked, her voice hesitant.

Claire nodded. "Almost a year ago now."

"I'm so sorry, dear," Mrs. Holbrook whispered. "You must still miss her very much."

"I do. But sometimes, when I hold a paintbrush, I feel her with me."

Mrs. Holbrook held out her right hand. "This was my mother's wedding ring. I feel the very same about her when I wear it."

A semblance of a smile touched Claire's lips but didn't linger. "My mother gave me her locket watch before she died, but I lost it the first night I got to Nashville." She sighed. "I went back to the shipping company some days later to find it, but . . . it was gone."

"Shipping company," Holbrook said, his wiry brows arching.

"Yes, sir," Claire answered. "That was the afternoon you and I first saw each other. At Broderick Shipping and Freight."

"What?" Sutton leaned forward. "You saw her at—"

Holbrook's hand went up. "You may take me to task later, Mr. Monroe, for my choice to withhold that information from you. But after seeing how thoroughly enamored you were with Miss Laurent at the reception that night, I thought it best, and I still stand by my decision."

Sutton felt Claire look over at him, but he didn't look back.

"Now . . ." Holbrook returned to Claire. "I remember that afternoon well, Miss Laurent. But I had no idea you had a *connection* with that company."

"I didn't—and don't. I was simply there looking for my reticule. Mr. Broderick had made *unwelcome* advances my first night there, at which time I grabbed my satchel and left. It wasn't until the next morning in church, where I met Sutton, that I even remembered I'd left my reticule behind."

Sutton had never met Samuel Broderick, but already he looked forward to throttling the man. "Claire . . . what were you doing there that first night? Why did you go there to begin with?"

"Because that's where my father and his business partner had arranged for me to stay when I first arrived in town."

Sutton exchanged a look with Holbrook. "Your father had a business partner?"

"Yes."

"And what is this partner's name, Miss Laurent?" Holbrook asked.

"Antoine DePaul."

Sutton got a sinking feeling, and witnessed the same in Holbrook.

"What is it?" Claire asked. "What's wrong?"

Sutton looked at Holbrook for permission and received a nod.

"Claire, the lawsuit Mr. Holbrook and I have been working on all these months, and that you've been so faithful to pray for me about . . ."

She got a wary look.

"We've been working with investigators to track fraudulent art on behalf of a client. Several clients now, actually. We've been gathering evidence for an upcoming trial. But the man we've been looking for is Sebastian Perrault. Does that name sound at all familiar to you?"

She shook her head.

Sutton nodded. "The majority of forgeries in this country in the past decade can be traced back to this man and his wide net of constituents. Perrault owns several galleries, all of which are quite small, except for the Perrault Gallery in New York."

A puzzled look swept her face. "Wait . . ." Her gaze drifted. "Perrault Gallery . . . New York. I remember seeing that name. . . ." She turned back, her eyes brightening. "That very first night in Nashville. The directions Antoine had written down for me were written on a piece of stationery with that gallery's name on it."

Sutton tried for a grateful look. "Unfortunately, that doesn't establish a connection between the two men. Perrault does an enormous amount of business with galleries both here in the United States and abroad."

"How well do you know this Antoine DePaul, Miss Laurent?" Holbrook asked, watching her over tented hands. "What kind of man is he?"

"I've known him since I was nine, or I thought I did. He was almost like a member of our family." Her sigh held regret. "And like an uncle to me. He traveled a lot, more in recent years. And when he took trips, he always brought home gifts." Her eyes narrowed, and she gave a humorless laugh. "Though, looking back . . . he always spent the most money on himself. He had a penchant for boots." She shook her head. "Alligator was his favorite."

Sutton sat forward. He and Holbrook stared at each other, and slowly began to smile. Even Mrs. Holbrook, who'd been quiet throughout, straightened in her chair.

"Fastidious dresser," Sutton said, recalling a remark in a deposition he'd read from a witness. "And always prided himself on . . ."

"His boots," Holbrook finished with him. "Vanity . . . thy name is Sebastian Perrault. Or . . . Antoine DePaul."

Claire looked between them. "You think Antoine is . . . Perrault?"

"I would bet my best black hat on it, Miss Laurent. Now, you said that DePaul arranged for you to stay at Broderick Shipping and Freight. I assume DePaul arrived in Nashville sometime after you?"

Claire nodded. "He was staying with Samuel Broderick. I saw his belongings the day I returned for my locket watch. I'm assuming he's still there."

"Authorities have been watching Broderick's store for weeks now." Sutton sighed. "No sign of the man."

"Then this will be of interest to you both," Claire said, her expression tentative. "Antoine DePaul saw us at the opera the other night, Sutton, and . . . he visited Belmont yesterday."

Sutton nearly came out of his chair. "Perrault was at *Belmont*?"

"I was going to tell you this morning, but . . . you had already left. He came to pressure me into painting for him again. When I told him no, he threatened to expose my past to Mrs. Acklen if I didn't give him five hundred dollars." She leaned forward. "I had already determined to tell you and Mrs. Acklen the truth, Sutton, even before he came. I give you my word."

Sutton felt Holbrook watching him, waiting for his response, and he nodded. "She's tried several times to talk to me about something, but . . . we kept getting interrupted." He looked over at her. He wanted to add that perhaps she could have tried harder to tell him about this, but the brokenness in her eyes wouldn't let him. "Did Antoine DePaul say anything else?"

"When I said I didn't have access to that kind of money, he said he would contact me within the week."

Sutton and Holbrook exchanged glances again, and Sutton guessed they were thinking the same thing. Sebastian Perrault would be contacting Claire again. And if Claire would help them—which her behavior now gave him every reason to believe she would—they were closer to catching Sebastian Perrault than they'd ever been before.

Only, Claire was going to get caught in the process too.

53

May I ask . . . what will happen to me?"

With her head bowed, Sutton couldn't see Claire's face, but he heard the fear in her voice. While part of him wanted to reassure her that all would be fine, the attorney in him couldn't. Not knowing what he knew. Seeing Holbrook's almost imperceptible nod, Sutton turned to her.

"Claire . . ."

She looked up at him, her desire to be strong clearly written in the rigid set of her jaw, but not the least convincing to him.

Pulling his emotions inward, he focused on the facts. "Forgery is a crime punishable by federal law. However, due to the specifics of your situation, it could be said that you find yourself in a rather advantageous position, considering the arguable duress under which you painted the forgeries and your obvious effort to leave that life behind. Any responsible jury deliberating—"

"Jury?" she asked.

"If it comes to that, yes." From his peripheral vision, he saw Holbrook nod. "But any responsible jury will take all of that into consideration when determining their verdict, especially if the defendant—you, in this case—aids in providing evidence. Which—"

"I'll do whatever you want me to do," she said quickly, scooting forward in her chair. "I'll tell you everything . . . I was going to anyway." Her eyes grew misty again. "I know what I did was wrong, so please don't hear me saying otherwise. At times, especially when my mother grew more ill, I felt as though I didn't have a choice. But we all have choices. I know that now. And I'd like to think that, if put in that situation again, I would make better decisions next time."

"And that," Sutton said, "is why I believe a jury will render a more lenient verdict in your case."

"I agree with Mr. Monroe's assessment, Miss Laurent." Holbrook rose and slowly straightened to his full height. "And you'll need to be willing to testify against Sebastian Perrault in court, which means facing him again."

"That won't be a problem for me, sir."

Sorting through the revelations of the past hour, Sutton studied Claire as Holbrook questioned her further. She'd been fighting to keep her mother alive, doing whatever she needed to do to make that happen. Another woman came to mind—along with images of wagons loaded down with cotton—and the similarities in the two women were undeniable.

"If it becomes necessary, Miss Laurent," Holbrook continued, "as it well may, can you prove that you painted that Brissaud?"

"Yes, sir. I can. Brissaud is known for painting a certain venue many times, but each time he includes something different. I included my mother in this canvas. She's painted down to the left, in the garden."

Sutton shook his head, joining in. "A touching gesture, Claire, but unconvincing in a court of law."

Her chin lifted. "In a moment of frustration with my father, I signed this particular canvas. If you were to scrape off the paint on the bottom right corner, you'll see my signature beneath the forged one. And if that isn't enough, look on the back of the canvas. I had to make the tiniest patch on the bottom right-hand corner. It will be evident . . . to the trained eye."

Accepting the challenge, Holbrook got up and left the room, and returned minutes later, satisfaction on his face. "One of the investigators would like to speak with you, Miss Laurent. But not here. At his office."

Claire stood. "May I ask what will happen to the painting?"

Sutton held her chair. "It will be confiscated as evidence and presented in the trial. Why?"

"It has special meaning to me, that's all."

Holbrook laughed softly. "I'm afraid it has special meaning to the Brissaud collector who bought it three months ago in New York too. Before he realized it was a fake, and that his investment was lost."

Claire frowned. "Will he be able to get his money back?"

Sutton felt the question directed to him. "That's part of what will be determined when we go to court." Then it occurred to him. "Claire, do you have any idea what the 'Brissaud' out there sold for?"

She shook her head. "It was stolen the night I left New Orleans."

Sutton paused before opening the door. "Your *Jardins de Versailles* sold at auction in New York for almost four thousand dollars." Her mouth fell partially open, as did Mrs. Holbrook's. "So from where I'm sitting, I just got a steal on *An American Versailles.*"

Never in all his years of knowing Adelicia and working for her had Sutton seen the woman so quiet. So still. So utterly and thoroughly shocked. He knew the feeling.

Only the sound of Claire's voice and an occasional soft cry as she recounted her story marred the otherwise thick and heavy silence. Sutton sensed it took everything she had, but she sat posture perfect, head held erect as she wept.

He stood slightly behind her, having declined to sit, preferring to be where he could watch them both. As surprised as he'd been to learn what Claire had done, her poise and grace under the pressure of the past two days had impressed him. She'd given deposition after deposition with never a complaint. And with never a differing fact.

But he knew she'd been dreading this meeting with Adelicia.

"So let me say again, Mrs. Acklen, how very sorry I am for withholding the truth from you and for placing you in the position that I have. I'm so grateful—" Claire's voice broke, and a moment passed before she regained control—"for the opportunities you gave me while I was here at Belmont. And for the way you opened your home, and yourself, to me. I wish I could be repaying you with something other than embarrassment and . . . public ridicule."

Already, the newspapers had grabbed the story, and of course, since Claire was Adelicia Acklen's personal liaison, the articles had both captured the front page. The stories were factual, for the most part, and were rife with the terms *counterfeit* and *fake*.

Claire bowed her head, finished with her part. But Adelicia still stared. Sutton wished she'd say something. The silence felt piercing and double-edged, even to him.

He and Claire had spoken at length about what she'd done but not at all about them. He loved her. He couldn't deny it and didn't want to. In that regard, nothing had changed. Inwardly, anyway. Yet they needed time to work through everything.

But one thing he was certain of—the Claire Laurent he'd grown to love was not the same person who had painted those forgeries. She'd given him a letter containing her thoughts after she'd heard *the question* so clearly in her mind, though *letter* wasn't quite the word for what she'd given him. It was really more of an outpouring of her heart onto the page, an outpouring that gave him deeper insight into her as a person, and an intimate look into her heart. And he treasured both.

As much as he'd thirsted for vengeance in his own situation, he ached for mercy now in Claire's. Justice wasn't as cut-and-dried as he'd once thought, and undeserved mercy held far greater appeal than ever before.

Adelicia drew in a breath and slowly exhaled. "Miss Laurent . . ."

Claire lifted her head.

"When I hired you as my personal liaison, I entrusted you not only with my personal and business affairs, but with my children, my family, my servants, my home, and my reputation. You ate at my table, you slept in my house, you sat beside me in church. Did I, or did I not, tell you that you would become an extension of me? That when people saw you, they would see me. That everything you did would reflect upon me. Does any of that sound familiar to you, Miss Laurent?"

Sutton knew Adelicia was within her right to speak in such a way to Claire, but a part of him still flinched, wanting to protect Claire. Wanting to defend her.

"Yes, Mrs. Acklen," Claire said, her voice soft, laden with respect. "You did, ma'am. And I tarnished that image. I'm deeply sorry."

Adelicia rested her hands on the desk, the feminine gesture oddly paired with the steel of her manner. "One thing I have learned in my life is that there are no private mistakes for people who live in the public sphere. Everything we do is subject to criticism. One must learn to live above all that, Miss Laurent . . . even when it cuts so deeply you think the wound will not heal."

Sutton detected the slightest waver in Adelicia's voice at the end, though her countenance denied it.

"It *will* heal, Miss Laurent. God himself will soothe the balm over the hurt, if you let Him. You will recover and move on. And you will be stronger for the scar."

Sutton knew that people—some of them Adelicia's peers—were reveling in this embarrassing situation for her. He also knew that, somehow, Adelicia would use it and harness it for the betterment of herself and her estate, just as she always seemed to do.

"And something you should remember for the future, Miss Laurent," Adelicia continued, her tone instructive. "Let no one define how you see yourself . . . save God alone. See yourself through His eyes and His strength, and you'll see who you *can* be despite being who you are." A dark brow rose. "But see yourself through your own eyes, and you'll be left to question, and to doubt, subject to the whims and wishes of others who *will not* have your best at heart. As experience has taught you in a rather harsh manner."

Moments passed, and finally Claire stood. She moved to the side of the desk, and with a grace and humility that caused Sutton to suck in a breath, she curtsied deep, her head bowed low. Adelicia's chin trembled the slightest bit before Claire rose and wordlessly walked to the door.

Adelicia stood behind the desk. "And just where, may I ask, do you think you're going, Miss Laurent?"

Claire stopped and looked back, her hand on the doorknob. "My belongings are packed, and"—she gestured to Sutton—"Mr. Monroe has offered to drive me into town. Reverend and Mrs. Bunting have opened a room to me in their home, until the trial is over."

"That's going to be most inconvenient for me, Miss Laurent. Because with my being gone to Angola, and you having apparently stayed here to traipse over hill and dale painting the countryside, we have much work to do."

Claire took in a quick breath. "But . . . I was under the impression that—"

"That I was dismissing you from your duties?"

Claire nodded, eyes watchful.

"Then your impression was *false*, Miss Laurent." Adelicia said nothing for a moment, and the words hung in the silence, rife with meaning. "Which, I trust, is—and henceforth will be—no longer the case."

Claire hiccupped a sob, fresh tears coming. Sutton looked between the two women, not just a little surprised, and felt his own chest tighten.

"Th-thank you, Mrs. Acklen. I . . . don't know how to tell you how much—"

"Yes, yes." Mrs. Acklen made a dismissive gesture. "You can thank me after I tell you—both of you—that come June the twenty-seventh there's going to be a wedding reception here at Belmont. Mine and Dr. Cheatham's."

Sutton raised his brow, though not surprised at the news. "Best wishes on your engagement, ma'am."

"Thank you, Mr. Monroe. You and I have a fair amount of work to do before then as well. But for you, Miss Laurent, I've already compiled the guest list." Adelicia smiled her sweetest and handed Claire a notebook. "We're planning to invite two thousand of our closest friends. Give or take."

Claire studied the notebook for a moment, then wiped her tears. "It will be my extreme pleasure to plan your reception, Mrs. Acklen. And almost three months away"—she managed a tremulous smile—"whatever shall I do with all that time?"

"I expect a good portion of it will be spent in court. I do hope you have a good attorney, Miss Laurent."

Claire nodded. "Yes, ma'am. Mr. Holbrook will be representing me."

Sutton felt Adelicia's stare. "Actually, Miss Laurent . . . there's been a change of counsel in your case."

Claire looked up at him, fragile hope in her eyes.

"Well . . ." Adelicia looked at them both. "It seems your fate is in very capable hands, Miss Laurent."

"Yes," Claire whispered. "It is."

Sutton and Claire were nearly out the door when he heard the all-too-familiar words.

"One more thing, Miss Laurent." Seated at her desk, Adelicia peered up. "Forgiveness may be an attribute of the strong, but this is one issue upon which I do not wish my strength to be tested again. Is that clear?"

"Perfectly, ma'am."

Sutton closed the door behind them, not missing the tiniest smile on Adelicia's face.

Epilogue

THURSDAY, JUNE 27, 1867
THE BELMONT ESTATE

Claire peered through a front window of the art gallery at the hundreds of clothed tables situated around the gardens, then at the endless array of twinkling lights strung from every tree and shrub and trellis and gazebo. "I hope it doesn't rain."

"Rain?" Sutton said behind her. "On the night of Mrs. Adelicia Hayes Franklin Acklen Cheatham's wedding reception? After you've planned everything to perfection? The heavens wouldn't dare."

She turned back only to find he wasn't looking at her. But seeing the focus of his attention warmed her.

He'd hung *An American Versailles* in the art gallery, but the placard beside the framed canvas clearly stated his ownership.

AN AMERICAN VERSAILLES
OIL ON CANVAS, 1867
CLAIRE ELISE LAURENT, ARTIST
ON LOAN TO BELMONT ART GALLERY
BY WILLISTER SUTTON MONROE

Willister. He'd used his full name just to get a smile from her. And it had worked.

He stood before the canvas and she came alongside him. The past three months had flown by in one sense, yet had crawled by in another. Due in part to the trial, then to planning Dr. and Mrs.

Cheatham's wedding reception, but mostly because of her and Sutton having to find their way with each other again.

It hadn't been easy. Her failure to be forthcoming had been as much of a disappointment to him as she'd imagined it would be. But she held on to hope that, in time, the affection he'd felt for her—that she still felt for him, more than ever—might return.

He pointed to *An American Versailles,* to a tree she'd painted just beyond the Belmont mansion where a boy knelt in the dirt. "How did you know I was burying those things for Zeke?"

"Because I saw you one night from my bedroom window."

He laughed. "You little sneak. You hid things for Zeke too . . . while I was gone to Angola."

"What makes you say that?"

"Because when I got back, he showed me everything he'd found that *I* hadn't hidden. And I never hid silver dollars."

Claire curbed a grin. "Those could have been there for years."

"Not likely, Miss Laurent." He reached for her hand and wove his fingers through hers. "Next time, if you want something to look like it's been there for years"—he brought her hand to his mouth and kissed it—"try dirtying it up a little before you bury it." His breath was warm, his lips soft. "And choose coins that weren't minted last year."

Claire laughed, but her eyes burned, her focus on their hands. He hadn't touched her like this since the night of the auction. "Thank you again, Sutton," she whispered. "For representing me in court."

He turned her hand palm up in his and traced feather-soft paths across her fingers. "Thank you for being the perfect witness. Your testimony in the fraud case made all the difference."

Evidence had revealed that the robbery of the gallery in New Orleans had been staged. Whether her father had been in on that part of the plan, she didn't know. Antoine had taken out insurance on the art—listing himself as primary owner—and had collected nearly twenty thousand dollars from the insurance company. Of course, most of the art had been forged, unbeknownst to the insurance company.

The trials had spanned ten weeks and had held Nashville—and every newspaper east of the Mississippi—spellbound. The juries—in each separate trial—had decided unanimously for the multiple plaintiffs. Antoine DePaul had been tried and found innocent of her father's murder due to lack of evidence. But he was later convicted on multiple counts of fraud—as was another art dealer from Perrault Galleries—and both men awaited their separate sentence hearings. As did Samuel Broderick *the second* who had been convicted of lesser counts of fraud.

Claire had no trouble imagining Antoine DePaul as the swindler that he was, but she *did* still find it difficult to believe that he might be capable of murder. That he might have killed her father was something she couldn't fathom, and was a question she guessed would never be answered.

She had testified against Antoine in court, and that was the last time she'd seen him. Or ever cared to again.

Shortly following the trial, Holbrook and Wickliffe had become Holbrook, Wickliffe, and *Monroe*. A surprising turn of events made possible by Sutton's contribution to the case. The name had a nice sound to it. Though Claire knew it wasn't what Sutton wanted to do with his life, it was a step, and every step changed the view. Who knew what God would bring next?

The jury for her trial had been generously lenient. Her "punishment" for the next year seemed anything but. Three times a week she held classes at the Worthington Art Center for any child who wanted to learn how to paint. The first day, thirty-six children had shown up.

She'd managed to make "quiet mention" to Mrs. Worthington about Mrs. Monroe's exemplary drawing skills, and Mrs. Worthington had wasted no time in extending a formal invitation to Eugenia Monroe to teach at the art center as well. Claire knew Mrs. Monroe still preferred Cara Netta LeVert for her son, but she was determined to win her over—

As soon as she'd won Sutton's heart again.

Sutton pointed to one of the gazebos in the painting. "I didn't see this at first."

She knew he wasn't talking about the gazebo but about the two people who stood inside. The images were faint, only shadows really, and one of them was about to fall out backward, in her mind, anyway.

"They're like hidden treasures," he whispered. "All the little facets you've put into this painting. Just like the party you planned for William."

She hadn't thought of that before. *Hidden treasures.* Like everything God had taught her in recent months.

Following the trial, all of the fraudulent art that had served as evidence had been auctioned off. At her request, Sutton had checked several times but there was no record of her *Versailles.* It was as if it had never existed.

But in a way, that was as it should be, she decided. Because that painting had never been hers. Not really.

God had given the gift and vision of that painting to François-Narcisse Brissaud. Not to her. She had simply taken it. Not only had she stolen from Brissaud, and from the patron who bought the canvas thinking it was authentic, she'd stolen from God, the Giver of all gifts. She'd also robbed herself. Because she'd cheated herself of the blessing of having to listen for God's inaudible voice, of waiting on His lead to show her what to create with the gift He'd given her.

Her gaze settled on the top portion of the canvas, the part that had taken her the longest to complete. And she recalled every painstaking brushstroke, every morning she'd arisen before dawn to be on that ridge, awaiting the sun's return, and for those precious fleeting moments she'd had to capture the beauty of the sunrise over the hill where Sutton's family home had once stood.

But it was the image within the sunrise she loved most, and that was barely visible. Even she had to look to really see it—a throne, high and lifted up, among the clouds.

Sutton reached for his coat on a nearby chair. "We'd better get on over there. Or *the Lady* will be sending for us."

With twilight nearing, they walked arm in arm the short distance to the mansion. Lanterns cast a shimmering spell over the gardens and a stringed orchestra tuned their instruments on the front lawn. When Claire and Sutton reached the top step of the portico, they turned and saw the first carriage.

Followed by another and another . . .

From all over the country, an endless stream of guests arriving for the wedding reception of Dr. and Mrs. William Cheatham, married just over a week ago by Reverend Bunting in a private gathering in the mansion.

Sutton sighed beside her. "Two thousand guests invited this time."

She laughed and shook her head. "And nearly every one of them accepted."

The front door opened behind them, and Eli stepped out in black coat and tails. "Good evening, Mr. Monroe, Miss Laurent."

Claire curtsied. "You look so handsome, Eli."

He bowed at the waist. "Why, thank you, ma'am. You look lovely, as always. And Mr. Monroe . . . how are you this evening, sir?"

"I'm well, Eli. Thank you."

Claire continued on inside but paused when she noticed Sutton wasn't following. She looked back.

"Eli, I'd like to . . ." Sutton briefly looked down. "I'd like to thank you for what you said about my father a while back. And also what . . ." Sutton lifted his gaze. "What you shared with me that *he* said. That meant more to me than you'll ever know." Slowly, he extended his hand, and Eli accepted.

Claire sensed significance to the moment and asked Sutton about it when they stepped inside.

But he just smiled. "I'll tell you about it later."

"Miss Laurent . . ."

Claire turned to see Mrs. *Cheatham* in a dress of flowing white silk, a veil of Brussels point lace floating about her shoulders. In true queenly form, a diamond tiara—a wedding gift from the Emperor and Empress of France, who had been invited to the reception but who had to politely decline—adorned her head. "You look radiant, Mrs. Cheatham."

"I concur completely, ma'am," Sutton added.

"I appreciate that." Smiling, Mrs. Cheatham turned to Eli, who now stood by *Ruth Gleaning* as well as an easel covered in a black drape. "I also appreciate this," Mrs. Cheatham added, then gestured. Eli removed the cloth with a flourish.

Claire couldn't believe her eyes. Her *Versailles,* with her *maman.* "Where did you get this?" But as soon as she looked at Sutton, she knew, and she loved him all the more for it. When she drew closer, she saw it. *Her* name in the bottom right-hand corner. And for a brief second, she was back in her bedroom above the gallery, looking out over the French Quarter, dreaming of her name someday being on a *masterpiece.*

"And to be clear, Miss Laurent . . ." Mrs. Cheatham stepped closer. "The painting is mine now. But you may view it anytime you like."

"What my dear wife probably hasn't told you," Dr. Cheatham said, joining them with Pauline and Claude in tow, as well as his own teenage children, Mattie and Richard, "is that she and Mrs. Worthington about came to blows in the bidding."

Mrs. Cheatham shushed him.

But Sutton laughed. "I wish I could have seen that."

Wishing she could have too, Claire felt Sutton's hand on the small of her back.

"So much for your talent not being unique," he whispered.

Mattie Cheatham sidled up beside her new mother, younger Pauline in hand, and Claire could see a close bond had already formed between them. Joseph was home from school now, and he and William, along with Claude, were already luring Richard Cheatham into their pranks on the girls. A full household indeed.

"Mr. Monroe"—Dr. Cheatham gave Sutton's shoulder a good-natured grip—"Adelicia tells me you're quite gifted with horses. I've recently purchased two thoroughbreds and would be obliged if you'd consider training them for me. As time permits, of course. I'll either compensate you outright or legally assign you a portion of their future winnings. Your choice."

A smile that did Claire's heart good broke over Sutton's face. "I'd be honored, sir. Thank you."

Prominently displayed on a side table was Adelicia Cheatham's copy of *Queens of American Society* opened to the page that bore Mrs. Cheatham's picture, along with the memory book Claire had made her. But a second copy of *Queens of American Society* also adorned the table, opened to a different page. Claire stepped closer.

"Have you had opportunity to read Mrs. Cheatham's portion yet, Miss Laurent?"

Claire turned to see Mrs. Routh beside her, the woman's spectacles resting midway down her nose. "Ah . . . *yes*, Mrs. Routh, actually, I have read it." She wasn't about to admit that she'd written practically every word. Only Mrs. Cheatham knew that. "She's lived a very full and meaningful life."

"That she has." Mrs. Routh smoothed a hand over the opened page, her forefinger lingering on the last paragraph. "It was most gracious of *Mrs. Cheatham* to include such kind remarks about me."

Claire nodded, knowing full well what the paragraph said, and getting the sneaking suspicion that Mrs. Routh knew their employer hadn't written it. "Mrs. Cheatham thinks most highly of you, ma'am. As do many other people. But then . . ." She met the woman's gaze. "I hope you would know that by now."

Mrs. Routh closed the book and held it to her chest. "I do," she whispered. "Just as I hope those 'other people' know that I think the same of them."

A while later, after toasts had been made to the new bride and groom and a waltz had ended, Claire spotted Mrs. Cheatham gesturing to her. Claire made her way across the grand salon and past *The Peri*. "Yes, ma'am?"

"Miss Laurent, why isn't the cupola lit and ready for our guests? I am *quite* certain I put that on your list."

"No, ma'am," Claire said gently. "We discussed the cupola earlier this week. With the redecorating you're doing upstairs, you expressly told me that you preferred our guests not—"

"Apparently one of us was not listening well enough, Miss Laurent. The servants are all disposed. Would you please take care of this personally? And straightaway."

Claire tilted her head. "Most happily, Mrs. Cheatham." Knowing she hadn't misunderstood but recalling everything the woman had done for her, Claire ascended the staircase, looking for Sutton, thinking he could help her with the task. She'd seen him dancing with his mother earlier, but he was nowhere in sight now. She'd lit the lanterns up there before. She could do it again.

On the second-floor landing, she retrieved an oil lamp and matches and continued up the stairs. She opened the door to the cupola and stepped inside.

"It's about time. . . ."

She jumped at the voice, then saw him. And the smile Sutton wore told her she'd been hoodwinked. Very happily so. "Why isn't the cupola lit and ready for our guests?" she mimicked her employer. "I am *quite* certain I put that on your list."

He laughed as he took the lamp and matches from her and set them on a table that wasn't usually there. Same for the bottle of champagne chilling on ice and two glasses. "She was most cooperative when I told her my intentions toward you."

Claire raised an eyebrow. "You have intentions toward me, Mr. Monroe?"

He pulled her close. "I do indeed." He leaned down and kissed her soft on the mouth. "And most of them are honorable."

She smiled, even as his expression sobered.

"I needed some time, Claire, to sort things through. But mainly for us both to get the trial behind us." He fingered a curl at her temple. "I've loved you since we hid all those silly clues together. And it took everything I had not to kiss you that night in the art gallery. I wanted to . . . so badly."

She traced a finger over his lips. "Like you want to now?"

His sharp exhale should have served warning. He lifted her in his arms, held her against him, and kissed her, deeply, cradling the back of her head. Then, gradually, he lowered her back down until her feet touched the floor again. But Claire could barely breathe, much less stand.

She gave a soft laugh. "I'll have you know that I loved you first. Because I've loved you since you fell out of the gazebo that same night. Long before we hid the clues."

His deep chuckle warmed her. "It's not a competition."

"Oh . . . look," she whispered, and peered over to see the gardens below. "It's even more beautiful from up here."

"Claire . . . I believe this belongs to you."

She turned back to see him holding something out to her. A necklace? No, it didn't look—

"Oh, Sutton . . ." Her mother's locket watch. She cradled the locket in her palm. "Where did you get this?" But as soon as she said it, she knew. "*He* had it . . . didn't he?"

Sutton nodded. "I put it on a chain for you, along with something else I've been wanting to give you."

A ring slowly slid down the chain, and even as his smile faded, hers bloomed.

"Claire, you've long held my heart. And it would be the greatest honor of my life if you would—"

"Yes," she said quickly. "I will."

His mouth tipped in a smile. "You're supposed to wait," he whispered, "until after I've finished asking you. I've worked a long time on this."

"Not nearly as long as I've been waiting for you to ask." She eyed the ring and then him.

He slipped it on her finger, then brought his arms around her, and Claire gave herself to his kiss. She couldn't imagine what a lifetime of loving Willister Sutton Monroe would be like. But she welcomed it—and eagerly anticipated the *masterpiece* that God would make of their life together.

Dear Reader,

The first time I visited the Belmont Mansion, I knew I wanted to write about this magnificent home and the people who'd lived there. While Belmont served as a "backdrop" for this story and I've gone to great length to remain faithful to history, I *have* taken creative license with historical personalities, as well as with the basement level of the mansion, which is no longer inhabitable nor open to the public. For more information on the historical specifics and for pictures of Adelicia's statuary, please visit my Web site (www.tameraalexander.com).

Adelicia had a great appreciation for art, and as the story portrays, she was one of the wealthiest women in the United States in the 1860s. The seed of her wealth came from her first husband, Isaac Franklin, a wealthy planter and slave trader, and was another story in itself. I desired to include those details of her life—and *did*, initially. But as writers learn early on, if story threads don't serve the main story, they must go. Which these threads did . . . during rewrite. Yet I do believe they are important pieces of Adelicia's life and to the history of Belmont.

As for the question Claire heard in the book, "Would you paint if you knew you were painting only for me?" that has its root in a personal experience. In 2003, after I'd pitched the idea for my first novel to an editor, she read the first few chapters, then told me she wanted to see it once it was completed. So I set out to finish it. And as I did, I heard this question so clearly in my heart during worship the next Sunday, "Would you write this book if you knew you were writing it only for *Me*?"

In that moment, I was certain of two things: One, it was God's inaudible voice, something I've "heard" only a handful of times in my life. And two, I knew the editor *wasn't* going to take my book. Still, I spent the next year writing and then submitted the manuscript. Hardly a month passed before I received the rejection letter. But . . . I gained invaluable insights through that experience.

First, I learned that only what we do for God will last. The lessons He taught me as I wrote *Rekindled*, my first published novel, are ones I'll carry with me forever. And second, from my earliest days of being a novelist I've realized who I'm writing for. And—just as Claire did—I'm determined never to forget that.

Adelicia Acklen didn't keep a journal, or if she did, it didn't survive. However, we do have letters written in her hand to friends and family members, as well as newspaper accounts detailing the lavish parties and dinners she hosted. One night, while I was writing, I was struggling with Adelicia's dialogue in a conversation between her and Claire when I remembered a letter Adelicia had written to her sister Corinne in 1860. I pulled it from my files and, oh . . . what a moment. Adelicia's words fit *perfectly*—without the least editing—into the conversation on the page. A God moment, for sure. (See Ch. 36, the paragraph beginning with the words, "Oftentimes, through the years . . .")

Attempting to sketch someone's character without having known them is tricky at best, and rife for misinterpretation. Yet, in researching, I quickly learned that the silent footprints we leave behind—letters written, mementoes saved, even purchases we've made—create impressions of the person we are. Or, to those coming after us, the person we *were*.

Never underestimate who's looking at your life and at how many people you influence. I doubt that Adelicia Acklen ever dreamed someone would write a novel about her life and her beloved Belmont nearly one hundred and twenty-five years following her death. And yet, here we are.

You and I are leaving lasting impressions. May we live authentic lives of faith that point others to Christ. After all, it's all about Him.

Until next time,
Tamera
Ephesians 2:10

With Gratitude to . . .

My husband, Joe—for acting as my first editor on this manuscript. You listened as I talked (and talked and talked) through characterizations and plot twists. Your patience and enthusiasm never waned, even when mine occasionally did.

Kelsey and Kurt—for your love and encouraging hugs and texts, and for the privilege and joy of being your mom.

Dad—for adding such happiness to our lives and for being such an encourager.

Mark Brown, curator of the Belmont Mansion—for your painstakingly detailed chronology of Adelicia Acklen's life, for opening the personal files of family history, for answering my endless e-mails and questions, and for sharing your love of history and your admiration for Adelicia Acklen.

Karen Schurrer and Charlene Patterson, my editors at Bethany House—for doing what you do so well, and for helping me to "see the forest for the trees."

Deborah Raney—for reading this manuscript in the early stages and offering insight and suggestions, but most of all for being your wonderful, encouraging self.

Natasha Kern, agent extraordinaire—for going the extra mile. You went above and beyond the call on this one, and I'm a better writer because of you (even if I do have less hair now).

Mandisa—for your CD *What If We Were Real*. I listened to it countless times as I wrote this story, and drew such inspiration from the lyrics, and from your gift of a voice.

My readers—for faithfully reading, and for sharing with me how these journeys we take together touch your lives. Such an encouragement! I pray you take a step closer to Christ as you read, just as I do when I write. After all, it's all about Him.

And to Jesus Christ—for ransoming this lost soul and for making an eternal lasting impression.

TAMERA ALEXANDER is a bestselling novelist whose works have been awarded or nominated for numerous honors, including the Christy Award, the RITA Award, and the Carol Award. After seventeen years in Colorado, Tamera and her husband have returned to their native South and live in Tennessee, where they enjoy spending time with their two grown children.

Tamera invites you to visit her at:

Her Web site	www.tameraalexander.com
Her blog	www.tameraalexander.blogspot.com
Twitter	www.twitter.com/tameraalexander
Facebook	www.facebook.com/tamera.alexander

Or if you prefer snail mail, please write her at the following postal address:

Tamera Alexander
P.O. Box 871
Brentwood, TN 37024

More Stunning Historical Fiction from

Tamera Alexander

For more on Tamera and her books, visit *tameraalexander.com.*

In the late 1860s, three couples carve out a new life in the wild, untamed Colorado Territory. Each person will be called upon to stand on nothing more than faith, risk what is most dear to them, and turn away from the past in order to detect God's plan for the future. By the time Colorado becomes a state, will they be united by love or defeated by adversity?

Fountain Creek Chronicles: *Rekindled, Revealed, Remembered*

Nestled beneath the Maroon Bells in the Colorado Rockies is an untamed land that holds the promise of a fresh start. As three women from the East carve out a place for themselves in the community of Timber Ridge, they seek to fulfill their dreams and hopes in a place where love has the power to change lives.

Timber Ridge Reflections: *From a Distance, Beyond This Moment, Within My Heart*